INTO *the* GROVES

BOOK FOUR *of the* **SANTA LUCIA** SERIES

MICHELLE DAMIANI

RIALTO
PRESS

INTO THE GROVES

BOOK FOUR OF THE **SANTA LUCIA** SERIES

RIALTO PRESS
P.O. Box 1472
Charlottesville, VA 22902

michelledamiani.com

For the people of Spello, who welcomed us home

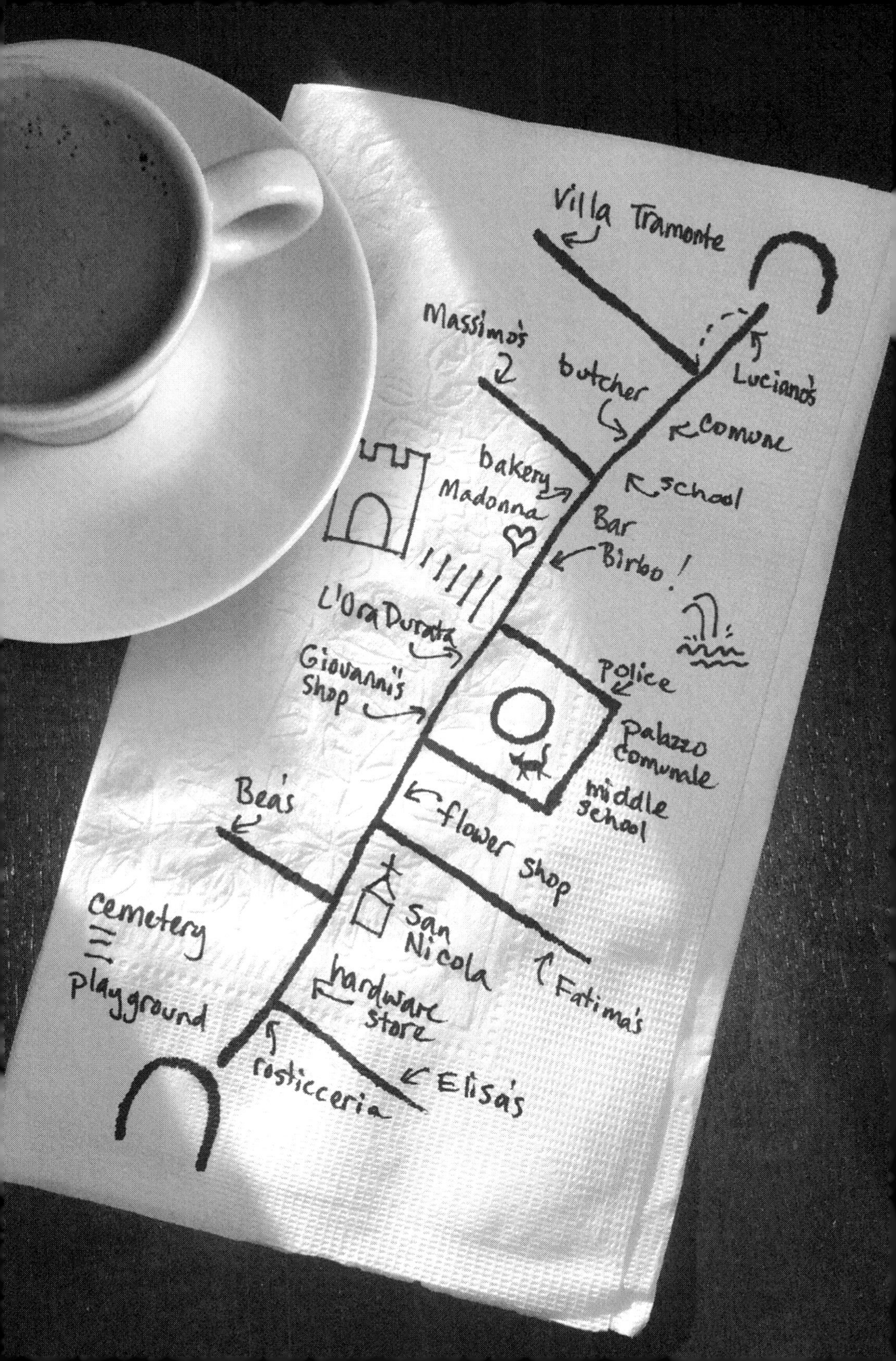
Villa Tramonte
Massimo's
butcher
Luciano's
Comune
bakery
Madonna
school
Bar
Birbo!
L'Ora Durata
Giovanni's
Shop
Police
Palazzo
Comunale
middle
school
Bea's
flower shop
cemetery
San
Nicola
playground
hardware
store
Fatima's
rosticceria
Elisa's

A NOTE ON THE ITALIAN

Italian words in the text are followed by the English translation or can be understood by context. For interested readers, there is a glossary in the back of this book.

CAST OF CHARACTERS

MAIN CHARACTERS

Chiara	*The owner of Bar Birbo, she therefore hears all the rumors and secrets*
Edo	*Chiara's nephew who lives with her and helps at Bar Birbo, he recently acknowledged to himself and others that he is gay*
Luciano	*A retired schoolteacher who lost his daughter and wife, which drove him to lose himself*
Vito	*Luciano's brother*
Enrico	*Luciano's nephew*
Massimo	*Father to Margherita, he was once married to Giulia, Luciano's daughter who died. A year later, he married Isotta, Giulia's virtual twin.*
Livia	*Massimo's relation, she comes to help with Margherita after Anna's death*
Pietro	*Livia's husband and a restaurant owner, he purchases the burnt-out L'Ora Dorata*
Leo & Sonia	*Livia and Pietro's twins who just graduated from high school and find work in Santa Lucia*
Anna	*Massimo's mother*
Elisa	*An 11-year-old girl who struggled in school until Luciano began tutoring her. She is Fatima's best friend.*
Fatima	*A 12-year-old immigrant girl from Morocco, injured in an accidental fire during the village festa at the castello. She is Elisa's best friend.*
Salma	*Fatima's mother*
Omar	*Fatima's father*
Ava	*The daughter of a florist, she is Santa Lucia's guerrilla gardener and perennially unlucky in love*

Fabio	Ava's brother
Alessandro	The owner of the derelict castle, newly arrived to Santa Lucia
Madison	His very American wife
Fabrizio	A writer from Bologna, he and Chiara recently began a relationship
Francy	Fabrizio brings Francy to Santa Lucia

VILLAGERS

Magda	Moved to Santa Lucia from Germany years ago with her husband who has since disappeared in Thailand
Bea	Santa Lucia's source of fresh eggs and fresh gossip
Antonella	Bea's granddaughter
Patrizia	Chiara's best friend who helps her husband, Giuseppe, in his butcher shop
Giuseppe	Patrizia's husband and the maker of Santa Lucia's famous chicken sausages
Sauro	Santa Lucia's baker
Giovanni	The joke-telling owner of the little shop on the piazza
Fabio	Ava's brother and her opposite In almost every way. He accused both the gay tourists and Santa Lucia's immigrants for starting the fire
Salvia	Ava's mother
Concetta	Elisa's mother
Arturo	Older villager who is sure his French wife is cheating on him
Rosetta	The school principal
Paola	The owner of the fruit and vegetable market
Marcello	The town cop, his mother is desperate for him to get married and give her a grandchild
Bruno	A cantankerous old farmer
Riccardo	A lawyer, he's a one-time resident of Santa Lucia, who now lives in Spoleto

AUTUMN

*T*he one-eyed dog stopped on Via Romana. Abruptly he sat and, under the ever-watchful gaze of Santa Lucia's beloved Madonna, he began scratching his left ear. Salami rinds and *mandarino* peels scattered across the street.

Scritch scritch scritch.

His leg thumped down as his attention caught on activity outside L'Ora Dorata, Santa Lucia's lone *trattoria*. The dog cocked his head as if trying to make sense of the warping light, rippling in waves. That whispering blue light, distorted like ancient windows bulging as the sand settles ever lower.

Could the dog see anything, though, his lone functioning eye obscured by a fall of what might have once been cream-colored fur? On Carosello, Santa Lucia's town dog, forever in quest to find scraps left for more beloved creatures, that fur was dingy. Almost grey.

The dog leaped up as if the bells of San Nicola had suddenly clanged. He peered into Bar Birbo. The waxed wooden door shut tight. No humans within to offer him a plastic tray of leftovers. He gazed up the street, toward the *macelleria*. A stop that often proved good for a pork bone.

Nose quivering, he gazed down the street again, toward the *piazza* and the wending warren of streets below. He contemplated this route past the playground, the cemetery, to his olive tree. Ancient. Gnarled. So ancient and gnarled it had the appearance of a fastidious woman at a party, lifting her skirts to avoid dragging mud. Leaving a little hovel below whispering branches, just right for a one-eyed dog.

As if realizing his tardiness to a prearranged rendezvous, the dog spun around and trotted up the steps. Cresting the stairs, he tossed a look at the women billowing cloth over an enormous table. The fabric smelled of endless seasons of charring wood, of feasts long forgotten. The tablecloth filled the sky like the sun, all goldenrod yellow. The women laughed as the cloth settled. The dog studied them for another moment, as they carried tureens and platters to the table.

Heaping quantities of food. Delicate, fragrant. Fresh. No scraps for him. Not yet.

Hearing voices from deep in the groves, the dog cut through the courtyard, through the breezeway, past the kitchen garden, filled with sunset-hued globes of winter squash surrounded by waving wildflowers to decorate tables across Santa Lucia. Carosello nosed through the dirt, aware that sometimes kitchen scraps found their way into compost.

At a sudden burst of swallows, wheeling across the achingly blue sky, the dog started, forelegs spread as if in play, an eggshell clinging to his muzzle. He stared after the birds, pirouetting together, in a dance that must make no sense to a small dog in a small town. His eyes followed the swallows, as they wove together beams of light into a curtain, a fall of dapper aquamarine. The dog's head roved back and forth for a moment before he shook the eggshell off his stubby whiskers.

Taking a faint path, he entered the groves. The dog brushed against wild mint, fennel, and fenugreek. Green and toasty smells rose all around him, obscuring for a moment the stale grease smell of his fur.

Carosello lifted his muzzle, testing the breeze. Left and right, he jogged, always toward the sound of humans. There they stood now, calling over the vines to each other. Divided from him by a rock wall. He trotted around the wall, looking for a tumble of rocks that marked the entrance.

The dog started to enter, to join the fray, wondering if scraps of panini might be left about, as they often were during the olive harvest. He stopped and sat, watching.

The people within the walled enclosure wielded flashing implements. Wresting huge bunches of grapes from the vines, they tossed them into waiting wooden crates. A voice warbled, and as the rest of the workers caught the melody, a song rose over the vines. A man's voice threaded among and between the others, a golden cord, holding the song together.

The voices soared along with the breeze. And the one-eyed dog carried on, picking his way past the brambles to enter the olive groves. The light seemed to part, to allow him entrance. As his tail waved like a ragged flag, the curtain closed behind him with a boom audible enough to make the swallows shiver and the workers in the grapevines look up in confusion, before they laughed, their voices rising into that hallowed blue light of Santa Lucia.

Bea pushed open the door to Bar Birbo. "*Buongiorno*, Chiara! You recover from the *vendemmia*?"

Bar Birbo's owner, Chiara, laughed in lieu of a response as she brushed the caramel-colored hair from her forehead. "*Ciao*, Bea. *Cappuccino stamattina?*"

Bea heaved her impressive bulk onto a stool. "*Sì, grazie.*"

Chiara bustled behind the counter, grinding beans, opening a carton of milk as she spoke over her shoulder. "I thought you would be there."

Harrumphing, Bea reached for the sugar packets. "I'm too old for that. Paid my dues."

Frothing the milk, Chiara smiled. "Luciano was there."

Bea shook her sugar packet. "No surprise. He wouldn't miss it. All those beloved children in one place." She lowered her voice. "How are they?"

Chiara served Bea her *cappuccino*. "It's hard to say. Sometimes they laugh and play and it's easy to forget. But then one of them cries, and it's a chain reaction."

"Poor babies. What an ordeal." Bea tipped sugar into her *cappuccino*. "No word on Massimo I suppose."

Chiara shook her head. "Nothing. And I'm sure Isotta and Ava would love to know if he died in the shipwreck."

Bea snorted and stirred her coffee.

Laughing, Chiara said. "I know, after Magda's husband came back from the dead..."

Bea used her spoon to gesture at Chiara. "Not her husband. His twin. Keep up, Chiara."

Chiara raised her hand to greet Patrizia as she said, "Keeping up has become complicated."

Patrizia hung her sweater, then turned to the women. "You talking about Gustav? Or Karl, I mean?"

Bea took a sip of her *caffè*, muttering, "I've never seen twins so identical."

Patrizia asked, "How was the *vendemmia*?"

Chiara began grinding more coffee beans. "A glorious day. Bruno stopped by and said he couldn't believe the vines produced so many grapes, given that no one ever sprayed them. That soil."

Nodding, Bea said. "My husband says the same. Mildew can't get a foothold in sandy soil." She thought for a moment. "Did Ale get the grapes typed?"

Chiara shook her head. "A professor from the University of Perugia comes next week."

Patrizia mused. "Maybe they're French?"

Bea frowned and turned toward her. "French? Why French?"

Patrizia shrugged. "Or from across the Adriatic, Croatia or something. They have to be from somewhere far away if Bruno doesn't recognize them."

Bea grumbled. "Or from a long time ago. You know the stories."

Patrizia accepted her *cappuccino* with a smile. "You had great weather. I hope it holds up for the olive harvest."

The bell over the door rang as Magda strode in. "*Cappuccino*, Chiara, *per favore*."

Chiara nodded. "*Subito.*"

Magda examined the women's expressions. As the faces slid away, peering at the *grappa* or the faded posters on the walls, she harrumphed. "You talking about me?"

Bea snorted. "Not for the past few minutes."

As Chiara said, "Can you be surprised?"

Magda's face creased into a rare grin. "No."

Bea threw her head back in laughter.

Magda peered into the pastry case. "Chiara, does one of those *cornetti* have apricot jam?"

Chiara nodded, her eyes on the coffee dribbling into the heavy white cup.

Nodding, Magda said, "I'll have one." She sat at the bar and waited. Feeling eyes on her, she glanced at Bea and Patrizia. "What?"

Bea let out an explosion of air. "What do you mean, what? What happened to that awful man? Did they take him back to Germany?"

In a softer voice, Patrizia said, "We've been worried about you."

A hint of Magda's old glower crossed her face, but seeing the genuine concern shining in Patrizia's eyes, the unaccustomed serious expression on Bea's, she breathed deeply. "I'm glad it's over."

Chiara used the antique silver tongs to select a *cornetto* with a generous fall of sugar. Sliding it on a plate, she said, "What a relief for you."

"No." Magda reached for a napkin. "I mean, yes . . . a relief to get that imposter out of my house. Out of our town." The women watched her every word. Magda's old hard edge prickled in the face of their interest. But then she nodded to herself. "But there's also a . . . liberation."

Bea's eyes glinted. "You did look pretty satisfied at the restaurant opening. Dancing with the mayor."

Patrizia put a hand on Bea's. "Now, Bea..."

Bea laughed.

Magda narrowed her eyes. "Dante was being polite."

Patrizia and Chiara smiled at each other.

Magda's face grew stony, and Chiara realized she had to get this conversational ship out of rocky waters. "Did you see Fatima leave, at the opening?"

Magda leaned forward. "I can't believe her parents let her go. Modeling! In Milan! I can't even count how many Muslim edicts that must go against."

Chiara shook her head. "Luciano told me at the *vendemmia*, apparently her agent has worked with girls like Fatima before. She has a reputation as strict, exacting. This may be what Fatima needs. A new path."

Patrizia gazed out the window at the Madonna, ethereal in her azure niche, spangled with fading gold stars. Slowly she said, "And being here, it's been so hard for her family. Maybe a new start is what they *all* need."

Magda grumbled. "Their new start is not what *I* need. Now I need to hire a new cleaning woman."

Patrizia ignored Magda. "I hope they all find what they're looking for."

The women all gazed toward Via Romana, as if expecting promise to land right in the street—bright, shiny, and clear as morning.

Isotta shifted her weight, moving young Jacopo to her other shoulder. "I'm sorry you have to leave again." She tried to keep the longing out of her voice. She had assumed that sometime in the two weeks between L'Ora Dorata's opening and the *vendemmia*, she'd have tamed her heart's tendency to lurch at the sight of Luciano's nephew. But on the contrary, she found her eyes also searching for Enrico, drinking him in as if she'd been parched for days.

How, oh *how*, had she wasted so much time thinking him attractive only as a friend? She tried to hang on to Ava's reasoning, that Isotta's entanglement with Massimo blinded her to Enrico's potential. It didn't ease Isotta's regret, though she appreciated the effort.

Enrico put the last of the lenses in his bag. "I know. It was a quick visit. But I have to get back—"

"To Carla. Yes, I know."

Enrico smiled awkwardly. "To work, I was going to say. But yes," he added gently. "That, too."

Isotta fought back a fierce wish that this Carla would evaporate off the face of the earth. Surely, without her, Enrico would rediscover the affection he'd once had for her, Isotta? She'd searched for some sign of lingering feeling, but the space between them had chilled like bedsheets past noon. She blushed at the thought of bedsheets, dipping her nose against Jacopo's hair, letting it tickle her face. She stammered, "I wanted to say . . . I wanted to thank you. When the children went missing, you spent so much time here. I don't think I ever told you how much I appreciated it."

He nodded politely. "Anyone would have done the same."

Isotta doubted that, but thinking about Enrico, his goodness, made her heart skip. To cover it, she added, "How nice of the university to give you the time off. Especially with your just starting."

"Since I'm focusing on research this semester, they didn't mind. Next semester when I'm teaching, I don't think the university would be so understanding."

"Glad the kidnapping happened the first semester then." Oh my God, Isotta thought. Had she ever been less articulate? To cover her embarrassment, she cleared her throat. "How long is the drive?"

"To Urbino? About two hours. Not too bad."

Isotta gestured to the boxes scattered around the living room. "So you'll be back soon then, right? To record the rest of these?"

His fingers grazed the papers stacked in the box on the table. "Absolutely. Thank goodness Luciano held onto them. What a remarkable find."

"And here I'd been begging him to declutter," she grinned. "Aren't you lucky he pretended not to hear me."

"Indeed," Enrico said. "In fact, I believe there may be enough here for a paper."

Isotta looked around doubtfully. "Really? About what?"

Gesturing more empathically, Enrico went on, "A new take on the story of the Jewish diaspora in war-time Italy. Why the experience impacted a unique subset of families and how they persevered. Did they rely on Catholic groups to support them? Jewish congregations? Where did they find resources, houseroom?"

As he stopped speaking, Isotta flushed, aware of how her eyes had been trained on his every movement. Focusing on the way his animation transformed what she once considered ordinary features as much as on his prospective research.

Was it her imagination, or did something flicker in his eye, a twitch of a smile? Realizing how long she'd been staring at his face, she startled and asked, "And Carla, is she a historian too?"

He cocked his head. "Carla? No."

"But she teaches at the university?"

"No. She manages the history department, but she doesn't teach."

Isotta didn't know why this information came as palpable relief. She waited for him to go on, but he stood and patted his pockets.

"Well, Isotta, a great *vendemmia* and it's been lovely to see you."

"Oh! We can walk you to the parking lot. Let me find his carrier..." She scanned the room.

But Enrico shook his head. "No time, I'm afraid. I have a meeting with the head of my department." He paused, running his hands again over the edges of the boxes. "You'll keep writing?"

"Writing?" She looked confused for a moment. "Oh! The children's book. I'd forgotten all about that with figuring out the next move. I can't come back here, I'd have to share a room with both children. And Massimo's..." she shivered. "That's a last resort."

Shrugging on his coat, Enrico said, "I suspect Ava and Ale would love for you to stay at the *castello*. It's felt more like a party than a recuperation."

Isotta nodded. "But it's not sustainable to have us all sleeping in the breakfast room forever. Ale will eventually have guests."

"I'm sure he has a plan for that."

"Or at least Ava does."

Enrico grinned. "Indeed." He hesitated before dropping a kiss on each of Isotta's cheeks. "Take care of yourself, Isotta."

Tears sprung to her eyes. "I will. You, too." She blurted out, "You'll be back for the *cinghiale* festival? You haven't lived until you've tasted Umbrian wild boar stew, cooked all day over an open fire."

He chuckled. "I'll try."

Isotta smiled. "And bring Carla! We'd love to meet her."

Enrico studied Isotta for a moment. "It's a few weeks away. We'll see."

Bruno shook his head. "*Non va bene.*"

Ale stopped pouring the inky grape juice from their vats into the waiting barrel. Glancing up at the old farmer, he asked, "What do you mean?"

"The barrels."

Ale regarded the wooden barrels. The ones he had spent all weekend scrubbing. He couldn't believe how tenaciously grape-must clung to wood. The smell had not been a treat.

Bruno gestured with his chin. "I will get you barrels. A winery across the valley sells outdated ones at a good price. Plenty of mileage."

Ale shrugged. "These are free."

"But—"

Ale cut him off. "Look, Bruno, I appreciate your help. I do. But I don't think you understand. I have *no* money. No money for barrels, no money for rootstock. If planting those clippings doesn't work to get new vines going, this vineyard will only last as long as the current vines do." What he didn't say . . . oh, what he didn't say. If he couldn't succeed, what kind of man was he? How could he convince Ava to one day join her life to his if he couldn't make a simple thing like *wine* work? He had to, and that was that.

"But, the wild—"

"Seriously, Bruno. I don't want to talk about it anymore. These barrels are fine. I cleaned them myself."

Bruno ran his hands over the stubble growing on his weathered cheeks and regarded Ale doubtfully.

Ale ignored him as he finished pouring the juice in the barrel. He straightened and sprinkled the purple surface with yeast. "I got the yeast you suggested. So you see? I'm not a total buffoon."

His face impassive, Bruno said, "Have you been punching down the caps?"

Ale nodded. "They never knew what hit them. I've been a punching *fiend*."

Bruno raised his eyebrows seriously.

Sighing, Ale said, "I know about the caps. I did my homework."

"Because if you don't do it well, you'll get bacteria growing on the skins and also you'll lack tannins and color since the must— "

"Bruno, I believe that's the longest sentence I've heard you utter."

Bruno didn't answer as he lifted a canister of the grape juice and poured it into a barrel. He paused and lowered his nose to the wood, sniffing inconspicuously. "*Non va bene.*" He muttered.

Perhaps Ale didn't hear him, since he said, "The guy from the University of Perugia comes Thursday, to type the mystery grapes. I hope it's not too late to press them. Should I add them to barrels of wine I have going, or make wine solely from those? Single denomination, or whatever?"

Bruno frowned. "It depends."

"I know, I know. Just making conversation."

Bruno looked at him quizzically. As if he'd never heard such a ludicrous concept.

Elisa poked at her breakfast.

Ava watched and said, "Elisa, you need to eat."

"I don't have to stay the whole day, right? You promised."

"Just an hour."

"And if Margherita cries before that, you'll come get me?"

Ava flinched at the storm brewing on Elisa's face. "Elisa . . . "

"No!' Elisa shouted, her voice shaking. "Promise! You have to promise you won't let—"

"Elisa, please calm down." Ava didn't know what made her say the exact thing that never worked.

"Don't tell me what to do! You can't tell me what to do!"

"I'm sorry! I don't want you getting wound up! You have a big day ahead of you."

"An hour! You said an HOUR!"

Ava turned to gather her breath, tucking her hair behind her ears over and over. She turned back to find Elisa glaring. Softly she said, "Only an hour. I promise. Margherita can handle it, we've been working on it. She might not like it, but she'll see you in an hour and then she'll learn that she'll always see you again." Ava didn't add that maybe Elisa could learn the same.

Elisa glowered at her yogurt cake.

"Tell you what. After I drop you off at school, I'll head straight to the playground. So Margherita has two people looking after her. Then we'll all come get you from school."

"Where's Isotta?"

"She's napping with Jacopo. He woke up early, his sleep is still all over the place."

"Well, obviously. Massimo never let us—"

Ava grew still. Might Elisa reveal anything, *anything* about her month on the road?

Elisa pushed her plate aside. "Let's get this over with."

They stepped outside into the castle courtyard and stood for a moment, watching the fog drift through the valley. Ava reached for her daughter's hand. "The view is incredible from here, isn't it?"

Elisa didn't answer.

Faltering, Ava asked. "Do you miss staying with Nonna and Nonno?"

Elisa shrugged. "I just like not moving." She hitched her backpack higher on her shoulders and stepped down the stairs that led to Via Romana. Ava watched Elisa's thin frame, the knot in her hair where she neglected to brush. Ava remembered how many knots Elisa had when she first returned to Santa Lucia. It had taken hours to brush them, to gently tease the hairs apart. The work should have been onerous perhaps, but with the fire crackling in the grate, and Isotta nursing Jacopo in the rocking chair as Margherita played with the paper dolls Elisa made her, while Ale and Enrico and Edo bustled about the table, putting out lamb stew and still-warm focaccia sent over by Sauro the baker, the time had been idyllic. Ava wished they could live in that bubble forever. Where nothing bad could happen.

As Elisa's head disappeared down the stairs, Ava raced to catch up.

They walked together in silence through the *piazza* and to the door of the middle school.

Elisa sighed in resignation. She gave Ava another baleful glance. "One hour."

"One hour. If you aren't here, I'll come up myself to grab you."

Despite herself, Elisa smiled. "You would not."

Ava shrugged, her eyes wide. "Don't underestimate me."

Elisa chuckled a little at the image. She let herself get swirled in with the assembling students. A few girls yelped, throwing their arms around Elisa and enveloping her, pulling her into the building.

Ava stood for several minutes, watching the last of the children evaporate into the middle school. The bell rang. Still, Ava watched. Waiting.

The *piazza* cleared of parents.

Ava watched. Waiting.

The bells of San Nicola tolled the hour, slowly, resolutely, deep with the tenor of generations. Ava looked up as if waking from a daze. Her eyes followed the birds darting across the sky. That sky. Was it always so lilting, wavering, blue upon blue?

She strolled down the hill, passing her parents' home. Her home, too, up until a few weeks ago when the children returned. Once the children tolerated separation . . . should she and Elisa move back with her parents? She hadn't known until she left how free she could feel without her parents' scrutiny and her brother's constant campaign of insults and criticisms.

Ava knew her parents grumbled at the unseemliness of their daughter living with a man, but really . . . could it be called "living" with Ale, when they all slept on mattresses strewn around the great room? The presence of so many prevented anything more daring than a swift kiss goodnight. And sometimes holding hands as they fell asleep, their mattresses snug against each other.

Not that Ava wanted more. Not yet. She needed to make sure she and

Ale fit together now.

She heard the swing before she spied Luciano pushing Margherita higher, higher. The little girl's laughter carried like birdsong, her curls trailing behind her as she reached up, up with her toes.

Luciano smiled at Ava's approach. "*Buongiorno*, Ava. I trust Elisa made it to school?"

"Barely."

Luciano waited.

But Ava just sighed.

Nodding, Luciano said, "She asks for Elisa every few minutes. But tolerates my answer that Elisa will be back soon."

Ava nodded. "Probably because of your idea to take them into the groves one-at-a-time for gradually increasing periods."

He cocked his head. "I wish I could take credit. But I believe it was Bea."

Ava darted a look at Luciano. She opened her mouth to speak, but then closed it again.

"Yes, *cara?*"

"I . . . I want to . . . apologize."

He smiled, his eyes behind their thick lenses creasing. "And what terrible offense did you commit?"

"We haven't talked about it . . . I couldn't, with the children missing . . . " Ava stammered. "But . . . Massimo betrayed your daughter with me. Even if Giulia never knew. It's an insult to her—"

Luciano held out a hand. "Stop."

"I've felt awful, dirty and mean, for years. When I let myself think about it, anyway."

Luciano shook his head. "Massimo betrayed my daughter. As he betrayed your innocence. You did nothing, *cara*, except get wounded in the process. I regret that no one had their eyes on you."

Ava's eyes swam with tears. "My parents had their hands full. With my brother."

"Fabio certainly took up a lot of space."

"He still does." Ava thought for a moment. "You don't blame me?"

Luciano turned from pushing Margherita, letting her laughter dapple like sunlight around them. "You, *cara*? How could I?"

The sun slipped behind the inky blue hills, rimming them briefly with a bold magenta line. For a moment, the landscape resembled a collage of postcards, cut out and glued together to increase the drama of the scene. The villagers didn't notice as they drifted into L'Ora Dorata.

For years, they had viewed the *trattoria* as a place for tourists. A hodgepodge of culinary influences that attempted to appeal to every possible visitor, and therefore appealed to none. Not having a local option in Santa Lucia, villagers ate at home. Or, for special occasions, they ventured into Girona.

Now, they surged forward, eager to taste the flavors of their childhoods, long forgotten. Rumor had it that on tonight's menu would be pasta with a rabbit *ragù*. Not tomato-based, but rather a white sauce, heady with the scent of wild thyme and layered with the richness of local pecorino.

The stone walls of the restaurant filled, almost overflowed, with burbling voices. Pietro, the man responsible for L'Ora Dorata's renaissance, crossed his arms and smiled, unable to believe his luck. Quickly, he skipped his fingers across the iron bar he'd nailed behind the register.

He turned to greet Ale and Ava, entering with Elisa. He wondered how in the world they'd been able to separate Margherita from Elisa, but as he approached their table, he heard Elisa whine, "What if she wakes up?"

Ava said, "Then Isotta will tell her you stepped out for a few minutes and you'll be right back."

"And she'll text you."

They must have had this conversation before.

Ava sounded drained. "And she'll text me."

More than once.

Elisa's shoulders sagged, but she took out her sketchbook without a word. Pietro glanced at her work, which had matured during her month-long kidnapping. Her lines were, if anything, more sure. She equivocated not at all, her hand sweeping over the page. He wondered if she'd had access to art supplies during her absence. Her thin frame certainly suggested she hadn't had enough food.

He reminded himself to tell the chef to load her plate well.

Ava turned to Arturo at the next table and asked him about the begonias he'd purchased at her father's flower shop. Arturo shrugged. "My wife can't keep them watered. You know she's so wrapped up—"

"Having an affair. Yes, I know," Ava said with a tired smile.

Arturo leered. "Speaking of affairs, I suppose you know about the mayor and Magda?"

Ava sighed. "That's a rumor, Arturo. As you well know."

Arturo nodded greedily. "Well, his children heard about this 'rumor' and I understand they are *not* pleased."

Ava drew back a touch. "You told them, didn't you? You can't resist making trouble."

Arturo blanched. "I only told Mauro. He told the rest."

Ava sighed and turned back to her table. "Oh, Arturo."

"What?" He lifted his arms.

Ava shook her head. Raising her voice, she asked, "Ale, are you getting the rabbit *ragù*?"

Ale blinked and then gazed from Arturo to Ava with a shaky grin. Ava's parents were joining them, weren't they? He'd counted on them footing the bill for dinner. His mind turned to his wallet, with proverbial moths flitting out of it. He shifted uncomfortably while working to maintain his confident smile. At the sight of Ava's parents strolling into L'Ora Dorata, he heaved a sigh of relief.

Meanwhile, Arturo grumbled and turned back to his bocce league, joining them in ripping chunks of bread and tossing back great gulps of the rough country wine they preferred with their *salumi*.

Ava greeted her parents and caught sight of Bea, now entering the restaurant with her family. A grin plastered across her face, Bea announced, "It's my birthday! My children *insisted* I not make dinner."

"*Auguri*, Bea," Ava said before adding cheekily, "Now why did you never teach your children to cook for you?"

Bea laughed. "I tried!"

Ava chuckled. "I think it was all a ploy to keep them coming to your house every night for dinner."

Bea and her family laughed and continued to their table. Catching sight of the enormous vase of flowers, Bea pushed past the rest of the customers, barely acknowledging Marcello, Santa Lucia's favorite police officer, dining with his parents.

Marcello joined his family in calling "*Auguri*" to Bea, but he didn't pay attention to their passing. Until his vision caught on Bea's granddaughter.

Wasn't it just a moment ago that Antonella had been a girl in a pinafore and braids? And now...he couldn't take his eyes off her liquid brown eyes, deep as the swimming hole he and his friends dove into to refresh on a summer day. He watched as Antonella cut through the room like sharp scissors through yielding fabric. A girl no longer, she seemed all woman—feminine, strong...and mesmerizing.

Unaware of Marcello following her with his eyes, Antonella sidled past her grandmother to continue her conversation with her father about her job in Girona at a product consulting firm. The secretarial work had been a bore, but she'd just found out that a senior marketing agent had taken a shine to her and requested her as his assistant. Antonella felt sure that now she'd get her foot in the business world.

She never noticed Marcello's gaze trained on her. Even as her grandmother and Marcello's mother winked at each other across the bustling restaurant.

Dante shook his head. "He won't tell me, Magda."

Magda grumbled before accepting her *cappuccino* from Chiara. "I'm sure he told you. You just delight in having all the information."

Dante laughed, his hand on his chest. "Me?"

"Yes! You *love* keeping me in the dark."

His voice lowered, "I do no such thing, Magda, and you know it. Perhaps—"

"This isn't my sugar!" She glared at the offending blue packet she'd ripped open.

Chiara nodded. "Regular sugar is right there, Magda—"

"I know!" She snatched up a white packet.

Dante leaned closer to Magda. "Seriously, Magda. I promise. Ale hasn't told me anything about the professor's visit."

"*You* introduced Ale to him. You *must* know if the mystery grapes have value."

"I *don't.*"

"I don't want to stop you if you're enjoying the repartee," Chiara smiled, scooping up the discarded packet of diet sugar. "But the wine expert got the flu, and they rescheduled. For next week."

Magda glared. "How do you know?"

"They stopped in last night before dinner and Ale mentioned it because he's concerned about the grapes over-ripening in the delay. He's also feeling sure the expert will tell him the mystery grapes are useless. He's distracting himself by working on one app project after another."

Magda looked mollified. "Oh."

Dante tentatively touched her hand.

Magda shook her head. "I'm still cross with you."

Dante's eyes widened. "But why? What did I do?"

Magda's brow contracted in fury. "I don't know, but I'm sure there's something." Her glare faltered, and she began chuckling.

Dante laughed as well, and soon they were both in merry peals of laughter.

Edo, entering the bar from the upstairs apartment, watched them for a moment before glancing quizzically at Chiara. She shrugged, rolling her eyes heavenward. He grinned, and they had to look away from each other to keep from laughing.

The sun hesitated in the sky, filling Santa Lucia with extra shimmer. Ava and Isotta reclined on the lawn chairs, watching Elisa and Margherita chase each other as the day waned. Neither mother could figure out how the ball figured into their game.

Ava nodded toward Jacopo, asleep in the crook of Isotta's arm. "Do you want help getting into him into his crib?"

"No."

Ava smiled. "You want to hold him as long as possible."

Isotta's eyes stung with tears. "Yes."

Ava turned back to Elisa and Margherita, who had flopped on the grass. "I know what you mean."

They watched for a few moments, the fall breeze drifting across their cheeks. A bird darted across the tapestry of the sky, an echo of the swallows that had chased each other south with the approach of cooler weather.

Isotta seemed to wake up from a dream. She smiled at Ava. "How are you, my friend?"

Ava lifted her hands to re-knot the hair at the nape of her neck. "It doesn't feel real. We went from all those days of worrying and dreading and needing, *needing* at such a basic level, you know?"

"Elemental, yes."

"Now they're all here. Back. And our life is filled. Not just with the glorious chaos of children, but all these . . . "

"Obligations."

"Yes! Everyone has their endless trying questions. About Elisa. About moving back home. About my brother, who seems to have taken Elisa's return as an invitation to return to his old habits." She sighed. "Everywhere I turn. Noise."

"I know what you mean. Tonight, the quiet . . . it feels a little magic."

As the breeze increased in strength, the tips of the olive trees swayed. Elisa noticed this and bolted upright before relaxing her body to bend like the trees. Margherita watched intently before spreading her arms and tilting from side to side, a kite caught in a swirl of wind. The girls lifted their arms high, letting their fingers drift in and out of the fading light.

Ava's breath caught. "They are so damn beautiful."

"I can't believe I never guessed they were sisters."

"Really? They look so different."

"Only because of Margherita's black curls," Isotta said. "Look at their upturned noses, the shape of their eyes, the set of their chin. Just like—"

"I know."

Isotta faltered. "I wish we knew."

"What happened to him? Me too."

"Luciano tells me he's sure he's dead."

"Ale says the same."

"So does everyone."

Ava said, "I'll believe it when I see it."

Isotta nodded. After a moment, she faltered, "Us being at the castle . . ."

"*Sì?*"

"You know what they say about fish smelling after three days. We're over three *weeks*."

Ava grinned. "Are you the fish in this scenario?"

Isotta didn't hear her. "And right when you and Ale..."

Ava reached over the expanse between the two chairs and rested her hand on Isotta's arm, letting her fingers brush against Jacopo's foot propped up at a ridiculous angle as the boy slept deeply. "Isotta. Please. I want you here. It's good for me. And the children..."

Isotta lowered her eyes. "It's good for me, too." She watched Elisa and Margherita as their tree-like swaying morphed into some kind of dancing game. "But at some point, we need to move on."

"I suppose." Ava frowned. "I'm sure Luciano is eager to have you back."

Isotta worried her lip between her teeth. "I don't know if I can move back in with Luciano."

Ava sat up straight, her eyes blazing. "What?"

"Two bedrooms? I can't sleep in one room with both children. Not for long, anyway."

Ava frowned. "How did his parents live there with *three* children?"

Isotta smiled. "They made it work. And right now it sounds blissful. Waking up to the sound of their breathing."

"To reach out and touch them when they're restless."

Isotta nodded. "But practically speaking. It can't be that way forever." Her lip trembled, "I can remodel Massimo's house with his money. Only..."

"Living in Massimo's house reminds you of moving to enemy camp?" Ava offered.

"*Esatto,*" Isotta nodded, grateful. "Besides, dividing the children... they're siblings, shouldn't they live together?"

Ava sat up straight. "Why are we ruling that out?"

"Ava."

"No, listen. This place has plenty of space. In the next month, we'll move the *passito* grapes into their barrels—"

"Already?"

Ava shrugged. "According to Bruno, the mystery grapes are reaching their pinnacle of sweetness." She shook her head, "Anyway, that room is *huge*. With some cash and time and labor, we can turn it into a suite of rooms."

Isotta hesitated. "It's a lot to ask of Ale—to let part of his birthright indefinitely, to have a single mother live under his roof. Even if I pay for rent and renovations."

Ava nodded. "We need to consider it. Ale's not talking about it, but I know the financial situation is stressful for him. This might resolve a few problems."

Nodding thoughtfully, Isotta said, "I'll know next week how much money I'm getting. If there's enough . . . but Ava, how would you feel with Massimo's money dribbling into the *castello* like this?"

Ava clasped Isotta's hand. "There's a funny rightness to it."

"Professore, welcome, welcome! Thank you for coming," Ale called as the gentleman from the University of Perugia stepped out of his Fiat.

"Gaetano, please," smiled the professor, adjusting his peacock blue scarf around his neck. His head swiveled as he took in the view. "Such a spot of heaven you discovered!"

Ale chuckled. "It's quite a story."

Gaetano's eyes behind his chunky black-framed glasses widened. "I'd be most interested."

Ale gestured to the town arch. "Do you want to see the vines first, or the grapes?"

"They aren't . . ."

Ale shook his head. "With the delay, Bruno, my, er, associate, suggested we remove the grapes from the vines and dry them to make—"

"A *passito*, yes, of course. An inspired notion. I do apologize for not being able to arrive for our initial appointment. Unavoidable." At Ale's nod of understanding, Gaetano said, "Let's see the vines. I'm desperately curious about what kind of soil you have that you'd be able to get any grapes whatsoever without spraying."

As they walked, Ale explained the history of the vineyard as well as he could, Gaetano peppering him with questions. Only some of which Ale could answer. Blushing, he said, "Bruno is meeting us at the *castello*. He'll be of better help."

"And a *castello*! What a fascinating story, Signor Bardi."

"Ale, please."

Gaetano ducked under an olive branch to arrive into a clearing, where a tumbling rock wall enclosed the vines. At the sight of a sunbeam breaking free and illuminating the vineyard, Gaetano breathed reverentially. "Magnificent. The slope, ideal. And perfect for sun exposure." He squinted. "Is the light always this . . ." He looked back at Ale in confusion. "I'm sorry. I rarely fail to find words. Descriptive language is my backbone. But this . . ."

Ale nodded. "I know what you mean. I don't notice it anymore, but when I first arrived, it hit me like a force."

"Like a force," Gaetano murmured appreciatively. He nodded to himself. "All right then, Ale. Let's see your vines."

Once in the vineyard, Ale led Gaetano to the corner. "Bruno couldn't recognize them . . . but he's local, maybe hasn't had too much exposure to grapes from outside the region. And we're so close to Le Marche, I thought, perhaps—"

Gaetano shook his head, his arm up to request silence. Murmuring to himself, he ran his fingers over the veins of a leaf, then down the ragged sides. He stepped back, examining the flow of the vines. Without a word, he pulled out his phone and began taking photographs. Looking up, he said, "I hope you won't mind—"

"Not at all. Whatever you need." Ale watched the man work, alighting like a butterfly over the leaves, the vines, the soil. Hands in his pockets, Ale crossed his fingers. He wanted this to succeed. He *needed* this to succeed. He'd sunk so much time, so much energy, so much hope into these vines. They couldn't fail him. His thoughts turned to the wine resting in barrels at the *castello*. According to wine blogs, it would soon be time to taste. The thought left him breathless. He imagined Ava's flashing eyes as she sipped the fruit of his labor, before leaning in to kiss him with breath perfumed by his wine. The image cracked, and he pictured her face, sour and petulant, as she shoved it away, complaining it tasted like funky vinegar. As all his ambition circled the drain. He wished one of his app ideas would pan out, at least a little. It would take the pressure off this wine business.

Ale startled at Gaetano's words. "May I take a leaf with me?'

"Absolutely. But this vine isn't that unusual, is it?"

"At the very least, it's unusual for this area, Signor Bardi. That's all I can say with certainty at this point."

Ale started to correct the formal terminology and then decided against it. "Would you like to see the grapes?"

"Please."

As Ale led the way back through the groves he said, "You'll be able to identify the varietal, even though they've been drying for over a week?"

"Undoubtedly."

They walked in silence until they crested the hill and arrived at the *castello*. Ale waited for Gaetano to make a noise of appreciation, but at the pause in their journey, Gaetano only said, "The grapes, if you please, Signore."

Ale nodded and strode to the drying room.

Bruno stood at the threshold, cap in hand.

Gaetano met him, hand outstretched. They had a few moments of whispered conference while Ale stood awkwardly. Then Bruno ushered Gaetano into the room. Feeling uncomfortable, Ale filled the silence. "You can see I've got barrels of wine from the other grapes over there. We think this used to be a ballroom, or perhaps a receiving room of some kind. In any case, it's big and airy, and Bruno thought it would be good for drying our mystery grapes for *passito*."

Gaetano stared at the grapes drying in a sea across the floor. "Net?"

Ale nodded. "Bruno said I could borrow his straw mats, but I Googled and found that nets from the olive harvest work just as well. And that I had, here at the *castello*."

Gaetano regarded Ale with curiosity before kneeling to pick up a bunch of slightly shriveled grapes. Ale started to explain that Bruno claimed they had at least another couple of months to dry and sweeten before pressing and fermentation turned them into dessert wine.

But at the serious gleam in Gaetano's eye, Ale said nothing.

Gaetano nodded to himself, muttering. He took photos, pressed a grape between two fingers and tasted. Ale lost track of Gaetano's examinations.

Finally, Gaetano stood. His face serious, he said, "Unless I'm much mistaken, Signor Bardi, this grape you have inadvertently discovered in your vineyard is the Prescia variety. Lost to the region in the 1800s when a louse obliterated the vines. But not, it appears, your stock."

Ale's mouth fell open. "The 1800s? But vines can't last that long."

"Vines can't. But many of our noblest varieties, Sagrantino to name a local example, have been in existence since the time of the Roman Empire. I refer you to Pliny the Elder, whose documentations serve as our treatise on ancient vines. As the vines themselves age, they lose their vigor, which is why we propagate, either by grafting onto hardy rootstock or, if the soil is good, directly into the ground. Your soil is exceptionally well suited—"

"Bruno told me that."

"Did he? Well, then. That knowledge informs our understanding of your vineyard. Perhaps unaware of the rarity of their grapes, previous owners kept the vines growing. They look to be nearing their demise—"

"Bruno told me that, too."

Gaetano nodded and turned to Bruno. "What prompted you to turn these grapes into *passito*?"

Bruno ran a hand over his grizzled face. "I tasted them. Seemed good for *passito*."

"Well said." Gaetano beamed. "Signor Bardi. You must trust your friend Bruno here. He seems to know quite a good deal."

Bruno frowned and gazed out toward the groves.

Chuckling, Gaetano said, "Now, make a good *passito* with these grapes, and you'll have winemakers clamoring to buy your clippings to plant in their own vineyards."

Ale rubbed his thumb. "Can't you tell the winemakers? Get them interested—"

Gaetano laughed aloud. "I'm afraid marketing is outside my skillset. Make a good *passito*, Signor Bardi. Make a good *passito* and people will line up for a taste of this history."

"*Buongiorno*, Magda! You're looking refreshed this morning."

Magda nodded. "Thank you, Chiara. I'll never again underestimate the power of sleeping in a house without a convict snoring in the next room."

Chiara chuckled. "Everything back to normal?"

Frowning, Magda said, "Nothing will ever be normal. Not ever again. Do you not know that?"

Chiara darted a look at Magda over her shoulder as the coffee dripped into the thick, white cup.

"No, things can't ever go back to normal." Magda tipped her chin onto her hand. "For years, I lived in a kind of purgatory. Was Gustav alive? Dead? It weighed me down. Now I'm free. Not just of Karl, thank God. But of that half-life."

As she foamed the milk, Chiara asked. "I'm not following. I mean, you still don't know where Gustav is, do you?"

Magda shook her head. "Not with any certainty. But I learned that when Karl escaped, the German police looked into Gustav's disappearance, in case Karl joined his brother. They discovered a story circulating through Bangkok about a German man who died years ago in a boating accident. The police suspect Karl learned the same story. It's what emboldened him to come here."

"And Gustav's parents?"

"Grieved him long ago. They knew he'd come home if he were alive."

Chiara set the *cappuccino* in front of Magda.

Magda sighed. "I'm returning Gustav's money to his parents."

"That's ... that's generous."

Magda said, "It's the least I can do. I see now, in a way I didn't before, that he was a good man."

Chiara smiled faintly. "Compared to his brother."

"*Especially* compared to his brother." Magda reached for the sugar. "But you don't have to play innocent, Chiara. Everyone loved Gustav."

"Well ... "

"After living with Karl, I understand. Gustav loved this town and that made him lovable. I've seen Gustav as a horrible person for years. I had to. Now I see he was a good person trapped in a bad marriage. Trapped with me."

"Oh, Magda." Chiara instinctively clasped Magda's hand and then winced, expecting Magda to pull her hand back with a remark. Instead, Magda squeezed Chiara's hand.

Magda said, "I've been trapped with me for years. I know it's no picnic."

Chiara smiled sadly, "Magda..."

Magda paused, stirring her *cappuccino* until the bubbles deflated. "And with that, I feel complete. That part of my life is over. Now, I've decided to begin."

"Begin?"

"And you should do the same, Chiara. *Begin.*"

Chiara narrowed her eyes.

Magda smiled indulgently. "All these years, you soak up our secrets, without ever divulging your own."

Paling, Chiara said softly, "I have no secrets."

Magda patted her hand. "Of course you do. You're more transparent than you think you are."

The bell over the door jingled merrily as a group of tourists walked in and stopped, gazing around with wide eyes, in the way of tourists unfamiliar with the idiosyncrasies and dynamics of Italian bars.

Dante rehearsed the festival preparations. He counted and recounted the fire extinguishers, checked every open flame like a nervous mother. Rubbing his hand across his forehead, he wondered for the hundredth time if he'd been right to acquiesce to Magda's insistence that the festival must be held at the *castello*. He wouldn't have given in at all, if she hadn't dragged Ale to him by the elbow so the castle owner could tell him that he'd be delighted to host the *sagra*. It would be magnificent advertising.

Each day since, Magda had ordered a different villager to tell Dante how having the *sagra* at the *castello* would ease their memories of shrieks shattering the night air. He suspected Magda badgered more than one of these villagers into this opinion, but he couldn't deny their fervor. Or the fact that last year's festival had been a tremendous success up until the fire torqued the *sagra* into something nightmarish. The crumbling *castello* as a wild backdrop, the moon rising and spreading ripples of silver across the olive trees. It had been a scene of surpassing beauty.

For better or for worse, the castle no longer crumbled. But it still offered a flavor of old Umbria. Only now it appeared neat and trim, with its village-sized turret and the arrow slits marching like soldiers beneath the parapet. How lucky that Ale had repaired the derelict *loggia* before he left Madison and lost his money. There wasn't another wooden balustrade like it in Umbria. Or even Italy. Too bad the plans of a fresco behind it didn't come to fruition. Though the sunflower yellow wall did work quite well.

As Dante scanned the scene, he had to admit that the *castello* fit just right with the rising scent of *cinghiale* roasting even now on the spit, guarded by farmers standing around and sipping new wine, as if observation were paramount to the process.

Dante sniffed the air. He couldn't smell the spice-scented *vin brulé*, so the women must not yet have prepared the mulled wine. He wondered if they would require an extension cord. Last year, without access to power, what did they use? Sterno, maybe? Dante began pacing.

He stopped as a group of workers carried an enormous cauldron up the stairs. Behind them came Giuseppe and other volunteers, heaving enormous tubs of wild boar that had been soaking in white wine, then red wine with herbs and garlic. Ready now for simmering over an open flame.

Crossing his arms, Dante nodded to himself. Charming! Artists, farmers, and craftsmen set up their stands as the scent of warming oil to fry *brustegnolo*, the flatbread scattered with scented sugar, rose into the air. He smiled, watching as Ava and Elisa made their way toward them.

Elisa stopped at a stand with renderings of olive trees, while Ava joined Dante. "I'm already hungry. How long will the stew take?"

Dante glanced at Giuseppe and his son-in-law, stirring with a long-handled spoon that resembled a paddle. "A few hours."

Ava groaned.

Elisa rushed up. "Did you see those paintings?"

Ava smiled and put an arm around her. "I did, but—" Elisa's shout of "Fatima!" silenced Ava's words. Elisa tore across the castle lawn to the stairs, where Fatima stood, arms wrapped around herself as she peered into the crowd. Fatima's face creased in a grin at the sight of Elisa.

Dante said, "That's Fatima? How could she have changed so much in a month?"

Ava didn't answer, just took in Fatima's poise, the way her ordinary clothes seemed to hang differently. She didn't look as if she'd lost weight—she'd always been thin—but nonetheless she seemed . . . willowy. The age difference between her and Elisa fairly creaked.

Elisa didn't seem to notice as she tugged Fatima toward the stands. Fatima seemed uncomfortable. As if she'd been forced into pants outgrown last season.

Ava stood on tiptoe to see over the rising tide of shoulders. "Her parents aren't here."

Dante made a non-committal noise, his attention caught by a surge of flame from the roasting boar.

Ava tugged his elbow. "Dante. Don't you understand? They left because they couldn't make a life here. Those lovely people . . ." Her breath caught, remembering all those times she'd knocked on their door to remind Elisa to come home and had a plate of something warm and savory thrust into her hands. She'd never been able to communicate well with Fatima's family. Hadn't even known that Salma spoke much English until the celebration of L'Ora Dorata's opening, when it seemed half the town spilled from the restaurant into the *piazza*.

After Fatima had left with Valentina's driver, Ava had seen the tears in Salma's eyes and slipped her hand in Salma's. Salma had seemed surprised at first, but squeezed back. Turning to Ava, she'd said, "I know it's ridiculous. We'll join her tomorrow. But even so . . . she's leaving us."

At Ava's stunned expression, Salma had offered her a faltering grin. "Your daughter is a treasure. I always meant to tell you."

That was it for conversation before Omar had recalled Salma to his side to gather their things and head home.

Ava tugged Dante's elbow again. "Dante? Are you hearing me?"

"Yes. Of course, I am. A sad situation, to be sure, but what can be done about it?"

"They needed jobs. They needed to feel safe. Fatima's brothers, their friends, you heard how they were harassed."

He frowned sympathetically. "Such a shame."

"Dante! You're the *mayor*!"

"Those boys got beat up in Girona, not here." He pushed his chest out.

Ava grumbled, "It could just as easily have been here."

Dante ignored her. "As for work, I'm afraid you don't know what a mayor does, Ava. Finding jobs for residents is beyond the scope of our job description. It's sad, of course, one wishes to be more helpful, but it's too late now. They've left."

"You know there are others. There's that family that lives just off the main road. They're thinking of following, leaving too. They need to *live*, Dante! They deserve a chance! After coming all this way—"

"There you go again, Sister." Fabio appeared at her elbow. "Putting your nose where it doesn't belong."

"Fabio." Ava recoiled. "What are you doing here?"

He shrugged, his eyes wide. "Am I not part of Santa Lucia?"

She grumbled while Fabio turned to Dante. "I hope you are humoring my sister, Dante. Everyone knows it's better to support your own people over outsiders."

Ava glared at her brother. "Who said anything about supporting outsiders *more*?"

Fabio said, "I don't hear you arguing on behalf of anybody else. And don't you remember the fire last year? Do you want more of those assaults?"

Ignoring her yelp of protest, Fabio turned to Dante. "I've been meaning to talk to you about that, Dante. You need to assign a councilman in charge of policing, the immigrants especially. Don't you think—"

Dante patted his shoulder. "I never like to get between quarreling siblings. Now, if you'll excuse me. I very clearly told the basket weaver to sit far from the roasting *cinghiale*."

Ava spun on her heel, away from Fabio who was now glowering at Dante. She scanned the crowd, looking for Elisa and Fatima, but lost sight of them amid the rising tide of villagers. Everyone seemed intent on being the first to arrive. Long before the festival was due to begin, the castle lawn stood filled with laughter, conversation, and the scent of simmering stew. The preparations advanced far more quickly, with so many hands to open tables, cover them with cloths, and spread wares.

Women ventured into the groves, returning with handfuls of olive boughs to stand into bottles on each table.

Ava blinked.

The olive boughs. Were they . . . *twinkling*? Like fairy lights? She shook her head, and the sparkling subsided. Must have been her vision. Perhaps without knowing it, she'd gazed into the sun for too long as it slipped over the mountains.

Tourists arrived, joining the villagers at the tables.

Dante was not the only one stalking the perimeter, studying each stall, looking for errant sparks. But every shred of flame—heating oil, bubbling fat, licking the haunch of *cinghiale* being turned on the spit—every flame behaved.

At the edge of the festivities, Dante almost ran into Magda, standing in the dark. "Magda? Why are you over here by yourself?"

Magda ran her hands over her arms. "People seem to be having a good time."

"It's a wonderful *sagra*."

"I guess I was right."

Dante grinned, his teeth flashing in the half-light. "You sound surprised."

"*Allora*," she breathed. "You never know."

"Yes, we do. You are always, *always* right."

"Always?"

Dante shrugged expansively. Drifting his hand over Magda's arm, he said, "Now come. Join the party."

Magda hesitated. Her words halting, she said, "Last year...I remember. Vale waved at me, but then I realized it wasn't me he wanted, it was Stella. I left. Alone. And later, that's when you found them. Vale and Stella."

Dante shifted his weight.

"That's why you didn't want to have the *sagra* here."

Still, Dante said nothing, just scanned the festival-goers drifting like shadows.

"I'm sorry, Dante. I'm sorry that happened. And I'm sorry I didn't think of it."

Dante smiled and took her hand. "In the magic of the evening, that feels long ago. Now. Let's join the party."

"All right, lovebirds," Bea commanded as she stepped into Bar Birbo's morning light. "That's enough of that!"

Fabrizio gave Chiara a swift kiss on the cheek before chuckling and taking his coffee to the little table where he spread his newspaper. Edo brought him his *cornetto* with a smile.

Bea nodded as if in confirmation before she settled on a stool. "*Cappuccino*, Chiara, *per favore*."

Chiara nodded and within moments the bar filled with the scent of grinding beans.

The bell over the door tinkled, announcing Livia's entrance. Livia paused to survey the bar before hanging her smart coat on the rack. Seeing Bea still wearing hers, she said, "I'll hang that for you, Bea."

Bea clucked. "No, thank you, dear. I run cold. In fact, I might just take yours."

The chortle of foaming milk rang through the bar as Livia greeted Fabrizio. "*Buongiorno*, Fabrizio. I haven't seen you since the opening."

He leaned back with a smile. "No, I've been wrapping up work in Bologna."

As Chiara handed Bea her *cappuccino*, Livia asked for a *caffè* and then turned back to Fabrizio. "I heard you write mysteries."

"Yes, that's true. Though I'm thinking of experimenting, trying something new."

Livia looked stern. "Fabrizio, you'll need to bear in mind that when writers change genres they lose readership, and thus, income. I have many good friends in the writing world, so I fancy myself a bit of an expert."

Fabrizio inclined his head. "I appreciate the advice."

Livia insisted. "I know how little authors earn. You can't afford to take risks—"

"Has anyone heard about our little Fatima? When will we see her on magazine covers?" Edo interjected.

Livia sniffed. "Not for some time, I would imagine. It takes years for a fashion model to get onto the main stage." She thanked Chiara for her coffee. "Also, you know she's not model material. Not like my Sonia."

Bea stirred her *cappuccino* as Fabrizio turned the page of his paper to study the sports page. Edo clattered dishes in the sink while Chiara nodded along to Livia declaring that if Sonia had been at the mall when Fatima had been "discovered" (her voice heavy with air quotes), it would be *she* in Milan. Not that she would let Sonia embark into that world. Restaurant management was much more important work.

As the bell over the door chimed again, Bea practically wrenched her neck trying to see who entered. She cheered, "Magda! Join us!"

Magda nodded absently. "*Cappuccino*, Chiara. It's gotten chilly already! Did you see the frost on the ground yesterday?" She unwound her scarf. "Bea, it made me think of your chickens. How are they faring?"

Bea smiled, pleased. "They didn't enjoy it. But they gave me extra eggs, so who can know the mind of a chicken?"

Magda chuckled, and she and Bea began exchanging egg-based recipes. Magda had heard of a dish from Spain with eggs and potatoes. Which sounded good with this coming cold. Bea shook her head, laughing. "Why would we want to eat food from Spain? They don't even *have* pasta."

Chiara and Edo exchanged looks with a laugh.

Livia rushed in, "Oh! The French do this marvelous thing with eggs where they put them in aspic. Quite elegant! I've told Pietro to serve them in his restaurants, but the man is so old school, he only serves dishes the locals expect."

Bea paled and muttered about how good that sounded. Fabrizio turned the page of his newspaper. The sound echoed through the quiet bar.

Chiara licked her upper lip, "Nonna used to put hard-boiled eggs in her *braciola*."

Bea said, "I've heard of that."

Magda leaned forward. "*Braciola* is actually based on a German recipe. Beef and eggs."

Bea and Chiara laughed until Bea wiped tears from her eyes. "Braciola! *German*! Oh, Magda. You are too much."

Livia pressed her lips together and then dropped her euro coin on the scuffed copper plate. At the sound, Bea turned. "Leaving already, Livia?"

Livia nodded.

Bea said, "*Alla prossima*! We'll see you soon!"

The door hardly shut behind Livia when Magda muttered. "What a tiresome woman."

Bea harrumphed her agreement and looked at Chiara. Who shrugged and said, "She means well. This is a hard town to break into."

All eyes turned to Fabrizio, who turned another page of his newspaper before looking up. "I happen to know that's factually true."

Peals of laughter from all three met Dante as he entered the bar. "I missed something?"

Magda moved over to make room for him next to her. "A spot of town gossip."

He waggled his eyebrows. "Oh, well then, do share."

Magda shook her head vehemently. "No way. You are the worst. You can't keep a secret to save your life."

Dante looked affronted. "And how would you know that? If you could see all the secrets I have stored up in here," he gestured to his chest, "You'd be shocked. Shocked! And also amazed."

Chiara darted her gaze at Dante as Magda narrowed her eyes. "Tell us one, then."

"A trick!" Dante yelped. "I can spot your tricks a kilometer away!"

As the two bantered, Bea widened her eyes at Chiara, and then Fabrizio. Who smiled before looking back down at his newspaper.

Bea announced loudly, "Did you all hear about Ale's *passito*?"

Dante broke off his conversation with Magda. "Bruno won't talk about it."

Magda frowned. "I heard there's not much of it. Anyway, are we sure this professor can be trusted? What do we know about him?"

Dante protested, "I recommended him."

Magda shrugged. "If it *is* true, somebody needs to talk to Ale about how to use this to Santa Lucia's advantage. Not just to line his purse."

Dante bristled. "I suppose you mean me. I'm the mayor, so I'm conscripted with this thankless task before I can even order my *caffè*. *Caffè*, by the way, Chiara."

She nodded.

Magda crossed her arms. "You expect me to do it? I hardly know Ale!"

Dante gesticulated, his hands moving to his chest and then out again wildly. "And I do? I've enough to deal with now that Fabio's breathing down my neck to appoint him to the town council, in charge of *policing* of all things. You can imagine how well that would go over with the department after the whole bones situation." Noticing Magda's gesture of annoyance, Dante got back to the topic. "And anyway, Ale's grapes aren't a civic matter!"

"Of *course* they are! How can you be so blind?"

Magda drained the last of her coffee and threw her euro on the copper plate before stalking out. Leaving wide eyes behind her.

Isotta shoved open Bar Birbo's door. At the tinkle of the bell, Chiara turned and said, "*Ciao*, Isotta. Riccardo isn't here yet."

Isotta nodded. "Can I get a *caffè*?"

"Of course, *cara*. No milk today?"

"No. Straight and fast. If you could mainline the caffeine, I'd prefer it."

Chiara watched Isotta slump onto a stool. She knew Isotta considered herself plain, but Chiara had always appreciated how Isotta looked as if she belonged frescoed onto a wall with a gold-leaf halo. Only now, with her hair lank and her face pale, her three-dimensional beauty had faded to a two-dimensional sketch of her former self. Chiara frowned and turned to make Isotta's coffee. "Rough night?" she asked, watching the drops of *espresso* squeeze through the La Pavoni with a practiced eye.

Isotta rested her chin on her hand. "So much yes. We moved to the guest room and both kids were up all night."

"It's a transition. *Piano, piano.*"

"But it's so painful for all of them. It makes me wonder why we're forcing it."

Brushing spilled coffee beans, Chiara asked, "Is there another option?"

"I don't know. I can't think straight."

Chiara tensed as a silhouetted figure approached the door. She breathed again recognizing Rosetta on her way to work, not yet Riccardo.

Isotta said listlessly. "Ignore me, Chiara. It's a hard day."

"Could you ask Livia for help? I'm sure she—"

Isotta shook her head. "She's offered, but what could she do with Margherita, if the child refuses to separate from Jacopo and Elisa? I can't ask her to hang out with all these children that are no relation." She sighed. "This meeting with Riccardo. I hope he's figured out how to list me as a beneficiary on Massimo's accounts. If I could renovate that castle room . . ."

"I'm sure he can. Riccardo is a gifted *avvocato*."

"But what if there's not enough money to renovate the space at the *castello*? I'd have to move into Massimo's, and Chiara, after everything that happened, I don't think I can."

"*Cara*, Massimo made a lot of money. I know, Anna bragged about it all the time. *All* the time. And he never spent it." Chiara looked up at the sight of Riccardo walking down Via Romana. "Here he is."

Isotta nodded, blinking back tears as she turned to greet Riccardo.

He entered the bar, in turn kissing Chiara and then Isotta's cheeks. "Isotta. I'm so sorry we keep meeting under difficult circumstances."

Isotta said, "I so appreciated all your help with Massimo. As difficult as he was with the custody, I know he would have been worse if you hadn't been in my corner."

Riccardo looked as if he wanted to say something, but he turned to Chiara. "*Caffè*, Chiara?"

"*Subito.*"

He turned back to Isotta. "How are the children?"

Isotta stared into her empty *espresso* cup. "Struggling. Elisa is up to half-days at school. She has periods where she seems fine, but others when she's . . . brittle. Margherita still protests being apart from her. Or Jacopo."

He nodded. "They need to learn to rely on their parental figures again."

She nodded and pushed her cup away.

Riccardo finished his *espresso* in three sips. "I wonder if we might talk at the *castello*?"

Isotta smiled. "Chiara said the two of you used to sneak in as children."

He laughed. "Teenagers, actually. We were bad. Or at least, my intentions were bad. Chiara, however . . . "

Chiara chuckled, "Breaking in was naughty enough."

As Isotta reached for her purse, Riccardo stayed her hand. "On me today, Isotta. Please."

Isotta tried not to let this rattle her. Was this a pity coffee? She steadied herself as she heard the coins clink onto the scuffed copper plate.

"Shall we?" Riccardo opened the door and led Isotta outside. After letting his fingers trail over the Madonna's skirts, he made idle conversation as they walked up the stairs to the *castello*. They walked around the perimeter of the lawn, where Riccardo noticed that the burnt olive trees had slight grey-green buds. Isotta stopped in surprise. She hadn't noticed.

She walked him through Ava's garden and popped into the renovated rooms. Riccardo lingered in the converted chapel. Isotta understood his reluctance to leave, the room seemed to hold the light. Finally, she led Riccardo to the breakfast room which, up until that morning, had been her family and Ava's collective bedroom. Isotta noticed that Ale had cleared away their surplus blankets and pillows and replaced them with a collection of tables scattered in front of the fireplace big enough to walk in. Ready for guests. And just in time as Ale mentioned yesterday with great significance that he had several reservations coming up. Thanks, no doubt, to Vito's and Enrico's stirring reviews.

Isotta gestured to the table closest to the fireplace, though it sat empty and cold. Isotta supposed she hoped for the mere remembrance of fire to warm her. She tugged her sleeves over her hands and waited.

Riccardo removed a sheaf of papers from his briefcase. "Well, Isotta, I'm sure you are eager to get to the point."

"I'm not sure eager is the word I'd use. But, yes."

He nodded. "So the good news is that there don't seem to be any legal hiccups to you accessing Massimo's account. There isn't any other next of kin, other than Margherita. Since the divorce papers hadn't been filed, we can get authorization for you to access his accounts even though he hasn't been declared dead."

She sagged, breathing a sigh of relief.

Riccardo hesitated. "The thing is, Isotta. Now, I need you to prepare yourself."

Isotta sat taller, clasping her hands between her knees.

"There is less money than expected."

"Less? How much less?"

Riccardo pulled out a sheet of paper and, taking a pair of glasses from his pocket, adjusted them on his nose before saying. "It looks like, all in all, Massimo was worth less than two thousand euros."

Isotta gasped. "How can that be? His job . . . Did he make less than he said? But that can't be . . . " Isotta remembered her own generous paycheck from the bank, and Massimo held a superior position.

Shaking his head, Riccardo said, "The bank paid him well. Each month I can see a hefty deposit entering his account. Enough to, given how little he spent, make you a rich woman. But it seems he transferred the bulk of that money to . . . well, to his mother."

"His *mother*?"

Riccardo nodded.

Isotta barked a laugh. "But *she's* dead."

"So it will go to you once he's declared dead. As inheritance, it works differently."

"How much does she have?"

"I can't access her account. But, based on how much he transferred to her, and reckoning that they didn't pay a mortgage—"

"They didn't?"

"The deed shows his father paid it off when Massimo was still a child." She nodded.

"Even calculating a handsome sum for utilities and groceries and cars, I expect that Anna was worth, given the amount transferred to her," Riccardo adjusted his glasses to read the number he'd penciled onto the page, while Isotta held her breath. "I'd guess at least 750,000 euros."

"Oh, my!"

"I'll have to do some digging to see if that's accurate. But you understand what this means, Isotta. We need to start the paperwork to declare Massimo dead. The process can take a year or more. Once that happens, you inherit all of it. Barring, of course, the possibility that there's a skeleton in a closet we're not budgeting for. Some next of kin we hadn't reckoned on, or something of that nature."

"Definitely possible with this family."

"Yes," Riccardo smiled. "The stories have reached even Spoleto. But until then, I'm afraid you have very little to live on. We should discuss your options."

"I guess I don't have any. Once the children are ready to separate, I'll have to move to Massimo's."

Riccardo nodded slowly. "It's roomy enough, surely."

Isotta tried to smile. "Oh, it's fine in all practical ways. If I could renovate so it felt less like a prison sentence, I wouldn't mind so much. But a few thousand euros? Even without a mortgage, I'll need to scrimp to make it last until I can get work." Her voice quavered.

"Remember, if he's discovered dead tomorrow, you could be a millionaire."

Isotta smiled sadly. "That's awfully tricky to wish for."

Francy strolled into Bar Birbo, his hands in his pockets and his eyes alive with suppressed excitement.

"You're looking happy this morning," Edo said, leaning across the counter to press his cheek against Francy's in a way that he hoped was chaste, or at least more chaste than suggested by the sudden fire that leaped into his belly.

"I am."

"Care to share?"

Francy inclined his head a touch before asking, "Can I have a *cappuccino*?"

"Milk in your coffee," Edo grinned. "There must be news."

Francy chuckled and then turned to greet Magda and Dante, arguing over the success of the *cinghiale* festival. Magda insisted, "The biggest turnout ever. My guests at Villa Tramonte assured me they'll tell their friends about it."

Dante shrugged. "I'm not denying that, Magda. I'm saying that it *might* have been a disaster. The unexpected does happen."

Magda said, "I suppose that's true. With our luck, Massimo could have shown up to hand out sugared almonds."

"Magda!" they all shouted.

She looked around, "What? It's true. You never know what will happen around here."

Edo shivered as he handed Francy his *cappuccino*. "So. Your news?"

Francy grinned. "You remember my friends Marco and Reuben?"

Edo scratched the back of his neck. "They were at your last show?"

"Yes, they live in Trieste."

"They're the ones who bring you coffee, yes, I remember. What about them?"

Francy smiled, his flush under his cheekbones spreading in pleasure.

"Their surrogate is pregnant."

Edo looked confused. "I'm sorry, what..."

"You remember them telling us about going to a clinic in the United States..."

"It's not ringing any bells."

Francy frowned. "Maybe that's when you were dragged away by Amelia."

"That sounds more familiar." Edo smiled at the memory. He and Amelia had hit it off, and she'd wanted to introduce him to her girlfriend, who had been raised in a small town outside Verona.

"And I never mentioned the backstory?" Francy's eyes flicked to Dante and Magda, who had stopped their conversation to observe theirs. "*Allora*, Marco and Reuben have wanted a child for years. They considered adopting, but the rules are so complicated nowadays. Even countries that gay couples used to be able to adopt from, they no longer can. Besides, they wanted a child from birth. Remember my other friends who adopted a son from a Ukrainian orphanage when he was two, and he had so many problems... lying, stealing, those rages..."

"I remember that. So sad, how much stress they're under."

"It's taken up their lives. So Marco and Reuben wanted a child from birth, and the only way to control that process is through surrogacy."

"But what is that exactly?" Edo thought he understood it, but the vague look of distaste on Dante's face made him wonder if perhaps he misunderstood.

"They get an egg donor, use their own sperm to fertilize the egg in a test tube, and then implant the embryo in a woman who agrees to carry and birth the child. Then they go home with their baby."

At a noise from Dante, they all turned.

Dante looked around. "What?"

Magda said, "What a surprise. You seem to have an opinion."

Dante said, "Don't you?"

Magda answered, "Why would I?" At Dante's incredulous expression, she sighed theatrically. "You forget, I'm German. We're much more progressive. Why should I care how other people get their babies?"

Dante muttered, "You never birthed one of your own."

Magda's eyes widened. "So because I haven't squeezed out a child, I'm not entitled to a position. Pardon my observation, but then as far as I can tell, you lack the basic equipment to have an opinion on the matter yourself."

"That's not the point and you know it."

Magda stood taller. "Is it not? Francy's friends, perfectly lovely people, right Francy?"

"Well, yes, but—"

"There you go. They want to have a child, and you get to decide that's wrong? Because they're gay, I presume. Dante, I wouldn't have thought it of you."

Dante's eyes filled with confusion. "No! That's not what I said! It has nothing to do with homosexuals."

Magda grunted and turned away. "Edo, Francy. I'm sorry you have to witness your mayor being this small-minded."

Dante leaped in, "No!" He took a breath and reached back for his air of authority. "You're taking my words out of context."

Edo mumbled. "I'm pretty sure we were all here for the context."

"It's the *surrogacy*. Don't you understand? Using a woman's womb like that? Like . . . like . . . paying rent on her body? It's prostituting that poor woman! That's why it's outlawed in any thinking society."

Francy pressed his lips together. "A thinking society, for instance, like the United States."

Dante lifted his chin. "We could go back and forth about the American moral compass, but most countries outlaw it because it's *wrong*."

Magda glowered. "So what you're saying is that when and if Edo decides to have children, Edo who you've known since he was a boy sitting here on this counter, his sole option should be adoption."

"Well, I didn't say *that*."

"That's good anyway," Magda clicked her spoon around her empty cup.

"I mean, raising children in a homosexual household. That can't be good for them, can it? Wouldn't they be more likely to be gay themselves?" He turned to Edo. "You've seen how hard it is to live in a world as a gay person. Would you wish that on a child?"

Francy clasped Edo's hand while Edo struggled to catch his breath.

Magda muttered, "I can't believe you think it's okay to say such things." She lifted her eyes to Edo. "Edo, I'm sorry. I wish we'd never horned in on your conversation."

Edo shrugged and said tightly. "I'm sure Dante isn't the only person thinking these things. It's rough to hear them, though. I'm not going to lie."

Dante pleaded. "It's nothing against *you*. I wish only for your happiness, Edo, you know that. I don't agree with surrogacy for anyone. It's simply not natural."

"Not natural?" Edo's voice went up at the last syllable.

Dante nodded as if pleased. "Precisely. I'm glad you understand."

Antonella dressed with particular care for her first day working with Signor Tocci. No longer part of the mass secretarial pool, she'd been *noticed*. All those hours drafting extra notes, asking crafted questions, it had paid off.

She stepped into the office and tried not to look smug as she glanced at the bullpen full of secretaries making long-distance calls for their bosses.

Antonella strode past the other women, imagining their eyes on her, wondering why she didn't take her customary place. Those that wondered would ask those with information. Soon *everyone* would know about her promotion.

She knocked smartly on Signor Tocci's door. At his "Enter!" she strode in, nodding in what she hoped was a professional manner. "*Buongiorno,* Signor Tocci."

He leaped up to shepherd Antonella to the chair beside his desk. After brushing the seat off and placing her in it, he stood back and appraised her.

"Excellent!" he announced before returning to his seat, a fatherly smile lighting his face.

Antonella tried very hard not to squirm. Since childhood, she struggled with a tendency to squirm when she couldn't intuit expectations. Her mother and her grandmother had been drilling her in preparation. No squirming!

She didn't squirm. Signor Tocci's direct gaze rested on her. Should she hold eye contact? Or would that appear challenging? Should she cast her gaze downward, modestly? Or would that appear spineless? Should she smile?

She squirmed.

Just a bit, a clench of her right upper thigh, pitching her slightly sideways.

As if it were the cue he'd been waiting for, Signor Tocci said, "So, Antonella."

"Yes, Signor Tocci?"

"I bet we're pleased to find ourselves out of the secretarial pool?"

Now modesty seemed to be called for. So even though Antonella wanted to say, "I've always been interested in business, and can't wait to learn about strategy and marketing," she said, "Yes, thank you, Signor Tocci."

He clapped his hands together, pleased. "I know you'll make excellent use of this opportunity. My assistants always go on to do great things."

Antonella lifted her portfolio off her lap and asked, "I wonder if you might want to—"

"In a minute." Dr. Tocci's smile twitched. "In a minute. I want to know the person I'll be working with so closely."

Eyes downcast again, Antonella nodded. "Of course, Signor Tocci."

"So, Antonella. How old are you?"

"Twenty-three."

"Good. Good. And you live in . . . "

"Santa Lucia."

"Ah, yes," he smiled. "The village up the hill. With the *cinghiale* festival and the *castello*. Plus, that light everyone talks about."

Never having heard her village described to her, Antonella wasn't sure of the protocol. But an answer seemed expected. "Yes."

"I haven't been up there in years. But I hear the new *trattoria* is surprisingly good. Maybe I'll drive up soon. You can show me the sights."

Antonella squirmed.

Signor Tocci tipped his head to the side in thought, a finger on his cheek. "Show my wife and me, that is. She loves village pottery. Does Santa Lucia have a pottery shop?"

Antonella's stomach swooped in relief. "We don't. Unfortunately."

He nodded. "I see. Perhaps that's why we haven't been."

"Yes, that would make sense. There's not a lot in Santa Lucia." Why did her stomach twist, as if she were criticizing her grandmother's *ragù*?

"You should get a pottery shop."

Antonella focused on keeping her bottom planted. How in the world would she do that? The admonition seemed faintly ridiculous. Suddenly, she wondered if Signor Tocci was a cousin of the owner or something.

Signor Tocci drummed his fingers across the desk, his eyes still fixed on Antonella.

She sat still, even as her mind whirred.

He nodded to himself. "You're quite attractive."

"Oh! I . . ." Her voice drifted off as she blushed.

"You don't need to be insulted. It's not a bad thing. Attractiveness is a valuable commodity in this business. Clients are more likely to hire an agency if their representative is attractive. We'll work with your wardrobe a bit, and your hair, obviously. But I'll definitely be taking you to meetings. You've studied my work already I imagine?"

"I tried, but I couldn't find anything recent on the website and—"

"I'll expect a little more ingenuity moving forward." He frowned. "Now I must tell you about my work and my accomplishments, which makes me very uncomfortable." He didn't look uncomfortable as he leaned back, his hands steepled under his chin. He looked like Carosello licking deep into a plastic tub of leftover pig parts outside the butcher shop.

Signor Tocci said, "You know about my work for Visia, at least."

With a breath of relief, Antonella said. "I do, of course. But I'd love to hear about it from your perspective. That marketing campaign . . . brilliant."

As Signor Tocci launched into a minute description of his work for Visia, Antonella strove for a rapt expression. This, at least, she understood. Her grandmother was always blathering on about town gossip and since childhood, Antonella had been expected to listen attentively, with her hands clasped on her lap. Nodding. And asking interested questions. She did that now, even throwing in the doe-eyed blink that she credited with making her Nonna's favorite grandchild.

It seemed to work.

"I made a good choice, hiring you." Signor Tocci nodded, breaking off his monologue. "I'm glad. We'll be working together closely, so you'll need to learn to anticipate me, to remember the logistics so I can focus on the more creative element. We'll fine-tune your eye, so you can offer feedback on products and marketing. You're from a small town without a real education, so you won't have skills. But don't worry, my dear. It's all teachable. Just pay close attention to me, to learn all you can. The more you tune into me, the better assistant you'll make."

Antonella nodded, her eyes wide.

"So do you know what I'm thinking about now?"

Antonella's mind raced. Had he dropped some clue?

He grinned. "I'll give you a little clue. I'm very very . . . *drowsy*."

"*Caffè?*" she ventured. Dear lord, she hoped he wasn't into speed or something.

"Excellent! Look how well you are doing, already."

Ava tied the red kerchief around Elisa's head, as Elisa tied a sky blue one around Margherita's.

Elisa moved the little girl's hair away from the knot in the fabric. "Why do we need these?"

Ava smiled. "You don't. But it's tradition. We all wear them when we collect olives. Always have."

"It seems weird."

Ava set her lips. Elisa tucked Margherita's curls behind the fabric and the little girl spun around to wrap her arms around her sister. The girls stayed clasped together before Margherita skipped across the room. She flung open the door and turned back, her feet tapping impatiently.

Ava asked Elisa, "You ready?"

"Can I bring my sketchbook?"

"Do I ever say no?"

Elisa's face shed its shadows, and she snatched up her sketchbook before joining Margherita outside. Ale, washing dishes at the sink, asked, "It's time?"

Ava called over her shoulder as she hurried outside, "Yes!"

He nodded and put the last dish in the rack above the sink, to allow the dishes to drip water into the basin. Toweling off his hands, he shouted,

"Wait for me!"

Isotta stood in the yard, helping Jacopo wave goodbye. Margherita's voice whined and Elisa's more distinctly complained, "Why can't Jacopo come with us?"

Isotta said, "I wouldn't want to intrude on your grandparents' tradition. When we do the castle's trees next weekend, we can all harvest together."

Elisa frowned at Ava, as she always did when lines between the families were drawn. "But we can take Margherita, right?"

Ava said, "Absolutely. That kerchief isn't just a costume, you know. She's your sister. She's coming."

Elisa grabbed Margherita's hand. Though the child threw one last searching look at Jacopo, she allowed herself to be led through the groves. Elisa, realizing she didn't know the way to the family plot, stopped at a junction and waited for Ava and Ale. Together they wound their way up the terracing. Eventually arriving at Ava's family plot of olive trees. Ava's parents, Savia and Bepe, greeted Elisa enthusiastically.

At the sight of Margherita, Savia stalled. Ava said quickly, "Isn't it wonderful that Isotta could spare Margherita so that Elisa could share this with her sister. After all, this is such a family event."

A voice behind her made her twirl around. "I'm glad to hear how much you're valuing family."

"Fabio?" She took a step back, colliding with Ale who rested a hand on her shoulder. "What are you doing here?"

"The same thing you're doing here."

Savia grinned, "See now? How nice! To all be together!"

Ava shook her head, furious. How many times had she told her mother that she never wanted to be in Fabio's striking distance again?

She looked up at Ale, her eyes alive with anger. He stroked her cheek, waiting to follow her lead. She glanced at Elisa, scuttling with Margherita away from Fabio toward her grandfather. Bepe unpacked the rakes, showing each one to the girls, demonstrating how to find a bunch of olives, and rake in just the right spot.

Ava decided to simply throw her mother an accusatory glare.

Which Savia ignored as she said, "Fabio, I thought you were bringing your girlfriend?"

He looked over his shoulder. "She took too long getting ready, so I told her to meet us."

Ava said, "How does she know where our plot is?"

Fabio laughed a short bark. "I guess she'll have a little adventure."

A thin young woman shifted from behind the trees. Fabio said, "Here she is! She must have chased me down."

The woman smiled tremulously as Fabio waved her forward. Ava noted her face...wider than would be expected given how thin, almost emaciated, her body was. A blur of acne scarring blotted her cheeks and over one eyebrow. The woman, more a girl, Ava noticed, twitched her hand up in a kind of greeting. She looked vaguely familiar, but Ava couldn't place her.

Savia pulled her in to kiss her cheeks, "Morena. I'm glad you could make it."

Ava said, "You've met?"

Fabio said, "As usual, dear sister, you've been so wrapped up in your life, you haven't been part of our Sunday lunches."

Ava blurted, "This is how you refer to my child's kidnapping?"

Elisa straightened, and Ava regretted her words.

Fabio chuckled. "Really though? Is it a kidnapping when the child is with her father?"

Darting her eyes at Elisa, Ava gritted her teeth to avoid answering. Ale watched, jaw clenching as his hand wound through Ava's.

Bepe called, "*Ragazzi!* Everyone take a rake. Ava, watch Margherita, they're sharp. Maybe she can help lay down the net instead. And then move the fallen fruit into the crates."

Elisa and Margherita took the net Bepe offered, spreading it under an olive tree. Margherita leaped up at a rabbit dashing into the underbrush, and Elisa guided her back.

Ava took her mother aside. "I couldn't have been clearer."

"Oh, Ava. Let go of old grudges! Remember what the priest said last Sunday."

Fabio chuckled. "Ava wasn't there."

Savia took Ava by the elbow and whispered, "Fabio has only ever wanted to be loved. And with your pregnancy, we had to give you all our attention. Don't you see? He needs us."

Ava sputtered, "All your attention? What the actual hell are you talking about?"

"Ava! Watch your language! See? It's like Fabio says. You make everything about you."

"Did you not hear what he said to me? About Elisa?"

"Take a rake, dear. Yes, I heard, and it's no more than many people say. You mustn't be so sensitive."

Ava stalked over to Ale. "I won't do this."

He pitched his voice low. "Do you want to leave? I can't believe they included him."

"I can," Ava said grimly. She looked over at Margherita and Elisa, squealing as they dropped olives from the net into the crate. "We'll play it by ear. But we need to be ready to get out of here. I won't stand for Elisa being torn down."

He nodded. "Or watching her mother get torn down." Ale inclined his head toward Morena. "Maybe he'll behave. With his girlfriend watching."

Ava snorted. "You don't have enough experience with Fabio. He doesn't work like a regular person." She grabbed a rake and began stripping the tree beside Morena. Her shoulders tight, she said, "I apologize for not greeting you properly, Morena. My brother and I have a . . . complicated relationship."

Morena giggled.

Elisa and Margherita ran by and Ava plucked the rake from Elisa's hand. Elisa laughed in acknowledgment. As Bepe stacked their filled crate in the waiting Ape, the girls began filling another with black olives, Elisa demonstrating to Margherita how to remove the foliage. A stack of leaves rose beside them.

She turned back to Morena. "I feel as if I know you. Do you work in Santa Lucia?"

Morena stammered, "I . . . I want to. But my parents say I need to finish high school first."

"High school!" Ava glared at her parents. "You knew this?"

Bepe stared at the ground, but Savia waved her hand. "She's in her final year, Ava. Let's not get dramatic. A ten-year age difference isn't a big deal."

"Whose math are you using? If she's eighteen and Fabio is thirty, that's *more* than ten years!"

"She's twenty."

"But you said . . ."

Bepe moved to Ava and whispered, "The school held her back a little."

Ava whispered back furiously. "This girl doesn't know what she's getting into. How can you be okay with this?"

Bepe said, "*Boh.* What can we do? You know Fabio. He won't change anything because we suggest it. Better that we get along."

Sensing Elisa's eyes on her, Ava smiled brightly while lowering her voice. "She's a *child*, Babbo."

"He's different now, Ava. He's got a steady girlfriend, he's got goals for himself. Why can't you give him a chance?"

"Goals?" Ava flinched as Fabio sidled up beside her and said, "Yeah, Ava, why not give your brother a chance?"

As the light dappled around them, sifting through the rustling olive leaves, Ava said, "Mark my words, Fabio. One day you'll get what's coming to you."

He regarded her with a grin. "Color me terrified." He laughed and walked to Morena, pulling her frail back against his paunch. Feeling his eyes trained on her, Ava closed her eyes, trying to erase the image of her brother grinding against this slip of a girl.

Ava stalked to the other end of the plot where Ale plucked olives, tossing them down to Margherita who caught them like a ball in a game. Elisa settled in the nook of a tree to draw. Her hand moved briskly, almost angrily, over the page. Ava watched as an image bloomed under her daughter's hand. Bones, erupting from earth.

Ice lacing her heart, Ava asked, "Elisa? What are you drawing there?"

Elisa turned the sketchbook upside down and picked at the bark of the olive tree.

"Elisa?"

Elisa shoved the sketchbook into her pocket and jumped down from the tree. She walked away without a word.

As the bar cleared, Edo turned to Chiara. "You're not going to believe this."

At the eager tone of Edo's voice, Chiara stopped slotting plates into the dishwasher. "Tell me."

"So, when Francy was here last week for the festival, he told me about friends of his who hired a surrogate in the United States. She's pregnant now, so you can imagine Francy's excitement."

Chiara paled, but Edo didn't notice as he ran on. "I knew nothing about surrogacy, it never occurred to me that gay couples could have children since I read in the paper years ago about all those countries forbidding adoption by gay couples. And wasn't there that couple that did adopt and then the Italian government didn't recognize the child as theirs?"

"I don't know, but, Edo—"

"I know, I'm getting off-topic. Anyway, Francy is explaining to me how surrogacy works, it's cool if you think about it, these women who offer their fertility to help people who can't have children. I mean, they get paid, obviously, but—"

"Are you two discussing having children?"

Edo's stopped talking as his arms fell to his sides. "No. I mean, someday I'd like to have a family, but it's not something we've—"

"Because you started dating like a minute ago," Chiara insisted.

"That's not true. We got together in the spring and—"

"But then you broke up. Because of your insecurity."

Edo stood back and crossed his arms. "Why is this relevant?"

Chiara shrugged. "The point is, your relationship is hardly in a place to talk about children."

Edo frowned. "And this is your business, how?"

"You're the one telling me. I just don't want to see you running behind butterflies, chasing impossible dreams that lead to disappointment."

"I'm trying to tell you what Dante said! I'm not planning on having a child!"

"Okay, okay. What did he say?" Chiara took out a clean dishrag and started buffing the La Pavoni, focusing on the corners.

Edo muttered to himself.

"Are you going to tell me, or do I need to hear it from someone else?"

"You aren't exactly a receptive audience."

Chiara didn't turn to him, but instead removed the nozzle from the La Pavoni and ran it under water to remove the accumulated milk foam. "I need to finish before the next customer asks for a *cappuccino*. I'm listening. Go on."

Edo muttered for another moment before he said, *"Allora.* So as Francy was explaining surrogacy, Dante gets all puffed up and says that he doesn't approve. And then—get this," Edo warmed up to the material again. "He likened it to *prostitution*."

Chiara carefully dried the nozzle.

"Did you hear me?"

"I heard you," she said.

"Well, aren't you surprised that our mayor is a homophobe?"

Twisting the nozzle in place, Chiara said, "That's unfair. How do you know he's against surrogacy because he's against gay people and not for some other reason?"

"Oh, come *on*, Chiara."

"What?" She turned to him. "Maybe there's another reason. Did you ask him?"

"I didn't have to, Magda was all over him. He insisted it wasn't because of the gay thing, but he talked about it in this super condescending way, as if he was doing us all a big favor by not being blatantly homophobic. Completely missing that denying gay people one of the few avenues we have to parent is wrong."

Chiara dried her fingers, one by one.

Edo said, "What gives? Why are you being so weird? You don't agree with him, do you?"

"It's a lot to take in, Edo."

"I happen to believe it's not all that complicated. And anyway, he also went off about children being raised in a gay home—"

"But for Dante, it *would* be complicated. You see that, right? You expect too much from people. He only recently agreed to a village-wide recycling program."

"So at least you admit he's behind the times."

"I think he's in *his* times just right. And maybe he deserves a little latitude. A chance to catch up."

Edo wondered who they were talking about.

56

The afternoon sun slanted into Bar Birbo as Arturo laughed. "Of course I knew Fabio was dating a high school girl. He tells me everything."

Chiara shook her head. "You're *friends*? Since when?"

Arturo shrugged. "Well, not friends *exactly*. He's twenty years younger than me."

Chiara's face seemed to say, "At least."

"I like him," Arturo went on. "And ever since the fire and then the bones, everyone turned against him. They all want to shut him up because they're afraid of the truth he tells. He doesn't deserve how everyone treats him. The police, even! The way they laughed at him!"

Dante muttered, "The fire . . . the way he treats women who reject him . . . him framing Elisa for her father's murder . . . "

Arturo raised his eyebrows. "Who says she didn't do it?"

Chiara recoiled, "*Ma dai*! Arturo!"

Arturo's face flushed a little. "Okay, that part might be an exaggeration. But sometimes you need to hear an extreme view to realize how you're in lockstep with the mainstream opinion."

Chiara stopped and thought for a moment. "That makes no sense."

Arturo shrugged. "I wouldn't expect you to understand. But Fabio is worth listening to." He gave Chiara a baleful glare and added, "He listens to *me*, too. Unlike some people."

"I listen to you!"

He shook his head, "Whenever I tell you about my wife cheating—"

Dante broke in, "Save it, man. You've been on that old saw for too many years."

"You see what I get? It's *nice* to have someone sympathize with my situation."

Magda pushed the door open and paused at the sight of Dante at the bar with his customary glass of wine. Finally, she stalked to the bar. "I'll have a *cioccolato caldo*, Chiara."

Chiara's raised her eyebrows, but she nodded and turned to reach for the box of packages.

Dante smirked at Magda who steadfastly watched Chiara stir the powder into hot milk. "Hot chocolate, Magda? Isn't that for children?"

Magda snorted. "Ah. And you are the authority, I suppose."

Dante lifted his wine glass. "I am partaking of an adult beverage."

Magda rolled her eyes. "Any toddler can toss back some wine. It takes more than that to be a grown up." Her words left off in a flood of muttering.

Leaning on his arms, Dante said, "Do you have something you'd like to say?"

She shook the hair out of her face and said with great condescension. "I just did. Perhaps it went above your head."

Dante looked affronted for a moment, and then broke into laughter. "Oh, Magda. You are something. Always keeping me on my toes."

She reached to take the saucer with pudding-like hot chocolate from Chiara with a smile particularly gracious and warm. "*Thank* you, Chiara."

Chiara looked from Magda to Dante. "My pleasure." She backed away and stepped to Arturo, hoping to keep him from listening to Magda and Dante. Initially, Arturo resisted her overtures, but then he brightened and turned to her when she mentioned Isotta's financial situation. Arturo mused, "All Massimo's money to Anna! Can you believe it? I mean, we all knew she had him under her thumb, but..."

Dante turned to Magda and murmured. "What's this show of yours about?"

"Show?" She carefully sipped her hot chocolate before deciding to use a spoon, given the silky, but thick texture. "Whatever can you mean?"

Dante narrowed his eyes. "Come on, Magda. I thought we were beyond this. What's all this insinuation that I'm a child when," his voice lowered, "You know very well that I'm not."

She blushed. "If you must know, I found your remarks about surrogacy childish. And stupid."

He recoiled. "You did?"

"You were there. Were you not listening?"

"I suppose I didn't take you seriously."

Magda's mouth dropped open. She closed it and glared at Dante before staring fixedly at the bottles of liquor across the bar.

Dante softened his voice. "I said that wrong."

"I certainly hope so."

Dante moved a bit closer. "I meant, I thought we were bantering. You know, you and me . . . we banter."

"*That* was not banter. *That* was me telling you off for being a small-minded stupid person."

"Small-minded! Me! The mayor that brought recycling to Santa Lucia!" Dante looked as if he had more examples of his broad-minded progressive thinking, but preferred not to reveal them.

"Under duress."

"Duress!"

"Yes! Not until we forced your hand! You kept coming up with excuses not to do it! From the cost to Carosello spreading trash around."

"That's not true." Though Magda's words rang some bells.

"It most certainly is. You are old-fashioned and ridiculous."

"*Ridiculous!*"

"You heard me."

Dante considered. "Look, Magda. We had a difference of opinion—"

"You called surrogacy a sex crime."

"I did not!"

Magda stared heavenward as if looking for patience. "Well, you might as well have."

Dante sipped his wine, noisily. A few drops escaped onto his shirt, where he swiped them with a wad of waxy paper napkins he snatched from the counter.

Magda said, "That will stain. You need baking soda."

"I know very well how to launder my own clothes."

"Not to hear Stella tell it."

He whistled. "Low blow, Magda."

She looked chastened. "You're right." She looked at him. "I apologize."

"I've been living on my own for almost a year now."

"I know. It's just—your words. You have no idea. Couldn't you see Edo's face when you said all that? Surrogacy is the only option available for gay men to have biological children. How can you call his one avenue for having a child something so gross?"

Dante blinked. "We weren't talking about Edo. We were talking about Francy's friends. It was a hypothetical conversation."

She snorted.

"What? Please. Tell me."

She sighed and looked directly at Dante. "Dante. It's hypothetical . . . until it's not. If or when Edo does decide to have a child, do you want your words ringing in his ears?"

He considered. "Maybe I shouldn't have said that."

Magda went on, "You shouldn't have *thought* it."

"You're controlling my thinking now?"

"I'm not controlling anything. But it's juvenile for you to assume that your way of thinking is the only one."

He tried not to smile. "Ah. And you never do that."

"No!" She stopped. And looked down, smiling. "Okay, maybe a little."

He said, "We're alike you and I, Magda."

She ran her fingertips over her bottom lip. "Maybe a little."

Ale tossed a shirt back to Ava. "This one is still damp."

Ava caught it and hung it back on the cord. She grumbled. "Nothing is drying in this cold."

Ale nodded. "I do miss my American dryer."

Ava looked up. "I get the appeal. Maybe when there's money."

He frowned and stared at the damp shirt in his hands. "When there's money," he muttered. His gaze swept over the room cluttered with Margherita's toys and Elisa's art supplies and piles of blankets for Jacopo. "It'd be nice to at least set the drying rack in front of the fire."

Ava removed the clothespins from a pair of Elisa's jeans before clipping them back on. "Damp!" She looked up, meeting his eyes. "I know it's not exactly a treat to have everyone here."

"I don't mean to sound resentful—"

"Well, you did," Ava snapped.

The pause between them stretched.

Ale tried, "Just last night you complained about the kids squabbling and the cold floor."

"It's different when I say it," Ava said under her breath. She closed her eyes as she ran a hand over her forehead. Opening them, she said, "Isotta has decided to move to Massimo's."

Ale inhaled audibly.

"I didn't tell you, did I? I haven't come to terms with it," Ava sighed. "I bit your head off, I guess. I'm sorry."

"You know your being herex is far more important than where we situate the drying rack."

"I know that. It's just ... hard." She turned her attention to hanging Jacopo's striped shirt.

"You and Isotta ... you're sure it's time?" He focused on disconnecting two clothespins.

"No," Ava said flatly. "But when am I sure of anything anymore? Besides, it's not my decision to make and I can't help with an alternative. There's no money for renovating a room here. And the children tolerate the separation. We need to move on."

"Hey," Ale wrapped his arms around her, letting his hands cup her face and tilt it to his. He studied her eyes for a moment before leaning down to kiss her. Warmly. Like he'd rarely been able to do with the tumble of families living together. Bringing his forehead to rest against hers, he said, "I'd love for you to stay. Once Isotta and the kids go."

Ava closed her eyes, breathing in the smell of Ale. Which used to be mostly like whatever detergent he wore, but with his work in the vineyard, more often than not he smelled of wind and green leaves. "You mean it?"

"You'd consider it?" His face broke into a grin.

Ava smiled weakly. "Even if my parents find it unseemly, we're better away from their house."

He thought for a beat. "Fabio?"

She nodded. "Did you notice? After the harvest, Elisa got...reactive. I mean, she's been that way since the kidnapping. Something sets her off, and she explodes or she clams up, usually one after the other. But she'd evened out a lot. Then, an afternoon with Fabio..."

"Like she couldn't be in her own skin anymore." He shook his head. "I can't understand why your parents are okay with it. Any of it. I can't even go into the hardware store, let alone hang out with the guy for fifteen minutes."

She shrugged. "Isotta says that if they didn't pretend he was normal, they'd have to see how crazy he is." Pausing for a heartbeat, she said, "Ale, I want you to know. My short temper notwithstanding...I'm ready. For this. Us."

"Moving in with me, you mean?"

"Well, I moved in with you a month ago," she said with a grin. "What I'm saying, is that it's not just for Elisa. I want to live here. With you."

He brushed her hair away from her face.

She ran her tongue over her lip. "This last month. Even with all these challenges, being with you has been..."

"I feel the same."

She lay her head against his chest, listening to the steady thump of his heart.

He ventured. "How do you think Elisa will take it, though?"

She closed her eyes. "That's the part I don't know."

While Signor Tocci grabbed his pen to gesture more expansively, Antonella checked the time. And groaned inwardly.

The last two weeks had been filled with these "sessions" where her boss regaled her with stories of his business conquests, while Antonella's mind wandered. She'd complained to her family about it, expecting them to commiserate with her disappointment that rather than learning the trade, she'd so far only learned to sit without squirming while her boss described, in exhausting but vague detail, his success. Instead, her family had admonished Antonella, insisting that all jobs had boring parts.

Then again, they'd no doubt been swayed by her first paycheck.

Antonella wanted the increase in pay to offset her boredom, but she almost wished she was back at the *rosticceria*, taking pizza out of the oven. Her stomach gurgled. She hated eating at work because Signor Tocci inevitably had an opinion about the caloric content of her food or how the nutritional value would impact her pores. She wondered if she could duck around the corner at lunchtime, without him noticing.

Doubtful, since at lunchtime he wanted long chats, of a more personal nature. Which were just as dull to Antonella, filled as the "conversation" was with recitations of the cars he'd owned or his wife's wardrobe. She'd perked up once at his casual mention of his pet mini-mallard duck and his wife's Texel guinea pig, but she hadn't been able to work the conversation back to pets, and he didn't relay any amusing anecdotes. Which was too bad. Antonella loved animals. She even had affection for her town's one-eyed dog. Petting the grungy thing whenever he allowed it. Though her mother always screamed in alarm and made Antonella wash her hands multiple times.

She tuned back into Signor Tocci's story of a business deal that had been about to nosedive until he saved it. As he took a sip of water, Antonella asked impulsively. "Such a great story, Signor Tocci! I wonder if you have any deals in the works now that we can work on?"

Slowly, he put down his water. He ran his finger around the rim of the glass, then placed the moistened finger in his mouth. He sucked the tip of his finger, watching Antonella. Before he removed it, wet now from his mouth.

Finally, he said, "Have you not been listening?"

"What? Of course, I have, Signor Tocci! The whole time!"

"I can't think you have. If you'd been listening, you would have heard how I described the nature of this business. There are active periods and build-up periods, while lower-level employees are hunting for businesses to approach. This is a *build-up* period."

"Right! I meant I'd love to help with soliciting new work. You see, when my family delivered olives to the *frantoio* for pressing this last weekend, I realized how the oil's distribution is limited to local markets. But with the right strategy, it could go global. We harvest a fraction of our olives and there are more all over the valley that don't get sold. If we—"

"Antonella. Please. Don't get ahead of yourself. This is a large firm. We won't handle small-scale operations like agriculture. And anyway, do you think you're ready for a project when you couldn't stay focused enough to mail those letters last week?"

"But... I'm sorry, Signor Tocci, but you said you were waiting on marketing materials..."

He shook his head, disappointed. "You still have a lot to learn, Antonella."

Antonella blinked back tears. Tears! She never cried! But she couldn't deny the sharpness behind her eyes. She worked to keep the tears from falling, from shaming her. She squirmed and berated herself again.

Signor Tocci handed her a tissue and waited while she blew her nose.

"Antonella." He leaned forward with a sad smile. "Are you on your period?"

"What! No!" Her hands clenched ineffectually on her lap.

He shook his head. "It's all right, really. Do you need to take the day off? To 'rest'? Perhaps return to the secretarial pool for a bit?"

"No! I'm fine." She couldn't go back to the secretarial pool. She couldn't! Her family would never forgive her. They counted on her income now, to let her father reduce his hours. His hands were growing more arthritic, and it was harder and harder to work on the farm equipment. She wrestled her emotions and plastered a smile across her face. "I apologize, Signor Tocci, for my outburst. It won't happen again. I'd love nothing more than to hear how in the world you saved the Visia account when they were about to move to another consulting firm. Goodness, that was fascinating!"

He regarded her as she leaned forward in her earnest entreaty. Antonella wondered if her shirt was gaping at the neck. Signor Tocci's comments about her wardrobe inspired her to wear her most modest clothing, but this one did have a tendency to open between the buttons if she didn't hold herself perfectly erect. She watched her boss stare at the buttons as they winked in and out of the fabric. Antonella fought the urge to make sure none had come undone.

Instead, she asked, "It's been two hours since your last *espresso*, Signore. Shall I fetch you another?"

"That would be fine," he drawled. "When you come back, I'll tell you the rest."

Antonella let out a relieved breath. "Oh, thank you!" Standing, she adjusted her skirt. Signor Tocci followed her movements, watching the play of fabric against her hips.

She nodded with a broad smile and strode out, trying not to feel his eyes lingering on her backside.

Ale and Ava conferenced outside the kitchen. Ale nodded, "It'll help, right? Not add pressure or something?"

Ava shook her head. "She's been withdrawn ever since we told her about Isotta moving out. Did you see her bite my head off at breakfast when I asked her to clean up her spilled juice? She needs something to look forward to. Something that's just hers." She smiled into his eyes and added, "An inspired idea, Ale."

He touched the tip of her nose with his finger and grinned. "Look at me, helping."

The two of them clasped hands and smiled at each other for a moment before Ava stepped into the kitchen. She watched as Elisa worked, surrounded by a scatter of sketches. Finally, she said softly, "Elisa? Do you have a minute? Ale has something to ask you."

Elisa looked up, blinking.

Ava and Ale sat down, and Ale began. "We've been talking, your mamma and I. I'd like to have a shop here in the *castello*, where we sell souvenirs."

"Souvenirs?"

Ale nodded. "Mementos. Like what you get when you visit the Coliseum or the Duomo."

Elisa shook her head, "I've never been to those places."

Ava said firmly, "I'll take you. I promise."

Ale went on, "Tourists like bringing home reminders of their vacation."

"And you want to sell those? Souvenirs?"

"Sort of. What I want to sell is art. Your art."

Elisa leaned back, stunned. After a few moments, she said, "My art? You want to *sell* my art?"

Ale nodded. "Actually, I want *you* to sell it. I thought you could help me clear out a room, turn it into a studio and a shop. You could work there after school."

Elisa thought about it. "But I'd have to talk to strangers. And do math."

Ale said, "Basic math. You can do it."

Elisa considered. "What if the tourists don't speak Italian?"

Ale said, "Aren't you learning English at school?"

Ava laughed. Elisa glared at her. "Oh, I'm sorry, Elisa. I'm remembering my English class in middle school. I didn't learn much. I had a coffee with Marco's mother the other day and she said the English teacher you have is about the same. I wound up learning by watching American TV shows."

Elisa looked interested. "American TV shows?"

"Sure! It's a fun way to pick up language. We can do that if you'd like. Together. It would be good for me, too."

"You do have a native speaker in your midst if you ever want to practice," Ale said to laughter from Ava and Elisa. "But anyway, Elisa. Lots of shop owners in small towns don't speak English. People find ways to communicate. Like a game."

Ava nodded, wondering if the shop might help Elisa's confidence. Elisa spent so much time with Margherita, Ava wondered if it might interfere with her maturity. At times, Elisa seemed an average teenager, talking about her worry that she and Fatima would drift apart, now that Fatima was so busy with photoshoots and "go-sees", whatever those were. Then, other times, Elisa grew as sullen as a toddler denied her favorite toy.

As much as Ava wished her daughter spent time with girls her own age, Ava couldn't help but notice how much Elisa bloomed in the face of Margherita's unconditional love. With Margherita, Elisa didn't weigh her words. Her thoughts flowed. Not for the first time, Ava wondered what had happened in the month they were gone.

In whispered conferences, Isotta relayed to Ava little bits of information from Margherita. From her, they suspected that Massimo dyed Elisa's hair right away, that the children ate fast food purchased by Elisa, and that Massimo had kept them moving, mostly by bus, with endless amounts of walking. Their feet had certainly been blistered. There had to be more though, if Elisa's jumping at any sudden noise was any indication.

She watched Elisa now as Ale said, "Plus, we can play store until it feels natural. We have plenty of time before we can count on tourists visiting." His tight face betrayed his continual calculation of euros dribbling into the *castello*.

Elisa thought. "Who decides which of my art I put in the shop?"

Ale laughed. "You, of course. We can even make postcards and plates and shirts."

"And I can make anything I want? *Anything*? You *promise*?"

Ava's lips condensed into a grim line as she studied her daughter. Ale tried to laugh through the fraught moment. "Absolutely."

Elisa sat a little straighter. "I'll do it."

Night settled over Santa Lucia. The moon hung low in the sky, lining the olive tree branches, the edges of San Nicola's bell tower, the arches framing the village's entrance with a thin rim of blue light. As the wind picked up, fallen bougainvillea petals tumbled down Via Romana, like so much leftover confetti. More than one cat shivered and hunkered down in a pot of *hosta*.

Bar Birbo shone, alight against the gathering darkness. Figures leaned against the bar or turned to each other. Antonella hesitated outside the door. She knew her parents and grandparents expected her home. But the day had been exceptionally long. Her cheeks hurt from smiling. Signor Tocci had started giving her work to do, but it seemed merely a vehicle for more stories of how he had rescued that deal with his wily charm, or he'd strolled into the design department in the nick of time. And so far, the work itself was no more challenging than taking notes or taking dictation.

In short, secretarial work.

She pushed the door open. Dinner could wait fifteen minutes. Nonna Bea was making *pasta al forno*, which likely would be behind, given the finickiness of their oven. She had time for one glass of wine. One quarter-hour where she didn't have to pretend she loved her job.

Chiara greeted her, cheerily. "Antonella! How is the big job in Girona?"

Antonella sighed and yanked a smile across her face. "Fine! Really excellent!"

Chiara glanced at the clock. "Isn't Bea expecting you? She stopped by on her way home this morning with a bag full of meats for a *ragù*."

"I have time for a glass of wine, first."

Chiara studied Antonella. Antonella shifted her weight and said, firmly, "Red, please, Chiara." She turned to the first villager she saw to her right and said, "Fabrizio, right? We met when I worked at the *rosticceria*."

Fabrizio smiled, "I remember! I don't know how you gave up that job, that *rosticceria* always smelled delicious. I would have gained twenty pounds if I worked there."

Antonella hit her laugh a little hard. "Then you understand why I had to leave. *Ciao*, Edo."

Edo smiled, "*Ciao*, Antonella. Peanuts and chips?"

She shook her head. "Just peanuts. Nonna will kill me if I don't eat a full plate."

Fabrizio and Edo laughed and then Edo said, "Speaking of eating all you can, have you seen Carosello lately?"

Antonella's hand stalled on its way to pluck a peanut from the bowl. "No. Did something happen?"

Giovanni strode into the bar, apron still on. "Does anyone know what in the world happened to Carosello?"

Edo laughed. Chiara handed Antonella her glass of wine, accidentally nudging Edo's arm. He flinched and whirled to stride to the La Pavoni, fidgeting with the levers as Chiara stood still, staring at him. Fabrizio watched the strained interaction, looking from Chiara to Edo, the question shadowing his face.

Antonella didn't notice, her eyes trained on Giovanni. She gulped a sip of her wine and reached a hand for Edo as he passed by. "Carosello. Tell me."

Edo startled, "Right! Sorry. He's fine. Only he's—now, prepare yourself—*groomed*."

"*Groomed?*"

Giovanni said, "Yes. His hair is so short you can see the pink of his skin—"

"And the flea-bites. Poor dog," Edo broke in.

"Those, too." Giovanni agreed. "But his tail and ears and eyebrows are left long."

Dante overheard this and called across the bar, "I can't tell if whoever did it meant for the dog to look more foolish or more respectable."

Antonella took another sip of her wine. "I don't think I've ever seen him groomed."

Edo shook his head. "I don't think I've ever seen him not covered with bits of trash. Let alone so sleek it's almost ridiculous."

She asked, "But who did it?"

Edo said, "We've been trying to figure it out."

Fabrizio added, "I think it's someone inspired by Fatima's glamorous career."

Giovanni murmured, "Maybe it's a miracle." Eyes drifted to the Madonna, who should be shrouded in darkness, but for some reason glowed, illuminating her niche of heavenly blue.

Into the quiet, Marcello strode in. "*Buona sera!*" he greeted the room at large. He stopped and looked around. "Did something happen?"

The stillness shattered and Giovanni said, "We were talking about Carosello."

Marcello frowned. "Somebody's idea of a joke? Poor dog."

Edo shook his head. "I think someone pitied his matted fur."

Marcello called to Chiara, "A glass of red, Chiara." As she opened her mouth he shouted, "Yes, I'm in uniform, but I'm off duty!"

She laughed and poured a glass from the bottle she had yet to cork and with a darting glance at Antonella, contemplating the contents of her glass, she set Marcello's wine beside Antonella.

Marcello hesitated for barely a moment before joining Antonella. "And chips, too, Chiara."

Chiara said, "Laura won't like that."

Marcello grumbled, "I'm not a boy in short pants!" Antonella glanced at him and smiled.

Chuckling, Chiara said, "Okay, okay. Edo, can you get Marcello his chips? I need to get another bottle of wine from the back."

Edo reached for a bowl in lieu of an answer.

Fabrizio started to follow Chiara into the back, but she lifted a hand, shaking her head firmly. He returned to his stool.

Marcello said, "Antonella. *Buona sera.*"

She nodded, a slight blush suffusing her cheeks. "*Buona sera.*"

"I haven't seen you for a while. Since you worked at the *rosticceria.*"

She hesitated and said, "You hardly saw me then. I think you were the lone police officer to never get a square of pizza."

Marcello patted his firm stomach. "Have to keep in tip-top shape."

Antonella followed his gesture with her eyes. She tried not to let her gaze drift up to Marcello's eyes crinkling above his high cheekbones, his hair where it curled against his collar. He'd grown more handsome since high school, as his face filled out until his square jaw set off his full upper lip.

She blushed properly now, realizing she was as bad as Signor Tocci. She'd always nursed a minor crush on Marcello. He had been a few grades above her in school, and was known for not just being good looking, but also sweet and funny. She'd been pleased when he'd gotten work in Santa

Lucia, but other than the brief eye contact at L'Ora Dorata, they'd hardly seen each other. She frowned, thinking how impossible it seemed in a town this small to not see everybody you knew every single day.

"*Tutto a posto*, Antonella?"

"Oh!" Antonella attempted to laugh. "I was thinking I need to finish this wine and head home."

He smiled easily. "And that's worthy of such a sad face?"

She shook her head, blinking. "I'm not sad."

Marcello took a sip of his wine. "That's good. A clear evening. A good glass of wine. Hot pasta waiting at home. What more do we need, right?"

Antonella nodded, relaxing a touch. "How have you been, Marcello?"

He beamed. "Santa Lucia is finally quiet."

Crunching a peanut, Antonella thought for a moment. "The children missing. Working with the German police to capture that guy, Magda's . . ." She screwed her eyebrows together in thought.

"Husband's twin brother," Marcello supplied helpfully.

"Right. It's hard to keep track now that I'm in Girona most of the time."

"You don't live there, though?"

"No, I still live with my parents. You?"

"I lived with mine when I moved back to Santa Lucia, but I have my own apartment now. You know it, I'm sure. The one next to the *forno*."

"I thought there was earthquake damage years ago and no one could live there."

"That's what I said! But no, the damage is to the apartment next door. Mine just had paint chip dust all over the place."

She sneaked a look at Marcello through her lashes. "And next to the *forno*. More good food to avoid."

Marcello guffawed. "Thank goodness I'm mostly home when the *forno* is closed. Though I did pop in last Saturday. Sauro made his cookies with wine must. Did you get any before he ran out?"

Antonella shook her head sadly. "No, I missed it. And it's my favorite!

By the time I got there, he'd run out."

Marcello bit his lip, trying not to laugh. "I may have gotten that last one."

Antonella swiped at him, her eyes dancing. "You rascal!"

Marcello's laugh rung through the bar. "I'm sorry. Maybe *that's* why you were so sad when I came in."

Antonella nodded somberly. "That's it. Grief. For my favorite wine-must *biscotti*."

His expression matching Antonella's serious one, Marcello said, "You know, I took an oath—"

"An oath?"

"Well, a promise of sorts. When I joined the *vigili*. That I wouldn't cause harm to anyone."

Antonella sniffed resentfully, but her eyes shone with merriment.

"Tell you what. Let me make it up to you. Dinner, maybe? Sometime next week?"

Antonella's breath caught, and she studied Marcello's face for signs of teasing. But his eyes rested, warm and open, holding her gaze. Her tongue darted to her lip as she pulled out her phone. "I suppose that's fair. When works for you?"

Marcello ducked his head beside hers to look over her shoulder as she scanned through her calendar. He said, "Your Thursday looks open. How about that?"

Antonella nodded, a smile lighting her face without her even knowing it.

Isotta shivered as she crossed the threshold of her marital home. Margherita peered up at her, and Isotta squeezed the little girl's hand. Hitching Jacopo higher on her shoulder, she said, "Just a draft, sweetheart.

Do you remember your house?"

Margherita peeked into the darkness, jumping when Isotta flicked on the lights. She yelped and ran through the kitchen, shouting, and then around the corner and up the stairs, shouting louder, into the dusty shadows.

From behind her, Isotta heard Luciano's voice. "It would seem that she remembers."

She smiled at Luciano. "I didn't know you were coming."

"I saw Ava at Bar Birbo this morning and she told me today was the day. I wondered if you might appreciate the company."

"Ava offered, but I . . . I thought I could do it alone."

Luciano shrugged. "And I am sure you could, *cara*. But . . . why?"

She shrugged. "I have to start sometime."

The two glanced up at the sound of Margherita's footsteps above them.

Luciano asked, "The suitcases?"

"Ale is bringing them later."

He nodded.

Tentatively, Isotta said, "How is Enrico? I hoped to see him at the *sagra* . . ."

"He had other obligations. But he and Vito are coming— "He stopped talking at the sound of Margherita, who now seemed to be jumping from the bed to the floor.

Trembling faintly, Isotta said, "Let's go upstairs."

She closed her eyes as she passed her old bedroom and then chided herself for being ridiculous. Nuzzling Jacopo's neck until he giggled, she reminded herself (again) that though that room had seen challenging moments, it was also the scene of her son's conception. She hugged him and tried to feel grateful. But only felt cold. She wished she'd remembered to come earlier in the day and turn on the heat.

Luciano watched her. "Why don't you acclimate Margherita, while

I return downstairs to locate the thermostat? If it is quite acceptable to you, I would like to open a few windows. I realize it will compete with the heat, but—"

"The fresh air. Yes, thank you, Luciano."

He turned back downstairs as Isotta flipped switches, illuminating her walk to Margherita's room. At the sudden light, Margherita paused her bouncing. Her curls formed a wild halo around her head as she said, "My room, Mamma! Toys!" She ran to her chest in the corner and pulled out a doll with a lolling head and no clothes.

Isotta sat on the bed and wondered when "Mamotta" became replaced with "Mamma." At first, it seemed a mistake, but soon the idiosyncratic moniker had faded away completely.

Margherita reached into the bookcase, throwing aside books until she found one with a rabbit. "Look, Mamma! Pretty Bunny!" She cocked her head and glared at the cover. "Not Pretty Bunny. Pretty Bunny is brown, Mamma. This bunny *not* brown. This bunny *black*."

Isotta laughed. As Margherita handed her the book, Isotta said, "I remember this one. Do you, my sweet?"

Margherita nodded solemnly. "Read it, Mamma."

Isotta turned Jacopo so he could see the pages. She opened her mouth to read when she felt her phone buzzing. Her heart clenched. She reached into her pocket. Riccardo. Her hand gripped around the phone. She debated answering it, when Luciano appeared in the doorway. "Luciano! Could you read this book to Margherita? It's Riccardo—"

"With pleasure. Why don't you leave Jacopo with us?"

Isotta nodded and nestled her baby onto Luciano's lap as Margherita sidled beside her grandfather, her thumb inching toward her mouth.

Isotta nodded to herself, and then turned away, speaking into her phone. "*Pronto?*"

"Oh! Hello. Isotta? Is that you?"

"Yes."

"Ah. The phone rang so long I expected to leave a message, and you sound . . . different."

"We just arrived at Massimo's." She thought for a moment. "I guess I need to start calling it home."

Riccardo paused. "I think that's wise."

Isotta's stomach twisted. She'd hoped without realizing it that Riccardo would correct her. Would tell her about a windfall he'd located.

He said carefully, "There have been some developments. Why don't we meet to discuss—"

"Can you tell me now?"

"Over the phone?"

"I'll be anxious until we meet. I'd rather be in problem-solving mode than terror mode." Isotta attempted to temper her words with a laugh, but the sound fell flat.

Hesitating, Riccardo said. "It's up to you, of course. And I can send you a follow-up with the numbers."

"All right."

Isotta moved further down the hallway until she sat on the steps, looking down into the living room.

"I started the process of declaring Massimo dead. I called the police in charge of the investigation—."

"No new details. I know, I talked to them yesterday."

"Yes. Well. With that process started, I ordered the bank to release details of all the accounts. Isotta, I know we were hoping we'd find Massimo's money in Anna's account, so you could access it, eventually. But unfortunately . . ."

She closed her eyes. "Just say it, Riccardo."

He sighed. "Her account is virtually empty."

"But . . . but . . . how could that be?"

"Honestly, I hoped you might have some idea. Did he have debts or . . . ?"

"No!" she laughed hysterically. "But, really, who knows?"

"I'll keep at it, see if I can unravel this mystery."

"Don't bother, Riccardo. I can't pay you."

"Isotta, remember our contract. You pay me a percentage of what you inherit, starting at 50,000 euros, which we have yet to hit. The money must be somewhere."

"You're right. I'm sorry."

"I imagine this is quite a shock. But you have the house, paid for. The car ... did they ever find the car?"

"No."

He paused. "I suppose you don't need a car. If you spend the money on food and clothes for the children, it should last you at least a few months. Until you figure out your next step."

"Yes. And thank you."

"I hope our next conversation brings better news."

At the sound of the thin wail coming from Margherita's room, Isotta stood. "You and me both."

Ava walked into the kitchen, her cheeks rosy with the cold. She stamped her feet while smiling at Elisa working at the table. "If I didn't know better, I'd think snow was coming." She called to Ale in the next room, "Ale! We need to figure out how to regulate the temperature in the chapel room."

The stone walls of the *castello* absorbed some of Ale's tenor but did nothing to mask his irritability. "The guy comes tomorrow! Or so he *says!*"

Ava frowned and turned to Elisa, "Is he working on his app?"

Elisa moved her nose closer to the paper. "I think so. I heard him on the phone speaking English."

Ava lowered her voice, "Does it sound as if it's going ... okay?"

Elisa looked up, her eyes unfocused. "Did you say something?"

Ava put a hand on her hair. "Never mind. You're in a zone."

Elisa blinked and turned back to her paper.

"What are you working on?" She looked over Elisa's shoulder. "I thought you were doing homework. Elisa, I told you not to do art on this table. It's where we eat, we can't have bits of paint and eraser all over it."

"I forgot, okay! God!"

Ava tried not to blanch. "It'll be easier once we get the studio set up."

Elisa continued to glower.

Trying to soften the moment, Ava said, "Ale said this weekend we'll clear the space. He found a table! Did we tell you? Luckily there's electricity running into the room, even if there isn't a heating vent. We can hook up a space heater to keep you good and toasty." She stroked Elisa's hair and looked over her shoulder at the table. "Is that what you're working on? Art for your shop?"

Elisa bit her lip and flipped her paper over. "I'm *trying*." She gathered her papers and walked out muttering about completing her math homework.

"Mamma! Nonna! I'm leaving!" Antonella called into the kitchen over the sound of her father and grandfather watching TV in the living room.

Bea lumbered toward Antonella, inspecting her dress. "Where are you going?"

"I told you. I'm having dinner with a friend."

Furrowing her brows, Bea scolded, "Why would you miss my risotto?"

Antonella's mother pulled Bea's elbow. "Mamma, don't you remember what it's like to be young?"

Bea's habitual smile took up its residence as she chuckled. "I suppose. But my risotto is better than my grandmother's."

"Your risotto is the best, Nonna," Antonella assured her. "I hope there are leftovers for *arancini*."

Bea tucked her wooden spoon into her apron. "I'll pack two with your mamma so you can have them for lunch tomorrow at the big office." Her voice rang with pride.

Antonella's stomach clenched. She smiled through it, "You're the best." She kissed her grandmother again before stepping out into the alley.

A faint breeze brought the scent of the olive groves across the cobblestones—green and silver, dusty and new. Antonella sighed and straightened her skirt. She hoped she hadn't overdressed. Or underdressed. She'd had so few dates. This fluttery feeling in her lower belly felt foreign and a little alarming. She breathed in the night air, threaded with starlight.

Accordion music tugged her up the hill. Graziano, practicing? Sure enough, his *cantina* doorway glowed yellow against the darkened stone walls. Antonella wondered at the open door; the room must be freezing. Suddenly, instruments joined Graziano and Antonella realized more musicians sat in the room. All those bodies probably heated the small space. Antonella stopped for a moment, listening, before the music chased her footsteps up the hill to L'Ora Dorata.

Within moments, she spied Marcello standing in the *piazza*, his hands thrust into his pockets and his head tilted back. Hearing Antonella's approach, he brought his chin down and grinned. "So many stars."

Antonella smiled, her eyes radiating warmth in the darkness.

Marcello said, "You look beautiful."

Ducking her head, Antonella blushed. "I bet you say that to all the girls."

"Just the ones I've offended by stealing their favorite sweet."

"You mean you make a habit of this?"

Marcello shrugged, smiling mysteriously. "Shall we? Pietro has our table ready." He offered his elbow.

Antonella hesitated for only a moment before taking his arm.

They strolled into the restaurant to Pietro's cheerful greeting. "*Buona sera!* So glad you're joining us for dinner. Antonella, I thought of your grandmother's stories of her visits to her aunt's farm in the valley when I created the special. Leo!" He called, but the young man was already at his elbow.

Smiling, Leo gestured to Marcello and Antonella. "Right this way."

Seated and scanning their menus, Marcello mused. "I didn't see you here the night of the opening."

"No. My grandmother came, but I hadn't met Pietro or Livia yet."

"Right. Because of your job."

Antonella nodded and took a sip of the bubbly water that Leo had brought.

"Do you enjoy it, your work? It must be so different from serving pizza and fried olives."

"It could not be more different," Antonella said, with more bite in her words than she intended.

Marcello put down his menu, his face serious.

She squirmed and reached for her menu. Affecting a laugh, she said, "I must have lost three kilos the first week after quitting the *rosticceria*. Not being surrounded by rising dough has its advantages."

Marcello looked doubtful. "Maybe you miss our small-town vibe, though?"

She pressed her lips together into a thin line. "I love breaking free of Santa Lucia."

"Free?"

"Maybe you feel differently. After all, you came back."

Marcello nodded, slowly. "When I left though . . . I couldn't wait to get out."

Antonella's eyes widened. "Really?"

Leo appeared at their table. "What can I get you both tonight?"

Marcello reached for his discarded menu. "We haven't even looked."

Leo lodged the pencil behind his ear. "Take your time. Let me just tell you that the special tonight is farro polenta."

Antonella laughed. "Pietro is right. That's right out of my grandmother's childhood. I'd forgotten. She used to make it all the time, but then ground farro became hard to find."

Smiling, Leo said, "My father has the chefs grind it. They're complaining so much, it won't stay on the menu much longer."

Antonella said, "Then I'll have that, please. While I still can."

Marcello lifted his finger. "This, I must try as well. And how is your *antipasti* platter?"

"Much like at the opening, but with more salumi."

Marcello turned to Antonella. "Sound good?"

"Delightful, thank you."

Nodding, Marcello nodded. "We'll have that, and...is a *mezzo litro vino rosso* all right by you, Antonella? I have to work the early shift tomorrow—"

"Perfect."

Food ordered, Marcello said, "So, you were saying how you can't get out of Santa Lucia fast enough?"

Antonella squirmed. "It's not that, exactly. I want to be somewhere where not everyone knows everything about me. Where I can start from the beginning."

Marcello reached for a piece of bread and began tearing it into pieces. "That part didn't bother me. For me, it was more...this is going to sound awful...but I needed a break from my family." He grimaced. "I sound ungrateful don't I?"

"No, I get it. I love my family, but..."

"Sometimes it's hard to breathe."

They paused as Leo dropped their carafe of red wine and two glasses, filling them before nodding and moving away.

Marcello mused, "The thing is, once I left, I got lonely. I missed life here, everyone stopping to say hello. You grow up with that, and you think it's like that everywhere. But I trained in Foligno, and nobody had time for each other. And I missed my family. Even Mamma, who doesn't know how to give it a rest."

"For me, that's my grandmother."

He chuckled, "Bea is something else."

"She has a lot of opinions."

Marcello popped a piece of bread into his mouth and chewed thoughtfully. "She does know a lot, your grandmother. I couldn't believe it when she birthed Isotta's baby."

"That shocked me and also didn't."

He laughed.

Antonella asked, "So you came back because you missed the very thing I'm trying to get away from?"

He laughed again. "*Allora*, I didn't miss everyone telling me to wear a scarf and how I shouldn't eat something because it wasn't good for my digestion. But by the second year of the academy, I kind of forgot that part. I only remembered how people would stop me in the street to ask me about my grandfather's health. That's when I realized everyone meddling was better than feeling all alone in the world."

Antonella's eyes swam with tears. She looked away, blinking, hoping Marcello wouldn't notice. Luckily he'd turned to thank Leo, bringing their *antipasti* platter.

She cleared her throat. "And has it been everything you thought it would be? Moving back?"

Marcello held out the platter, "Take your favorite before I finish whatever you had your eye on."

She laughed and took a piece of *capocollo* as Marcello said, "Five minutes after moving back, I thought I'd made a huge mistake. I'd forgotten how much my mom believes she gets a say in my life. But . . . this will sound weird . . . but after what happened with Massimo and what we learned about how Anna tried to kill his wives, I've realized . . . Mamma is a genuine peach."

Antonella choked on a piece of salami, coughing and laughing intermittently.

"Are you okay?"

She took a sip of water. "I couldn't believe that whole thing with Massimo. I thought I understood the whole Italian men and their long apron strings—"

"Guilty as charged."

"But that . . . that took *mammoni* to a whole new level."

Marcello nodded.

Antonella thought and said, "You were in the thick of it, too, weren't you? The kidnapping?"

"Accidentally. Isotta started banging on the door looking for Jacopo when I'd come by for supper."

"So horrible."

Swirling his wine, Marcello said, "But this town . . . they showed *up*. It's what I mean. People pull together. When it's good, when it's rotten. They pull together. Tighter than any police squad I've served on."

Antonella nodded. "I suppose that's true." She took a sip of her wine. "And you live on your own now. That must help with your mother being in your business."

"She finds a way." He grinned. "But it's easier to bear. Especially since I can always go to my own apartment."

"Sounds dreamy."

"It is. And the apartment is great. You should come see it sometime. "He cocked his head in thought. "Maybe tonight?"

Antonella stiffened. "Oh, I don't think that would be a good idea."

Marcello nodded. "Sure, I understand." But he didn't look as if he entirely did.

❧

Ava stood in the doorway of Elisa's room. "Are you all ready for bed?"

"Yes."

"You brushed your teeth?"

"Oh! I forgot!" Elisa leaped out of bed and ran down the hall into the bathroom, where Ava heard the taps turning. She could never decide if Elisa's tendency to neglect her teeth stemmed from her general difficulty remembering or because dental hygiene hadn't been a regular part of her childhood.

Elisa sprinted back down the hallway. An apparition in her flowing white nightgown as she flung herself onto the bed, burrowing under the heap of blankets.

Ava tucked the blankets around her. "I've wanted to ask how you're doing, with the children gone."

Elisa frowned. "Fine."

"Elisa. You must miss them."

Elisa picked at her blankets. "I get that we couldn't all stay on the floor together forever."

Ale appeared in the doorway. "But the extended sleepover situation was fun."

Elisa grinned. "Like camping. Indoors."

Ale nodded. "Especially the last night."

Ava and Elisa said, "With the fire." And laughed.

He said, "I wish s'mores would make their way to Italy."

Elisa drew her knees to her chin. "S'mores?"

Ale stepped into the room and kissed the top of Elisa's head. "I'll tell you tomorrow."

She nodded. "Goodnight, Ale."

"Goodnight." He turned to touch Ava's cheek, saying, "I have at least a few hours of work to do. I may be close on this iteration. You okay on your own tonight?"

Ava nodded. "Another date with my catalogs." She smiled into his eyes.

"We'll manage. Don't worry."

He smiled faintly and walked out of the room.

Ava's eyes followed him. When she turned back, she noticed Elisa's grin. "What?" Ava said.

"Oh, nothing," Elisa said airily.

Ava bit her lip in thought before saying. "So. Elisa. Making sure, since you aren't exactly forthcoming with information." Elisa blinked and looked away. "Are you okay with our decision to stay here, rather than moving back in with your grandparents?"

Elisa said slowly, "I liked having them around."

Ava nodded.

"But Fabio is mean. And weird."

Ava chuckled. "Agreed, on both counts."

"And now that he comes to Nonna and Nonno's house a lot. With Morena." Elisa shivered. "I miss it there, but I'd rather be here."

"Only . . . you wish Margherita and Jacopo could be here, too."

"At least they visit us here. I can take care of them."

Ava smiled. "And you're good at it. I don't know how you do it. I'm wrung out after fifteen minutes of both of them."

"I did it for a month."

Ava waited.

Nothing. When would Elisa open up? Ava considered her words. Her daughter could fly off the handle so easily. "It's such a help for Isotta. But I do want to make sure you're keeping up with your schoolwork."

Elisa tensed.

Ava tensed in return. "Elisa?"

Elisa shook her head. "Talking about school is boring."

Adopting the most gentle voice she could muster, Ava said, "Elisa, this isn't the olden days when you would do anything to avoid your parents finding out about your bad grades."

Elisa narrowed her eyes. "How did you know?"

"Know what?"

Elisa looked away. "Fatima must have told you. Or Luciano."

"About . . . " Ava prompted, her shoulders tightening.

"Stefano! About *Stefano!* And how I paid him to fix my report cards!"

Ava looked slapped. "What—"

"Stefano. I *told* you." Elisa pulled her hair behind her ears.

"How did you pay him?" That house Elisa lived in with her adoptive parents—dark, with crumb-strewn cupboards and a couch with broken springs, splattered with fossilized dribbles of soda.

Elisa mumbled.

"Elisa, you know I can't understand you when you talk like that."

"I stole it, okay! I could never find enough coins in the street, so I took money from people's pockets! Now you know! So there!" Elisa's pale face trembled with tears.

Ava closed her eyes and put a hand over Elisa's. "Oh, Elisa."

"Aren't you angry? Didn't you hear what I *said*? I *stole.*"

"It breaks my heart to think of how scared you must have been to do something like that."

Elisa dismissed Ava, but then glanced at her face, noticing her mother's eyes, wide with sadness.

"I hate that your parents pressured you so much," Ava said. "That's what I'm trying to tell you. I don't need you to bring home good grades. I just don't want you feeling overwhelmed by schoolwork. I know you missed a lot."

Elisa's chin trembled. "I might not pass well. Like in science or math."

"Unless you plan on being an engineer, I don't think that much matters."

Elisa stared at her hands. "With Margherita and Jacopo, I feel good. I thought maybe when I'm older I could be an art teacher or something."

"That's a wonderful idea." Ava considered and said carefully, "I'd love to see your work. For the *castello.*"

Elisa withdrew her hand from Ava's. "I'm not ready."

Ava wondered if Elisa would ever really be ready.

Marcello swung his baton as he strolled through Santa Lucia. The day had dawned fine. Chill, but clear, a little icy bite to the air. He paused at the scent of coffee. Nodding as if in agreement, he veered into Bar Birbo.

Edo looked up from putting a box of milk into the under-counter refrigerator. He smiled. "*Buongiorno*, Marcello."

Marcello swung his baton with a little extra jauntiness. "*Buongiorno!*"

"*Caffè?*"

"*Come no?* Why not?" He leaned on the counter.

As Edo ground the beans, he said over his shoulder. "*Una bella giornata.*"

"A very beautiful day," Marcello smiled. "Crisp, you know?"

Edo nodded.

As he set Marcello's *espresso* in front of him, Edo said, "How was your dinner at L'Ora Dorata?"

Marcello blushed faintly. "With Antonella, you mean?"

"I'm not referring to the *farro*. Though that is rumored to be excellent."

Marcello frowned. "You talked to Leo."

Edo grinned. "I did, yes. But he's not the only one who pays attention to Santa Lucia's favorite police officer."

Marcello straightened as his eyebrows furrowed.

Edo said gently, "She's a lovely girl."

"She is." Marcello softened. "And easy to talk to. It's so funny, isn't it Edo, how you can go to school with someone for years but because you aren't in the same grade, you don't pay attention to them at all? And then one day—pow! It's like, where did *you* come from?"

Edo nodded. "I felt like that about Ava. I mean, not exactly what you're describing since . . . you know. I'm not into her. But I never even noticed her enough to hang out until last year. She finally seemed my age or something."

"*Esatto!*"

Edo hesitated. "You and Antonella. I see it."

Marcello stirred his coffee. "She's not interested."

"What do you mean? I heard from several people that she looked smitten."

"I invited her over, and she got all weird."

"*Ma dai*, Marcello. Of course, she did! Imagine what the old ladies would say! Imagine what those same old ladies would tell her *grandmother*."

Blushing lightly, Marcello stammered, "I wasn't . . . I didn't mean . . . I didn't ask like *that*!"

Shaking his head, Edo said, "I'm not arguing. But if those ladies spied her entering your apartment . . . what would they *say*?"

Marcello took a sip of his *espresso*. "I didn't think about it."

Edo shook his head. "You've dated a lot, I'm surprised this is the first time this has come up."

"I haven't dated a Santa Lucia girl," Marcello said.

"Ah."

Shaking his head, Marcello said. "You may be right. But the way Antonella acted after I asked her . . . she didn't just seem nervous. There was something else. Like the idea . . . repulsed her."

Edo frowned. "That doesn't match what I heard. Any chance you're reading too much into it?"

"Maybe. But, I didn't get the feeling she wanted to be anything more than friends."

Ava ran her hand over the rough-hewn table. "I can't believe you're okay with Elisa making a mess of this."

"It's just a table," Ale shrugged.

"It's hundreds of years old!"

Ale shrugged again. "It's ugly."

Ava's laughed reverberated through the room. "No denying that."

"It's the right height, the right depth, and a splatter of paint across its surface will only improve it."

"It's generous, anyway." She paused. "Thank you. For this. But also for how hard you work to make us all fit together."

He took her hand. "I can tell it's not always easy."

"You're supposed to tell me everything is fine! That I'm reading too much into this!"

Ale grinned. "I got in trouble for that. Now you have Ale 2.0."

"Ale 2.0? What in the world are you talking about?"

"Never mind." He grinned. "Elisa is settling in though, don't you think? She goes to school, for a full day and doesn't complain about being separated from Margherita and Jacopo."

"She still has nightmares."

"But she lets you hold her. Calm her down. Remember, when she first came home? She couldn't even do that."

"Yes, that's true. Sometimes."

"I know it feels as if the road before us is pockmarked and treacherous, but really it's more open than the road behind us."

Ava smiled, biting her lip.

"What?"

"Sometimes I forget you're American at all, your accent has become so local. But then you say the oddest things, and I remember." She turned to the studio. "This has certainly helped. Her having a place to work."

"Us believing in her, if nothing else."

Ava nodded. "And having a space to leave messes where I won't nag at her probably helps, too."

"Maybe I'll build a room for my dirty socks." Ale grinned.

Ava laughed. "Tell you what. When we finally finish the *castello*, why don't you do that?"

Ale's face fell.

Ava stopped. "Did I say something?"

"No." He turned to the desk. "Looks like she's using it, anyway."

Nodding, Ava said, "She won't talk about it though. At all. It's this big secret, but how can it be if she's going to sell it?" She lifted the papers and started turning them over.

Ale drew in his breath. "Are you sure we should be looking at her work?"

Narrowing her eyes, Ava said, "I don't see that we have a choice. I don't want her getting carried in the wrong direction."

Ale tilted his head to show he didn't follow this logic.

Ava held up a sketch to the light coming in the doorway. She gestured to Ale. "Can you switch on the light?"

"Ava, I'm not sure about this. Teenagers need their space, don't they?"

"It's fine, Ale. Just switch it on, okay?"

Ale shook his head but followed the wire to click the switch. The room flooded with light.

Ava let out a sharp, "Oh, no!"

Ale looked up, worried. "What is it?"

The images . . . they were not what Ava had been hoping for. No persimmon trees glowed against a sunrise. No cats socializing in an alley. Instead, the pieces were bold, disquieting. An olive leaf so blown up it appeared distorted. A girl standing with her back to the viewer, the earth around her bare and lonely.

"Ale . . . what does this all mean?"

He shook his head. "I can't believe a teenager made these. When I was her age, I couldn't draw a recognizable human, let alone make something with so much power."

"But . . . but they're disturbing!" Ava held out a drawing of a simple landscape, so covered in blue pastel it seemed draped in ocean water. "Every painful thing that's ever happened to her is on paper for the world to see!"

"It's so brave," Ale murmured, examining a flower blooming from bones, cross-hatched quickly and thoroughly so it felt more dark than light.

"Ale! What's wrong with her?"

He looked up. "What do you mean?"

"All *this*!"

"Ava, darling . . ."

"Don't tell me to calm down!"

He smiled. "I wouldn't dare. Listen, I've known more than my share of artists in New York. The thing about them—"

Ava cut in, holding up another drawing. "Am I doing a horrible job? Does she feel this . . . desperate?" Ava rifled through the drawings. "Aren't there *any* cheerful ones?"

He touched her elbow. "Like I was saying . . . it's not that artists feel more tortured than other people. It's that they can open themselves to it, to allow the darkness. Ava, think about it. You of all people know how much work it can take to press all the hard stuff down so you can go about your day, moment to moment. What Elisa does here is find a way to channel it."

Ava wailed, "I want her to be normal!"

"No. You don't."

"Don't tell me how I feel, Ale! This is how I feel, and you have to deal with it."

"Oh, I can deal with it. That's no problem. Only, I don't believe you."

Ava glared at him. "I can't believe we're back here again."

"Ava. Listen. Your whole life, you were told you had to be a certain way. Of all the things I know you want for your daughter, it's the freedom to be who she is."

Ava looked down, scratching at a bit of paint on the table until it flaked off.

Softly, Ale said, "She's not normal, but she's as abnormal as any of us, as extraordinary as any of us. She's just better at owning it, better at expressing it."

Ava looked again at a painting of a rock wall with stones missing, like an old man with gaps for teeth. She shivered. "Maybe . . . is this the stuff she needs to work through to get to the pretty pictures again?" She looked up at Ale, pleading, "Do you think so? Do you think maybe once she starts making good art again, she'll leave all this . . . stuff behind?"

Ale handed her a sketch. "Look at it. And just *feel* it."

She forced herself to focus on the weeds growing out of the wall, wild. In her heart, the line between stability and instability shook on the knife's edge of losing control. Tears sprang to her eyes that had nothing at all to do with her worry about her daughter. And what people would say.

Ale whispered. "You see?"

Ava nodded.

Ale put his arm around her shoulder. "We all have darkness, Ava. Elisa is just honest enough to own it."

In a small voice, Ava said, "I want her to be happy." She looked up at him. "When will she be happy?"

Isotta unsnapped the top button of her shirt. She looked down and frowned. Then snapped it back with a sigh. Jacopo's babbling recalled her attention, and she brought her face to his, whisking across his bare snub of a nose. The sensation sent the child into a fit of giggles.

Luciano looked up with a smile from setting the table. "His joy is infectious."

Margherita popped between Isotta's arms to rub noses with her brother. "I do it, Nonno! Listen how he laugh!"

Jacopo's eyes grew wide as he followed Margherita's face as it drifted toward him, her curls brushing against his face. His laughter filled the room.

Luciano chuckled, "I didn't know babies could belly laugh."

Isotta ran her hand over Margherita's hair. "Margherita is better than cartoons."

Glancing at the clock, he said, "I'm sorry Elisa can't join us."

Isotta nodded. "She'll come after she gets home from Spoleto."

"How good of Ava to make sure Elisa maintains her relationships with her brothers."

Isotta nodded. "Sometimes I think..." She stopped herself.

"What is it, *cara*?"

"I'm probably too fragile." Isotta's eyes welled with tears and she shook her head to drive them away before Margherita noticed them. Any shift in her mood too easily alarmed the child. Striving for a light tone, Isotta said, "I worry that Elisa has all these half-relationships. You know, two half-siblings she doesn't live with and two adoptive brothers she rarely sees. You fill a grandfather role, but aren't. I fill an aunt role, I suppose, though I'm not. A mother who missed her childhood."

Straightening a napkin that already lay straight, Luciano said, "Elisa's early years were so impoverished, I suspect she feels her patchwork family covers her completely."

Isotta considered. "I suppose you're right." She grinned suddenly. "Did I tell you about seeing Elisa and Ale at the *fruttivendolo*? He was telling her the English words for vegetables, pretending horror at how few she knew, dramatizing the pronunciations until they were both in hysterics."

"Ale is a good man."

They both looked up at a knock at the door. Luciano regarded Isotta. "Are you ready, *cara*?"

"For lunch?" she quipped.

Luciano stared intently at Isotta.

She nodded. "Yes. I'm ready."

Luciano opened the door. Vito stepped through it, stopping only briefly to kiss his brother's cheeks before flying to Isotta on the couch with Jacopo now pulled against her like armor. Vito crowed, "Look how he's grown! In a week! I tell you, Isotta, that child is absolutely gorgeous! And Margherita! I adore your crown of dried flowers!"

Margherita patted the battered chain of camomile blossoms now sitting askew on her head. "My sister makes me a princess crown."

Vito rocked back on his heels. "You like princesses, child?"

"Yes! And pirates. Pirate princesses is my favorite."

He beamed at Isotta. "Her language growth is a wonder!"

Margherita leaned into Isotta, who said. "It's like I'm getting to know a whole new side of her."

"Astonishing! Astonishing..."

From behind Vito, Isotta noticed Enrico walking in and greeting his uncle. He stepped to the side and introduced a thin woman, not much taller than Elisa, with coffee-colored hair that fell in waves halfway down her back. Carla.

Luciano hesitated only a moment before he welcomed Carla. Enrico guided her to Isotta, who tried to stand, but couldn't, with Margherita now leaning across her lap as Jacopo bounced on her legs.

Enrico grinned. "Please, keep your seat. You have your hands full. Or your lap, rather." Enrico blushed faintly, as if he'd said something indecent. He shook his head and in more measured tones, added, "Soon you'll have Degas on your knees as well."

Isotta grinned tremulously at Enrico's sudden change of expression. "Doubtful. I gave Luciano an earful about feeding animals processed meat. The cat stalked off as if I'd betrayed him."

Chuckling, Enrico turned with a smile lighting his long face. "Isotta, this is Carla."

Carla offered her hand, which felt like a bundle of cool sticks in Isotta's loose grip. Carla laughed merrily, "How charming you look here, Isotta. Surrounded by children. Pure and maternal as the Madonna herself."

"It's good to meet you, Carla."

"The pleasure is *mine*. I've heard so much about you! Enrico quite goes on and on. I'd come to believe you might be a figment of his imagination! But here you sit. On the sofa."

Isotta pulled Margherita closer.

Enrico glanced at Isotta before kneeling beside the child to say, "Margherita. I love your crown."

The little girl sucked hard on her thumb and nodded. Then she pulled her thumb out with an audible pop. "Elisa makes me a pretty crown and I wear it *all day*."

He nodded with equal sobriety. "Now, I'm not sure of the rules for princesses. Do princesses eat Tronky bars?"

Margherita cocked her head to the side and grinned. "Princesses *love* Tronky bars!"

Pulling the candy bar from his pocket, Enrico said, "That's very good to hear. I thought I would have to eat this all by myself."

Margherita laughed. "Princesses so good at helping!"

To Isotta, Enrico said, "I should have asked, but I couldn't help myself. Last time, Margherita opened my world by introducing me to Tronky bars. I never ate candy as a child, so I'd missed that."

Isotta said, "You didn't? I had no idea—"

Carla's laugh tinkled, though her eyes stayed hard. "You didn't know, Isotta? How Enrico's mother forbade sweets? I'm surprised."

Isotta rested her cheek on Jacopo's hair. "I suppose I should help Luciano with lunch."

Carla said, "You're weighed down with all these babies. I'll help him.

You stay here and chat with Enrico. It seems you have a lot to catch up on."

Enrico leaped up. "Oh, no. I'll come with you, Carla." He darted a glance at Isotta but didn't meet her eyes. "You okay, here?"

Isotta nodded and watched the couple stroll into the kitchen. Was it her imagination, or did Carla sway her hips triumphantly?

Antonella scurried out of Giovanni's with the packet of pasta under her arm. Her head ducked, she almost crashed into Marcello entering the shop. "Oh!" she said. "I didn't . . . I mean, how are you, Marcello?"

Marcello blushed. "I'm picking up wine for Mamma." He paused. "I haven't seen you."

"Oh, work. You know." Antonella cringed at the sound of her affected laugh.

Marcello said, "You still enjoying the freedom?"

"Absolutely!" Her smile faltered. "How about you? I was thinking about what you said at dinner about the officer who might retire . . . "

"You remembered."

Antonella's eyes widened. "Of course. I asked Nonna. She said that his wife complains about his bunions all the time. She doesn't live close to our alley, but Nonna heard from somebody who heard from some-body . . . you know how it goes."

Marcello grinned. "You see? Small towns have their benefits."

Antonella grew serious. "I'm seeing the advantages, to be honest."

He leaned down to look seriously into her eyes. "Everything okay?"

"Oh, yes!" Antonella said, airily. "Life outside of Santa Lucia is fabu-lous. In fact, I'll be out of town next week, pet sitting for my boss!"

"Pet sitting? What's that?"

"You know, babysitting for pets."

"Like feeding and walking and stuff?"

"Yes."

Marcello frowned. "Isn't that what neighbors are for? Why would he ask his assistant to do that?"

She waved her hand. "It's a bit of a special circumstance. The pets . . . they aren't simple, like dogs or cats or fish or whatever."

Scratching his chin, Marcello said, "What, does he have an alligator or something?"

"Nothing like that," Antonella smiled.

Marcello gestured for Antonella to go on.

She blushed. "Okay, it sounds silly, but you know how people are about their pets."

He said nothing.

"He has a miniature mallard duck and a Texel guinea pig."

"A what?"

"I didn't know either, I had to Google it. It has long fur, like an angora rabbit but in a guinea pig."

"He has a *duck*? In his *house*?"

"Oh, that."

"Who is this guy?"

"My boss, I told you—"

"He keeps this duck and this pig . . . "

"Guinea pig."

"In his *house*."

"Kind of. I mean, the animals live outside in a special cage during the day, and then I'm supposed to bring them in to watch TV with me at night."

"You can't be serious right now."

Antonella giggled behind her hand.

Marcello's shoulders relaxed. "You were kidding. Thank the Madonna! For a minute—"

"Oh, no, Marcé," She placed a hand on his arm. "I'm serious. But it wasn't until I saw your face that I realized how crazy the situation is."

They both stopped when the bells of San Nicola reverberated through the evening air.

She shook her head. "I have to go. Mamma is waiting for this." She held up her purchase, and then let it drop as if suddenly realizing how foolish she looked waving a pack of pasta.

Marcello held out his elbow. "Why don't I accompany you home and you can tell me more about this duck situation? I suspect there's more that you haven't divulged."

"No, that's it."

"Humor me."

She threaded her arm through his, and they began strolling down Via Romana.

Marcello inclined his head toward her. "You know, you hear those tales about small towns filled with nuts. But this guy lives in Girona, right?"

"Yes."

"And he's married."

"Yes."

"To someone who accepts his duck and pig wandering through the house."

"The duck is his, but the guinea pig is Micia's."

Marcello sputtered. "Whose?"

"Micia. His wife."

"*Micia*? His wife is named *kitty*? This is too good. I believe I must take you to another dinner so you can fill me in on how this 'pet sitting' goes. Maybe they have mermaids in jars."

Antonella squeezed his arm. "I won't be back for a week. But after that, yes, I'd like that."

The bell over the door tinkled, and Edo whirled around. Seeing Francy, he hurried from behind the bar. "You're back!"

"I am. And glad to be so." He dropped a light kiss on Edo's cheek. Seeing no one in the bar, he let his lips drift to kiss Edo more fully, breathing in for a moment before pulling back.

Edo sighed happily. "You dropped your bags off already?" Edo peered around Francy, hopefully.

"No bags."

Edo groaned. "You're just here for the day again?"

Francy frowned sadly. "I could hardly steal that."

Glancing at the clock, Edo said, "Chiara should be back from her walk with your dad soon. Then I can duck out."

"Good." Francy ran his hands over the counter as his face grew thoughtful.

"Francy? Is everything okay?"

Francy smiled through his lashes. "I don't want to ruin what little time we have."

"Tell me." Edo's mind filled with the things he didn't like to talk about—his embarrassing insecurity that caused him to dump Francy when he thought Francy might dump him; the fact that he still hadn't told his family he was dating; his concern that Chiara harbored some secret repugnance for his "lifestyle."

"It's Fabio."

"Fabio!" Edo walked back around the counter and ground beans for Francy's espresso. "What did he do now?"

"I saw him in Girona on my way in." Francy perched on the stool directly across from Edo.

Edo frowned. "Why did you stop in Girona?"

"Gas. And the bank. I want to stay as long as I can tonight, so . . ."

Edo grinned. "Good. So. What happened with Fabio?"

Francy sucked in the corner of his lip. "I saw him walk out of a cosmetics store with his girlfriend. I overheard him berating her, saying she needed too much make-up to hide her acne. And why didn't she wash her face properly with the bar he got her."

"*Uffa.*"

"It gets worse. He stormed down the street and when she hesitated, he whirled around and called her, like a . . . "

"Like a dog?"

"Yes, painful to watch. She ran to catch up to him. Then he spun around, and she cowered. She *cowered*, Edo. Like he might slap her. Do you think he does? Hit her?"

Edo handed Francy his coffee. "To tell you the truth, I wouldn't put it past him."

"The things he said to her, about how dumb she is, how useless. It's almost worse than watching him hit her."

"I know what you mean."

Francy stirred sugar into his *espresso.*

They both looked over at the door as it opened. To their wide eyes, Fabio strode in, Morena mincing behind him.

Fabio broadcast loudly enough for passers-by to turn. "I thought I'd find you damn homos here."

Francy stood.

Tired before he even began, Edo said, "What do you want, Fabio?"

"What do I *want*? I'll tell you what I want. Tell them what you told me, Morena."

Morena mumbled something incomprehensible.

Fabio glared at Francy and shouted, "You hear that?"

Francy shook his head. "No, I don't." Softening his voice, he asked Morena. "Can you repeat that?"

Morena offered up a grateful smile before Fabio cut in. "Come off it. You heard her. She *saw* you. She saw you trailing us in Girona, not a half-hour ago."

Francy crossed his arms over his chest. "Trailing you? I'm afraid I don't follow."

"But you did! That's the point! You *followed* me!"

Francy snorted and turned back to the bar. "You're out of your mind."

"Am I? I'm smart enough to know all you homos are the same. Eyeing the rest of us decent folks like meat."

Edo's mouth dropped open as Francy turned around, aghast. "What are you talking about?"

"You know what I'm talking about. Everyone does. And, once I get the *assessore* position in the town council, we're going to put a stop to this. You all, trying to get in our pants."

Francy took a step toward Fabio. "That's what this girl told you. That I was trying to get in your pants. She said that."

"She didn't have to! I know how you operate. Contaminating normal society with your bad morals."

Francy threw a hand out to stop Edo as he strode around the counter. "No, Edo. Wait." He turned to Fabio. "Fabio, I expect this will strain your limited capabilities, but I wouldn't look favorably on you if you were the last man on God's fertile earth, served up with a bow complete. You see, you *repel* me. So, please. Do us both a favor and get gone."

Edo tried not to smile.

"What are you saying?" Fabio turned to Morena. "Did you hear what he said? What did he say?"

She shook her head and stared at her feet.

Fabio shook his fist at Francy. "You like to think you're some big fish. *But I know the truth.* And I'll make sure everyone knows, too!" Grabbing Morena, he whirled them out the door.

Into the silence, Edo whispered, "What the hell was that?"

Francy shook his head.

Ale pushed open the door. "I heard the shouting from the *castello*. What's going on?"

Edo said, "Fabio."

"Fabio?"

Ava ran in. "Was that Fabio I heard?"

Edo nodded. He peered at Francy's grim face before saying, "He seems to think Francy is trying to turn him."

"Turn him?" Ava snorted. "Leave it to my brother to have zero understanding of who is grossly out of his league." She put a sympathetic hand on Francy's arm.

Francy patted Ava's hand. "It's fine. Unfortunately, it's part of the score."

The door opened and Chiara walked in, her eyes wide. "What's going on with Fabio?"

His voice tight, Edo responded, "He came in with some words."

Fabrizio shrugged off his coat. "Words? About what?"

Francy looked away for a moment and said, "Take a guess."

Chiara's face grew still as she busied herself emptying her pockets of lint and loose change.

Fabrizio watched her for a moment before turning to Francy. "Son..."

Francy shook his head. "Nothing I haven't heard before." He glanced up at Chiara, investigating a particularly curious receipt. "But he said something... troubling."

Edo nodded, "That he would make sure everyone knew. He hit that pretty hard."

Ava nodded. "Rumor mongering is part of his schtick. He couldn't convince anyone that I was a teenage slut," her voice turned to ice, "or at least I never got wind of it. His stock is plummeting, as you'd say, Ale, right?"

Ale nodded. "Right."

Francy shook his head. "Still. The standards aren't the same for anyone who is the least different. We have to represent all the time, we can't ever have a whiff of scandal. With my tour just getting traction, if he tells some news outlet—"

"He won't!" Ava and Edo shouted.

Ava shook her head. "He wouldn't even know how. I promise. He'll tell his stupid friends who still hang out in the hardware store. And that will be the end of it."

Francy said, "I hope so. Because if he goes farther . . . musicians in Italy have been ruined for less."

Isotta looked up at a knock on Massimo's front door. Her front door, she amended mentally. She sighed and put down her pencil.

She smiled when she saw Enrico. "I didn't know you were back."

Shadows from the streetlight obscured his face. "*Buona sera*, Isotta. I hope it's okay that I drop in without an invitation."

She stood back to allow him to enter. "Of course."

He followed her into the kitchen. "My father decided last minute to visit Luciano. I thought I'd tag along. I called, but . . . "

Isotta moved papers from the table, revealing her phone. She picked it up. "I forgot to turn the ringer back on after the kids' nap." She stacked the paper out of the way. "Can I get you anything? A cup of tea? A glass of *grappa*?"

"Do you have *camomilla*?"

Isotta smiled. "Just like your uncle."

Enrico looked around. "The transition . . . how has it been?"

"Fine," wished Isotta.

Enrico studied her pale face, the shadows under her eyes. Her shirt that gaped at the collar with the weight she'd lost.

She shook her head to break the eye contact. "It will be fine," she said softly. She brought the cups to the table. "Milk or sugar?"

He grinned. "Real men take their herbal tea straight."

She laughed and winced a little at the effort.

Enrico said, "Isotta. Talk to me. We're friends, right?"

She bit her lip and nodded. "I can't sleep. I keep waiting for him to burst in. I can't *sleep*."

"But the locks—"

"I know. It's not rational. But he's here . . . *everywhere*. This house is full of him. Of her. Anna. I can't escape them." Her voice caught. "I've opened the windows until we all froze. I've moved the furniture, and Luciano gave me fresh bedding. Nothing works. They're always right behind me."

"Sounds as if you need an exorcism."

"Don't mock me. Please."

He shook his head, seriously. "I'm not. I promise. I don't mean like in the movies. I mean, we need a way to get rid of the ghosts. Not actual ghosts, the lingering feelings."

"I tried burning incense. That didn't work either."

He nodded in thought. "And the children?"

"Jacopo isn't sleeping well, but that might be because he's in my room and I'm tossing and turning. Margherita's nightmares are subsiding. I think. It's hard to keep track." She shook her head. "Enough about my tale of woe. How are you? How's Carla?"

Enrico rubbed a thumb over the handle of his cup. "I'm fine. We're fine."

Isotta tried to nod companionably. "Good. That's good. And the research?"

His eyes brightening, Enrico said, "Not only is Luciano's house a treasure trove, but Ale said he found boxes of old documents in an unused room at the *castello*. And I talked to Edo, he said he was pretty sure they have some at the bar as well, he needs to talk to Chiara about it, and then I can make my way through more documents."

Isotta smiled, "You'll get a real sense of what Santa Lucia was like at the time people took refuge at Luciano's."

He regarded her appreciatively. "Yes."

She nodded. "Plus, Ale and Edo. Good guys to know."

He chuckled. "They are. It's hard, sometimes, to stay on task. Edo, particularly, is quite the storyteller." His face growing serious, he added, "They think the world of you too, you know. They find ways to work that into every conversation."

She flushed. "They do? Oh ... well, that's nice to hear."

Enrico leaned forward. His hand twitched toward hers. Then he straightened, as if suddenly aware of his surroundings. He gestured to her stack of papers and cleared his throat. "Speaking of work, how is the book coming?"

Isotta took a cautious sip of her tea. "I've been thinking of taking it back out. When I worked on it, I felt good—peaceful and invigorated at the same time." She sighed. "But I need to focus on looking for work. I expect Luciano told you."

Enrico nodded. "What a shock."

"Yes. It forced the separation sooner than I would have liked. Plus, you know," the edge of her voice sliced the air, "added an unpleasant layer of insecurity."

Enrico's face grew serious. "No idea where the money went?"

Isotta shook her head. "My money is on gambling."

"Massimo or Anna?"

She shrugged. "Both of them? I don't know." She rotated the cup on the table. "Riccardo got me Massimo's final paycheck. It's substantial, which helps. But if he received that every month ... there should be a small fortune."

He nodded.

Isotta went on. "As it is, I've calculated I have a comfortable three months or a tight six months before I have to find a source of income. And leave the children."

"Your parents?"

"I can't ask them. At least this place is paid for."

He considered. "I think you should work on your book."

She looked up. "Why?"

"So much is out of your control here. You deserve something that's yours. Some lightness."

She found she could no longer hold his gaze. "I wouldn't know how to illustrate it."

Enrico thought for a moment. "Elisa?"

She shook her head. "Her art is . . . I couldn't ask her to contain it."

A pause. "Maybe that doesn't matter when you're doing it for yourself." He darted his gaze to her. "My mother and I, we used to write books together. Comic books, really. She would draw the figures and speech bubbles and I'd fill them in and we'd read them together, laughing. Before she got too sick."

Seeing the tears in his eyes, she clasped her cup with both hands and leaned toward him. "I'd love to see them."

He smiled. "Someday. Perhaps."

When the leaves crisped on the trees and the persimmons glowed from bare branches, Ale discovered his wine had irretrievably, absolutely, and unambiguously failed.

He'd wondered, of course. Even suspected. Hard not to, with Bruno scowling at his barrels. Plus, when his impatience led him to try a sip a week ago, he'd known something was wrong. He'd gagged, inhaling the funky scent. But hoped that this was part of the process, typical of wine at this stage.

He asked now, "What went wrong?"

Bruno shrugged. "The barrels."

Ale lifted his hands. "But, Bruno, my ancestors stored wine in those barrels for generations! How could—"

"The bacteria. You can't keep that old bacteria on the inside of the barrels. It goes wild. It's like asking rogue warriors to make nice at the dinner table."

"I *cleaned* them. The barrels." Ale protested.

Bruno harrumphed. "Not well enough."

Muttering to himself, Ale said, "And here I thought I've come so far."

Bruno patted his shoulder. "Next time. Use steel."

"I can't afford steel!"

Bruno shrugged. "I told you I could get second-hand ones. Even second-hand wood barrels would be better. Just wash them better next time, eh?"

Ale chanced another sniff of the quote-unquote wine. "But something else went wrong, didn't it? I mean, this is awful. In a way that nature would be hard-pressed to replicate."

Bruno chuckled. "Hard-pressed. That's funny."

Ale grumbled. "It wasn't meant to amuse."

"Happy is the man who makes witticisms without effort."

"How did you get so philosophical all of a sudden? And are you going to answer my question or are we going to continue to banter as if we're at a cocktail party?"

"Cocktail party?"

Ale shook his head. "Never mind."

"The self-flagellation is useless," Bruno offered. "Making wine is science. Making wine is art. You haven't learned it. You've been following directions from a book."

"Who reads books? I followed wine-making blogs."

Bruno shivered. "Worse and worse." He held the wine up to the light. "There's a change in tone when the wine is ready for pressing, a shift in the nose when it's time to rack. Without years of practice, without being guided by those signs, why would you expect to have that knack? To say nothing of the intuition you need to determine how many whole bunches, with stems, to add for structure. When to shift the temperature up or down." Bruno shrugged. "On and on."

"So you're telling me I need a Mr. Miyagi, and even with that, I might not create a decent bottle."

"Mr. Miyagi?"

Ale sighed. Sometimes it got tiring explaining the references his mind reached for as easily as most people reached for a salt shaker. "Karate Kid. Wax on, wax off?"

Bruno stared for a moment before he opened his mouth wide, hooting with laughter. "Mr. Miyagi! Yes! You do, you need a Mr. Miyagi!" Bruno poked his own chest, leaving a dent in the padding of his chest hair underneath his heavy cloth shirt. "Lucky for you, *I* am Mr. Miyagi."

"You'd help me? After all this?"

Bruno looked around. "What am I doing right now?"

"You've already offered too much. Lending us your destemmer. Your barrel crusher. Coming for the *vendemmia*. Lending the small barrels for the *passito*." Ale looked away so Bruno wouldn't see his eyes filling with tears he couldn't explain.

Bruno watched Ale curiously.

"You would guide me through the process? The whole one?"

"Fertilization to corking. Not labels though, I have no eye for decoration."

Ale thought of all the labels he'd sketched out, the legal pads strewn over the table, covered with names for the vintage he'd been sure would make him a wine star. He hung his head.

Bruno frowned in thought. "You are from New York."

"Yes."

Bruno nodded. "Then perhaps you do not understand our people. Those vines stand in my valley. You stand in my valley. It is enough."

Ale chewed his thumbnail. "That's very generous. But. *Allora*, I don't think it's worth my time. Or yours. I'm going to cut my losses. With my luck, the *passito* will fail, too." He ran his hands over the soft wood of the offending barrels. "I'm done."

"They are your vines, of course." Bruno shrugged. "But you'll make better wine from the vines you cultivate than the ones you abandon."

Antonella knew Signor Tocci had left the house already. She *knew* it. And yet she couldn't stop herself from knocking, or from calling "*Con permesso?*" as she opened the door.

Silence.

She exhaled.

This wouldn't be so bad.

Yes, it was weird that her boss asked her to take care of his duck and guinea pig while he and his wife vacationed in the Canary Islands. And it hardly signaled her moving up in the ranks. She still felt like a glorified coffee bringer. Frankly, she had more responsibility when she was in the secretarial pool. Her cheeks flushed now as she remembered how her voice grated her heart whenever she asked, "And *then* what happened?" She'd realized Signor Tocci liked it when her voice grew breathy. And a little lost.

Antonella cleared her throat.

This would be fine. She liked animals. Loved them. Maybe this was a test of sorts. If she proved herself worthy with his pets, perhaps Signor Tocci would trust her with his accounts. She sighed at her stupid optimism and began flipping on lights.

"Oh!" She exclaimed as the first switch lit an enormous painting of Micia. In a negligee. At least, Antonella assumed it was Micia. It resembled the photo framed on Signor Tocci's desk. Though Antonella wasn't sure if it would be better if this portrait was of his wife or not. She leaned closer. The airbrushing skills of the photographer were prodigious. Micia shimmered like plastic. Except for her breasts, which heaved out of her lacy number. Were those her nipples outlined in the material?

Antonella forced herself to look away. It was difficult, akin to turning away from a bus crash in process. But she felt indecent, staring at her boss's scantily clad wife.

She flicked on another light. No surprises here. She switched on the next light to reveal another hallway. She moved to a darkened room and flicked on another light, revealing another portrait of Micia. This time in a red nightgown and matching feathery mules. Micia's breasts looked, if anything, more voluminous.

Antonella shook her head and decided to rip off the bandage, walking through the house and coming to terms with one racy portrait after another. Here Micia leaned forward suggestively, there she reclined on a velvet chaise. Every picture starred Micia, solo, except one where she held what must be her guinea pig.

Antonella hoped the creature wasn't a metaphor for something. But it did remind her of her obligation. She went in search of the binder Signor Tocci promised Micia would leave her in the kitchen. Luckily, the kitchen boasted not one near-photo of Micia.

The binder was indeed prominently placed and Antonella flipped through it, her mouth falling open. No wonder Signor Tocci needed her to stay in the house rather than popping in twice a day. The animals required hours of care. She checked the clock. She was already twenty minutes behind schedule!

She cast her eyes around the room, hoping there wasn't a camera recording her dereliction of duty. She couldn't find one, but didn't rich people sometimes hide them in stuffed animals or pillows? She straightened her skirt and resolved to always behave as if she was being watched. And to only change in the dark.

The conversation stopped when Pietro walked into the bar. Not because anyone disliked the man. They didn't. In fact, they felt much affection for him. But he never seemed comfortable with people. Or, more specifically, he never seemed comfortable *interacting* with people. Unless he had the buffer of food to hold, discuss, or offer. Without that, he habitually shrank to the side.

Nodding acknowledgment of Pietro's arrival, the villagers returned to their conversations.

His fingers tapped back and forth on the counter. Chiara withdrew her hand from Fabrizio, who seemed to be reading her palm, and approached Pietro. "*Buongiorno*, Pietro. What can I get for you this morning?"

"*Solo caffè, per favore*, Chiara." As the bell over the door tinkled, Pietro looked over his shoulder. He turned back as his wife stalked into the bar. "Better give me a *cornetto*, too, Chiara. *Vuoto*."

"Plain? Are you sure, Pietro? I would think a man of your particular talents would appreciate our filled *cornetti*. The apricots come from Calabria."

He shook his head politely. "Another time."

Chiara waved a greeting at Livia as she turned to prepare Pietro's *caffè*.

Livia stood for a moment in the middle of the room, like a high schooler at a discotheque waiting to be asked to dance. When conversations resumed, she stared at her husband's back. "*Con permesso*," she muttered as she pushed in between Pietro and Paola, who owned the *fruttivendolo*.

When Chiara handed Pietro his *espresso* and *cornetto*, it didn't look as if the couple had exchanged one word. They stared fixedly ahead. Livia announced, "Nothing for me, Chiara. I'll share Pietro's *cornetto*."

Chiara couldn't help noticing Pietro wince. She nodded and made her way to the other end of the bar. Before she took even a few steps, a hissing sound made her examine the La Pavoni. Was pressure building in the lines?

But no, the hissing came from Livia, steadily whispering at Pietro. Who shoved bites of *cornetto* into his mouth instead of answering. His mouth worked as he chewed, all but pointing at his face to demonstrate his inability to participate in the conversation.

Chiara wanted to walk away, but Livia's anger mesmerized her. Particularly with Pietro's complete refusal to engage. Chiara thought she heard the words "restaurant" and "Sonia" and wondered if perhaps something had happened to their daughter, who Chiara knew to be away consulting. The girl seemed nice enough, if a little edgy for Santa Lucia.

At a curious glance from Fabrizio, leaning over the counter to catch her eye, Chiara smiled and took up her place across from him. Arturo, standing beside Fabrizio, jerked his thumb toward the couple. In a low, greedy voice, he whispered, "What's going on with them?"

Chiara affected a casual shrug. She looked up at the clatter of coins skidding across the scuffed copper plate to see Pietro walking out of Bar Birbo, his wife watching as the door closed behind him.

Ale poured the last of the wine into Ava's glass. She looked up. "You should have taken it. I'm done."

He nodded and swapped glasses with her.

She glanced at Elisa, who was swirling pieces of her salad into novel shapes. Resolving not to say anything, Ava hunted for a mushroom.

Ale took a breath. "The wine failed."

Elisa looked up in alarm, as Ava said, "Oh, Ale, I'm sorry. I know you were hoping...how bad is it?"

"Apparently, it will make medium-quality vinegar."

Ava murmured, "Do you want to talk about this later, maybe?"

Ale shook his head. "No. You both worked hard. You deserve to know."

"Oh, Ale," Ava soothed.

Elisa said, "You aren't going to make wine anymore?"

Ava narrowed her eyes at Ale, watching him carefully.

Feeling her gaze, he looked into the shadowy corner of the room. "*Allora*, Elisa. I'd wanted this to work. *Needed* this to work. None of my app ideas lead anywhere, and I figured wine must be a sure-fire way to generate an income. After all, country people have been making it for thousands of years without science or thermometers or how-to guides. How hard could it be? So discovering that even my fallback is fallible? Well, giving up seems like the easiest course of action." Ale felt two sets of eyes boring into him. He'd never realized before how Elisa and Ava had the same intent stare.

Tightly, Ava said, "Don't leave us in suspense."

He shrugged and smiled bravely. "Bruno is on board. The rest depends on you two."

"Us?" Elisa and Ava yelped.

He nodded. "You. You see, it'll take a lot of work. I can't afford to hire anyone and according to Bruno, we need to begin now. I'm already behind in pruning. I thought I had more time, but again, I was relying on blogs and Bruno informed me that there's a microclimate here. I have to plant the canes from pruning to repopulate the vineyard since it's dying out."

To Ava's astonished expression, he added, "Plus, he's supportive of my wanting to keep to old school methods. Which means thinking about fertilization. He spent about an hour explaining the importance of compost. And worms. We want to find every worm within a two-kilometer radius and re-home them to the vineyard."

Elisa grinned. "Worms? Why worms?"

Ava answered, "I can't believe I didn't think of it." She turned to Elisa. "Worms oxygenate the soil by creating channels with their tracks. And they eat things a garden doesn't need and then they poop out a rich soil."

Elisa laughed. "That's funny. I want to be on worm duty. Margherita and me."

Ale chuckled. "Worms help with fixing nutrients in the soil, too. Good when there's run-off, which depletes the soil. And Bruno predicts a wet spring."

Ava frowned. "He does? How does he know?"

Shrugging, Ale said, "I guess the old farmer version of an old wive's tale. He sounded certain, though. He may have used the word 'biblical'."

Ava lowered her voice. "I thought for sure you'd walk away."

Ale said, "I thought I would, too. But then... I remembered the *vendemmia*. Waking up that morning, watching the sky, afraid of rain. Cutting the grapes from the vines all together. Tasting one, and imagining the wine." He stopped himself, "I did a poor job of imagining that, as it turns out."

Ava said, "Hey..."

He shook his head. "It's okay. Wine is complicated but, like many good things... worth the complication."

Ava grinned at him with shining eyes as Elisa smirked and reached for her sketchbook.

He touched Ava's nose with his forefinger and said, "The point is, I liked how small I felt that day—part of a place, a process, much bigger than me. It's strange looking back on it. You'd think I would have realized how arrogant it was to think the wine would bring me instant glory. I need to stay small. Step by step."

"That will make the wine drinkable?"

"No," Ale snorted. "What will make the wine drinkable is that Bruno is going to help."

Ava's laugh filled the kitchen.

Ale added, "And even then, who knows? I asked Bruno about our odds, and he said to 'put it in God's inbox'. I kid you not."

Elisa glanced up from her sketchbook to grin at Ale.

A simple gesture, but suddenly, Ava found that she didn't care how many times she had to clean up Elisa's smears of paint. All that mattered was this. Them sitting together, around the table. Together.

Ale smiled. "So what do you think? Family project?"

Ava and Elisa looked at each other and nodded. Ava asked, "The *passito?*"

Ale shrugged. "We won't know for a while. It could be great, but . . . an unknown grape, we're going with a lot of gut work. At least that's Bruno's gut work, though. Thank the Madonna I was so distracted by the winemaking I didn't notice Bruno doing what he wanted for the *passito.*"

Ava said, "Remind me to bring Bruno a cake." She added, "And you said you hit on a promising app idea, didn't you?"

Ale shrugged. "Maybe. I'm more interested in the predictive code that powers that app."

Leaning forward, Ava said, "And! We've got some bookings!"

He smiled. "I'm glad you thought of listing the *castello* on those high-end websites."

"I didn't, actually. I ran into Antonella at Giuseppe's and we got to chatting. She's working for that firm in Girona and has lots of ideas."

He nodded and raised his glass, "Cheers to Antonella then. I'll have to buy her a meal."

Ava laughed. "Let's not get ahead of ourselves. Maybe a *cappuccino.*"

Ale smiled wanly, but the smile didn't reach his eyes.

Elisa piped up, "Plus, the postcards and shirts and stuff are coming in soon, right? For me to sell?"

Ava muttered and turned away. When everyone looked at her, she smiled brightly. "Won't that be fun?"

Ale nodded thoughtfully. "But that's your money, Elisa. We decided."

She shook her head. "We're all in this together. Like that book with the three men on the cover. Or is it a comic book with three mice?"

Ale realized first. "The three musketeers?"

"Yes. Yes, that."

Fabrizio's voice rose, "I don't understand why you won't tell me."

Chiara shook her head. "Edo is moody sometimes. What more is there to say?" Her smile stretched wide as she greeted Magda, "Magda! How good to see you!"

Magda frowned briefly before hanging up her coat. "Wine please, Chiara."

Dante, opening the door behind her, echoed, "Wine, please, Chiara."

Chiara grinned before uncorking the wine.

As Magda and Dante began one of their spirited debates, Fabrizio leaned across the counter to press a cheek against Chiara's, murmuring, "I'll go. I want to get some writing done before you're off tonight." Raising a hand to say goodbye to Magda and Dante, he cast one more curious look at Chiara. She poured the wine with great intensity and missed it. He sighed and walked out.

Magda turned to Dante. "What's wrong with a woman president?"

Dante put up his hands. "I didn't say there was anything *wrong* with a woman president. I said nobody should vote for a woman *because* she's a woman."

Magda bristled. "Listen, women in politics are like a dog in church. They aren't welcome, and they have to fight to belong. Don't you think they deserve every advantage? Or is it that you don't think they are up to the job?"

Dante frowned into his wine. "It's a brutal world. Could a woman handle it?"

Magda turned to Chiara. "Are you hearing this?"

Chiara chuckled, "Don't mind me, I've got dishes to do."

Magda frowned. "One of these days, you're going to have to offer an opinion."

Dante insisted. "I'm not suggesting that women aren't smart enough. Or capable." He smiled at Magda, leaning toward her a touch. "How could I think women aren't smart or capable? Knowing the women I do..."

Magda blushed and dropped her eyes to her wine.

Dante went on, "But politics are brutal, you know they are. Is the world ready?"

Magda muttered, "They have a woman prime minister in Germany. Even in England. Why not here?"

Dante shrugged. "It's different. You know that. If we elect somebody before the people at large are ready, they'll chew her up and spit her out and we'll never get another one. It's a question of timing."

Magda looked into Dante's warm eyes. Her scowl softened. He held her eye contact, his hand sliding across the counter to touch hers lightly. She stiffened, sending her fingers into a spasm. Dante lifted his hand for a napkin as if that had been his plan all along.

Their conversation continued as they stood and headed out the door. Without thinking, Dante dropped enough coins on the scuffed copper plate to pay for both of their glasses of wine. Chiara raised her eyebrow at Magda, who didn't notice as she beamed up at Dante.

Dante inclined his head toward Magda, listening intently as the two of them strolled out of Bar Birbo.

Magda shivered as the cold air enveloped them.

"You okay, Magda?" Dante's eyes searched hers.

She nodded, not chancing speech.

He grinned. "I'll walk you home."

Grumbling with a smile, she said, "I know the way."

Dante placed a gentle hand on her back. "Allow me this touch of chivalry."

She hesitated before taking the arm he offered. They began walking up the hill in silence. As if testing the waters, Magda leaned briefly against

Dante. At the sudden closeness, she wished she'd washed her hair. Before feeling grateful that the darkness hid her flush of unaccustomed nervousness.

From the shadows, the end of a cigarette burned orange with the wafting tar smell of an MS-brand cigarette. A voice, reedy with malice, wafted across Via Romana. "Well. How sweet." Fabio stepped out from the alley, taking another drag from his cigarette.

Magda felt Dante's arm tighten. Authority ringing in his voice, Dante said, "What do you want, Fabio?"

Fabio snorted. "I'm more curious about what *you* want, Signore Sindaco. Is your divorce even final?"

Magda took an involuntary step backward.

Catching sight of the movement, Fabio sidled toward Dante. With a leer, he said, "I suppose there's no accounting for taste. I, myself, have never enjoyed the smell of rotten cabbage." He wrinkled his nose in distaste before snorting at his joke. The laughter rose like smoke above Via Romana, as Fabio strolled down the street and disappeared into the darkness.

Antonella slammed the car door and breathed deeply. She had to admit, as the sun slanted across the valley and the sky bloomed pink and purple, she was glad to be back. She inhaled the scent of woodsmoke, the wild herbs that lined the parking lot. Yes. It was good to be home. She wondered if she'd feel as grateful to be back if her time away had been less . . . odd.

"Antonella!" She turned at the sound of her name.

Marcello stood at the entrance to the parking lot, his arm waving above his head.

She smiled and waved. "*Buona sera*, Marcé."

He strolled toward her, waving his baton. "Bea said you'd be pulling in soon. I thought I'd walk you home."

"Has Santa Lucia been taken over by some bad element?"

He chuckled. "Nothing like that. But I had to hear the rest of the story. About the duck."

"Oh, the duck." She smiled wearily as she opened the trunk of her car. "Did he prove a handful?"

"He was sweet, actually. As charming as a duck could be. I just hadn't expected a duck and a guinea pig to demand so much attention."

Marcello pulled out her suitcase and held out his arm for her to take as they began walking up the hill. "I'm intrigued. Tell me everything."

She grinned up at him. "So I was there for a week, right? Every single morning, I had to take the duck and the guinea pig out of their outdoor pen and let them roam around the yard for twenty-five minutes."

"Twenty-five? Exactly?"

"Exactly. This was underlined in the notes. Very important."

He grinned. "What then?"

"Then I had to place them on their chairs—"

"Their *chairs*?"

"You heard me. Don't act as if you didn't," Antonella nudged Marcello with her hip. He nudged her back. She went on, "They each had a chair and a special suction cup bowl. For their breakfast."

Marcello stopped walking. "For their *breakfast*? Do they also read the paper?"

"In the morning? Heaven forbid! News is their evening activity. Watching it, though. Not reading it."

Marcello doubled over, laughing. "Now you're pulling my leg."

Antonella widened her eyes. "Me? Never." She tugged his arm. "Are you walking me home or not? Nonna will wonder where I am."

"She knows I'm walking you home. She won't worry about you getting home safe."

"Well. She may worry about something else."

He raised his eyebrows. "Nah. I'm a gentleman." He tightened his arm. "Now. Tell me more."

She shrugged. "That's pretty much it. After their breakfast, I put them back in their outdoor pens. At midday, I put them into special cages with toys I had to rotate out each day. And in the evenings, I put the duck in the kitchen to waddle ahead while I carried the guinea pig into the TV room. The duck plopped himself on a fresh sheet of newspaper and preened while I brushed the guinea pig."

"With the news?"

"The news, it turns out, is critical. One time I deviated, who wants to hear about all the bad stuff happening in the world all the time? The duck quacked and quacked and refused to settle down until I turned the channel and he saw his news anchor. I think the duck has a crush on him."

He shook his head. "Are all rich people like that?"

She shrugged.

"How was the rest of the house?" he asked.

"About what you'd expect," she said lightly. "Nothing too unusual." Part of her wanted to tell him about the portraits of Micia, the supplements that crammed every drawer. How she screamed when she caught sight of the extra toupee in the guest bathroom. But she knew she couldn't. She wouldn't be able to admit to anyone how disorienting the experience was. She'd focus on the duck. Who was pretty sweet. As long as he had his eyes trained on his favorite news anchor.

Dante hesitated before pushing open the door of the hardware shop. Interacting with people you despise was the curse of living in a small town, but it couldn't be helped and procrastinating would intensify the discomfort. No, better to take the ball at the bounce and treat Fabio like any other villager. Of a village he, Dante, was mayor.

As soon as he stepped in, Dante felt awash in discomfort. He hated being with Fabio, who never followed the social conventions that made life predictable and comfortable. He hated the dim light. How could a shop that sold lightbulbs have so many burned out? Did the owner know that Fabio kept the hardware store this dark?

In a thunderclap, Dante realized what he hated most of all. The hardware store, it reminded him of Vale. Because of Vale, he'd rarely had to come to this hardware store. Because of Vale, he'd lost his marriage. Not that he missed Stella, if he were honest with himself. But the sordid affair left him vulnerable to speculations about his manhood that he found in poor taste.

As Dante entered, Fabio smirked and closed his newspaper. Perhaps he also remembered the rumors. Dante gathered his strength in his chest, using it to prop himself higher. "Fabio. You're looking well."

Fabio's smirk still played about his face.

Dante cleared his throat. "I need an insulating strip."

Fabio pointed down the edge of the store that seemed draped in the visual version of spiderwebs. Dante found the package of insulation and carried it to the register. Fabio nodded and punched the price into the cash register, nodding in appreciation at Dante's use of exact change.

Gesturing to the paper, Dante said, "What's the news?"

Fabio frowned. "I'm looking for an article. I spoke with a journalist who assured me he took my story seriously, but I haven't seen it."

Dante wished he hadn't asked.

Fabio mumbled. "You'd think they'd get a pervert like that off the streets." He looked up. "You think *you* would get a pervert like that off the street."

Dante looked confused. "Are you referring to something in particular?"

"Francy. He followed me in Girona, trying to get me to switch to his side, if you know what I mean. They're all the same."

Dante shook his head. How had he missed a piece of gossip about Santa Lucia's closest brush with celebrity? "Pardon my ignorance, Fabio. But you can't possibly be insinuating that you believe Francy was trying to . . . turn you gay? That's what you told a newspaper?"

Fabio bristled. "Imagine what he's doing to little boys at his concerts! Everyone ribs me about the bones and ignores what's right under their noses. It's shameful. Well, I for one won't stand by and do nothing. It's time to act! Rise up! And stand for what we believe in!"

Dante stared at Fabio. "And what's that? Exactly?"

Fabio started. Perhaps no one had asked him this before. He stumbled over his words, "Loyalty . . . to what made Italy great in the first place. Ancient Romans . . . they fought for what was right! Firm morals and protecting the people!"

Shaking his head, Dante said, "Firm morals? You know those ancient Romans were all sleeping with their houseboys, don't you?"

Fabio recoiled. "What? You're making that up. That's nasty."

Dante picked up his bag, tired of the conversation. "Look it up. And while you're at it, I'd thank you to not besmirch the name of our villagers to the press."

Glaring, Fabio said, "The *assessore* position . . . I deserve it. I've earned a place on the town council. I'm one of the few people around here that cares about the important things. When will you appoint me?"

Dante shook his head. "Get a clue, Fabio. You are a small man with limited capabilities and should stick to what you know. Selling u-bends."

"You're the mayor! You're supposed to stand by villagers! You're going to put Magda on the council, aren't you? Fill the seats with foreigners! Ruin everything our ancestors built!"

"I'm not listening to your garbage, Fabio. That's beyond the scope of the office."

Fabio stared at him levelly before his grin stretched over his face.

"Then maybe we need someone new in the office."

"Chiara, I wish you'd tell me what's going on with you and Edo. I keep waiting for it to get less tense and it doesn't," Fabrizio said, his eyes going dizzy from following Chiara around the bar.

"I told you before, he's moody. He acts as if I'm about to jump down his throat."

"Well, are you?"

"No! But I wish he wouldn't be late all the time."

The door opened and Edo strolled in with Ava, the two of them chatting animatedly. They stopped when they noticed Chiara staring.

Edo unzipped his coat. "Am I late?" He held out his hand for Ava's jacket and checked the clock.

Chiara grumbled.

Edo asked loudly, "What was that, Chiara? I can't seem to hear you."

"You were supposed to be here an hour ago! Fabrizio's about to leave."

Edo drew out his phone. He held it out. "It's eleven o'clock."

"What? No, it's not, it's noon!"

Fabrizio chuckled. "Did you forget to set your watch back?"

Chiara reddened. "Oh. Was that today?"

Edo shook his head, opening the drawer to pull out his apron. "I'll change the bar clock as soon as I make coffee for Ava. She has to pick up a package at the *posta* before they close for *pausa*."

Chiara couldn't miss the chill in Edo's words and mumbled, "I didn't know. I thought you weren't coming."

Edo asked, "Why in the world would you assume that?"

"Because of that time when you and Francy went for a walk and you lost track of time . . ."

"That was ages ago, Chiara. And I didn't lose track of time, Francy dropped his keys and we had to find them."

"Right. Now I remember."

Edo shook his head and turned to Ava. "I'm happy to help with pruning. The *vendemmia* was fun. More than I thought it would be. Should I ask Francy if it fits with his tour schedule?"

Fabrizio touched Chiara's hand to get her attention. "You'll walk me to the car?"

She nodded slowly. "Yes. Let's."

As they walked out the door, Fabrizio pulled her closer. "Are you sure everything is okay, *cara*?"

Chiara sighed and leaned on his shoulder. "I'll be honest. Edo and I had a...strained moment. He was telling me about...well, it doesn't matter what. The point is, I didn't react the way he wanted me to and I think he's angry. But the thing is, with Francy and Edo. It's strange to have everything be okay. Suddenly. It doesn't work that way."

"Maybe it does for them."

"Why should the rules be different for them?"

Fabrizio kissed the top of Chiara's head. "My theory? Francy's buying the bar put too much pressure on the relationship. I think they needed the break-up to come together as equals. Then, again, take that for what it's worth, it's not as if Francy is forthcoming." Fabrizio stopped and looked back, realizing Chiara had stopped walking several paces behind him. Her mouth gaped open.

"Chiara?"

"When you say Francy bought the bar..." She shook her head. "No, I must be misunderstanding you."

Fabrizio's face stilled. "Oh my God."

"How can this be?"

"I forgot. I wasn't even supposed to know, of course Francy wouldn't want you knowing. Please, I'd appreciate you not telling him I slipped up."

In a cold voice, Chiara said, "I see. So I'm the only one not allowed to know to whom, exactly, I'm so indebted?"

"It's not a big deal, really, Chiara."

She snorted. "Your son, my nephew's once-in-awhile boyfriend, saved me from ruin. Nobody thought to share this information with me. And that's not a big deal?"

"Our shared accountant mentioned it in passing, I didn't know either."

"It wasn't your life on the line."

"Can't you see this as a magnanimous gesture and move on? He probably did it to impress Edo. He's been smitten with him from day one."

Chiara, remembering their shared dinner, when she first met Francy, mumbled, "Not exactly from day one."

Elisa jumped when Ava stepped into the room. Ava smiled. "You excited to see Fatima?"

Dragging her fingers through the back of her hair, Elisa said, "It's been months."

"How long is she here?"

"Just until tomorrow. Then her parents have to head back to Milan."

At the sound of the knock, Elisa flew up, throwing open the door. "Fatima!" She cried, falling into her friend's arms.

Fatima wrapped her arms around Elisa. "It's good to see you."

As the girls broke apart, Ava said, "Fatima. We've missed you."

Fatima kissed Ava's cheeks politely before stepping back a bit awkwardly.

Ava guessed, "Strange to be back?"

Fatima nodded. "It's quiet. And everyone is so friendly. People I didn't even think knew me want to stop and talk. I'd forgotten . . ."

Ava laughed, "You have to budget extra time to walk across town, that's for sure. And that's just for us normal villagers. I bet everyone who sees you asks when they'll see you in magazines."

Fatima laughed, the sound ringing hollow within the stone walls of the *castello.*

Seeing Elisa's glare on her, Ava said, *"Allora,* I'll let you girls have your reunion. I left money in case you go to the *rosticceria."*

Ava noticed Fatima shifting her weight. Was she not allowed to eat pizza? Or maybe the talk of money made her uncomfortable. Maybe Fatima now made more money than anyone in Santa Lucia now. Or maybe not. Ava didn't know how long it took for a modeling gig to turn a profit.

They watched the door close behind Ava, then Fatima turned to Elisa. "Let's walk in the groves. Like old times. In Milan, there's concrete and cars everywhere. I miss trees. And birds that aren't pigeons." She took a breath, "Unless it's too cold for you?"

"No. You know I have the *sangue bollente.* Ava's always griping about my hot blood when she's trying to wrap another scarf around my neck."

Fatima nodded. "Ready, then?"

Elisa shrugged on her coat. "Sure." As they stepped out of the door, Elisa asked shyly, "Do you want to see my studio?" She held back a proud grin at the word.

"Studio?"

"I told you. The room Ale set up for me to make and sell art."

"Right. Sure. I'll see your room." Fatima's gaze lingered on the waving olive trees.

Elisa paused. "Or we can see it later..."

Fatima exhaled in relief. "That's probably better. Let's use the daylight while we have it. I told Sonia I'd drop by."

"Oh. Okay."

"She's just in town for a few hours. So..."

"I got it."

They set off for the groves, Fatima weaving her hands through the wild herbs lining the path. She sighed. "I missed this."

Elisa, pushing a branch out of her way, didn't respond.

Fatima said, "I want to see the vineyard! How's Ale's wine coming along?"

Elisa frowned. "I told you. It failed."

"Right, right, I knew that." Fatima paused. "I meant, I remember you and Ale and Ava are going to work on it. Redouble your effort. How's that going?"

"Redouble our effort?"

"That's something Valentina tells us. Or me anyway."

Elisa narrowed her eyes at the bitter edge to Fatima's words.

Fatima rushed on, "I bet working on the vineyard is fun. Fresh air, and all that."

Elisa bit her lip. "Modeling . . . is it as glamorous as you hoped?"

Attempting to laugh off the abrupt change in topic, Fatima said, "Did I hope it would be glamorous?"

"Yes."

Fatima shrugged. "I mean, it's fine. The clothes are cool. I don't hang out with the other models that much since I live at home, but they seem nice."

"And Valentina? How is it working with her?"

"At least she doesn't smell like cigarette smoke and tell me . . . " The rest of her words ran into a mumbling undertone.

Elisa stopped walking. "What?"

Fatima shook her head. "There's a learning curve, Valentina says. She said a couple more good shots and I'll get a contract in Dubai or Singapore."

Elisa sucked in her breath. "So soon?"

Fatima shrugged. "Maybe."

"And your parents . . . "

"Valentina was right about that. The more I respectfully follow their rules, the more they see me as competent and responsible. Which is funny if you think about it. Anyway, I'm not getting a ton of work yet, but the income has helped so much, that softens the blow."

Elisa shook her head.

Fatima considered Elisa for a moment. Her friend stood on the tender path into the groves, the arms of the olive trees arching above her, framing the azure blue of the sky. The color of the Madonna's niche. For a moment, the sun seemed to throb, magnified by the silvery branches. Fatima blinked, pressing her hands against her eyes. When she could see again, she noticed Elisa turning away.

Fatima watched her for a moment and then ran to catch up. "How's Margherita?"

Elisa turned and walked backward. As awkward and bumbling as she could be in a classroom, her feet never wavered on the path, finding purchase and surety without hesitation. "She's great. I see her and Jacopo every day. And sometimes Isotta leaves them both with me so she can run an errand or something."

"Two babies? Sounds like a lot of work."

"Less work than being kidnapped together."

"Oh, Elisa. I'm sorry. I didn't mean to bring it up . . ."

Elisa shook her head and gestured to the vineyard. "Here's the vineyard."

Fatima's eyes stayed trained on Elisa. "After the fire, I thought about it . . . the fire . . . all the time. Do you do the same?"

"Every day." Elisa looked away and gestured to the vines. "Ava is planting roses at the end of each row. Ale says people do that because problems in the soil show up in the roses before the grapes. And since our soil is so good, we don't need to do that, but Ava thinks it'll be pretty, and it's good to look like other vineyards."

"Elisa."

Elisa kept her eyes on the vines. "There are old artichoke plants there now. I don't know why."

"It's me."

Elisa ran her bottom lip back and forth between her teeth and turned to Fatima. "Is it though?"

Fatima said nothing, just kept regarding Elisa steadily.

Elisa shook her head. "Nothing's the same."

"I know. And I'm sorry I've been so absent. It's...harder than I expected. At the end of each day, I want to sleep. But I miss you."

Elisa cast her eyes down. "I miss you, too."

"And I'm here for you."

Elisa stepped toward the rock wall surrounding the vineyard. She ran her chilled hands along the rough stones.

Fatima said softly, "Elisa. When Massimo took you all...for us it was terrible. For you, it had to have been worlds worse."

Elisa squinted up at the wavering sun. "Every morning, when I woke up, I didn't know where I was. I had no idea how any day would be. Or even...what Massimo would be."

Fatima stilled, her body taut as if afraid to break the spell. The wind bent the olive trees in the distance. They dipped and waved their silver arms.

Elisa went on, trance-like. "Some days he was nice. He'd buy Margherita whatever candy she wanted. He'd worry if we didn't finish our lunch. But other days, he woke up in a panic, and left us for hours on a floor somewhere. Or worse."

Fatima reached for her friend's hand, but then let it drop.

Elisa shook her head. "He didn't hurt us. Not the way everyone thinks. But he could be...rough. Especially with the little ones when they wouldn't stop crying. I did my crying in the bathroom, so he was easier on me. Not loving or anything. Just not...awful, you know?"

"Elisa. That sounds..." Fatima couldn't finish the sentence.

"I'm making too much of it. He didn't hit us or anything."

"You are not making too much of it."

"The police had all these questions. About how he...touched us. So I know. It could have been worse."

"Anything could be worse. It doesn't mean it wasn't traumatic."

Elisa shook her head at the clinical sounding word. She took a deep breath and looked directly into Fatima's eyes. "I don't want to talk about bad things anymore."

Fatima nodded. "Promise me you'll tell me the minute you find out what happened to him. I can't stand that I'll be a million miles away and he'll turn up or something."

Elisa scratched her elbow. "Okay. I promise."

Fatima took her hand again and squeezed. "Show me the vineyard."

Leo walked into Bar Birbo to find the bar filled with villagers. He paused at the entrance and then approached the counter. Edo smiled hesitatingly when he saw him. "Leo. What can I get you?"

"*Cappuccino, per favore.*"

Edo nodded and turned to grind the beans.

At the other end of the bar, Arturo, Dante, and Paola waved their hands emphatically as they shouted and pointed.

As Leo accepted his *cappuccino*, he asked, "What's getting them so mad?"

Edo watched the villagers for a moment. "They're not mad. Rosetta wants the steps to the middle school fixed and Dante is telling her he'll get the stonemason on it and Arturo is remembering how the middle school and the primary school used to be in the same building. And he's sure none of them remember the quality of the original stone."

Leo chuckled. "I'd forgotten."

Edo shrugged easily and stepped to the register to collect coins from the villagers before they cajoled each other into the street.

Leo stirred sugar into his coffee. "It's strange. Being on this side of the bar."

Edo nodded. "I was thinking the same thing."

Leo took an appreciative sip of his coffee. Finally, he said, "I want to apologize. I should never have tried anything with you. It's kind of a dick move, right? Trying to pick up somebody who already has a boyfriend."

Edo shrugged. "That's not all on you."

Leo harrumphed.

Edo went on, "No, really. I gave off signals I probably shouldn't have."

Leo raised his cup and nodded. "Things seem good now. With you and Francy."

Edo beamed. "They are."

"I really am glad."

Nodding, Edo said, "And things with you? Your girlfriend seems nice."

Leo grinned. "Yes, she is."

"So . . . you're straight now?"

"Oh, Edo. We've been down this road before. I don't feel the need to define it. I like who I like. Gender doesn't matter to me."

"So you've said." Edo shook his head as he rinsed the dishes, stacking them in the dishwasher. "Don't take this the wrong way. But I miss your energy around here."

Chuckling, Leo said, "I promise I won't let it go to my head." He narrowed his eyes. "Chiara?"

Edo's eyes flicked to the window and the empty street beyond. He lowered his voice anyway, "She's . . . snappy. Tense. And I can't get it out of my mind . . ."

"What?"

Edo shook his head. "It's probably nothing. I can be too sensitive."

Leo leaned forward and studied Edo's face. "No such thing. What happened?"

With another look out the window, Edo said, "It's when I was telling her about Francy's friends who are using a surrogate to have a baby. Or actually, I was telling her about Dante's reaction—"

"Poor, I'm guessing."

"How did you know?"

Leo shrugged. "That guy is old school. You can tell." He lifted his chin. "Go on."

"That's it, I guess. I had to stop telling her about the conversation because she got . . . tense. She's been that way since."

Rotating his cup, Leo said, "Maybe she thinks you and Francy will get some ideas and have a baby of your own?"

"I guess that's possible. But why would *that* make her so weird?"

"You don't think that would be . . . rushing things?"

"I don't mean *now*. But someday maybe. You never know." Edo blushed. "She's always said she has no problem with my being gay. "

Sighing, Leo said. "You have to know this by now. Nobody likes to think of themselves as homophobic."

Edo paled at the word. He whispered, "You think she is?"

Leo chuckled, pointing at Edo with his spoon. "Oh, Edo. You are so transparent. *You* think she is."

"That . . . that's not . . . " He stopped, unsure of how to finish the sentence when he realized that Leo had articulated with alarming exactness the diffuse anxiety he'd felt. "But she'll get over it, right? People do. She just needs time . . . "

Leo lifted his hands. "*Boh.*" He stood and dipped his hand into his pocket.

"On the house," Edo said. With a smile, he added, "L'Ora Dorata's soft launch . . . it was really special. Consider the coffee an inadequate thank you for including us after everything."

Leo looked surprised. "Of course. I'm glad we can stay friends."

"Me too."

Leo hesitated and then asked casually. "By the way, have you seen my dad around these last few days?"

WINTER

*C*hiara and Edo watched as Livia rushed down Via Romana, her vision fixed on the horizon. Edo glanced at Chiara, "Pietro hasn't come home?"

Chiara shook her head. "I don't think so. When did Leo tell you he was missing?"

Edo closed his eyes to remember. "Wednesday. And he'd been missing for a few days. Leo's been managing the restaurant alone."

"Sonia came back to help."

"I hadn't heard that."

Chiara nodded. "Patrizia told me this morning on our walk."

Edo walked to the window and watched as Livia scurried through the *piazza*. She disappeared around the corner. The dappled afternoon light drifted through the streets, quiet now save for Carosello stopping to scratch his ear. His voice lost in thought, Edo said, "Pietro doesn't seem the type. To disappear."

Plucking the broom from the corner of the bar, Chiara began sweeping. "He doesn't. But I remember when the kids went missing, Livia mentioned something about how Pietro disappeared once."

"Right." Edo turned from the window. "It's not the first time."

"No. In fact, she mentioned it so casually, I wondered if perhaps there were more."

"If he makes a habit of it," Edo wondered aloud, "why worry now? And why avoid coming in here?"

Chiara shook her head. "Maybe she doesn't know if he's okay . . ."

Edo nodded, gazing out the window again. "Is that Fabio?"

"Where?"

"Smoking his ridiculous MS cigarettes." Edo gestured with his chin. "The guy gives me the creeps. He won't come in anymore. But this is the second time I've caught him staring, as if we're a movie he hates but can't not watch."

"Ignore him. He's looking for a reaction." Chiara swept the sugar packets and other debris into the dustpan. "Anyway, about Livia. She always wants to present *la bella figura*. It must be awful for her to be the subject of gossip." Chiara replaced the broom and washed her hands. "I get that."

Hesitating for a moment, Edo said, "Chiara, is everything okay?"

She didn't answer until she had dried her hands. "Why wouldn't everything be okay?"

Edo rolled his eyes. "I don't know where I get these notions."

"There's just a lot on my mind." Chiara shrugged. "Nothing important."

Edo finished straightening the sugar and regarded his aunt levelly. "If you say so."

She lifted her chin. "Edo."

He sighed. "It's not my place to presume. *You* know what's going on with you, right?"

Chiara said, "Yes." But she didn't sound so sure.

Marcello knew he should return to the station. His beat ended already. But Antonella would pull into the parking lot at any moment. And as much as he wanted to seem nonchalant about how he felt about her, he had to admit that he looked forward to those moments when he walked her home from the parking lot. He liked watching her eyebrows crease and wave, like butterflies across her forehead. He liked watching her dig into her purse for a piece of *panino* she'd saved from her lunch for Carosello. Most of all, he liked hearing her voice. The cadence, the pauses. Maybe it was growing up with Bea for a grandmother, but Antonella knew how to listen, to have that listening be full of meaning. And when she spoke, she was clear, articulate, as if she'd been mulling her words for days.

Plus, Marcello acknowledged to himself and nobody else except sometimes Edo, Antonella was gorgeous. Her smile made his heart sing, and he could drown in her eyes.

Madonna mia.

What had he come to? "Drown in her eyes" indeed.

He shook his head.

He knew he thought about Antonella too much, maybe because he never got to spend enough time with her. He wanted Antonella to agree to another dinner, but so far she'd sidestepped his flirtatious hints. Well, the time for flirtatious hints had passed. He would tell her he loved the moments they spent together and he wanted more of them. He wanted to take her to dinner—here or Girona or on the moon. It hardly mattered.

In the back of his mind, he could hear his mother cheering for joy. After years of begging her son to get a steady girlfriend, to get married, and finally give her grandchildren, she practically crowed in delight whenever he mentioned Antonella. He thought he'd been discreet about his feelings, but apparently not. He was fairly certain he'd started blushing whenever Antonella even came up in casual conversation. To his mother's satisfaction and endless amusement.

A pair of headlights crawled up the hill, along with the telltale whine of Antonella's ancient Fiat Punto. Marcello started walking back up the street so he didn't appear to be loitering, waiting for her. Then he remembered, he wanted to move from silly flirtatious games to something more.

He needed to quell the tickle in his heart when he thought of her. He spun back and waited.

The car swung around to park in her customary spot. Marcello waited for Antonella to climb out of the car. It seemed to take an awfully long time. Or maybe it just seemed so because of his impatience? He started walking to the car but didn't want to scare her, approaching out of the darkness like that. Instead, he paced under the streetlight. So he wouldn't take her unawares.

Finally, the car door creaked open and Antonella swung her legs out. Her shapely legs appeared pearly in the early moonlight, but Marcello thought that must be an illusion. Didn't she wear stockings to work? Marcello couldn't figure out why women shoved themselves into stockings. But he hadn't mentioned it, reasoning that raising a woman's stockings as a topic of conversation was not nearly as suave as he liked to imagine himself.

Instead of climbing out of the car, Antonella dropped her head into her hands. Her shoulders shook. Marcello lunged forward, then stopped. His jaw worked as he wondered what to do.

Antonella slammed the car door. The force spun her around and she almost lost her footing, grabbing wildly to the car. Her ankle gave out, and she sagged before standing again, tucking her hair behind her ear helplessly.

Marcello couldn't stand it anymore. He left the safety of the circle of lamplight, hailing her heartily to advertise his presence. "*Ciao*, Antonella! Welcome home!"

She winced, pressing her hip against the car. "Marcé?"

He tried to guffaw. But not being practiced in guffawing, he landed well south of mirth. "Who else?"

She looked down at her foot. "I . . . I think I twisted my foot . . . the heel of my shoe . . . "

"Let me take a look at it." Marcello squatted down to study the shoe.

He tried not to notice the shape of her legs, the way they disappeared suggestively into the mysterious darkness of her skirt. He asked, pointing at the offending shoe, "May I?"

She bit her lip, nodding.

He picked up her foot, encased in the sensible pump. Keeping his mind on the task to quiet the trembling of his heart, he squeezed and turned the heel of her shoe. It gave, wiggling in a way a heel shouldn't wiggle. Darting another gaze up to Antonella who watched him seriously, her eyes overlarge, he put his hand lightly on her ankle.

She grimaced.

He stood. "You'll need to get the shoes to Luigi."

She shook her head. "I have another pair."

"In the meantime, you shouldn't walk on the ankle. I think you twisted it."

"You're a doctor now?" she snapped.

Marcello reminded himself that her ankle likely caused terrible pain.

He said, "Let me carry your bag. Lean on me and we'll get you home."

She looked as if she wanted to refuse, but when she put any weight on her foot, she gasped. She handed him her bag, grumbling, "Just my luck. If I'm not well by Monday..."

Marcello didn't know marketing required two good ankles, but he decided it would be best not to annoy her by asking. Instead, he lodged her bag on his shoulder and held out his elbow. Usually, she slid her hand through with a smile, winking about how Santa Lucia's police officers offered the most personal service. Or some funny remark like that. This time, she hesitated before putting her arm through his. Was it his imagination, or was her touch fainter?

She leaned on him enough to keep from hobbling, and they made their way up the street, her watching her step as he screwed up his courage.

"So, Antonella."

She didn't answer.

"You know what I was thinking about today?"

She shook her head.

"I was thinking about how people used to think we were going out. Remember? When I was dating a different Antonella?"

He sneaked a glance at Antonella, and her face seemed to close. He shook his head, aware of the terrible error he'd made. What girl wants to be reminded of another girl you've dated? He had to get out of this one. "That seems like so long ago! I hardly knew you then!" He softened his voice, "I feel as if I know you now. I want you to know how much—"

"Don't."

Marcello stopped walking. "Don't?"

In the feeble moonlight, her eyes shone. "Please, Marcello. Just . . . just don't. I want to go home."

He nodded, pretending to understand.

At the sound of the key in the lock, Livia threw open the door. Her face pale and her normally polished hair now standing on end, she had never looked less like herself. "Hello, Pietro. How nice of you to stop in." She gestured that he should enter. "Will you be staying long?"

"Livia . . ."

Livia waited. "Was there more? Or are you waiting for praise that you remembered my name?"

He wrung his hands together. "So much anger."

Laughing mirthlessly, Livia said, "Are you coming in, or did you want to further entertain our neighbors?"

His fingers waved against each other momentarily before he reached for his suitcase and stepped into the house. "Leonardo?"

"At the restaurant. Where else could he be, when you left without so much as a by-your-leave?"

He nodded and began walking down the hall. He stopped as Livia's voice ricocheted against the walls. "No explanation, Pietro?" The fierce tilt of her chin belied the suffering in her voice. "You think you can disappear for two weeks and then stroll back in here as if nothing is wrong. Particularly after what happened to those children..."

Pietro put a hand to his forehead before turning around. "You knew I wasn't kidnapped. Don't pull that."

"I want to know where you've been for two *weeks*!"

His voice quiet, Pietro said, "Two weeks? It was ten days."

Livia grumbled.

"Besides, I told you I was going. I'm sorry the job took more time than expected, but—"

Livia's voice iced over. "What in the world are you talking about?"

"The consultation. I told you it would be a week. It took longer. I should have told you, but you were so cross with me for leaving in the first place, I didn't think you'd want to hear from me."

"That's not why I was upset! And you know it!"

Pietro crossed his arms over his chest. "What was it then?"

"That was weeks ago! I can't remember!"

Pietro grumbled, "Perhaps the problem is you're upset with me so often you can't tell one time from another."

"Maybe if you spoke to me, if you listened to me, I wouldn't be nagging at you!"

Pietro looked away and said nothing.

Livia struggled to control her shaking voice. "Admit it. You're inventing this 'consultation'. Like you've invented excuses every time you've disappeared, whether or not you've told me in advance or just slipped away into the night, like this time. I'm tired of it, Pietro."

He shrugged.

She went on. "You make me feel like a crazy person. But I *know* you didn't say you were leaving because Leo and Sonia didn't know either."

"You didn't tell them?"

Livia raised her hands to her temples as her mouth dropped open. "Are you mad?"

He looked away.

She yelled, "You didn't answer any of our calls or texts! You could have at least picked up the phone!"

"You made it clear my conversation wasn't welcome."

"You could at least return your son's calls!"

"I lost my charger."

"Oh, yes, because the place you went has no chargers. Where is this alleged job anyway? You're not thinking of buying another restaurant, are you?"

"No." He said, sounding exhausted. "L'Ora Dorata is my last."

"Then *where were you?*"

"For the final time. I was consulting about a restaurant purchase. In Ravenna."

Livia thought. "You never said anything about Ravenna."

"You didn't ask."

Shouting now, Livia's face turned red, "I won't take this anymore!"

"Then leave me." At the floundering expression on her face, Pietro added softly, "It's not so easy, is it?"

Dante brought the evening air with him into Bar Birbo. "It feels like snow," he said as he took off his hat and hung it on the wooden rack.

Edo glanced up from emptying the dishwasher. "I heard rain."

"The air has that bite." Dante shrugged off his jacket and settled on a stool. "Better make it red tonight, Edo."

Edo reached for a wine goblet.

Dante hummed tunelessly. "I wonder if anybody will be out tonight."

Edo's eyebrows went up. "Are you expecting anyone?"

"No...no. Is Chiara here?"

Pouring the wine into the glass, Edo said, "It's been so quiet, she and Fabrizio went for pizza in Girona."

"How nice."

Dante turned at the sight of a shadow passing the doorway, the greeting on his open lips. He closed his mouth, as Carosello continued jogging down the street. "His hair is growing back."

Edo nodded. "Peanuts?"

"Do you have those fennel crackers?"

"I thought you didn't like them."

"I like them. With red wine. Sometimes."

Edo nodded.

The bell over the door chimed and Dante stood at Magda's entrance. "Magda! *Buona sera!*"

Magda beamed at him before catching sight of Edo's smug expression. Scowling, Magda struggled to remove her coat, her back turned to the counter.

"Here let me help you with that." Dante let his hands rest on Magda's shoulders and then pulled off her coat, hanging it on the rack beside his hat.

Edo straightened his face. "What can I get you, Magda?"

Her eyes glanced at Dante's place. "I'll have red wine, too." Taking a seat, she added, "Oh! My favorite fennel crackers! Peanuts, too, please Edo."

Edo stifled his grin.

Dante turned to Magda. "Is it raining yet?"

"Rain? It's not going to rain tonight." Her eyes danced in anticipation.

"Sure it is. I heard it on the news! Edo and I were just talking about it. Right, Edo?"

Edo finished pouring the wine and then raised his hands, "I'm not getting involved."

Magda glowered. "Involved? It's weather, not a Mafia operation. Watch out, Edo, or you'll turn into a closed book, like Chiara."

Dante chuckled and placed his hand beside Magda's on the counter. Edo caught himself staring and busied himself with corking the wine. He straightened as the bell over the door tinkled again. "Marcé! *Tutto a posto*?" Relief warmed his words.

"It's *cold*!" Marcello shook his head.

As Edo started a *caffè* for Marcello, Magda and Dante settled into their familiar pattern of by turns nattering with each other and empathizing with each other about everyone else's stupidity.

Setting the *espresso* in front of Marcello, Edo said, "Your mom came in earlier today. She's looking well."

Marcello nodded. "Thank the Madonna, no trouble this past year. She's in fighting form." He added the last with a shade of bitterness.

Carefully, Edo asked, "Does she have something to fight about?"

"The usual. Why I'm depriving her of grandchildren. You know." His cheeks pinked. "Or maybe you don't get that pressure from your parents."

"I get a different kind," Edo said lightly. "I thought your mother had lightened up."

"She did. When she thought I was dating Antonella."

Edo frowned. "Aren't you? Dating her?"

"I'm not sure if we were, but we're not now," Marcello said. "She won't even look at me."

"Did something happen?"

Marcello shrugged. "Beats me. Maybe I was too pushy. Are these things genetic?" He smiled wanly.

"Pushy is hardly how I'd describe you."

Edo wiped down the counter, taking note of Magda and Dante, their heads close together in whispered conference for a moment before Magda announced. "You can't tell me you believe that!"

Edo turned back to Marcello. "Maybe you should talk to Antonella? See how she feels."

Marcello sighed. "I fear the way to be less pushy is probably not to push for a conversation about our 'relationship'."

"Maybe." Edo ran the cloth through the running water. "But is the alternative giving up?"

"She's not interested. My hands are tied."

Wringing the water from the towel, Edo shook his head. "I've seen you walking her home from the parking lot . . . talking. She likes you." He shot his gaze at Magda and Dante laughing, their heads thrown back.

"She's easy to talk to. Sweet. Funny." Marcello sighed. "I liked her. I thought . . . well. Never mind. It does no good to dwell."

The bell over the door rang as Chiara and Fabrizio stepped into the bar, stamping their feet. Chiara smiled broadly, "It's snowing!"

Edo looked into the darkness beyond the window and spied great white flakes drifting through the street.

Dante laughed, "I told you, Magda!"

And Magda retorted, "You said rain, not snow!"

And Marcello breathed, "It's so pretty."

And Edo murmured, "Will you look at that?"

The morning sun trickled down the cobblestone streets of Santa Lucia. Bea's rooster, for the first time in weeks, crowed as if to announce a moment of great significance. Patrizia chuckled to herself as she pushed open the door of Bar Birbo.

Chiara turned with a tired grin, brushing the bangs off her forehead. "*Buongiorno*, Patrizia. Something funny?"

Patrizia unbuttoned her wool coat but kept her scarf tied around her neck. "Bea's rooster sounds sure of himself this morning."

Chiara chuckled. "Good for him." She started grinding the beans for Patrizia's *cappuccino*. "How is Filamena?"

"Much better! The nausea stopped in her second trimester."

Chiara noticed Patrizia's satisfied smile. "What aren't you telling me?"

"Oh, Chiara," Patrizia laughed. "It's . . . nothing."

"Why does your nothing sound like something?"

Shaking her sugar packet, Patrizia chuckled.

Chiara waited. She took a sip of her *espresso*.

"*Allora*, I'll tell you but *promise* not to tell anybody. It might not happen, and I don't want a million questions or people assuming there's a problem if plans change."

"In Santa Lucia? I don't know what you could mean," Chiara smiled.

Patrizia laughed. "They might move back. To Santa Lucia."

"What!"

"I know! Can you imagine, having her here, getting to help with the grandchildren every day . . . "

Chiara turned to wipe the coffee grounds on the back counter into the sink. "I thought they had to stay closer to Rome. For Paolo's work?"

Patrizia laughed. "It's so funny. It was the day after you and I talked about how people are always on their phones and we complained about technology changing our lives . . . well! The very next day, Filamena told me that Paolo's company is thinking of allowing the employees to work from anywhere. Computer commuting? Something like that." Patrizia sipped her *cappuccino*. "They don't have the details yet. But oh! Wouldn't it be wonderful?"

"It would." Chiara considered for a moment. "I bet she and Isotta would get along well."

"I thought the same thing!"

At a sound from the street, Patrizia turned. She laughed at a tabby cat, attempting to knock the lid off a trash bin. Turning back she said, "That reminds me, I saw Livia in the *piazza* yesterday. So early, it was still dark."

"What were you doing up?" Chiara frowned.

"I couldn't sleep so went to the *forno* right when Sauro opened."

Chiara nodded.

"So Livia was in the *piazza*, not just feeding the cats, but chatting with them. Petting them, scratching their heads. Like she was a pied piper of cats instead of rats."

Chiara scratched her cheek. "I never pegged Livia as an animal lover. They don't have any, do they?"

"Me either. She's so . . . you know."

"I know. She wants to be important, the person with her hands on all the *scopa* cards," Chiara mused.

Patrizia shook her head, chuckling. "Remember her cake?"

"Do I? It took days to get the metal taste out of my mouth."

Patrizia giggled. "She needs to leave the cooking to Pietro . . . who is back! Did you know?"

"I heard." Chiara watched the tabby cat perch on the edge of the trash bin, using its paw to fish in the contents.

Patrizia thought for a moment. "But cats . . . why spend time with cats? They don't make anyone feel important, as you say."

Chiara guffawed. "I had one growing up that did."

"But not *town* cats. They're half-wild."

"Yes, that is odd." Chiara put down her towel to gaze out the window.

Patrizia nodded. "Very odd. That woman is a puzzle."

"Carla. How nice to see you again," Isotta lied. She clamped Margherita between her knees to finish braiding her hair, but the child dashed away with one braid undone.

Isotta wished she resembled less of a wild woman with a wild child. She had set her alarm to get up before the children, to allow time to apply make-up and iron her skirt. Insisting all the while that she wanted to look nice for Luciano's Christmas gathering.

But alarm clocks had nothing on Jacopo, who woke up screaming at the injustice of cutting his first tooth. She had offered him a cold washcloth to suck, praying it would soothe him back to sleep for a few hours. But then Margherita sprang out of bed, babbling about the party. She turned up her nose at the promise of sweets if she woke up with the sun, stubbornly refusing to climb back into bed.

Exhausted and out of tricks, she'd jostled Jacopo in her arms while begging Margherita to at least lie down. But Margherita simply sang more and more loudly, drowning out Isotta's pleading. Isotta couldn't take it. She couldn't take it anymore. She turned away, choking on angry words rising like bile in her throat.

Feeling guilty for her imagined outburst, Isotta let Margherita eat anything she wanted out of the fridge while allowing Jacopo to nurse until she felt raw.

Now she sat smiling with pretended delight in wrinkled clothes and frizzy hair, as Jacopo drooled all over her chest.

Charming.

Just charming.

She started to rise to greet the incoming guests at Luciano's door, but Carla held out her hand. "No, please. I insist. Don't trouble yourself. You seem to always be covered with children, don't you?" She laughed merrily before calling to Enrico, stalled at the door as Ale, Ava, and Elisa had entered the house. "Enrico! You rude fellow! You're neglecting your duty by not greeting poor Isotta!"

She turned to Isotta and simpered, "Enrico is always so kind to others. I can't imagine why he's ignoring you."

Isotta stammered, "Well, he's saying hello to Ava and Ale, so—"

"What fashionable people! They're the ones that own the *castello*?"

Isotta appraised her friends. Fashionable? She supposed so. Ale had dressed in one of his super-tailored, American outfits. Not a suit, but the jeans and light-blue micro-chevron patterned shirt elegantly defined his figure. He'd packed his stylish clothes away long ago, claiming that Armani didn't coordinate well with dirt stains, so he must have rummaged for this one. He did look fashionable. So much so it lent an air of elegance to Ava's customary jeans and a somewhat nicer-than-everyday sweater, her hair falling loose around her heart-shaped face. Isotta knew it was only a matter of time until Ava twisted her hair into a knot.

Carla smiled at Isotta's silence.

Isotta realized she hadn't responded. "Oh! Yes. I mean, Ale owns it."

Carla patted Isotta's arm with a simpering smile. And then wiped her hand on the couch before walking toward the gathering. Isotta busied herself making sure the snaps of Jacopo's pants didn't twist into his chunky little legs. She didn't need one more reason for him to fly off the handle.

She looked up at a hand on hers. "Hey," breathed Ava. Isotta smiled to see Ava's hair already swept back in its loose bun. That was fast. "I met . . . *Carla.*" She said with significance.

"Oh? Yes, she's lovely, isn't she?" Isotta said in a strained voice.

Ava arched her eyebrows. "Not the word I'd choose. She's a cold fish, that one."

Isotta watched Carla wind her arm around Enrico's waist as she leaned her head on his shoulder, listening raptly as Ale spoke. Usually, Ale's restrained gestures showed his American-ness, his arms locked to his sides at the elbow. But today, his hands bounced and waved.

Isotta said, "He looks excited about something."

"He and Bruno drew up plans for repopulating the vineyard. Bruno won't say for sure it'll work, but according to Ale, he nodded slightly, which is almost a guarantee." Though Ava's tone was sardonic, Isotta knew it was all for show. Ava loved Ale's newfound passion.

Though Isotta's heart twisted a bit seeing the three of them working in the vineyard, calling silly jokes over the vines, she was thrilled for Ava. "Where's Elisa?"

"She ran into the garden with Margherita as soon as we walked in."

"It's so cold!"

Ava shrugged. "You know those two. Now, how is our prince this morning?"

Jacopo scowled at being transferred to Ava's lap but settled in when he noticed the flash of her necklace.

"Watch out for that," Isotta sighed. "He's grabbing everything."

"Oh, it's his if he wants it." Ava laughed until she noticed Isotta's still face. "I'm joking, Isotta."

Isotta nodded, her lips pressed together. "What's wrong with me?"

"You've got a lot to manage." Ava snuggled Jacopo closer. "But at least . . . you're so lucky to have this dear boy."

"You want him?" Isotta ran a hand over her eyes. "You can keep him."

Ava's arm twitched around Jacopo. "You don't mean that."

"Of course not." Isotta smiled wanly. "I'm just tired."

Ava whispered, "You're so *lucky*." Catching Isotta's curious look, Ava offered a tremulous smile. "Let's go find the girls. Elisa is wearing the shirt with her design."

Isotta said in an undertone, "You feeling less worried, about Elisa's art?"

"No." Ava shrugged. "I might if she talked more. But she's a clam."

Isotta said, "She's a teenager. I wrote horribly morbid poetry when I was her age."

"You did?" Ava frowned. "Were you . . . unhappy?"

Isotta pressed her lips together.

"You were! This proves my point," she searched for Ale as if to tell him, but he and Enrico were deep in conversation. Probably about grapes. "Ale keeps insisting that the goriness in her art is a process, not a sign that she's cracked."

Shaking her head, Isotta said, "Funny to imagine Ale talking about 'process'."

Ava rolled her eyes. "I'm not even getting into his theories on art being her therapy and how Elisa is tapping into the darkness we all feel."

Isotta grew quiet.

Ava nuzzled Jacopo's cheek to his delighted cackling. Finally, she said, "Anyway, the image on the shirt is less troubling. Still powerful, but not so . . . chaotic."

Isotta grinned. "I'm glad you approve since I'm wearing mine. Not that you can tell since it's covered with the long-sleeve shirt. And all the drool."

Ava laughed. "Elisa will be pleased."

Isotta's next words died on her lips at the sight of Enrico approaching. His gaze met Isotta's and he held her eye contact, even as Carla wound herself around his arm. Enrico looked away, his jaw uncharacteristically set.

Isotta stood and kissed his cheeks. She blushed when she realized she'd lingered on his right side, distracted by the scent of his smooth cheek. She looked away, embarrassed. "Enrico. So good to see you."

"Isotta." He nodded. And then gestured to Margherita running through the hallway. "I hope it's okay, I brought Margherita a Tronky bar. I'm bribing her to nag you until you work on your story."

Isotta blinked back tears. "I have, actually. After we talked last time."

He nodded and in clipped tones said, "Good, that's good. I'm glad to hear it." Ava watched the interchange and grinned into Jacopo's hair.

Carla tittered into her hand. "That's Enrico for you. Charitable to a fault. Come now, Enrico," she pulled his hand. "I smell something wonderful in the kitchen and I promised your father I'd help. These two probably have all sorts of motherhood stories to share. Dirty diapers and whatnot."

Enrico pivoted to follow his girlfriend.

Edo caught sight of Fabio lurking on the edge of the parking lot, smoking those stinking cigarettes. He mumbled to Francy, "Don't look now. It's everyone's favorite Looney Tune."

Francy looked up from pulling his suitcase out of the trunk and followed Edo's gaze. He didn't smile. "Looney Tune?"

Edo shrugged. "I watch a lot of American TV. Plus, you know, I'm dating an international superstar, so I need to learn the lingo."

Smiling, Francy admonished, "One song. In Spain, not America."

"Read my lips. *International. Superstar.*"

Francy grinned. "I'll do something to those lips, you can count on that."

Edo placed his hand on Francy's chest. "I do declare!"

Francy paused in thought. "Scarlett O'Hara?"

Edo nodded, a grin twitching up the corners of his mouth.

Francy said, "How much American TV did you watch, exactly?"

"All of it." Edo thought. "Looking back on it, I think it was the one place I ever saw gay people."

"Not in cartoons or *Gone with the Wind*, surely."

Edo laughed, tiptoeing to land a kiss on Francy's mouth.

Francy stiffened.

"What's wrong?"

"That guy. Fabio. He's still watching."

"Who cares?"

"Edo."

"Okay, okay." Edo backed away from Francy. "I guess we have time. A whole week! It feels like a present."

Francy slammed the trunk of the car closed and darted his gaze to the edge of the parking lot. He couldn't see Fabio in the shadows, but he saw the lit end of the cigarette redden briefly. "Nice that shows don't book

Christmas week, right?"

Edo nodded happily, yanked Francy forward, out of the parking lot. Fabio watched them, letting loose a stream of muttering as they passed.

Edo squeezed Francy's hand. They said little as they dropped off Francy's suitcase at the house he and Fabrizio shared. Then continued up Via Romana to Bar Birbo.

Edo called, "Look who I found!" He beamed as a chorus of welcomes met them. Leaning his cheek against Francy's, he whispered, "That's better."

Francy smiled weakly. To Chiara, he said, "Are Ava and Ale stopping by today? Or will we not see them until tomorrow?"

She didn't seem to hear his question as she scrubbed the side of the sink, so Edo answered as he opened the drawer to pull out his white apron, tying it swiftly around his waist. "Tomorrow. They're coming for an *aperitivo* before Christmas Eve dinner."

Francy nodded. "That will be nice." To Patrizia and Giuseppe he asked, "The *macelleria* closed for the holiday?"

Giuseppe nodded. "Only just."

Everyone turned at the sound of the bell. Fabrizio took off his hat, setting his hair on end as he stamped his feet and looked around with a grin. "Francy! You made it!"

Francy kissed his father's cheeks with a tight grin.

Holding his son's face between his gloved hands, Fabrizio searched his eyes. "*Tutto a posto?*"

Francy shrugged and turned back to the bar, accepting the glass of red wine Edo poured him.

Corking the bottle, Edo said, "We ran into Fabio. Always unsettling."

Patrizia inhaled audibly. "Did he … do something?"

"No." Edo shook his head. "Didn't even make a real appearance. But still, the guy reeks of trouble."

Giuseppe scowled, "He holds onto trouble like Carosello with a bone."

Unwinding his scarf and hanging a bag of cookies from the *forno* on the hat rack, Fabrizio asked, "He's given up trying to publish a story about Francy, though, right?"

Edo nodded. "He's moved on." He paused. "To Dante."

Francy sputtered on his wine.

"*Dante*? The *mayor*? I thought Fabio harassed people he found weak or vulnerable in some way. Beneath him. Why Dante?"

Chiara and Patrizia exchanged glances before Chiara returned her attention to the sink. Patrizia watched her, curious, but Chiara didn't notice.

Edo said, "They won't talk about it, but we suspect Magda and Dante are seeing each other."

Francy sputtered again and pushed away his wineglass. "I'll save this for afterward." He looked up at Edo. "Is this true?"

More glances exchanged. Edo finally answered, "Neither of them has confirmed it."

Francy chuckled. "And everyone is too scared to ask?"

Giuseppe guffawed. "The boy has the measure of it!"

Edo went on. "Fabio is saying that someone should root out weak politicians."

"Weak? Is that how people see Dante?"

Edo said simply, "His wife cheated on him."

Francy nodded slowly. "I had forgotten that part of the story."

Edo said, "Basically, Fabio says that Dante is being led around by his pants."

Francy nodded. "Sounds as if *he* wants to run for mayor."

Patrizia said, "He's too young."

Chiara said, "And he'd never win."

Francy ran his fingers around the base of his wineglass. "I wonder though . . . he could do some damage, even without running. Couldn't he?"

After Magda pulled on her jacket, she ran to the bathroom to check her hair. She leaned toward the mirror—did she smear her mascara? Blushing, she chided herself. Mascara at her age!

The anger quieted the butterflies as she stepped out of the house with her overflowing tote bag, shoving the door to make sure she'd locked it securely.

Adjusting her scarf, she set off down the cobblestone street, checking her watch. She'd never been able to quell her German habit of arriving on time. In Santa Lucia, being ten minutes late was considered early. This time, she'd budgeted additional time, hoping for the distraction of a neighbor to chat with. But the streets lay empty. Not even Carosello. Not even a cat. Only the wind setting the potted *hosta* leaves nodding as Magda passed.

She slowed her steps. It wouldn't do to be early. She found herself loitering in the *piazza*, waiting for San Nicolas's bells to announce the hour.

She waited, the cold biting at her ankles. She peered down, did her pantyhose have a run?

No.

She stood back up. Jumping when the church bells clanged. She wondered ... should she wait longer? People always startled at her punctuality.

To hell with it. This was the time she was invited, this was the time she'd appear. Leaping up before she could talk herself out of it, Magda tried to focus on the alley's twists and turns that led to Dante's door.

She lifted her hand.

And knocked.

Almost before she'd finished knocking, the door was thrown open.

Dante.

Standing in a wooly sweater that brought out the green flecks in his eyes. He smiled, and the tension around Magda's heart eased. He murmured, "You're here."

She frowned. "You invited me."

Chuckling, he stood back to allow her to enter. "I'm glad."

She thrust the bag into his arms.

Surprised, he said, "What's this?"

"German pastries. Umbrian wine. I didn't know which direction to go."

He touched her hand. "This is perfect. Thank you."

She whispered, "They've arrived?"

He nodded. "Most of them. Lorenzo comes later, and the rest are away."

Not for the first time, Magda wondered at the audacity of bringing seven children into the world. "You warned them?"

"You mean, did I tell them I invited you for dessert? Yes."

"They... they were okay with that?"

"Maybe a little confused. But they didn't say anything. To me, anyway. Who knows what they were whispering when I left the room."

"Oh, no."

"I'm joking."

Magda wondered.

As Magda and Dante entered the living room, the conversation halted. He pushed Magda forward. "You all remember Magda?"

A young woman leaped up from her place on the ground beside the coffee table. She approached Magda and said, "Magda. You probably don't remember me. Luella."

Of course Magda didn't remember her. All children seemed much the same to Magda, and then they left Santa Lucia just as they became interesting humans. But Magda stretched her lips over her teeth. "Luella, how nice to see you again." She reached back to remember what Dante had told her about his youngest daughter. "How was your drive from Rome?"

Luella said, "I took the train. Cars in Rome..." she shivered with a grin.

Magda searched for something of Stella in her daughter, but Luella was a carbon copy of Dante. Down to the thick hair waving back from her forehead.

Dante took Magda's tote bag into what Magda assumed was the kitchen as Luella lead Magda toward her siblings. "Hey, *ragazzi*. Stop your gossiping. Say hello to Magda."

One by one Dante's children stood and shook her hand or leaned to kiss her cheek. This wasn't as bad as she feared. For an army of children, she'd girded herself as if for battle. But they were polite. If a bit distant, which was fine by her.

Perhaps they were as confused by her presence at their holiday table as she was. Did this mean she and Dante were "dating"? He'd crossed no physical line with her. Maybe he thought of her as his buddy. She had assumed his Christmas invitation indicated something . . . *more*. But as he puttered in the kitchen, she began to wonder.

And also wondered if she should have accepted. She so easily tired of being pleasant with strangers.

Talking to Mauro now, she asked about his older brother stationed overseas. Magda worked so hard to nod, she almost missed Mauro's question. "You don't have any family here?"

"No. I'm from Germany."

He smirked. "Obviously." At her frozen expression, he added. "Your accent. It's terrible." Mauro turned to his brother, stoking the fire. "Have you heard how she says her s's? Like from a war-time German textbook."

They laughed as Magda's face flushed. "Everyone understands me."

Mauro nodded, his face suffused with condescension. "I'm sure they do. Not pretending at all."

Luella said, "Mauro. Be nice. Babbo . . ."

He spat, "Haven't you heard what people are saying about Babbo because he's dating *her*?" He turned to Magda and glared. "But really, I'm sure you think you're worth all of that, right?"

Magda's cheeks flushed as she stammered, "Dating...who said..."

Mauro rolled his eyes. "You must think we're morons. We have friends in Santa Lucia. We know what's happening."

Dante walked in with a tray of desserts. "To the table, everyone! Wait until you see the German sweets Magda brought!"

With a gasp, Elisa stopped walking. She blinked, doubting her eyes. Running down the cold cobblestones, she called, "Fatima? Fatima!"

Fatima turned mid-laughter, her hair rippling in the slight breeze. When she saw Elisa, she faltered. "Elisa! I was going to come by later. To surprise you." Beside Fatima, Sonia snorted, and Fatima knocked her with her elbow.

Elisa worried her lip between her teeth. "What are you doing here?"

Fatima shrugged. "Everything in Milan shuts down around Christmas, and since we don't celebrate...Sonia picked me up at the train station."

Elisa narrowed her eyes. "Where are you staying?"

Shaking her head, Fatima said, "I'm not. I'm getting a late train back."

Sonia watched the conversation with some amusement. "Why don't you play with your little friend for a bit. Then we can get ready to go out. Did you bring the clothes?"

Fatima pointed to her suitcase, far too full for a day trip. Sonia shook her head. "I can't believe they let you keep them."

"Not the shirt you wanted, don't get too excited."

"The red flowy one you wore for that Instagram post?"

Fatima shook her head as Elisa shifted her weight, crossing her arms over her chest before letting them fall awkwardly to her side again.

Sonia frowned. "Damn. I would have rocked that shirt."

"No doubt," Fatima grinned. "But you'll like the samples I brought." She glanced at Elisa, staring at the ground, before saying to Sonia, "So we'll meet at your house?"

Sonia took out her phone. "In an hour?"

Fatima nodded. "Sounds good."

Sonia smiled indulgently at Elisa, "Have fun, you two!" Elisa had no idea why Sonia laughed as she waltzed into L'Ora Dorata.

Elisa scowled. "I didn't know you had Instagram."

Fatima shrugged. "We have to, all us models. To build our brand, as Valentina says. You can follow me."

Elisa gazed up the street where Carosello jogged past two cats curling against each other on a bench. "I don't have a phone."

Fatima laughed.

Elisa glanced at her. "Why is that funny?"

"It's not, I guess."

Elisa muttered, "I can get a phone. Ava told me."

Fatima threaded her arm through Elisa's and started walking up the street. "Where do you want to go?"

"We could go to the groves." Elisa chanced a glance at Fatima, striding beside her. "I don't suppose you actually want to play."

Fatima's laugh scraped against the stone walls of Via Romana. "Do you?"

"No."

Gesturing into Bar Birbo, Fatima said, "Should we get coffee to warm up?"

Elisa hesitated. "Or . . . we could go to my studio. Ale put a space heater in there. It's warm."

"Perfect!" Fatima snapped her fingers. "Let's do that. It shouldn't take long, right?"

Elisa's step faltered. Still, she led Fatima up the castle stairs and through the courtyard to the room that looked out to the kitchen garden. No flowers bloomed, but Ava kept the dried stalks and the poky tops of the flowers, claiming they added 'winter interest'. Elisa had laughed, thinking Ava had been joking, but she'd found the desolate garden a wonderful place to sketch. All her garden drawings looked like negatives, with the images of the plants and flowers in black with the most vivid blue backgrounds Elisa could manage.

Pausing, Elisa considered telling Fatima about it, but it seemed like too much to explain.

As Elisa stepped through the door into her studio, she relaxed into the scent of the ancient stone floors, the tang of paint thinner, and the curls of pastel crayons. Switching on the portable floodlight, she said, "It's not ready or anything."

Fatima blinked at the sudden light. Her eyes grazed the heavy table splattered with paint and covered with heavy sheets of paper, the boxes stacked in the corner, and the easel propped in the corner by the window. She moved toward it, hesitating before touching the edge of the frame. Fatima's mind cleared as she admired the painting, a view of the groves through the window. Though on further inspection, they didn't seem so much through a window as reflected by a mirror.

Elisa opened one cardboard box, then another. "Ale ordered prints and postcards. And these t-shirts." She stood, holding one. "I wanted you to have this." She shoved it into her friend's hand.

Fatima waved the shirt open. She spread it out on the desk to examine the design. It looked almost like a woodblock print. Of two little girls walking through olive groves, holding hands. One had braids, the other pigtails. The olive trees rose over them, as a steeple rises over a cathedral. The colors didn't quite fit the lines, creating a sense of chaos around the girls, though the figures themselves were painted neatly. Boldly. Fatima breathed. "This is beautiful, Elisa. Thank you."

"Sure," Elisa smiled, her lips tight. "It's us, you know."

"I know." Fatima's voice shook. "This means a lot to me."

Elisa shrugged. "It's just a t-shirt."

ONE COLD JANUARY EVENING

Snow drifted through the muted January air, shavings of diamonds across black cobblestones. Heaven's breath made manifest. By morning, it had disappeared. As if it had never been.

Chiara twisted the key, unlocking Bar Birbo. Standing in the doorway, she shivered in the breeze. She breathed deeply, stepping out into the street to run her hands over the Madonna's pedestal with its dusting of snow. Or was it simply cold dust? She ran it between her fingers, her eyes fixed on the Madonna. Before turning back into the bar.

The morning passed in a steady stream of customers. She and Edo pivoted around each other like a choreographed dance. It could have been old times, save for the sparks at odd moments that they both tried to ignore.

Magda didn't take part in Bar Birbo's play that day, but most every other regular customer let loose the merry tinkle of the bell over the door. Even Livia made an appearance; trepidatious at first, but after that initial awkwardness, she sat at the edge of the bar swapping stories of political scandals with Ava's mother. Together, they warmed to their topic, bemoaning the church's lessening influence on society.

Fabio loitered outside smoking for a few minutes, as if drawn by his ideal conversation. But he no longer crossed Bar Birbo's threshold. Chiara wondered where he drank coffee. She shrugged, turning her attention to Luciano and Vito, arguing about which filling best suited a *cornetto*. So hard to believe these brother spent years rarely seeing each other. With Vito's visits increasing in number and duration, nowadays the brothers walked shoulder-to-shoulder, listening with single-minded intensity to each other's words. Stopping every few paces to gesture, unable to walk and focus on their conversation at the same time.

Like schoolboys, they'd reverted to playing physical pranks on each other. Isotta had told Chiara how once, when she'd been visiting Luciano, she'd clutched Jacopo at a sudden booming at the door as if a giant kicked with reckless impatience. Luciano, though, had rolled his eyes. He opened the door to find his cat, eyes beseeching for mortadella. Helpless giggling had drawn them outside and around the corner to an alley where Vito hunched, doubled over with laughter.

The sound of Bar Birbo's bell broke Chiara's reverie. She looked up to find a stranger standing in the doorway, hands clasped at her waist. Chiara shot a look at Edo, who shrugged and continued to froth milk. So not a friend or former classmate of his, though they looked the same age.

The young woman, her hair in a neat braid down her back and her cheeks blazing red, approached the bar. Chiara wiped her hands and greeted her with a smile. "What can I get for you?"

Chiara had to lean far over the counter to hear the woman's words. Not a woman, she realized. Late teens, at the oldest. Chiara shook her head to indicate she hadn't understood. The stranger took a breath. "Pietro Bertelli. Do you know where I might find him? His restaurant is closed."

"Pietro?"

The stranger nodded.

Chiara cocked her head, wondering why this girl might be looking for Pietro. Maybe a friend of Sonia or Leo's? They appeared about the same age. Chiara turned to Livia. "Do you know where Pietro is?"

Turning from her conversation with Savia, Livia appraised the young woman. "At home, I expect."

The woman nodded, bringing her braid over her shoulder to fiddle with the end of it. It was a motion both innocent and seductive. Chiara wondered again at her age. And who she was. Livia didn't know her, so she couldn't be family.

The stranger said, "Would you mind pointing me to his home?"

Chiara could feel the bar crackle with supposition. Maybe it was her own history, but Chiara couldn't help wondering if perhaps Pietro had gotten mixed up with an underage girl.

Livia stood. "Not without knowing who you are."

"I'm Sonia."

"Sonia?"

The villagers darted looks at each other.

The girl nodded, her face wan. "His daughter."

The winter chill had crisped and faded the thistle surrounding the parking lot. Elisa set another prickling orb in her basket and put her gloves back on. Deep in consideration of how to weave the image of the dried flower into her newest piece, she startled at the sound of her name.

She looked around and spotted Sonia, leaning against her car.

Elisa looked behind Sonia as if expecting to see Fatima. Seeing nothing but the fog, wending its way into the darkening hills, Elisa said, "I didn't know you were in town."

Sonia shrugged, pushing her curls out of her face. "My dad wanted to meet at the old grain storage room. He's thinking of buying it and putting in sheltered outdoor seating."

"Okay." Elisa paused. "See you later."

"Have you talked to Fatima?"

Elisa stopped. "No. She's in Dubai."

Sonia chuckled under her breath. "You didn't hear."

Focusing on breathing, Elisa said in a casual tone, "Hear what?"

"She flamed out. Blew it."

Elisa shook her head. "Mamma got me a phone and Salma emailed me a photograph. Fatima looks incredible."

Sonia gazed out over the hills. "It takes more than looking incredible to be a model, Elisa. Surely, you know that?"

Not knowing the proper response, Elisa shrugged.

Sonia narrowed her eyes at Elisa. "They kicked her out. Of Dubai. Couldn't work with her. She blew it."

Softly, Elisa said, "Where is she? Dubai?"

"They didn't want her anymore." Sonia shrugged. "Looks like she'll get one more shot in Japan."

"Looks like?"

Sonia shrugged again. "According to Instagram, that's where she's headed next. She isn't talking to me. I totally get why photographers in Dubai couldn't stand her. She won't listen to hard truths. Goes cold."

"I don't understand."

Sonia's half-smile winked in the gathering gloom. "I guess that's why she likes you, right?"

Elisa took a step toward Sonia. "Fatima. What happened to Fatima?"

Blowing out a breath of exasperation, Sonia said, "She must have told you. Even in Milan, she could only get good shots if Valentina was there. Otherwise, she got defensive at the tiniest things. Come on, models *have* to stay rail-thin. That's not a surprise. Why should it bother her if a clothing company complains that she's fat?"

"She's not fat!"

Sonia appraised Elisa without comment. Digging into her sleek handbag, Sonia pulled out her keys. "I have to go."

"You didn't tell me anything!"

"I told you all I know. The girl takes great pictures, but she doesn't have what it takes. I mean, it's not rocket science—follow directions, stay thin, trust the photographers, forget about the cameras."

"And you think that's easy?" Elisa scowled. "You never knew Fatima at all."

Sonia cocked her head. "I know I wouldn't blow an opportunity like this because I'm stubborn or whatever."

"Fatima isn't stubborn. She knows her mind. She has to, you know what happened to her . . ."

Sonia made a dismissive noise. "Plus, she probably shouldn't have shown up for her shoots hungover."

"Hungover! But Valentina said—"

"Turns out, when a girl wants oblivion, she'll find it, no matter how many people she has watching." To Elisa's open-mouthed astonishment, Sonia added, "All I'm saying? Your friend is bad news."

Livia didn't know how she arrived home. She had a vague memory of someone walking beside her, murmuring platitudes. By the time she came to on the threshold of her home (well, rented home, and she could never ignore the rumors that a body had been found buried in the slope behind the house), Pietro had thrown open the door and whoever was beside her had melted away.

Her voice empty of curiosity, Livia asked, "Is she still here? That girl?"

Pietro's hands were still. He shook his head.

Livia nodded and stared at her feet. Her keys fell to the ground as she swayed. Pietro lunged forward, catching her before she fell. Acid rose in her throat and she pushed him away. "I suppose you have nothing to say for yourself."

"Nothing you want to hear in the doorway, no."

Livia stared at her husband, this stranger.

He opened the door wider and backed up.

For a rash moment, Livia considered running. Escaping this moment. She stepped through the doorway.

All the lights were on, blazing against the early evening.

Livia dropped her purse on the table but kept her coat on as she sagged onto a kitchen chair. An acrid scent drew her gaze to the counter where something charred and crisped lay forgotten on a baking tray. Livia shivered, her mind returning to those bones buried in the back.

Pietro sat across from her.

The clock's ticking resounded through the house. Had it always been so loud?

Livia looked up as Pietro drew a breath. "I met her before I knew you. Sonia's mother."

"I'm Sonia's mother."

Pietro looked at his hands. "You know what I mean."

"No. I'm afraid I don't." Livia wondered if she should be yelling. Throwing electronics. Tearing Pietro's recipes. But she felt spent already.

Pietro said, "There's too much to explain. Maybe it would be better if I just left."

Livia's head jerked up. "If you think you can drop this bomb into my life and walk away unscathed, you have another thing coming."

"Livia . . . I'm thinking of *you*, here."

Livia lifted an arm to cut him off, then ran her hand over her face. "There are few things I'm certain about right now. But this I know. Of the many things you've been thinking about, I am not one of them. Any more than that lamp." She gestured to the living room. "That lamp you only notice when it won't switch on."

Pietro stared at the lamp as if mesmerized. As if seeing it for the first time.

Standing, Livia went on, "Pietro. I don't know what happened. But I know you've ruined me. So let me be clear, you do *not* get to dictate what I get to know. You do *not*," she sobbed, "get to take everything away and not tell me *why*."

"Okay, Livia. Jesus. Calm down."

She recoiled as if slapped. "Who *are* you?"

He sighed, his fingers waving against each other as he counted silently. The red things in the room? The blue? It no longer mattered. "Livia. I've been two people for so long, I can't even answer your question."

It couldn't be her imagination.

Carla must be coming to Santa Lucia to plague her. Why else would she tag along for Enrico's day trip when he'd be spending the entire visit tagging the contents of dusty boxes?

Luciano seemed to guess Isotta's feelings. At least, when she opened the door to find him standing on her doorstep, he shifted his feet apologetically. "Enrico is coming for a few hours so the three of us can finish documenting our father's legacy." He scratched his chin and regarded her with a sheepish expression. "We wondered, Vito and I . . . we wondered if you might invite Carla for a visit."

Isotta's face twisted. "Me?"

Luciano sighed. "Carla seems to have taken a liking to you."

"I find that doubtful. She positively sneers at me."

Pushing his overlarge glasses higher onto his nose, Luciano said, "I won't pretend to not understand. But I suspect that comes from her feeling insecure. Around you."

Isotta stood stock still, her hand gripping the doorknob. A peal of laughter erupted from her with such force she had to double over.

Jacopo's cry prompted her back to standing but didn't mute her laughter. She held up her finger and walked into the recesses of the house, her laughter trailing behind her like a cartoon speech balloon.

She returned a few moments later, wiping her eyes, Jacopo perched on her hip. The boy popped his thumb out of his mouth at the sight of Luciano and held out his hand, twisting at the wrist.

Luciano widened his eyes. "Is he waving now?"

"Oh, who can say. All I know is that with his new cold, he's not sleeping." Margherita appeared at her side, an apparition with a cloud of dark curls waving around her face. Isotta put a hand on the child's head. She looked back up at Luciano. "My manners are terrible, I'm sure, but really... the very idea. It's ludicrous. I mean, have you *seen* Carla?"

"I have."

"Well, then."

He shook his head. "The two of you are very different. It is no wonder you fail to notice your charms in the face of your rival's."

She glared. "Rival? That's a bit harsh."

"It's no less true." He shrugged. "She sees how much Enrico values you. Which spurs her to put up a kind of act. But I assure you, she does like you. She asks question after question about you."

"If nosiness passes for respect nowadays, we'll need to give Arturo a good citizenship award." She shook her head. "You're not selling me on entertaining Carla. Plus, Riccardo needs me to complete all this paperwork. And, as you can see, Jacopo's nap was short. It's not as if I'm swimming in time."

"Can you ask Livia—"

Isotta shook her head. "She offered so many times when the kids returned, but I was overwhelmed. I think I offended her. She barely looks at me."

"Perhaps you could take this opportunity to repair that relationship?"

Isotta studied Luciano. "Why is this so important to you?"

His eyes behind his glasses widened. "I'd like the time with Vito and Enrico, to sort our family legacy. Carla means well, I'm sure, but she demands a lot of attention."

Isotta switched Jacopo to her other hip. "Okay. I'll do it." Unsure if she had agreed out of wanting to help Luciano or softening with his criticism of Carla.

She phoned Elisa, who agreed to take her siblings to the park and bring them back by Jacopo's naptime.

When Carla's smart one-two rap echoed through the walls, Isotta muttered a prayer for fortitude. Before she opened the door with what she hoped was a winning smile. "Carla! I'm glad you could stop by."

Carla looked a little confused at this display of warmth but smiled and followed Isotta into the kitchen. "Where are those adorable babies that are always hanging all over you?"

"With their sister. I suppose you know about—"

"Oh, of course. Enrico tells me *everything*."

Isotta momentarily tripped but then regained her composure. "Good. That's good. You can imagine it's a lot to explain. It's always nice when other people take the trouble of doing it for me."

Carla sat down and beamed at Isotta. "And they haven't found your husband? Well, your marriage wasn't all that good anyway, right?"

"Er...well, not exactly, no, but—"

"Poor, poor Isotta. So unlucky in love." She looked meaningfully at Isotta. Isotta wondered if Enrico told Carla about their mistimed attraction, or if Carla had picked up on it from Isotta herself.

Isotta turned to the counter. "Cake? I should tell you it's not home-made, I picked it up from the *forno*. So glad for an excuse to buy almond cake! It's my favorite."

Carla cocked her head to the side. "Just a sliver for me. I have to watch my figure, you know."

Without meaning to, Isotta glanced at Carla's trim body, as lean as a racehorse, and just as sleek. Isotta looked down at herself. Six months after having Jacopo and she wondered if she'd ever feel taut anywhere in her body again.

Carla grinned. "That Massimo...a rascal for sure, but he was a real looker, wasn't he?"

Isotta startled at hearing Massimo spoken of in the past tense. "How do you know what he looked like?" She couldn't see Luciano taking out the old photo album.

Shrugging, Carla said, "I Googled him."

"You Googled my husband?"

"Sure." Carla frowned playfully. "Now, you're not going to get bent out of shape, are you? It's in the public domain. What's the big deal?"

Isotta's hands shook as she brought the moka and cups to the table. "Nothing, I suppose." But the weirdness of it was undeniable, she felt sure of that. She wished she could duck out and text Ava.

Carla rested her chin on her hand and looked dreamily into the corner, which Isotta realized was riddled with cobwebs. "He looked like a movie star, didn't he? Such a waste . . ."

Isotta wondered if the waste was his untimely demise or his attaching himself to someone as ordinary as herself.

Into the silence, Carla slid, "So different from Enrico, right?"

Isotta looked up. "What was that?"

"Massimo. His killer looks. I bet when Enrico flirted with you, you were like, 'Are you kidding me with this?'"

"Enrico never flirted." In a clap of thunder, Isotta realized that's why it had taken her so long to respond to him. Massimo's flirting had been supercharged. He couldn't turn it off. Enrico, he approached attraction like he approached anything. With reason and thoughtfulness. She sighed.

Carla waved her hand. "Whatever you call it."

Isotta frowned. "How can you say this about your boyfriend?"

Carla shrugged. "I'm experienced enough to spot a good thing when I see one. Enrico might not fit the mainstream image of handsome, but he's better than that. He's gorgeous."

"He is." The words flew out before Isotta could stop herself.

Carla's eyes narrowed. "Too bad it took you so long to figure it out, eh?"

Isotta picked up her cup and then put it down without taking a sip. "I don't think we should be talking about this."

"Does it violate your sense of propriety?"

"Yes. Actually. You're dating Enrico."

"And you wish you were."

Isotta said nothing.

Carla took a delicate sip of coffee and winced faintly. "Before Enrico and I started dating, we'd talk at university functions. It was impossible to miss how smitten he was with his ingenue in backwoods Umbria."

Ingenue? Backwoods?

"I couldn't understand why in the world any woman wouldn't snap Enrico up."

"Maybe because he's not a fish or a trump card."

Carla smiled. "Oh, Isotta." She pushed the cup away. "Then when I came here, I watched you. I saw how your eyes followed him. But it's too late. You see that."

Isotta turned the saucer around and around. Finally, she looked up. "Why are you here?"

Carla shrugged. "You're like family to Enrico, right? And he and I, well, the way things are going, he and I will be family, too. It's right that you and I get along."

"This is getting along? You've done nothing but be nasty to me."

Carla looked affronted. "What can you mean? Such an accusation! No, Isotta, I haven't been nasty. What I'm doing is laying down the boundary. If the lines are clear, we'll get along just fine."

Pietro's story came out. Piece by piece. "I dated her in high school. When we grew serious, her father said he'd cut her off if she didn't break it off. Their family had a lot of money, a lot of standing. And I was the son of a greengrocer, with nothing but dreams of opening a restaurant." Pietro looked down, opening and closing his fingers against his palm like underwater sea creatures.

Livia watched and then looked away.

"So that was that. Sonia ended our relationship."

Livia's head whipped toward Pietro. "Sonia? Her name is Sonia? *Our daughter's name?*"

He blushed. "There's a lot in this story I regret. That may be the worst."

Livia flushed and moved to stand, but forced herself to keep seated. She had to get this horror over with. "This can't be happening."

Pietro paused before continuing, expressionless now, almost robotic. "We never stopped loving each other, Sonia and I. But she got married soon afterward, to an awful man. A man that . . . did vile things. Hurt her. While running her father's business into the ground. I didn't know all this at the time. You and I had gotten married. I wasn't in touch with her."

"You wanted to get married so fast. We didn't even have a proper wedding. Everyone assumed I was pregnant. Even though you didn't touch me until our wedding night. Like a good Catholic."

He blinked as if surprised to find her in front of him.

She mused aloud. "You used me to forget her."

He hung his head and said nothing.

"You . . . you told me you'd never had sex before. You lied, didn't you?"

"Yes."

"You'd had sex with Sonia."

"Many times." When the words left his mouth, he moved awkwardly as if trying to take them back.

Livia shook her head. "No wonder our marriage never flourished. You built it on a lie."

He said nothing.

"I see," she said blandly. "Continue. You married me, you wished you had married someone else. Continue."

Pietro pressed his lips together. "A few years after we got married, I ran into Sonia again. I swear I didn't seek her out."

"You get no gold star, Pietro," Livia breathed, and then her face stilled. "Wait. A few years after we got married? When exactly?"

He looked away and said nothing.

"When I was pregnant? With twins?"

His nod was almost imperceptible.

Her body released backward, slumped against the chair as she muttered, "I thought my body, so big, it repulsed you."

Rather than answering, he continued, "When I discovered her, she was poor. Alone. Her father had died of a heart attack, perhaps brought on by the stress Sonia's husband caused, dividing them all, probably embezzling. He moved with Sonia to Arezzo and then abandoned her."

Livia didn't respond.

"I took her to dinner. And one thing led to another."

"Did she know you were married?"

He paused.

"Don't lie to me. For the love of all that is good and holy in this world, don't you dare lie to me. Not now."

He nodded. "She knew."

Livia's eyes welled. Though she didn't know why the tears waited until this part of the story. But maybe they were waiting for her to say—"You named our daughter after her."

He nodded, mute now.

"Our *daughter*. My *girl*. You named her after the woman you loved."

"A mistake. You and I were talking about names and you asked what girls' names I liked and Sonia came out before I knew it—"

"Maybe because you were thinking about her?"

Pietro looked away.

Livia nodded, her question answered.

Pietro said, "You liked the name. I couldn't figure out how to talk you out of it."

"And at some point Sonia got pregnant, and you decided to name that girl Sonia too? How much of an homage does one woman need?"

"It wasn't about an homage, it was about . . ." Pietro's voice trailed off.

Livia suddenly understood. "Balance."

Pietro looked up, surprised. "Yes."

"A lack of balance tempts the evil eye."

"Yes. How did you . . ."

"We've been married over twenty years."

He nodded.

She sighed. "Well, I guess it worked. You lasted a long time, all those disappearances. I never knew. I wonder what threw off the universe now." She'd said it mockingly, but Pietro's face stilled.

"Margherita, *please*," Isotta begged. She hated the sound of her voice. "*Please* stop jumping. If you wake Jacopo from his nap . . . you know he has a cold and—"

"I's a FLYING pirate, Mamma! I fly and fly and *fly*!" Margherita jumped from the sofa to the chair to the table, then back to the sofa.

Isotta peered over her shoulder. Was that Jacopo? The house settled around her in eerie ways.

"MAMMA!" Margherita shouted. "Look at me now! Look how I fly! Did you see?"

"I see, *cara*, but please, stop yelling!" Her voice swelled to a whispered scream.

Margherita began singing as she leaped back around the furniture.

Isotta felt her hands closing into fists. She started walking away, desperate to slow her racing heart.

The child's voice followed her. "Why aren't you watching me, Mamma?

MAMMA!"

From Jacopo's room, Isotta heard the whimpering that always pre-
ceded his howl of waking.

She spun around and yelled at Margherita, "Look what you did! You
woke up your brother! I told you! I *told* you! But would you listen? *No!*"

Margherita paled. She tried to laugh, running to the electrical cords
to pull them from the wall.

Isotta yelled, "What are you *doing*? Stop it!"

Margherita struggled with the cord to the lamp, and it popped out
suddenly. With a thump, she stumbled, her shoulder knocking the table.
The lamp teetered and then fell onto Margherita's shoulder before shattering on the floor.

"There!" Isotta shouted. "Serves you right!"

Margherita lifted her arms. "I's hurt, Mamma. Hold me!"

"No!" Isotta stalked out of the room and yanked a wailing Jacopo out
of his crib. She stormed into the living room where Margherita cried pit-
eously, her arms limp at her sides.

Isotta glared at her as she jostled Jacopo to quiet him. "You're being
awful, Margherita!" Isotta yelled, "Just awful! Can't you see I'm at the end
of my rope? Can't you see I have no more *left*?" She took a breath.

Margherita looked up, her face streaked with tears. "Why you so
crabby, Mamma?"

Isotta's heart tore. She sagged to the floor beside Margherita and
pulled the child onto her lap beside Jacopo. Tears filled her eyes as she
kissed one curly head and then the other. What was wrong with her?

After a few minutes of silence, Margherita cheerfully helped Isotta
clean up the lamp, and then shyly brought her a book to read. Isotta said,
"I love this one!"

Margherita settled on Isotta's lap and nodded with great seriousness.
"I like pirates. They have swords. They aren't afraid."

Isotta read the book, treasuring the feel of her children, their quiet, as she turned the pages with hardly a rustle. When she closed the book, Margherita slapped the cover and shouted, "Again!" Rousing Jacopo who had nodded off.

Isotta thoughts cast back to Margherita's earlier words. Carefully, she said, "Did you notice, Margherita, how the pirate was scared? He was scared of not finding his gold. But he kept looking and then he found it in the end." She paused, weighing her next sentence. "Margherita, are you scared of anything?"

Margherita stood up and put her hands on Isotta's cheeks, bringing their faces nose to nose. She whispered. "Yes."

Isotta's breath caught. What was Margherita scared of? A faceless boogeyman? A fleeing life on the road? Isotta's lip quivered as she wondered . . . *her*? Softly she asked, "What are you scared of, *cara*?"

Her face still so close, Isotta could smell her cotton-flower shampoo, Margherita whispered. "The dark, Mamma. The dark is so scary. Jacopo, he scared of the dark, too."

Isotta felt her breath leave in a rush. The dark. "The dark is scary, that's true." She ran her lip between her teeth. "I have an idea. Why don't we have a treasure hunt like in the book? And we can go into the dark, like the pirates go into caves. We can practice getting braver and braver?"

Margherita clapped her hands. Then she stopped. "But you come with me, right?"

Isotta laughed. "Oh, yes. I want to play, too. But why don't you and Jacopo stay in your room for a minute while I set up?"

"Come on, Jacopo!" Margherita ran up the stairs. Isotta followed, calculating how many coins she had in her purse and where she could hide them. Should she make a map? No, Margherita was too young to follow one. She'd just hide the treasure in the kitchen and turn off the light.

For the next half-hour, Isotta hid coins in one darkened room after another, following as Margherita crept in and then located the coin with a shout of unadulterated glee. Then Isotta made dinner as Margherita played with Jacopo in the kitchen, noting informatively, "I sharing my treasure so good, Mamma. You see?"

"I do see, *cara. Grazie.*" Isotta noted that Jacopo, thank goodness, seemed to have no desire to stick the coins in his mouth.

Before long, she tucked the children into their beds. Back downstairs, she tried to read, but the words made no sense. She kept thinking she heard one of the children calling. Though every time she tiptoed to their room, she found them curled tight as seashells.

She was glad she'd hit upon the idea of moving Jacopo into Margherita's room. It made juggling naps complicated, and many mornings she found Margherita in the crib with her brother, one arm thrown carelessly over his belly. But they both slept more soundly.

Isotta's thoughts went to the parenting books she read about healthy sleep patterns. She argued with herself, wearily, that Italian children had been sleeping piled like puppies since time immemorial. Then she had a flash of anecdotes she'd read online about children unable to function on their own. Round and round, her thoughts cycled. A merry-go-round.

Isotta decided to go to bed. On the way, she stopped one more time in the children's room. Light from the hallway drifted over their faces. In separate beds for the moment, Jacopo in his crib with his thumb falling out of his mouth, his long black lashes standing out against his rounded cheeks. Margherita with her wild curls fanned around her quiet, elfin features.

Isotta's heart caught.

She turned at a brushing sound from outside, like a hand running over wood grain. Tense, she waited.

Nothing. She continued to her bed. Worries about money, worries about leaving the children to go to work chased by Anna's whispers that she didn't deserve these children and Massimo's admonishment that she would never be good enough. And layered through it all, she heard Carla's voice, warning her away from Enrico.

The whirling thoughts jabbed her out of any real sleep.

"M*adonna mia*, there's more?" Livia said.

"Yes."

"More children?"

"Children?" Pietro dipped his head to the side. "Of course. But that wasn't what—"

"You had *more* children with her? After telling *me* that two was plenty? That we couldn't afford more and live on a restaurant owner's salary? After telling me that God knew more than the Church and wouldn't want us to overpopulate the planet?"

Pietro said nothing.

"You *know* how I love children! How I always wanted a house full of them, like I had growing up. A tumble of brothers and sisters."

He shrugged defensively. "You have nieces and nephews. Margherita."

"She's not mine! I'm not even in that picture!"

"She loves you," he said uneasily.

Livia choked back a laughing sob. "I barely see her! I've asked Isotta if I can look after Margherita. I wanted to help. But Isotta must know the same thing *everyone* seems to know. I am so disagreeable, so . . ." her voice hitched, "unlovable. I can't even keep the man I married."

"Stop! You are *not* unlovable! Our marriage was broken before it began, but you have been a wonderful mother and—"

"Nobody likes me!" Livia wailed, suddenly undone. "Why didn't you just leave me?"

"It wouldn't have been fair to you."

"And this *was*?"

Pietro stared at his hands, rubbing his knees as the clock ticked on. "Isotta does like you, I remember after Jacopo was born, she told me how appreciative she was to have you in their lives."

"She said that?"

"She did." He nodded. "You know how it's been. Isotta doesn't want to leave the children with anybody. Her parents asked for Jacopo for the weekend, and she said no, remember?"

"I hadn't heard that."

"Maybe because you aren't in the bar enough."

"Nobody likes me there."

"They don't know you." He thought for a moment. "Give Isotta a little time."

"Time. Time is what I'll never get back. You took it all. I can't have children now. You're the one who has children." She stopped. "How many children?"

He shook his head. "It will upset you."

"Tell me. Shouldn't I know how many siblings my children have?"

Pietro's jaw worked. "I have five children."

"Five? You allowed me two children and yet you allowed Sonia *three*?"

He shook his head slowly. "No. I have…I *had* five children with Sonia." His eyes shone, and he looked away.

The clock continued to tick, relentlessly marching, counting the moments, the minutes. The long minutes.

The word caught and rang in the air, twining with the metronome rhythm of the clock. "Had…had…had…"

Livia broached, "You're not telling me something."

He shook his head. "It's not your problem."

Livia raised both hands to her hair, brushing it backward until she could feel the skin on her temples rising like goose flesh. "It's *all* my problem. You've gone and created a whole other family. Teeming with life, with children. Giving them everything. Giving me nothing but an income. Like I've been some sort of employee. And now my life...it's tainted! You've made a mockery of me!" Her voice rose. "I'll be a laughingstock. You realize that, right?"

He hung his head.

"You want me to leave." Realization struck Livia. "Once I leave, the way is clear, isn't it? You'll bring your little harlot here to parade her around, her and your five precious children. What a sweet image!" Livia's mouth stretched in a caustic approximation of a smile.

At Pietro's silence, Livia nodded, as if she'd scored a point.

It didn't last.

As surreptitiously as possible, Antonella removed her coat from the rack, but her grandmother did not miss the gesture. "Where are you going? It's cold! And dark."

Shaking her head, Antonella said, "I need some air."

Bea looked over at Antonella's mother, snoozing at the other end of the couch. Standing, Bea brushed the hair off her granddaughter's forehead. "Is everything okay, child? You've been so quiet."

"It's fine." With a small smile, she said, "Aren't I too old to be considered a child?"

Bea kissed her granddaughter's cheeks. "You'll always be that little girl yelling that Carosello got into a fight with a cat."

Antonella said playfully. "Carosello was around when I was a girl?"

"Maybe it was another dog," Bea said, her forehead creased in thought. "Now...don't tell me you're headed out alone."

Antonella closed her eyes. "This is Santa Lucia. The biggest risk is that Arturo will hound me until I tell him your recipe for *pasta alla norcia*."

Bea snickered. "Don't tell him."

"Tell him what? You won't even let me in the kitchen when you make it."

"Good girl." Baa's face grew serious. "Are you meeting that police officer? Marcello? You can tell me, *cara*. I'm very liberal-minded."

"No, Nonna." Antonella sighed. "I told you a thousand times already. You made too much of that."

Bea looked chastened. "Be careful then. The cobblestones get slippery in the fog."

"I know." Antonella slipped out the door with a faint, "I love you." She cast one more glance at Bea settling on the couch with a groan of appreciation for soft couches and warm blankets and the handsome man on the screen pointing ominously to a series of storm clouds approaching their boot-shaped peninsula.

The cold air struck Antonella like a slap. As if the night were an overworked blade. She wrapped her arms around herself and strode as if compelled through Santa Lucia's twisting, turning alleys until she arrived at the steps that led up, up. Into the groves.

She stepped firmly, willing her footsteps to drown out his words, the feel of his hands on her shoulders.

Shivering, she ordered herself, "Don't think about it! Focus on how to get *out*."

But she couldn't. And she knew she couldn't. Her father had quit his machinist's job. The thought of his hands, curved and hardened around their work scars made her want to weep. She couldn't stand the thought of him having to return to torquing gears, forcing his twisted fingers to wrap around tools.

As the wind stung her face with air particles that felt individually frozen, Antonella admitted her other reason for staying. She couldn't go back to the *rosticceria*, where her biggest puzzle was how to fit two slices into a box along with three *arancini*.

Edo had mentioned they may need help at Bar Birbo. Her abraded heart clung to the comfort of a life at the bar. Working with a man who was a) not a lech, and b) gay, chatting about this and that with people who had known her since she was in pigtails... well. It did sound appealing.

But she knew that wasn't for her. She wanted work that excited her with strategy and impact. If she left her firm, she'd have to move to a big city to get this kind of work. How could she afford that on a starting salary if she couldn't live at home?

She had watched the news enough to know about Italy's job crisis. She'd combed the papers for new options and found nothing. She was lucky to have this one, and she had to hang onto it, despite the feel of her soul eroding.

Her only joy now was the ease in their household as her father read the paper aloud in the morning to her mother bustling around the kitchen. Her father offering commentary, as her mother quipped in return, their shared laughter.

Wasn't that worth the revulsion that grew every day as she drove down the hill to Girona? As she entered her office building. As she took her seat in front of Signor Tocci. As he watched her, wolf-like. Waiting to comment on her clothing, the shift of her shoulders. Waiting to find an excuse...

She leaned against an olive tree for support as the memories broke over her.

"Antonella, you look so sad today. Boyfriend troubles? I know young men can have so many demands. In the bedroom, you know. You can tell me about it. I can help. Offer a man's opinion." He chuckled at her blush, leaning forward to stroke her knee. "Don't be embarrassed. You're a small-town girl. You can't yet understand how normal sex is. How pleasurable it can be."

And

"Why are you tense? Here, open your collar a bit so I can show you these pressure points on your shoulders. You know, not all bosses would do this. My last assistant says it's what she misses most about working for me." His hand drifted across her shirt and he apologized for his mistake, even as he cupped her breast like the glide of a bird.

And

His intake of breath as she leaned over to pick up a box of scattered paperclips. "You know you're wearing the wrong underwear for the snugness of that skirt. A thong is what you need. Here, let me show you. I have some bookmarked to order for my wife. I'll get you a pair. You'll wear them to our meeting with Zinc. A fashion house will be turned off by a woman wearing panties that belong in the back of Nonna's drawer. And they'll know. They'll know like I know. If you want to be taken seriously, you need to dress the part. Now come sit beside me. Let's order you something more appropriate."

And

"You know, no woman in this business wears her shirt buttoned so high. Are you ashamed of your large breasts? You shouldn't be. Men find large breasts very attractive. Now, unbutton one button, let's see how that looks." His eyes fixed on her fingers as they trembled, slipped, unbuttoning a button while trying to keep the shirt from gaping open. His panting breath, "One more. Let's try one more. Yes. Yes. That's good." Before he suddenly rose, standing in front of her, his groin at her eye level. She looked away, repulsed. He paused before striding out of the room to the bathroom.

An avalanche of memories...words, glances, touches, innuendos.

And mixed with the revulsion, she felt a creeping shame. She must be inviting his advances. Or wouldn't she be able to stop them?

She had tried everything she could think of. She wore pants, but he told her to go home and change, pants on a woman were an insult to their God-given assets. She offered ideas for projects, like a catchphrase for copy he labored over. He'd rolled his eyes.

She didn't know what else to do. Many of Signor Tocci's previous assistants transferred to promotions at other branches. She just needed to wait it out until her turn came for advancement.

The cold bit into her skin.

Starlight seeping from behind the clouds barely illuminated her steps, but she walked without tripping, the path as known to her as the maze of alleys between her house and her grandmother's. She walked without the clarity she had hoped to find. But she suspected that wasn't because the magic of the groves eluded her so much as there was no answer. What she needed more than a solution was patience, and hope that Signor Tocci would tire of her quickly enough to send her up and out of his slippery grasp.

Pietro's eyes streamed with tears. Livia had never seen him look so lost. All the fight had left him. If he'd ever had any. Which he must have, to continue this charade for so many years.

His voice a rasp, Pietro whispered, "You don't have to worry. Sonia won't be parading here. Or anywhere." He paused. "She's dead."

Livia snapped to attention.

"Dead?" She shook her head. "But..."

"That's what Nia came here to tell me. None of the children know about you. Or Sonia and Leo. They only know the locations of my restaurants. Nia went to all of them before she came here. She went to all of them. To tell me... to tell me..."

"Don't."

"That her mother." He gasped. "Is dead."

Silence.

Livia whispered. "What happened?"

He shook his head angrily. "She kept saying something was wrong. I ignored her. Thought she was trying to get me to stay longer. She got weaker, said it was hard to breathe. It didn't alarm me. Not much alarmed me out of my need to have everything always be okay." Pietro's voice broke. "Nia said she went to wake her mother and found her . . ."

"Oh, *Madonna mia.*" The sneer had drained from Livia. A movie played over and over in her brain, the horror of that innocent girl going to wake her mother and realizing she would never hear her mother's laugh again.

Pietro wept, "The children . . . they're with a neighbor. Sonia had to cut off ties with her family once she had my children. So you should stop thinking," his voice rose in indignation, "that her life was so charmed while yours was cursed."

Livia blinked. "It's a sad story. It doesn't make mine less sad."

Pietro paused and then hit his head with his hand, over and over. "Stupid! I'm so stupid! How did I ruin so many lives? And she's *gone!*"

Livia stood and said, her voice wavering. "It's a mess. Your mess." She glanced at the clock, still relentlessly ticking. "And it's about to get messier. Your son will be home soon."

"What? I can't . . ."

She shook her head. "I don't think you want me telling the story. And you'll have to explain why I'm not here."

"Where are you going?"

"I'll see if Magda has a room available."

"Magda!"

"Or Ale. Either one. You don't leave me much choice. Everyone will know by now, so it's not worth pretending they don't."

"Stay with me!"

She shook her head, aghast.

"Just for a little? I'm alone, and I need—"

"You're alone? *You're* alone? You left me long ago. You broke me. You don't get the leftovers."

"What do I say? To Leo? You always told me what to say, what to do!"

She laughed, without humor or ire. "Look how far that got me. My desperation to be part of your life pushed you deeper into the arms of another woman."

And with that, she picked up her purse and walked away, into the still and waiting night of Santa Lucia.

WINTER CONTINUES

*M*agda shook her head. "I can't believe I missed all of that. What did Livia do?"

Chiara set Magda's wine in front of her. "She almost fainted. Scared the girl almost to death. Someone, I can't remember who, volunteered to take Sonia—"

"Sonia! His daughter is named *Sonia*?"

"Apparently." To Magda's incredulous expression, Chiara said softly, "I know. I can't imagine how Livia is managing. I never ever would have thought Pietro capable . . . maybe there's a misunderstanding. Maybe Sonia is a niece. A niece who considers him a father."

"Then Livia would have recognized her."

"Or maybe it's bad, but not as bad as it seems. Like maybe he had a brief affair and didn't know the mother got pregnant. And her being named Sonia is some weird coincidence."

Magda put down her wine. "Oh, Chiara. Ever the optimist. Odds are, it's *worse* than it seems."

Chiara nodded. "That's what Savia said. Or something like it. That nothing about this could be simple."

Magda stared into her wine. "Nothing ever is, is it?"

Chiara's hand paused, reaching for the dishtowel. "Magda?"

Magda closed her eyes as if summoning strength. "I met Dante's children."

Chiara looked confused, and then the pieces fell together. A smile worked at the corner of her mouth but stalled at the paleness of Magda's face. Casually, she said, "You must have met them before."

"I had, yes. Some of them, anyway. But not as . . . not as . . . "

Chiara's eyes flicked to the door. She debated putting up the closed sign, but she feared breaking Magda's vulnerable moment. At Magda's inability to finish the sentence, Chiara supplied, "As Dante's . . . friend?"

Magda released her breath. "Yes. Friend."

"How did it go?" Chiara worked to keep her voice interested, but not curious.

"Not well." Magda's voice landed like a boulder into a shallow pond.

Chiara tried to respond, but before she could, Magda went on, "With one of them, it was okay. Luella. But his son, Mauro. He said . . . awful things."

Chiara's heart rose in her throat at the uncharacteristic tremor in Magda's voice. She whispered, "What did he say?"

Magda waved her hand dismissively before wiping her eyes. "Oh, you know. Stuff about how I was ruining Dante's life. But, why Chiara? Why would it? What's wrong with Dante dating me?" Immediately Magda grew pale. "I misspoke, Chiara. Dante and I aren't . . . dating."

Chiara cocked her head to the side. "You're not?"

Magda shook her head. "Our relationship is very . . . chaste."

Scratching her cheek, Chiara said nothing.

A faint blush suffused Magda's cheeks. "We argue. A lot. Too much for dating people, right? Like when he said that dumb thing about gay people using surrogates, Chiara, I was so mortified." In a gesture that about defied understanding, Magda reached across the counter and took Chiara's hand in her own.

Chiara stiffened and withdrew her hand.

On an ordinary day, Magda wouldn't fail to leap on the gesture. Chiara so carefully curated her reactions and rarely let her emotions show.

But Magda was too caught up in her story to notice. "He can be so short-sighted. I was embarrassed. And he got so testy I figured I made up the whole feeling between us. But, even when our fighting crosses an invisible line, the next day, I see Dante . . . and his face . . . it shines. And something in me. It breaks. Every time."

"Oh, Magda." Chiara had witnessed a lot of love stories bloom in front of her during her tenure at the helm of Bar Birbo's La Pavoni. Still, her eyes widened in wonder hearing Magda's. "It does sound like romance. Of a sort."

Magda shook her head. "I never would have expected it. I hated him for so many years. Even longer than he hated me."

Chiara grinned. "But you were saying. About Dante's son."

Scowling, Magda said, "Mauro, right." Magda said bitterly, "What a merry Christmas for me."

"This was *Christmas*?"

"Yes. Did I not mention that part?"

Chiara shook her head. At Magda's silence, Chiara asked, "But . . . what did Dante say?"

"As soon as he walked in, they were all smiles. Like it never happened."

"But what happened when you told him?"

Magda turned the base of her wineglass. She took a sip. She patted her mouth with a napkin.

"Magda! You didn't tell him?"

Magda shook her head and pleaded with Chiara, "I told him I was sick. I left. I haven't seen him since."

"Well, no wonder he keeps coming in, ordering wine and taking an hour to finish it. Looking over his shoulder the whole time."

"He does?"

"Yes! Magda. He *likes* you!"

Magda shook her head. "I told you. Nothing has happened between us. Maybe I made up the whole thing."

Chiara insisted, "Magda. A man doesn't invite just anyone to come to his house for Christmas to meet his children."

Magda stared into her wineglass. "Maybe he was being kind. Knowing I was alone."

Chiara held back a grin. "Does that sound like Dante?"

Glaring, Magda said, "He's wonderful, Chiara. You just don't know him like I do!"

Triumphantly, Chiara clinched, "Exactly."

Magda slumped forward. "What am I supposed to do?"

"Talk to him. Tell him what happened. Tell him how you feel."

"What? That's ... that's ... "

"Scary, I know."

"But ... but what if he gets annoyed?" Magda asked, her eyes wide.

"He won't."

"What if he does? Just say ... "

Chiara could not miss Magda's beseeching expression. "Then Magda, I hate to say this, but it wouldn't have worked. But I believe, with all my heart, that he will listen and be grateful you opened yourself to him."

Magda stared at Chiara. "I swear, I do not understand how you people do this. All the time. With other people."

"Open up?" Chiara asked. "Well, according to you, I'm no expert at that."

"I don't mean that, I mean ... "

Chiara grinned. "Love them?"

Magda sat back as if Chiara had thrown her a bocce ball. "I ... I ... " she stammered, "I never said anything about love."

"It's okay, Magda. I love you so much I'll do it for you."

Pietro loitered in the kitchen, making coffee. Finally, Leo emerged from his room, yawning and stretching. "Good morning, Babbo."

"It's noon."

Leo shrugged and took down another coffee cup. "I got in late." He scratched his head. "Where's Mamma?"

Pietro slumped in a chair as if the wind had been knocked out of him. "She . . . had an errand."

"Is there enough in the moka for me, too, or should I make another pot?"

"You can take it all."

Leo looked over his shoulder. "You okay, Babbo?"

Pietro shook his head. "Why don't you sit down, Leonardo?"

Leo stalled. "Can I make my coffee first?"

Pietro nodded, his eyes serious. He waited, as the kitchen filled with the sounds of the sugar bowl hitting the counter and the spoon clanking onto a saucer.

What seemed like years later, Leo slouched into his chair. "*Che c'è?* What's up?"

Pietro watched his hands, waving over each other. "Your mother . . . she's not on an errand."

"Is she okay? What's happened!"

"I don't mean to alarm you. She's fine. Physically, anyway. She's . . . not here. Because . . ." Pietro muttered, "You think I would have figured out how to say this."

"Babbo, you're scaring me," Leo said, his face pale.

Pietro took a breath. "I've been having an affair. For years now."

Leo's face hardened, and he looked out the window. "That's between you and Mamma."

Pietro said softly, "I wish that were true. But it does concern you. And Sonia."

"How?" Leo glared at his father, his jaw working. "How in the world can this concern me?"

Pietro watched his hands moving across his knees. "With this woman. I had another family. You have brothers and sisters."

Leo stared in disbelief. "Oh, God."

"I know this doesn't excuse anything, but I didn't mean for it to happen. She was my first love, I ran into her after your mother and me—"

"I swear to God, I don't require details." Leo straightened, his eyes flashing.

"I want you to understand—"

"Understand! *Understand*! You've been cheating on Mamma for *years*? You have other *children*? And you expect me to *understand*? What kind of asshole *are* you?"

Pietro hung his head. "I deserve that. But Leo, your mother didn't get this angry—"

"Well, she should have." He stood and moved to leave, but then came back and sat down.

"How many children?"

Pietro shook his head.

"Tell me!"

"Five." In a pleading voice, Pietro added, "You'll love them. Remember, you always wanted brothers..."

Leonard's waving hand came close to hitting Pietro. "Five. When Mamma always wanted more...she chose your wishes over God's, and meanwhile, you were procreating like a damn rabbit!"

Pietro's voice hardened. "She shouldn't have told you that."

"She didn't have to!" Leo yelled. "You two argued about it so loudly it was as if you *wanted* us to know! Sonia and I would huddle under her sheets, scared, listening as you criticized her religion! Talking about 'financial freedom' and 'global overpopulation'. Meanwhile, you knocked up some woman over and over again? No wonder you mocked Mamma's faith, you had none of your own!"

Pietro's head fell again. "I really am sorry."

Leo laughed harshly. "Anybody can be sorry once they're caught."

"I know I made a mess of things. I knew it the whole time. But I couldn't keep everything in balance. I couldn't stop loving Sonia—" as soon as the word left his mouth, Pietro looked desperate to choke it back.

"Sonia! You named my sister after the woman you cheated on Mamma with? Oh, my God. Is there no end?" He added, almost to himself.

"I can explain—"

"I don't need an explanation! I need you to not have done this! Any of this!"

"Leo, please!"

"No! You don't deserve anything from me!" He drew in a shuddering breath. "Where's Mamma? She needs me right now. Sonia too."

"You'll abandon me? I didn't do anything to you."

"*Madonna mia*," Leo breathed incredulously.

"Okay, yes. It's difficult to swallow. But, Leo, don't let that blind you to all the years—"

"Can't you see? All these years, you've straddled two families. How can you think this wouldn't impact us? My God, it's made you a disaster. Look at you!" Leo waved his hand at his father, whose fingers drummed a counting drumbeat on his knees. "Now, *where's Mamma?*"

"At Magda's. Or Ale's . . . she wouldn't tell me—"

"And you blame her for that, too, I suppose? Like you've blamed her for everything." Leo staggered backward. "Oh my God. This. This is why Mamma has all those controlling habits. She's been accommodating your sins without even knowing it." His voice filled with tears.

Pietro said softly, "Call her."

"You don't tell me what to do. I can take care of my mother." Leo pulled out his phone and dialed as he stormed out, not even bothering to close the door behind him.

At her hesitant knock, Enrico threw open the door. "You don't have to knock. This is your home."

She hugged her papers closer to her chest. "Not according to the postal service."

"Still." He drew back and gestured her into the house.

As she walked in, Isotta said, "It's strange. It's no longer where I sleep, but it does still feel like mine, you know?"

"I know." He closed the door. "Luciano misses having you here."

"I see him almost every day, but it's not the same. Timing is good though since your father has a place to stay. I heard he might move in?"

"He's been renting an apartment since my mother passed. But it's not ideal."

"Such a good man your father is. I hope he'll move here." Isotta set down her papers.

"I, as well." He smiled as he handed her a cup of thick and dark coffee. "Watch out, I make it strong."

Isotta grinned. "I think I can take it." She winced at her own words. Did that sound too flirty?

Enrico took a sip and recoiled. "I think I overdid it. I foamed some milk if that helps. And here's the sugar. I guess you know that."

Isotta smiled faintly.

Enrico said, "Okay. Enough stalling. Let's see it."

Isotta frowned for a moment. "Oh! My book!"

He grinned. "Yes. Your book. I'm honored that you're willing to share it with me."

She smiled tremulously. "*Allora*, if it wasn't for you, there wouldn't *be* a book."

He looked into her eyes. "Yes, there would. You always had this book inside you. You only needed to give it wing."

Isotta bit her lip, hardly daring to break the eye contact. How could this be the same Enrico who grew quiet and distant with Carla around, as he focused on everyone in the room but her? Each time she saw them together, she decided that Carla had probably had the measure of it and that Enrico wanted nothing more than to shove her off, politely but firmly. But without Carla . . . Enrico warmed again.

Finally, she blinked and laughed awkwardly. "Fine words. You haven't read it yet." She drummed her fingers on top of the pages.

He shrugged without taking his eyes from hers. "I know it's challenging to share your work for the first time."

She murmured, "I'm being silly. It's just, I have only these little moments that I can work on it, so I have no idea. It could be dismal." She stood and began laying out the papers. "All right. Here we go then. It's the story of a girl who drops her stuffed bunny in an olive grove. The fairies are confused about why this rabbit has an ear falling off and no fur around its nose, so they gather around it and inadvertently bring it to life."

"Pretty Bunny." Enrico chuckled.

She smiled. "Exactly. When the rabbit comes to life, it resembles a normal rabbit, but because it's always lived in a house, it doesn't understand the rules and manners and habits of the woodland animals. Chaos ensues."

"It's an entertaining premise. Now, stop distracting me so I can read."

Isotta smiled at Enrico's aggrieved tone. "If you insist."

"I do," he said, pulling the pages closer. He read for a few minutes. Which stretched to ten minutes. Isotta shifted in her seat as he pulled the first pages back and started again.

He looked up at her with shining eyes. "I think you have something here."

"You do? You're not just saying that?"

"What good would that do you? No, it's funny and charming and just the right amount of sentimental when the girl comes looking for her stuffed rabbit."

"And finds the tag?"

"Right. There are some rough places, but it seems you had fun with it."

"I did. I'll be honest, I started it because I felt myself spiraling. Things are . . . hard. I needed a way to get my feet underneath me. Working on it, it's given me some lightness. Like you said," she added shyly.

He smiled and read the page closest to him again. "Whatever your process has been, it's worked. I don't know much about children, but your book seems to meet children where they are. Without looking down on them. The writing is sharp and interesting like every word is meaningful. The imagery is compelling. And the cadence, which is the hardest part to do, you've nailed that. It reads like poetry without being poetry."

Isotta sat back, stunned. Not so much at his praise, but at Enrico's indefatigable ability to be Enrico.

Enrico looked up. "What?"

Isotta sat forward, running her hands from her temple down her hair. "Nothing. I'm taken aback is all. I knew you'd be polite, but I had this fear . . . '

"A writer is her own worst critic. I'm not saying it's perfect. It needs some work. My hunch is that it's too long by at least a third. I'm imagining reading this to Margherita . . . I'm not sure it could hold her attention."

"It doesn't."

He smiled reassuringly. "Illustrations will help. Have you talked to Fabrizio about getting an agent?"

"He writes mysteries."

"Sure, but you know how it is . . . one person knows another person. Would you feel comfortable sharing this with him?"

Isotta flicked her eyes to the papers before settling her gaze on Enrico. "An hour ago I would have said no. But now . . . yes. I think I'm ready."

Ale approached the barn-sized wooden door and hesitated.

He strode back toward his car then turned back, his fists shoved into his jacket pockets. It was time to face facts. The apps were going nowhere, despite that pretty bit of code. It had been a pipe dream; only a unicorn of an idea had a chance of rising above the fray and gaining an audience. He was not made to birth unicorns.

His best financial hope was the *castello*. After all, he couldn't know if the wine would be any better than last year. Yes, Bruno had snapped twigs and prodded soil and sniffed infinitesimal budding growth and pronounced the signs "good." Ale couldn't take that assurance to the bank. And Bruno still wouldn't let Ale taste the *passito*, citing some superstition. So who knew the value of their ancient grape?

He had to diversify. Hence his hopes of negotiating a partnership with the *frantoio*. Perhaps sharing advertising, or at least increasing his access to oil for selling at the *castello*.

It wouldn't bring in much, but Ale had to do something. His financial outlay was low since he owned his home, but groceries, utilities, supplies . . . they added up. Ava's landscaping brought in a bit of an income, which she dropped onto the table with a kiss on his forehead ("what's mine is yours, Ale, we'll get there"). But he'd left the envelope in a drawer.

Who knew he was so old school?

But not old school enough. Because the thought of hitching his entire livelihood to what the earth could give him frightened him to the core.

Olives and grapes.

Both tempestuous, both fickle, both susceptible to drought and hail and a surfeit of sunshine. And bugs. One mustn't forget about bugs. Ava and Francy had convinced him to make the wine organic, insisting that the grapes had grown without chemicals for decades, they might as well take advantage of the vines' innate hardiness. Nowadays, he spent his weekends among the vines with dish soap and a bucket, delighting in the removal of every beetle.

Odd to admit, but he loved the work. App development resembled slamming his head against a wall. But standing out in the vineyard on a fine day with Ava and Elisa and Isotta and Margherita, and sometimes even Luciano, Vito, and Enrico (he could do without Carla; the woman seemed pleasant, but Ale didn't miss the shrewish looks she shot at Isotta), learning country songs and tenderly caring for every tendril and leaf bud. It filled him with good feelings.

But it also scared him to care for something so irascible.

Olives and grapes.

Ale rang the bell. He heard the echo of footfalls before the door yanked backward, revealing a man about his age, trim, with wildly curling hair pulled half back to free his vision. The man grinned, "You must be Ale. I'm Tommaso. I'm glad you could make it."

Ale nodded. "Thanks for taking the time."

Tommaso gestured inside, and Ale couldn't help but notice the olive-leaf tattoos snaking their way up his arms. Feeling himself studying the design too closely, Ale said, "Nice ink."

Tommaso nodded his thanks. "Do you want a tour of the operation, or should we head straight to the office?"

Ale said, "I don't want to take too much of your time . . ."

Tommaso looked at him blankly.

"A tour, please."

Tommaso nodded and walked Ale around the floor, showing him where the olives arrived, the stems and leaf removal process, the grinding machine, and how the wheel pressed the macerated olives until their luminous green oil flowed into the waiting vats.

Despite himself, Ale found himself excited. He'd always loved processes, and this one was such an interesting mix of old-world customs and new technology. He longed to ask how the *frantoio* had changed over time, but he needed to get down to business.

As they crossed the salesroom, Ale noticed the tins of olive oil lining the shelves. He lingered, taking one down. Ale studied the simple label—text with no accompanying image. Holding up the tin, Ale asked, "Did you ever think of putting a rendering on your label?"

Tommaso scratched his chin and said, "Antonella said the same thing."

"Antonella?"

"Antonella Benedetti. Do you know her?"

"I do. Or Ava does anyway."

Tommaso nodded thoughtfully. "She said a rendering of your *castello* would make the olive oil appeal more storied, more particular."

"She did?"

"Yes. But I assumed there might be licensing issues with using your *castello* as our featured image."

Ale almost laughed aloud. "Not at all. I'd be honored."

Tommaso's serious face illuminated with a smile. "That's good to know."

Ale had a sudden thought. "Actually, if you're interested, I have a piece that might work. Ava's daughter, Elisa, has been selling her art at the *castello*. She did a painting that might work, a view of the *castello* surrounded by olive branches. It's a little abstract, perhaps less like a photo than you would like—"

"That could work. Will you bring it by sometime?"

"I'll bring it tomorrow." He put the oil back on the shelf, his mind alive with the breakfast room set about with tins of olive oil, all festooned with images of the *castello*. As if to himself, he murmured, "And Antonella suggested it. Who would have thought?"

Tomasso shrugged and led the way to his office, saying over his shoulder. "She and I went to school together. I figured with her working at that consulting firm in Girona, she might have ideas. I tried to hire the firm, but apparently we're too provincial. She felt terrible and sat down with me for hours to draw up a plan to widen our distribution. Didn't charge me at all."

Expansive now, Ale asked, "And how is that going?"

Tomasso turned, offering Ale a seat. "Quite well. She encouraged us to apply for demarcations and awards. And connect with wineries. Things we hadn't thought of." Tomasso lowered his voice to a conspiratorial whisper. "I shouldn't be telling you this since it's not announced, but we're a finalist for Slow Food's new olive oil award."

Ale's face grew as serious as Tomasso's. "If you win that, that will generate incredible interest in your oil. And in the area."

Tomasso's grin spread slowly across his face. "So. Let's talk business."

"Magda! Magda, *wait!*" Dante put on a burst of speed to catch up with Magda, making her way to the parking lot.

She turned slowly. "*Buongiorno*, Dante."

"*Buongiorno?* You haven't spoken to me in weeks and '*buongiorno*' is all you have to say? I thought you were sick!"

"I am."

"Some sickness. You leave Christmas early, my children were so concerned about you. Then weeks go by! That kind of sickness you should head to the hospital!"

She shook the hair off her face, standing tall. "Maybe I am."

His voice dropped, and he placed his hand on her shoulder, his eyes searching hers. "Are you? Really?"

She pressed her lips together for one last shot at defiance but then deflated. "No."

"Then . . . what's going on?"

"I . . . I'm having second thoughts. About you and me."

He smirked. "You assume there's a you and me?"

Eyes flashing, she snapped, "See, this is why we never get anywhere, Dante! Everything is a joke to you!"

He frowned. "That's unfair."

"It's not, though. Our relationship has . . . changed. You *know* it has."

"You mean how you don't hate me anymore?" He winked.

"You don't hate me, either."

He paused. "No. I don't."

"But . . . it's more than that. Isn't it?"

He paused again. As if waiting for her to grin and pull the rug out from under him. But she gazed into his eyes levelly. He slowly said, "It could be."

"Otherwise, why would you invite me for Christmas?"

He stiffened. "Maybe I felt sorry for you."

She turned away and headed for the arch that led out of Santa Lucia.

He put out a hand to stall her. "All right! That's not why."

She stopped, and turned. "And."

"Why do I have to say it?" he grumbled.

"Because we're grown-ups. Not children. We shouldn't shrink from conversations because we're both worried someone will take all our toys away."

"You put it with your usual delicacy."

She smiled, tentatively. "You don't like me for my delicacy."

He shuffled his feet. "I'm not sure I like you at all right now."

"Dante. Don't you see? All this round and round. It's dizzying. We're too old to be dizzy. Let's be happy instead."

He looked at her, surprised. "That doesn't sound like you." He narrowed his eyes. "You've been coached by Chiara, haven't you?"

"No! Well . . . maybe a little," Magda conceded. "She can be very persuasive."

Dante moved closer. He picked up Magda's hand and clasped it between the two of his. He took a breath and said, "You're right. We've been foolish."

"Speak for yourself. *You've* been foolish."

"Magda."

She bit her lip, smiling. "Force of habit."

"There's a lot of habit to overcome. Are you sure it's worth it to try? We've both . . . you know . . . "

He lifted her hand against his chest. "Maybe it's better for us to stay how we are. Neither of us can get hurt while it's only harmless fun."

Magda looked away, over the hills.

Suddenly Dante startled. "Is that why you've been pretending to be sick? You didn't want to be hurt again? Your feelings for me scared you." His hands wrapped around hers, squeezing imperceptibly.

Magda's gaze rested on Dante's face, fixed on hers. Her vision darted to the olive branches waving gently, a visual tinkle of chimes. "I wouldn't use those words. But I won't deny there isn't truth there."

"Oh, Magda. I guess the game between us went on too long. I assumed you knew how I felt. Since that day we accidentally met in Perugia. But, actually, since before then . . . "

"Before then? You had feelings before then?" Magda watched him with a curious mixture of doubt and eagerness.

"I'm not telling you anything until you tell me how long you've been waiting for this moment."

"Ha!"

"*Ma dai*, Magda. If we're changing course, you need to give a little, too."

"Are we, though? Changing course?"

He stroked her cheek, down to her chin, where his thumb lingered. He moved a little closer, his lips brushing hers as he whispered, "I think we already have."

Ava walked into Elisa's studio, carrying a box of blank canvasses.

Elisa dropped her pencil and leaped up. "I can get it."

Ava shook her head. "It's not heavy. Just bulky. Where do you want me to put it?"

Elisa gestured to the corner of the studio where Ale had hung shelves. Ava dropped the box and turned, looking around. "You warm enough in here?"

Elisa gestured to the space heater. "Plenty."

"So how's life in an artist's studio?"

Pressing her lips together in thought, Elisa said, "I like having space to work. Without getting in trouble for leaving marks everywhere."

Ava pursed her lips together. "It's not fair to expect us to clean up after you—"

Elisa held out her hand. "I'm doing the best I can!"

Ava writhed, wanting to say, "Are you, though? It's not complicated to clean brushes..."

Elisa moved back to her chair and Ava drifted closer. "Can I see what you're working on?"

"No."

Ava sighed. "Elisa, I'll see it eventually." She gestured toward the walls. "You put it right there to sell."

Elisa shrugged. "Once I put it up, you won't criticize it."

"I'm not criticizing!"

Elisa looked up at her, her eyes hard.

"I'm not, Elisa! I'm trying to help! Do you want to sell your work or not?"

Using her pencil to tuck her hair behind her ear, Elisa said, "Not if it's not my work. I have to do it my way."

"But some of your work is so *pretty*. Everyone who sees your cheerful landscapes says how much they love them. It's this other kind..." Ava flicked her eyes to a stack of canvases in the corner, stormy with depths of black.

Elisa's jaw set. Ava felt her own jaw set in response. Ava watched the flush creep up Elisa's neck as tears shone in her eyes.

Ava's heart lurched. "Elisa...I've been thinking. Or Ale and I have been thinking, actually."

Elisa looked away and didn't respond.

"There's an art teacher in Girona who—"

Elisa looked up. "An art teacher?"

Ava smiled. "I don't know how good he is, but I asked around and my cousin's neighbor takes lessons with him and likes him." She didn't mention that the art teacher had a soothing effect on her cousin's neighbor. Ale wanted the lessons to support Elisa, but Ava just hoped somebody else could encourage Elisa to express herself in ways that were less...unsettling.

Elisa frowned. "You're doing this so I make prettier art."

"No!" Ava lied.

Elisa shook her head. "Besides, we can't afford that."

"I don't want you to worry about stuff like that. We're fine."

Shaking her head, Elisa said, "I'm not a child."

"You're right." Ava nodded. "You've just had so much worry in your life. I guess I try to spare you."

Elisa rolled a pencil on the table.

"Ale thought we could propose a swap with the teacher. That's what my cousin's neighbor does. Maybe I could do landscaping. Or Ale is getting all that oil from the *frantoio*. Which is going to have your painting on it! Isn't that exciting?"

Elisa sat back, thinking.

"You don't have to, Elisa. I'm not trying to get you to change your art." Ava couldn't help the untruth.

"You couldn't if you wanted to."

Ava smiled tremulously. "I thought maybe it would be fun for you. To learn some techniques or . . . well, I won't pretend I know what I'm talking about."

Elisa grinned. "It wouldn't be a burden? My having lessons? Are you sure?"

Ava felt tears sting her eyes. How could a child so good be so...odd? "I promise. Besides, spring is around the corner. With more tourists, you'll make more sales. We all will."

Elisa mused, "Spring...sure."

Frowning, Ava asked, "What is it?"

"Fatima said she might come home in spring."

"You texted her?"

Elisa shook her head. "FaceTime. Not for long. I tried to ask her about what Sonia said, but she had to get ready for a shoot."

Ava said, "Adolescence is tricky. She'll figure it out." She tried to sound more confident than she felt. When in reality, she imagined drinking and drugs being Elisa's next great move. Standing, Ava said, "Well, I'll let you get back to it."

Elisa nodded, pulling her paper back toward her. She didn't say goodbye as Ava left, her mind absorbed in her hand moving across the paper. Ava turned to ask her to please, please, put her brushes away before she came in. But seeing the hair falling across her daughter's face, the shadows from the single lamp hollowing the area under her cheekbones, she instead closed the door softly behind her.

Pietro unlocked the restaurant, his hands barely able to turn the lock. Tired. He was so tired.

The pasta chef arrived behind him, and together they paced the kitchen, over and over. No flour. Five eggs. And not enough tomatoes for a family's Sunday dinner.

Pietro racked his brain, wondering how their ingredients had walked away. He called Sonia. The phone rang for so long he started preparing to leave a message when she clicked on and snapped, "What?"

"Sonia? It's Babbo." At the lack of response, he said again. "Hello? Can you hear me?"

"I hear you fine."

"Oh. Okay. I didn't . . . okay. Listen, we're out of supplies here. No flour, no eggs, I haven't checked the walk-in but—"

Sonia barked in laughter. "And this is my problem, how?"

"I wondered if you knew what happened."

"Okay. I see. So you don't call to tell me about your *entire other family.* With *my* name all over the place, like some bizarre landmark. My *name.* But you call me when your supplies run low. Thanks. I feel so valued."

"I thought your mother would tell you. She did, didn't she? She must have." Pietro started pacing, making sure he crossed the kitchen in thirteen steps, back and forth.

"Shockingly, she expected *you* to tell me. But since nobody said one word, Leo finally explained it all." She paused. "You are unbelievable."

"I know it's a lot to take in."

She barked in laughter again.

He tried another tack. "Where is Leo?"

"You only now noticed he got a job in Girona?"

"I guess he didn't keep up with the supplies."

Her voice was a tonal eye roll. "I guess not."

"Can you tell me how to order—"

She hung up.

He stared at the phone in his hand and resumed pacing. Somewhere there must be papers, lists with his providers. Invoices maybe? He began throwing open drawers. He didn't have much time . . . the children would arrive this evening.

How could Leo have left him in this lurch? He stood in thought. No, it must have been Sonia who kept the restaurant coasting, this whole time. His daughter, Livia's daughter . . . Sonia had filled in his gaps without him knowing. How odd that having so many Sonias had never confused him before. This must be what happened when the fragile walls that held together the compartments of life crashed around a person.

For so many years he moved within whatever chamber he inhabited and didn't spend any time considering the overlap. Not until now did he consider what those compartments had cost Livia, who had, he realized, raised his children alone. Not until now did he consider what it cost Sonia. His dear Sonia.

His divided house.

His crumbled house.

He should leave. Leave Santa Lucia. He was tired of avoiding Livia. Anytime he caught sight of her wan face, he wanted to die. He should move. But . . . L'Ora Dorata. He had poured himself into the restaurant. Just standing back and watching the restaurant fill with villagers calling over tables, swapping chairs, laughing, ordering another carafe of house wine that he'd chosen to go with the night's specials . . . he *couldn't* abandon it.

He frowned.

He'd sunk too much into the restaurant. He needed to keep it going or he'd drown in debt which wouldn't help Livia. Or any of his children.

He would have to stay. While his children attended school, he'd prepare the restaurant for the evening. He'd be home for his children in the afternoons. He'd have to head back to the *trattoria* most evenings. The younger children would be asleep anyway. He'd make it work.

Somehow, he had to make it work.

He checked his watch.

The children would arrive soon.

Patrizia dusted the cold off her jacket before hanging it on the rack. She breathed in the familiar scent of wax from Bar Birbo's wooden door, almond from the pastries, and the ever-arching scent of grinding beans. Chiara looked up from the La Pavoni and greeted her oldest friend.

Grinning, Patrizia fairly sauntered to the bar.

Reaching for the milk, Chiara said, "You look happy."

"Filamena had the baby last night."

"What!" Chiara yelped. "Already!"

Patrizia nodded placidly, reaching for the sugar. "A week before her due date, but..."

"How's the baby?" Chiara's worried eyes searched Patrizia's face.

"Perfect." Leaning forward, Patrizia said, "Her husband is in that haze of happiness, so in love with his new little girl. So Filamena asked him again about moving to Santa Lucia and he's going to talk to his boss."

The women straightened as the tinkle over the door announced Dante's presence.

"*Caffè*, Chiara," he said, lifting his finger.

She nodded. "You're in early."

"An enormous amount to do," he sighed importantly.

Chiara looked around the bar as she pumped his coffee. "Did Santa Lucia agree to take on the World's Fair or something?"

Chuckling, Dante said, "You got me there, Chiara." Chiara and Patrizia exchanged expressions of wonder as Dante went on, "The thing is, what with Magda and I seeing each other, I haven't been in the office lately. I'm dreading the mountain of paperwork."

Chiara ventured, "I wonder if this is why we've hardly seen Magda."

Dante accepted his *espresso* and shrugged. "That I cannot speak to. Magda is her own woman," he added fondly.

Patrizia smiled. "She is at that."

Turning at the sound of the door, Dante cheered, "And here's Marcello! One of the fine folks keeping this town running while I've enjoyed a bit of a sabbatical."

Patrizia whispered to Chiara, "He's in a good mood."

Chiara waggled her eyebrows, but her grin faltered at Marcello's somber expression. She blurted, "Your mother, is her health—"

"*Sano come un pesce*, Chiara, healthy as a fish. Thanks for asking." He turned his gaze to Dante. "I'm glad you're here. The office hasn't gotten your signature on the election paperwork."

Chiara said, "Election paperwork?"

Dante sipped his coffee, "Arranging for the police officers' presence during the election this spring. But that can wait, surely?"

Marcello scratched the back of his head. "Normally, yes. But since this time you're not running unopposed—"

"What?" Chiara yelped. "Who is running against Dante?"

Marcello's gaze moved from Chiara to Dante to Patrizia. "None of you have heard?"

They shook their heads, Dante's eyes wide.

Muttering almost to himself, Marcello said, "Such a strange situation."

Chiara leaned over the counter. "Marcello! You can't keep us in suspense. Who is running for mayor?"

"Arturo Calugi."

Dante, Chiara, and Patrizia looked at each other for a few dumbfounded seconds before they burst into peals of laughter.

Chiara said, "*Arturo*? Marcello, are you sure? The man has never shown an interest in local politics."

Patrizia said, "That's unfair, Chiara. You know how upset he gets about the *posta*'s hours when he forgets to pick up his check."

Chiara burst into fresh laughter.

Dante smirked. "What is that fellow on about? Does he hope that as mayor he'll have access to better gossip?"

Marcello slumped onto a stool. "I wouldn't brush this off. He came in crowing about his outside backing."

Dante grinned, eyes flashing. "I'll head in and sign the paperwork. And make my way through whatever else is waiting for me in that pile.

No doubt George Clooney is looking to build a villa on the edge of town, in the earthquake zone. Or a villager is requesting an ordinance to ban eating pizza with a fork." He laughed at his good humor.

Marcello shook his head, "But he said there's a fool-proof strategy—" He stopped as Dante's hand came down on his shoulder.

"You worry too much," Dante clinched. "Mark my words. This is Arturo's newest ploy for attention."

The days turned unseasonably warm, the sun drawing villagers outside. Once again, neighbors paused outside Giovanni's *alimentari* or Paola's *fruttivendolo* to swap recipes and gossip and opinions, particularly about the weather. Thoughts turned toward spring, coming around the turn of the next calendar page. Spring, when the *gelateria* would open again, when outdoor tables would be filled with men playing *scopa*, when the streets would fill with the buoyant greetings of friends and neighbors.

Fabrizio stopped Enrico and Carla as they made their way to Giuseppe's to buy chicken sausages for lunch. "Have you seen Isotta?"

Carla stiffened and Enrico shook his head and said, "We've barely arrived. She's coming for lunch in about an hour. Do you want us to pass along a message?"

Carla wound her arms through Enrico's and beamed up at him.

Fabrizio bounced on his toes as he said, "I'll try her house. I have excellent news. Excellent!"

Enrico nodded seriously. "Isotta could use good news."

Carla's grip on his arm tightened. "What do you mean?"

Enrico startled and looked from Fabrizio to Carla. "Oh, you know. The usual. Money. Being a single-parent. I can't imagine it's easy."

Fabrizio nodded. "I feel for her." His face brightened. "But at least the financial piece might get a *tiny* bit easier." He leaned forward confidentially.

"I showed her book to my agent, who walked it over to a colleague who specializes in children's books. She's certain she can sell it."

Enrico gripped Fabrizio's arm. "Oh, please find her."

Fabrizio nodded gleefully. "Don't tell anyone, okay?"

Enrico assured them they wouldn't.

The couple watched Fabrizio lope up the street and make a left into the alley lined with waxy green *hosta* plants.

"Good for her. Oh, *good* for her." Enrico sighed to himself. Grinning from ear to ear, he added, "And you know, even though she won't make much, imagine what a boost this will be!"

Carla frowned until his gaze turned to her. Then she put on a dazzling smile. "Lucky girl! She's been wanting this *forever*."

His face regained a measure of implacability. "*Allora*, not forever."

"True, that's true." Carla considered. "Only since you gave her the idea. What a friend you've been to the poor duck."

He put his hands in his pockets and grinned slightly in thought.

"I can't help but wonder, though, if she'll drop the charade. Now that she's gotten what she wants."

The grin left Enrico's face as if it had never been.

"Charade?"

Carla put her hand on her chest. "I've said too much, haven't I? I never learned to keep my mouth shut. Ever since I was little, the truth spills out, even when it makes things uncomfortable."

"What truth? What charade?" Enrico's gaze met hers with urgency.

Carla sighed and said with reluctance, "It's just...when we had our coffee, she let something slip. I'm sure it was supposed to be in confidence. You know how women are when we get together. The walls drop and we confide *all* our secrets." At Enrico's continued stare, Carla went on. "Oh, darling, it's nothing that awful, don't look so serious! We were gabbing about men and she mentioned how *handsome* Massimo was, it made it hard to see *you* as a romantic partner. She said something so funny about that, but I can't remember what it was . . . " Carla screwed her face in thought. "Oh! Right! She said your personality was as somber as your visage. Isn't she clever? Such a way with words!" Carla laughed.

Enrico did not.

Carla went on. "I teased her, you know how good-humored I am, until she said that you did have your uses. I had no idea how helpful you'd been to her! You quite undersold it. She said it was worth your hangdog expressions—was that the word? I might have that wrong, don't quote me—for all the *assistance* you've given her."

"She's been . . . using me?"

Carla frowned. "Darling, don't take it personally. I'm sure she didn't mean it that way. Let's not blame her for being mercenary. At some level, aren't we all? I know you and I wouldn't have gotten together if you hadn't needed me to get you into meetings with the head of the department." Her laugh tinkled once more.

Enrico's gaze drifted up the street, where Fabrizio had disappeared. He ran his hand over his forehead. "I thought we were friends."

Laying a sympathetic hand on his arm, Carla said, "You *are*, darling. Good friends! That's what I'm *saying*. You just use the friendship for your own needs. You pity her, so taking care of her makes you feel good about yourself. She enjoys your attention and having your support. Really, are the two of you so different? If anybody is using anybody, you are using *her*. Which isn't fair, if you think about it. You should find new ways to feel like a generous person."

He shook his head.

Carla said as if realizing for the first time, "Gosh, I hope this doesn't make lunch awkward!"

He turned and trudged down the street. "It won't. It doesn't matter."

But the light in his face had gone out.

Carla bit her lip with suppressed merriment even as she put her arm around him for solace.

"Antonella, *ciao!*" Ale called, rushing down Via Romana.

She gritted her teeth and turned to face Ale.

He stopped running when he reached her. "I didn't think I'd catch you!" Catching sight of her serious face, he said, "What's the matter?"

She attempted a smile. "Nothing, I'm fine! *Che c'è?*"

He shook his head with a grin. "I wanted to thank you."

"Thank me?" Antonella's guard dropped, and her face moved in its usual fluid lines.

Laughing, Ale said, "Yes! I spoke with Tommaso, and he told me that you'd suggested using the *castello* on the oil tins."

"Oh, that."

"Yes, *that!*" Ale grinned. "You have no idea what a help you've been."

"Sure I do. Tommaso told me sales are up."

"No, I mean a help to *me.*"

Antonella stared at him. "Oh. No, you're right, I didn't know that."

"Well, maybe I'm getting ahead of myself, maybe being the featured image on more widely distributed olive oil won't lead to anything, but it feels like a step in the right direction." He smiled and added, "Tommaso couldn't say enough about how helpful you were. You must be learning a lot at that company you work for."

"A ton."

Ale waited for more, but at the lack of give, he pressed on. "Do you work with a lot of food producers?"

"No." At his confused look, Antonella added, "I'm not given a lot of responsibility at work."

"Oh. Well, you must have a lot of talent then."

"I don't know about that, but I have a lot of ideas."

He smiled. "I bet that—"

She didn't look as if she'd heard him as her words found a rhythm.

"What I wish I could do is combine my strategy work for the *frantoio* with other suppliers. To create a way for people coming to our area to learn about history through our food production."

Ale frowned, trying to keep up. "Like a tour group or something?"

She laughed. "Not exactly. I'm picturing a packet of promotional materials we could distribute to tour guides. Or bloggers, or really anyone. We just need some way to accumulate and distribute information about all local producers with traditional roots."

"Like the *castello*."

She smiled authentically for the first time. "I can't wait to try your wine."

"I wouldn't get too excited," he said. "So your idea, how do you keep bad producers out?"

She shrugged. "I'm not sure. But I know enough producers myself to get that ball rolling. There's the cheese farm over the hill . . . you've had their pecorino?"

"Extraordinary," he said, but Ale's eyes suggested his mind ran in another direction.

She mused aloud, "Saffron, of course. Lentils. Trevi's black celery. I don't know how to include festivals, but that would be . . . " Her words trailed off at the sight of Ale's stark expression. "Ale, are you okay?"

He clutched her arm and she couldn't suppress her flinch.

"Antonella, you've given me an idea."

Isotta finished tucking the children into bed and tiptoed down the stairs. Ava turned from making tea and said, "Asleep?"

Isotta nodded, flopping into a chair. "Hopefully. You never can tell. Margherita still gets those nightmares. And Jacopo is cutting another tooth."

"Which one?"

"Upper right."

Ava laughed. "Oh, he's going to look ridiculous. One tooth in the bottom center and now this."

Isotta smiled. "I know. Ready the cameras."

Ava shook her head and murmured with unfocused eyes, "That sweet, sweet little boy."

Cocking her head to the side, Isotta said, "Ava? Do you and Ale ever think about—"

"Oh!" Ava blurted. "Did I tell you about how much Elisa is loving her studio?"

Isotta considered her friend for a moment as she took a sip of her tea. "You didn't need to. Elisa came by after school today. Covered with paint and grinning ear to ear."

Ava nodded, crossing her legs and leaning back. "Ale's genius move."

Isotta shook her head. "Definitely." Isotta let her mind wander as the women sat in companionable silence. "How is Ale? I feel as if I've hardly seen him."

Ava put down her cup. "Neither have I. He's got some new idea, and he's been working non-stop. I have a picture of what he was like in his New York days."

Isotta frowned. "App or *castello*?"

Ava shrugged. "He won't tell me. Since he's in front of his computer, I'm guessing app, but he could be doing some strategy for the *castello*." Ava sipped her tea. "I saw Enrico. By the way."

"Today?" Isotta's voice scaled up.

"No, but nice job keeping your crush under wraps." Ava grinned. "When he was here with Carla."

"Oh."

"Isotta. You need to tell him how you feel."

"I did!"

"Months ago! And you *hinted*, you didn't tell."

Isotta set her jaw. "What's changed since then? It's not as if I've grown more irresistible..." At Ava's frown of protest, Isotta added, "This is not me selling myself short. He's not gotten any more single. And my complicated life has not grown more attractive to outsiders."

Ava thought for a moment. "Where could the money be?"

Isotta sighed. "I wonder that every day. Riccardo is researching offshore accounts, but I can't picture Anna setting up something like that. My guess is she gave it to a relative for safekeeping."

"And that person isn't coming forward to help you now?"

Isotta shrugged. "It's only a guess."

Ava thought. "I still think you should tell Enrico."

"Did you not listen to me—"

"I heard you!"

"Shhhh! You'll wake the children," Isotta smiled.

Ava grumbled. "I heard you. But you don't see how he looks at you. I think he's still in love with you. But he feels too bad cutting Carla off. Especially if he's not sure you still like him."

Isotta shook her head. "Ava, you are like an incurable romantic crossed with a sixth-grade girl. Relationships don't work that way. Enrico is with Carla now. I have to accept it."

"Well, no offense, Isotta, but you are doing a crummy job of accepting it."

"*Ma dai.*"

"You deserve more than this! You deserve to find happiness! After what happened with Massimo, you deserve a man like Enrico."

"Maybe later." She smiled at her friend. "For now, I'll be glad that my best friend, who also deserves happiness, found it."

Ava scowled, grumbling. Then her face cleared. "The book though."

Isotta grinned. "The book, yes."

"When do you meet with the agent?"

"I did. Over Skype. Last week."

"What! And you didn't tell me?" At the look on Isotta's face, Ava said, "I'm sorry. I know it's hard to juggle everything. I'm just . . . what happened?"

"It went well. She sent me a contract and I've forwarded it to Riccardo."

"Wow!"

"It's not money, you know that right, Ava? This contract stipulates how much the agent will get if she sells the book to a publisher."

"Isotta." Ava shook her head. "I can't believe I've been yammering on, and you have this wonderful thing happening!"

"To be honest, it doesn't feel real at all. So remembering to talk about it is like remembering a dream."

"The sleep deprivation probably doesn't help."

"No," Isotta agreed.

Ava sipped the last of her tea. "Okay, but the minute you get an offer from a publisher, the minute it happens, I want to know about it."

Isotta smiled. "Deal. But Ava, this is only for fun. The agent said it herself, children's authors make little if anything. The money is still running out."

"Between Luciano and me, we can take the children . . . "

Isotta shook her head. "No, you need the freedom to be outside when the weather is good. And Luciano can't keep up with two children. Maybe for an hour, but with the tantrums Margherita has been having lately . . . I'm going to have to put them in nursery."

"Leave them?"

"I don't see another way. I talked to the bank, they're willing to hire me, but they don't do part-time."

"Leave them *full-time*?"

Isotta's eyes welled with tears. She said again, "I don't see another way. Thinking of it, though . . . " she lifted a hand to her heart.

Ava murmured, "I know. I can't believe this is where we are."

Leo sipped his coffee. It had been so long since he'd crossed Bar Birbo's threshold, he had to struggle against the old awkwardness. Or maybe it wasn't the old awkwardness so much as the darting eyes and stiff body language of the other customers—undoubtedly curious about how he'd taken the news of his father's betrayal. That must be it, because as the last villager left the bar, Leo noticed his awkwardness vanish. He leaned toward Edo. "I'm guessing you heard."

Edo turned to him, relieved that Leo took a direct approach. Nowadays, Edo found pretending to ignore the unsaid thing to be increasingly complicated. "I didn't want to bring it up . . ."

Leo shrugged. "Better out then buried."

Edo nodded in thought. "It must have been a shock. Your father, he doesn't seem the Casanova type."

"Definitely a surprise." Leo cocked his head. "Though it explains a lot. He's always distracted, especially when he's out of the kitchen. Plus, I'm sure you've noticed all his nervous counting and touching."

Edo considered. "How does that relate?"

"I'm not sure. But I think he always felt on the verge of losing control." Leo shrugged. "Maybe all those tics made him feel as if he was controlling something."

Edo smiled. "You almost sound sorry for him."

"Do I?" Leo frowned. "I'm not. He did this to himself. To all of us."

Edo hesitated. "I'm sorry it's meant you've moved to Girona."

Nodding, Leo said, "Me, too."

"But things are good with your girlfriend?"

Leo's smile was so broad, Edo couldn't help but grin. "Better than one would expect, given that she's a vegetarian."

"A vegetarian! And yet you're still seeing her?"

He laughed. "I even met her family."

Edo suppressed a grin and said, tentatively, "Just the one?"

Leo stopped for a moment before throwing his head back and laughing. Wiping his eyes, he said, "Yes, my slacker girlfriend only has one family."

"Why the lack of effort?"

"I know, right?"

"Whew." Edo grinned. "I thought it might be too soon."

Leo shook his head with a smile. "Never. Not with me. Laughing makes it easier."

Edo nodded. He picked up the discarded cups and saucers and stacked them in the sink. "So, have you met them? Your father's other kids?"

Leo shook his head. "No. He sent Sonia and me an email, saying the kids moved in with him. He wants us to come by." He stopped suddenly, "Have *you* met them?"

Edo said carefully, "Just Nia."

"Nia?"

"Sonia." He paused. "She goes by Nia, apparently."

Leo turned the word over in his mouth. "Nia. Stupid name."

Edo nodded noncommittally.

Softly Leo said, "My poor sister."

As if summoned, Sonia pushed open the door. She stopped when she saw Leo at the bar. Then they rushed toward each other, a blur of words, of tears, of tension released as laughter. He grabbed her hand and then pulled her toward the bar. "Edo, *un caffè* for my sister. With a dash of *forza*."

Edo nodded, turning to grind the beans.

As he pressed the water through the La Pavoni, he heard Sonia say to Leo. "How's Mamma?"

Leo shrugged. "About the same."

"Of course." She shook her head and then smiled at Edo as she accepted the coffee. "Can you believe Babbo didn't even tell me?"

"I can. Turns out he's a huge coward."

"The hugest." She stirred sugar into her coffee. "I thought for sure Mamma would already have left Santa Lucia."

Leo paused. "I think that's why she wants to talk to us today. She doesn't want to leave looking ashamed or guilty."

"Right! He's the one who should go!"

"But the *trattoria*," Leo shrugged. "How can he? You did the books for him. You know how much money he sank into it."

Sonia grumbled her response.

After a few moments of quiet, she said, "You don't think she'll go back to him. Do you?"

Leo laughed. "Mamma? With all her pride? No way."

Sonia said, "I think she loves him though. No matter how weird both of them got, it always seemed as if she loved him."

Leo shook his head. "Love won't be enough to see her through this one. It's over."

Isotta and Ava rushed toward each other, hands outstretched, their families riding in their wakes.

Ava spoke first. "You got the call."

"Yes."

"What do you think?" Ava tried for a jocular tone. "Found or dead?"

"Oh, Ava . . . "

Ava shook her head irritably. "I'm sorry. After so long, it's surreal."

"I know."

They gazed steadily at each other with wide eyes. Ale left Ava's parents and sidled up to Luciano. "Do you know anything?"

Luciano shook his head. "The police called and asked her to come in. That's all."

Ale nodded and asked. "The children?"

Luciano's eyes never left the two women still holding hands in the *piazza*. "With my brother." Luciano looked around. "Where's Elisa?"

Ale didn't seem to have heard.

"Ale... Elisa? Does she know? That we may find out what happened to her father?"

Ale shook his head. "She's at her art lesson. In Girona."

Luciano nodded and said without thinking, "She loves those lessons..." The women were moving now, hand in hand, into the police station. The families followed.

The chief waited in the doorway. He nodded, his face serious. Ava tried to read his expression, but his eyes merely flicked to each family member entering the station.

"Follow me," he said, leading the way to the conference room. Everyone hurried to settle and turn their attention to the chief. Who cleared his throat. "As you have no doubt surmised, we have some news. About Massimo." He hesitated, looking around the room, commanding attention he already had. "His body has been found."

At the questioning murmur, the chief held up his hand. "I regret to inform you that he is dead."

Dead!

How could something so inevitable feel so shocking?

Savia's voice rose above the noises of disbelief. "When? When was he... the body... found?" She put an arm around her daughter as she waited for the chief to answer.

"Yesterday. The body... it must have drifted for all these months. It washed up in Greece."

Greece!

Ava hesitated. "How can you be sure it's him?"

The chief said, "I don't think you need to concern yourself with grisly details. You can trust us to—"

Luciano's quiet voice boomed throughout the room. "Answer the question."

The chief, unused to interruption, mumbled. "His watch . . . "

Ava shook her head. "He could have given his watch to someone. How about dental records?"

The chief chuckled knowingly. "I'm afraid you've been watching too many crime dramas. We don't need dental records. The size of the body, the remaining hair, the scraps of clothes . . . *plus* the watch."

All eyes stared at him.

Savia said, "Check the dental records."

The chief glared. "It's not necessary. He's dead. It's over."

Luciano said, "You would be surprised."

The chief shook his head, frustrated. "Isotta, you are the next of kin. Do you insist on—"

"I do." She smiled tremulously. "Dead isn't dead around here. I want to sleep at night. Knowing. Knowing he won't show up at my house."

Ava took her hand and squeezed.

Dead.

Snatches of memory swirled through the room. Savia remembered Massimo as a teenager, wheeling Giulia on a scooter through town. Luciano remembered Massimo and Giulia telling him and his late wife about the new baby, the baby she was carrying when she died. Ava remembered his hungry eyes for a brief moment before she shivered and forced herself to think about other things. Ale saw her tremble and remembered his first sighting of Massimo, striding through the streets of Santa Lucia, the very picture of a purposeful life. Isotta remembered . . . so much. She remembered their lunch together in Rome. She remembered the first time he touched her. She remembered longing for his affection as he turned away. She remembered him forcing her to dye her hair and dress like Giulia. She remembered him standing up to her parents, saying the things she'd never been able to say. She remembered his face in the lamplight as he found her laboring in the dark recesses of the castle. She remembered his strong arms around her as he pulled her up, lifting her, carrying her as if flying up the ladder, into the air again. She remembered his face when he first held his son. She remembered his disdain as he handed the baby to her, her shirt wet with milk. She remembered when he whispered to Jacopo, calling him by a name not his own. She remembered him adjusting Margherita's hat at the park, her eyes on him wide and adoring. She remembered the look on his face as he said goodbye that last time. His face smug as he nodded, turned, and stepped out of Luciano's house, out onto the street, his arm curved around their baby.

She put her head on her folded arms.

And wept.

SPRING POPPIES, SWALLOWS RETURN

*T*he rain began.

Softly at first, a lover's touch.

Then harder. More insistent.

Relentless.

Bar Birbo filled with farmers, unable to work on their land. Watching, helpless, as water soaked their world. Women stood in windows, reluctant to head into the damp that would wreak havoc on their hair. Finally, style be damned, they threw on kerchiefs or plastic hoods and tumbled forward, into the street. The fear of being behind the gossip curve worse than the fear of appearing disheveled. They too filled the bar, patting their hair as they swapped stories on Dante's refusal to take Arturo's run for mayor seriously and his surprisingly logical relationship with Magda. On Enrico's discovery of a brief Nazi presence in Santa Lucia. On Ale's unlikely friendship with Bruno and Tomasso, both of whom were seen having dinner at the *castello*. On Isotta's getting an agent to sell her children's books. On Elisa's t-shirts, which had somehow become a hot item, with people asking every shop keeper in Santa Lucia where to find them.

And most of all, on Massimo.

Dead.

Which *most* people believed, but not all.

Weather couldn't keep villagers away from the opportunity to chat about news, small and large. As the rain grew steadily, achingly, more bruising. The pummeling water seeped through any umbrellas sturdy enough to stay right-side-up in a wind that made a mockery of them, tossing them up and into another alley, like a predator batting about a small animal. Turning life into a toy. A plaything. So went the safety of umbrellas. Skittering down another alley, with another villager in hot pursuit.

Ava opened the door and tried to smile in greeting. "Luciano. Thank you for coming."

He nodded, tapping his umbrella on the step before entering. "Of course, *cara*. You've told her?"

Ava shook her head. "She never talks about the kidnapping. Or him. I . . . I don't know how she feels about him. I wanted to wait for you."

He nodded.

Ava hesitated. "Elisa swings between two states since she's been back. Either she's deep into her drawings, which have these flashes of peace about them but are mostly . . . dark." Luciano nodded as he removed his jacket. "Or she's irritable. With me, anyway. She seems perfectly fine with everybody else."

"I imagine you're the riskiest person to connect to."

Turning to put the moka on for coffee, she asked, "What do you mean?"

He shrugged and sat at the table. "The stakes are simply higher."

Turning, Ava crossed her arms over her chest as she leaned against the counter. "He won't say it, but Ale thinks I'm too hard on her."

"Are you?" The words flew out, swift and sure.

She dropped her head. "Maybe. I try not to be. But it's as if I can see the two paths in front of her, happiness or misery. I have to put her feet on the right road."

He shrugged. "Elisa is Elisa. She's always saved herself."

Ava blinked back tears, taking two cups down from the cabinet. "Isn't that my job?"

"*Cara...*" Luciano murmured. "You can't rescue her from her journey."

"Her life has been so hard. When I think of it all—the abuse, the abandonment, the kidnapping. Plus, my giving her up to start," her voice throbbed. She put her hand up to forestall Luciano's words. "Whether I had a choice doesn't matter. It happened. Isn't that all too much for a person? I set it all in motion, shouldn't I fix it?"

He shook his head and pushed his overlarge glasses up his nose. "I suspect trying to fix it may only entrench it. She's an adolescent. She'll do the opposite of what her parents want." He grinned. "No matter how well-intentioned the parent."

Pouring the coffee, Ava said, "I don't think I'll ever learn how to do this. I suppose I should be glad I only have the one child." Her voice crackled with pain.

Luciano murmured, "We, none of us, know how to do this. Parenting. Living. We take it one step at a time."

"That's pretty profound, there, Luciano." Ava eked out a grin.

"It is," he nodded. "It's something I learned from Elisa. Long ago. Her core is strong, Ava. You'll need to trust it."

Ava sighed. "I guess there's no use putting this off. I'll get her." She didn't notice how her hair had fallen from its customary knot at the base of her neck. The rubber band, forsaken on the floor.

The sound of rain filled the kitchen as Ava dashed to the studio to collect Elisa.

Luciano waited. He stared at the rubber band, stark on the buff-colored stone. As the wind howled up through the valley, Luciano tipped his head back, closing his eyes.

Elisa grumbled as she shook off the rain, but she brightened when she spotted Luciano. "Maestro! What are you doing here?"

Ava interceded. "Do you want some coffee, Elisa?"

"Coffee?" Elisa looked suspicious. "You never let me have coffee."

Ava poured a cup and set it in front of Elisa, pushing the milk and sugar containers closer. Darting a quick look at Luciano, who nodded, Ava pulled up a chair close to Elisa. "Elisa. I have some news. About your . . . about Massimo."

Elisa straightened and with a strangled voice said, "What about him?"

Ava closed her eyes. "They found him. He passed away."

Elisa sagged against her chair. "He's dead?"

Tightening her lips, Ava whispered. "Yes. He is."

Elisa dropped her head into her hands, her shoulders trembling. Just as Ava reached for her, Elisa picked up her head, her face pale. "Am I supposed to be sad?"

Ava's eyes pleaded with Luciano. He leaned toward Elisa and said, "You could be. Or you could be angry, remembering what he did to you and your brother and sister. Or you might be happy to not worry about him coming back. Or you might feel nothing."

Elisa snorted. "I never feel nothing."

Ava's eyes widened.

Luciano went on, "My dear, there is no doubt that Massimo's passing leaves us all with a complicated series of reactions. None of them are wrong."

Elisa studied her hands, gripping one another. She looked up, "Can I go now?"

Ava started. "You don't want to talk about it?"

Standing, Elisa said, "I'm in the middle of a painting." She strode out the door.

Ava pressed her head into her arms, folded on the table. She dragged her hands down her face as she sat up and looked at Luciano. She whispered, "You see what I mean?"

Isotta tensed at the sound that was almost a knock. She waited. The sound echoed again, more assertive this time.

Her heart beat in her chest. She wondered if she would always have this reaction. Or if, when the dental records came through, she'd finally stop imagining Massimo at the door, stymied by the knob not turning, then swearing when his key didn't fit in the lock. Knocking, then pounding at the door.

Jacopo turned in his sleep.

The small motion prompted Isotta to fly to the front door. She knew it couldn't be Massimo. She *knew* it. And yet she couldn't help but peer through the peephole with hesitation.

Darkness. Only a shadowy figure. Tall. Restless.

Trying to control her heartbeat, she took an unsure breath and flicked on the outdoor light. A glare flooded the doorstep. She blinked, flinching away from the peephole before her eyes adjusted and she leaned closer.

She exhaled. And threw open the door.

"Enrico. What are you doing here? So late?"

"Did I wake the children?"

She shook her head.

He crossed his arms over his chest, let them fall, then put them on his hips. She watched his awkwardness, stepping back to allow him to enter.

Three steps into the house and he stopped, watching her.

Tired now, she indicated he should take a seat in the living room.

He waited.

She sat down on the couch, and he sat beside her, leaving a gaping space between them.

Quietly she said, "What's going on?" Her mind clamped, and she yelped under her breath, "Luciano?"

He took her hand. "Everyone is fine. I got here a few hours ago. Did you hear about the bullet holes my father found behind the paintings and postcards Luciano had hung all over the house?" She shook her head, confused, and he went on, "Luciano had done it so long ago, he'd forgotten why. I suppose we all figured it was Luciano being Luciano. Anyway, Luciano called me as soon as he found them . . . it's a sign that the Jews and other refugees were caught, information I need to fit with the puzzle."

"Enrico, this is all very interesting. But it's been a long day. Can you tell me about it in the morning? I promise I'll make a much more receptive audience."

He shook his head in annoyance. "I'm sorry, I wanted to explain why I'm here, but that's irrelevant. The point is . . . Luciano told me. About Massimo. And I had to see how you are. I knew I should wait until tomorrow. Really, I shouldn't be here at all, knowing what I know," he added with a tinge of bitterness. "But I found myself at your door before I even realized."

Isotta nodded. "Where's Carla?"

He cocked his head to the side. "Carla? She's in Urbino. Why?"

"I guess I wondered if she'd be behind you."

"No," he said, his voice tinged with ice. "I'm glad you two are great friends now, but tonight it's just me."

"Great friends?" She shrugged helplessly. "I don't know what you're talking about. But I don't know anything anymore."

He shook his head. "It doesn't matter. It's a conversation for another day. Right now, I only want to know how you're taking the news."

Her eyes searched his, and she sounded out the words tumbling in her head. "I know I should be relieved. What he did . . . to Ava . . . to the children . . ."

"To you," Enrico said softly.

"To me. Yes . . . and I am. Relieved." She drew in a ragged breath. He put his hand on hers as she struggled to find her next words. At the touch, Isotta began to cry. "But I'm so *sad*. At the tragedy of it all. Massimo...I can't help thinking of him at Jacopo's age. Innocent. His mother...you know the story..."

"Parts of it."

Isotta sighed. Relieved that she didn't have to say the words that turned her stomach.

"I don't know if that happened. It's hard to imagine anybody doing that to a child."

"But we know he did it to Ava."

"Yes." She shook her head. "As much as I hate to believe him, or I guess hated to believe him..." She gulped as she realized she had to change the tense. "His mother messed with him. If all that hadn't happened...maybe he would have been a good person. Maybe he wouldn't have died alone. In water surrounded by fire."

Enrico put a hand on her shoulder as she dropped her head.

"What a waste. What a terrible, terrible waste. We each get one life and she doomed his. Because of that, my children won't ever know their father. All they have is me, and I can't..." Her voice shook as she looked up at with eyes wide and frightened. "I can't ever be enough. I can't hold it together all by myself. I've been snapping at Margherita. Tonight, she wouldn't eat her dinner and I yelled and it freaked her out, and that freaked Jacopo out. It was horrible."

Enrico's jaw worked as he listened.

"Who knows how much I'm wounding her, both of them? Jacopo doesn't understand, but he knows when things are loud and scary." Isotta looked at Enrico, tears streaking her face, "What if I doom them?"

"Hey," he said with the ghost of a smile. "You will not doom them. All parents yell at their children from time to time."

"But I *know* better!"

"It's not about knowing, Isotta. Yelling isn't a strategy, it's a reaction."

He paused. "Then what happened? Tonight?"

She shrugged. "I held them both. I apologized. I realized they were both exhausted, so I gave them a long bath with bubbles and read extra stories and tucked them in early."

"You see?"

"See what?" She ran her hand across her eyes.

"What kind of ruinous parent apologizes, then looks to find reason, and then solves the problem?"

She stared at her hand, clasped in Enrico's. She hadn't even noticed he'd taken it. "It's so much responsibility. What if I can't do it?"

"Hey." He tentatively put his hand on her chin, lifting her face so she had to look him in the eyes. "It's normal to doubt. But those children are lucky to have you."

Tears reformed in her eyes.

He wiped them away with the soft pads of his thumbs. "As for Massimo. It *is* tragic. We don't always get the lives we deserve."

She closed her eyes briefly.

He said softly, "You'll be okay, Isotta."

She pulled her lower lip inward and nodded.

He smiled and leaned to kiss her cheek, right as she blinked. When her eyes opened, she saw his face approaching and with jackhammering heart moved to meet his lips with her own.

At the touch, a wild current raced through her. She felt him hesitate before pressing against her. Her hands felt more like light than substance as she lifted them, winding them around his neck, letting her fingers run through his thick hair.

He groaned and wrapped his arms around her, pulling her against his chest and turning her so she found herself straddling him. His hands ran up her back and down her waist, fluttering, holding her close.

Her entire being, her entire consciousness lost, lost to the moment. She could only feel his lips on hers, those gorgeously full lips— so soft, so luxurious, yet so insistent. Hungry for her.

She gasped as his hands drifted under her blouse, touching her waist.

With trembling fingers, she felt for the buttons on his shirt, kissing him with an abandon she'd never known. She touched his chest, and he groaned again. His fingers stroked her sides, her belly, finding their way up, up within her shirt. She worked another button free, and another, and ran her hands over the definitions of his chest.

His breathing fast now, he began lifting her blouse over her head. She trembled, already feeling their bare chests against each other. The magnetic heat, sated but not sated.

She leaned back to allow him to lift the shirt.

His hands stilled.

She opened her eyes and found him staring. With eyes wide and unfocused, as if coming out of a spell. "What are we doing?" he whispered.

She placed her hands on his cheeks and brought his face toward her own.

He turned his head, gulping air. "No. Isotta. We can't do this. We're both dating people. We can't get . . . swept up this way."

She hesitated in her confusion and ran her fingers down his exposed chest, and back up to his chin, where she traced his mouth. "I am? That's news to me."

"Tommaso."

She shook her head.

He put his hands on her waist and she smiled, anticipating his touch again, but he lifted her and placed her beside him. "Anyway, there's Carla."

Her hands clasped on her lap and she stared at her interlaced fingers. They moved convulsively, empty of his touch. "Carla."

"Yes, Carla." His voice acrid, he added. "You remember. My girlfriend."

"You kissed *me*!"

"On the cheek!"

"I didn't know that! Your aim is terrible!"

They stared at each other for a moment, and then looked away, chuckling. He said, "Or maybe my aim is just right. I won't lie, Isotta, I've been wanting to touch you like that since the day I met you. I guess that got loose somehow. But it can't happen again."

"Why?" Isotta asked.

"*Why?* Isn't it obvious?"

"If you still feel like that about me, shouldn't we be together?"

"It's not that simple."

"Why?" She asked again.

"First of all, that's unfair to Carla."

"Right. *Carla.*"

He ignored her tone. "Second of all, I know how you feel about me. This isn't real. This is your grief running away with you. Looking for distraction."

She stared at him. "You don't know anything."

He looked at her steadily. "I won't be the thing you want because you can't have it. I care about you, but I won't be played with that way."

She shook her head. His words made no sense.

He rose to leave, buttoning his shirt. "I'm sorry . . . for everything."

She shook her head again, staring at her hands.

He said gently. "I'll see myself out."

She nodded and watched him leave, closing the door behind him.

"He's *dead*?" Fatima's face loomed closer until Elisa could only see the top of her head. She pulled the phone back as if to maneuver Fatima into focus. "Oh, Elisa. I'm . . . shoot. I'm stuck. 'Sorry' seems kinda the wrong word."

"Anyway. I promised to tell you. You're probably busy, so . . . "

"Elisa! Holy smokes! I'm not too busy for this, and if I were . . . this is more important. This is . . . *everything*." Elisa heard the sadness throbbing in her friend's voice.

"Well, there's not more to say, honestly. He's gone," Elisa frowned. "I guess I don't have to worry about that monster leaping out of my closet ever again. But he's, you know . . . my father."

"Oh, Elisa." Fatima's face adjusted until she filled the frame.

Elisa shook her head. "So what's new with you? You taking . . . care of yourself?"

Fatima rolled her eyes. "I assume that's code for asking if I'm partying?"

Elisa blinked.

"Look, it's not easy. Not that I thought it would be nothing, but it's harder than I imagined." Her voice grew small and Elisa imagined the millions of miles between Santa Lucia and Tokyo. "They put these clothes on me and order me to twist this way and that and complain that my face is all wrong, my collarbone doesn't jut out enough, blah blah blah, until . . ." She shook her head.

"You're in the room again. That little one. With the smoke."

Fatima exhaled. "I should have known you'd get it."

Elisa shrugged.

Fatima's lip quivered. "I don't know what to do."

"Come back."

"I can't."

"Why not?"

Fatima shook her head. "I just can't. I can't let everyone down. I've already failed Valentina. She had all these high hopes for me. Then I get kicked out of Dubai. Sent packing to Tokyo."

Elisa chuckled. "Like Carosello."

Fatima's grin wavered. "Yes, I suppose so. Like Carosello." She laughed at the image. "I *am* trying. My Instagram profile has tons of followers. But anyone who hires me for actual work ends up complaining that I freeze too easily."

"Can you just model on Instagram?"

"That doesn't pay. I post to drum up interest, so I'm seen as a desirable commodity. But at this point," her voice reached an artificial level of cheer, "I fear my reputation precedes me."

Elisa chewed her fingernail. "Will you get kicked out of Tokyo?"

Fatima shrugged. "If I don't 'redouble my efforts'."

The words rang familiar to Elisa, but she couldn't remember where from. "Do you want to? Redouble them, I mean?"

Fatima shook her head, the frame tilting for a moment. "Kind of. I'd like to not fail. That would be a bonus."

Elisa snorted.

Fatima went on, "But maybe you're right. It would be better to come home."

Elisa thought for a moment. "To Santa Lucia?"

"No. I couldn't, with my parents in Milan now. But ... my tutor said I'm ready to take the college entrance exams."

"So fast!"

Fatima shrugged and tried not to look too pleased with herself. "The other girls, I don't connect with them. I thought I could by partying, I thought I'd find a way to fit in. But it turns out, partying is just another smoky room. Especially the next day. The next day is the worst. So I've been studying. More than I've been working, unfortunately."

"College. Wow. I'm not even in high school yet."

Fatima laughed, "Well, neither am I, really. Anyway, I'm sitting for the exams next week."

"In Tokyo?"

"They have places foreigners can go. My tutor set it up. After that, I guess I need to figure out if I should keep trying to make modeling work."

"But Fatima ... do you *like* it? The modeling?"

"Sometimes. I love it here, in Tokyo, for sure. It's exciting with all the lights and the food is so interesting and the culture is ... wow. But modeling ... when I hit a groove, I like it, but it takes a *lot* to hit that groove—the right job, clothes that don't bunch around my neck, a gentle photographer. When I'm just taking photos with one of my roommates, that's fun, even though we aren't close. Maybe because I can do it how I want. And I like taking photos, too. I can see the world through your eyes or something." She shook her head. "I don't know. It took so much to get my parents to let me do this. Shouldn't I see it through?"

Elisa shrugged. "Maybe you have."

Edo opened Bar Birbo's waxed wooden door and stood back to let Fabrizio in. "You're up early."

Fabrizio nodded. "I couldn't sleep." His eyes searched Edo's.

Chiara stepped into the bar from the upstairs apartment, her face lighting at the sight of Fabrizio. Her greeting stalled at the sight of his stiff expression.

"Listen," Fabrizio said. "Have you seen Arturo's campaign posters? They're all over the *piazza*."

He dropped a pink flyer spattered with rain on the counter with obvious distaste.

Chiara tied her apron as her eyes scanned the paper. "Edo," she said, her voice tense.

He finished moving the umbrella stand closer to the door and stepped to the counter saying, "What is it?"

He read the words, his face pale. In a strained voice, he said, "He's accusing Dante of being *gay*? That's what this means, right?" He held out the poster of a photo of Dante, doctored to look as if the mayor assumed an effeminate posture with a headline that read, "Santa Lucia deserves a real man."

Fabrizio frowned, "I assumed it referenced Stella. You know. Dante's wife leaving him for the town handyman. People certainly did make hash of that." He shook his head. "Or maybe it's because he's dating Magda. I've heard that making the rounds."

Running her hand over her eyes, Chiara said, "Only Fabio cares about that. And the guys he runs with."

Fabrizio slumped onto a stool. "Do you think he's behind this? Fabio?"

Chiara shrugged. "I wouldn't put it past him. He's been loitering outside the bar, glaring at Dante and Magda. I know he sees Magda as an interloper. She's foreign but makes good money here."

"Stop it." Edo's voice rang through the bar.

Fabrizio and Chiara startled.

In a strangled tone, Edo said, "It's not about the affair. Or Magda. Look at the posture. Look at the photoshopping on the face. Look at the *pink paper*. This . . . " he held the paper up by the corner, "insinuates that Dante is *gay*. And probably, by extension, that Magda is the best he could do for a beard."

Fabrizio and Chiara studied the flyer again before glancing at each other and then looking away. Chiara said, "It doesn't necessarily mean that."

"What else could it possibly mean?"

Chiara shook her head. "It's trying to paint Dante as weak, sure, but—"

"Gay, Chiara. *Gay.*"

Fabrizio ran his eyes over the flyer. "I think he's right, Chiara. I'm sorry, Edo. I should have recognized that."

Chiara shook her head. "No way." She turned around and flicked the switch to grind the coffee. "Arturo wouldn't do that. He knows Dante isn't gay, it wouldn't be fair. He wouldn't stoop that low."

Edo stalked to the bar's window and raised his hand to his forehead. Then he spun back and strode to the counter. "I'm not sure which bothers me more, that you refuse to see the obvious or that you think that calling someone gay is a low blow or that you think it's a perfectly fine low blow as long as it's true."

Her eyes implored Fabrizio. "Back me up, Fabrizio. Calling a candidate gay is slander, a political death knell. That's a fact."

Fabrizio closed his eyes, shaking his head.

Chiara prodded. "Fabrizio?"

"I like to think I know what you mean, Chiara. But I get how it sounds to Edo."

She spun around, dropping the cup of *espresso*. It crashed but didn't break, spilling coffee all over the floor. "I'm not saying that being gay is bad. You *know* I'm not! I'm saying it's unfair to saddle Dante with that label when he's not even gay!"

Edo crossed his arms over his chest. "So if a journalist had written an exposé on Francy because he's gay, he would have deserved that?"

"It never happened!"

Edo shrugged, "So it's okay to use homosexuality as a slur as long as it's true. Because maybe you sort of agree with it."

Chiara sputtered. She hunched over to clean up the coffee. When she rose, she said, "We're on the same side. Arturo is wrong to do this. That's what we need to focus on. Why we think it's wrong . . . we're saying the same thing."

Edo glared. "You think we are, and that's frightening."

Fabrizio cast a sad glance at Chiara and shook his head.

Yanking an apron from the drawer, Edo said, "Look, it would be easier if you just admitted that you have some prejudices to work through. I'd understand. Or at least I'd try. I get that it's a lot to change."

Chiara's hands curled. "But that's not true!"

Fabrizio watched, tension straining his face as Edo said quietly, "It is, Chiara. And you know it. There have been too many times—"

The tinkle of the bell over the door shattered the quiet. Livia and Savia walked in, deep in conversation.

Livia's eyes caught Edo's. "Edo. I can't imagine what this must be like for you." At his stare, she added, "The flyers."

Edo attempted to smile, but wound up grimacing as he tied the apron around his waist, fumbling over the knot.

Savia said, "*Cappuccino*, Chiara." Seeing Livia start to order, Savia amended, "Two, please." She turned back to Livia and said, "Like I was saying. I saw Bea laying into Arturo the other day, and I thought for sure he looked contrite. Like he realized he had no call to be running for mayor."

Livia shook her head. "I was there, remember? It looked to me as if he only wanted Bea to stop talking."

Savia chuckled. "I suppose that makes sense."

Livia said, "Is anyone falling for this? I mean, who would vote for Arturo over Dante?"

Fabrizio pushed the flyer farther away from himself and said with a sigh, "You'd be surprised."

The woman kept following her.

Antonella ducked into a new aisle at the *farmacia*. She peered behind her, and the young woman appeared again, this time looking flustered. At Antonella's glare, the woman picked up a box of diarrhea medicine and examined the front. Then she turned it over and studied the dosage recommendations.

Antonella backed away and darted down another aisle. For a few moments, it seemed to work. Antonella found Signor Tocci's vitamins and started searching for his cough drops. She should have looked for them first, since not every *farmacia* carried them. The last one hadn't. But yes! Here they were!

When Antonella started walking to the register, she startled at the sudden appearance of the woman, standing right beside her. And no longer pretending to read the box of diarrhea medicine still clutched in her hand.

Coldly, Antonella asked, "Can I help you with something?"

The woman pointed at her with the box, her mouth open as if to say something, but then she let the box fall to her side.

"Why are you following me?" Antonella said through clenched teeth.

"Are you Antonella?"

Antonella's mouth went slack.

"You work for Signor Tocci."

Still, Antonella said nothing.

"I saw pictures of you with him on Facebook."

Antonella shrugged, attempting an air of nonchalance. "What about it?"

The girl stepped closer and murmured, "Are you okay?"

Antonella dropped the vitamins. They knocked against a stack of melatonin, and bottles began rolling all over the aisle.

The woman made an involuntary noise and then crouched to help clean up the bottles. They both stood again.

Antonella whispered. "What do you mean?" She studied the woman now, her chestnut hair thrown into a sloppy ponytail on the top of her head. She was either statuesque or endowed with large breasts, it was hard to tell from the man-size t-shirt she wore.

"I'm Francesca. Francesca Simone. Has he mentioned me at all?"

Antonella suddenly recognized her as the glamorous young woman hanging onto Signor Tocci's arm in the photo on his desk. "Oh, yes! It's nice to meet you."

Antonella held out her hand, which Francesca ignored. Instead, she repeated, "Are you okay?"

Antonella tittered, "Okay? Why wouldn't I be?" What was going on? Why was Signor Tocci's old assistant spying on her? Did Signor Tocci send her? Well, she wouldn't give anything away. She plastered a huge grin over her face. "I'm marvelous!"

Francesca frowned. "I find that hard to believe."

"What do you mean? Everything is so so great." The words rang false, even to Antonella.

Francesca raised one eyebrow. "Is that so? So nothing has happened at work? Nothing...unexpected?"

"Unexpectedly *fantastic* maybe!" Antonella was giving Francesca no fodder to deliver back to Signor Tocci.

Francesca studied Antonella for a moment. "I know you're lying. The question is why."

"What! Why would you—"

"You haven't talked to any of us, have you? His old assistants?"

Now Antonella frowned. "How could I? You're all working at headquarters or other companies...you've all moved on. Bigger and better jobs." Antonella struggled to keep her voice even.

"We're all right here." Francesca held her arms out around her.

Antonella followed Francesca's gesture with confusion.

Francesca clarified. "Well, not right here, literally. You know what I mean."

"I don't."

Francesca shook her head. "We were all fired. We stayed in Girona."

"Fired!"

Francesca nodded and looked around to make sure nobody overheard. "Some gave into him more than others. But even those that did...*everything*," Francesca said meaningfully, "every one of us got fired. Nobody has lasted for more than a year."

Antonella's mind struggled to keep up. "He's done this...to other women?"

Francesca snorted. "You thought you were the first?"

"The way he talked about you, the photos..."

"You look chummy with him on Facebook, too. Photos lie, Antonella."

"The way he talked about you . . . as if you were so close."

Antonella didn't miss Francesca's shiver of revulsion. "Closer than I ever wanted. But I was one of the lucky ones. He fired me before he'd played with me too long." She added lightly, "He said I'd grown tiresome."

"Tiresome. He says that about me sometimes."

"When you won't unbutton an extra button?"

"When I make excuses to avoid sitting on his lap so he can rub my shoulders."

Francesca paused. "He's breaking out new material. He must like you."

Antonella paled.

Francesca leaned forward, insisting, "Look. Nobody told me, so I assumed it was my fault. Like I led him on."

Antonella nodded, hanging onto Francesca's every word.

Francesca continued, "I didn't think I could tell anyone. I thought they'd blame me. I kept hoping he'd change, or I'd come up with some way to stop him and save my job at the same time."

Antonella considered. "You never told anyone?"

Francesca's laugh cut through Antonella. "And burn every bridge? I hoped to get a reference from someone there, at some point. If I exposed him, I'd lose even that chance. Workplaces aren't inclined to believe women," Francesca added with a trace of bitterness.

"And did you? Get a reference?"

Francesca hung her head. "No. Once I crept out, I found I couldn't even pick up the phone. Every time I tried, I wanted to throw up."

At the look of shame suffusing Francesca's face, Antonella put a hand on her arm. "Hey. I get it. I do. Every day when I drive to work, I get sick."

Francesca put her hand on Antonella's and said nothing. Until, finally, she whispered, "You need to be the one who quits. Before you're fired."

Shaking her head, Antonella said, "I can't. You don't understand. My family, we need the money. And I'm learning some. It's hard, like chasing crumbs, but I am. I want to get a job where I use all this someday."

Francesca frowned. "Trust me, it's not worth it. He'll fire you soon. Then what will you have? Don't sacrifice yourself for... for *him*."

Antonella shook her head. "I'll be okay." She only wished that were true.

The bell over Bar Birbo's door jangled as Ava and Elisa ran in, Ale following behind them, an umbrella held high. They laughed as he exclaimed, "I can barely keep hold of it!"

Ava shrugged off her coat, grinning. "*Cioccolato caldo* for all of us, Chiara. I hope you didn't put it away for the season."

Chiara reached for the box. "Not yet, thank goodness. It's been a popular item."

Ava hung all three coats on the rack, greeting Bea and Paola. Ale leaned on the bar, scrolling through his phone. Meanwhile, Elisa took her sketchbook and roll of pencils to the room by the falls.

Paola nodded to Ava. "She's gotten so tall."

Ava nodded. "I know. I can't keep her in pants that fit."

Bea nodded knowingly. "It's not just her height." She dropped her voice. "She *stands* taller."

Paola added, "I used to feel so badly for her, scuttling up and down the street as if something chased her. I gave her fruit whenever I could. Hoping to fatten her up a little."

Ava put her hand on Paola's. "I didn't know that. Thank you."

Chiara put the three hot chocolates on the counter without a word. Ava started to pick up the tray when she noticed Chiara's face. "Everything all right, Chiara?"

"What? Oh. Yes. It's all fine." Chiara turned away to wash the backlog of dirty cups in an uncharacteristic tumble by the sink.

Ava darted a look at Ale, but his eyes were on his phone. His eyes widened. "Ava ... "

"*Che c'è?*"

He looked up. "I figured out why people have been buying the shirt."

"What do you mean?"

He held out his phone.

"What am I looking at?" Ava startled. "Oh, my God! Is that *Fatima?*"

Bea and Paola huddled around them. "Fatima? Where?"

On the screen, Fatima sat on a chair in a Japanese temple. Her long legs stretched out to the sides, toes tilted inward. Her body leaned forward and slightly to the right, with her hands gripping the center of the chair, so that she resembled a lanky pyramid. A pyramid with the anticipation of motion, an inhale of breath before song. Fatima's gaze lingered into the camera, her expression challenging, defiant. But her barely parted lips suggested a softness, a kind of tenderness. The whole photograph seemed charged with contrasts and opportunities.

Elisa, hearing her friend's name, appeared from the side room. "Fatima?"

Ava held out the phone. "Look at this ... "

Elisa gingerly plucked the phone from Ava's hand. "Wow. I can't believe that's her ... she looks so ... intense."

In a quiet, almost reverent voice, Ale said, "Look at what she's *wearing.*"

Elisa yelped. "My shirt! The shirt I made!"

Ava murmured, her fingers hesitating above the screen, "The painting of the two of you."

Everyone looked more closely, Chiara turning to dry her hands.

Because of the way Fatima angled her shoulders and neck, the shirt's design was unmistakable. Worn almost like a royal sash.

Ava breathed, "How did you find this?"

Ale's eyes were still wide. "Tomasso told me to get on social media as a way to promote the *castello*, the *frantoio*, the area ... you know. I started an account yesterday and decided to search for hashtag-Santa-Lucia, and this came up first. Did you see her caption? It's in English first, and then Japanese, don't know how she did that—wait, it's Fatima, she's probably fluent already—but then look at the Italian..." He scrolled down.

Ava read aloud, "Loving this shirt designed by my bestie in Santa Lucia. Remembering always, home is where you love the most."

Everyone looked at Elisa. She blinked. Creeping to Ava's side, she rested her head on her mother's shoulder. Ava's hand shook as it wound around Elisa's shoulders, stroking her hair.

Ale scrolled further. "There are hashtags for Umbria, Le Marche, even Girona. Tourists must be getting on Instagram and searching for what's around and seeing this. It's getting a lot of play." His eyes widened at the screen. "She has a serious number of followers."

In a small voice, Elisa said, "I wonder if she'll ever come home."

Ava ran her fingers through Elisa's hair as she soothed. "She will, *cara*. She will."

A sudden lightening of the rain prompted villagers out of their homes. They flooded the streets, the shops, and Bar Birbo. Chiara and Edo could hardly keep up with drink orders as voices filled the bar, surrounding them in a continuous clatter of opinions.

"Can you believe how long it rained?"

"Who says it's over? The farmers say to expect more."

"Who are you going to believe? Dirt-streaked country people or your own eyes! Look! A patch of blue!"

"Blue? Try grey."

"You always see everything in black. I bet you think Dante will lose the election, too."

"I hope he does."

"What! After all he's done for Santa Lucia!"

"What has he done? Tell me. Because as far as I can tell, all he's accomplished is strutting around as if he's royalty. While his wife sleeps with the town handyman."

"Arturo's wife is having an affair, too! Why doesn't that bother you?"

"That's never been proven. Besides, it's different."

"Why?"

"It just is. And look at Dante now, taking up with that horrible German woman!"

"I wouldn't say she's exactly *horrible*."

"You would, and you know it. How many times have I heard you complain about how she cuts in line at the *macelleria*?"

"Dante's love life is none of my business, and it shouldn't be yours either."

"Well, I heard that his kids worry about his sanity. That should tell you something."

"Probably Mauro. He's always been a pill. They should all stay out of his business. He can sleep with anyone he wants as long as he keeps doing good for the community."

"What good? You haven't said one thing."

"You haven't given me a chance with all your harping on his personal life. They're *loads* of things! He ... he ... "

"See?"

"He tried to get that arts festival here."

"Trying isn't doing. All talk, no action, that's Dante."

"Oh! And remember? When we almost had to cancel the *sagra* because VUS scheduled the line repair? He arranged to have it at the *castello*. *That* was action."

Laughter.

"What? Why are you laughing?"

"The *fire*. How could you forget? The worse *sagra* ever! That poor little girl. Half killed. His fault, if you think about it. I don't know how he sleeps at night."

"You don't care about that girl! You never mentioned her the whole time she was in the hospital! Besides, she's fine now. Didn't she leave Santa Lucia? A model, jet-setting all over the world."

"*Buongiorno*, tutti! Are you all talking about Massimo, and his empty bank accounts? Where did the money go?"

"We were talking about Dante."

"Ah, Dante! It's about time someone ran against him. And do you notice, he's not even *trying* to get elected. I think he quit long ago."

"I don't care what you two say. You mark my words, if you elect Arturo, you've given a big win to Fabio. He wants that councilman position so he can put a chokehold on the police department. Plus, I heard he's behind the entire campaign. Arturo is just a puppet. Think about that. Now . . . I'm going to gather greens while there's still sunshine."

A crack of thunder, and all conversation in the bar stopped as if it had never been.

Hail rioted against the cobblestone streets.

As Francesca predicted, Signor Tocci's hands became more insistent. He no longer invented a pretense to touch her neck, but instead at any moment stood behind her, rubbing her shoulders in a brotherly fashion for no more than a moment before his hands slid down her chest, opening her collar a little with his fingers. Shivering when he touched the tops of her breasts.

In some ways it was easier now that she knew. She no longer blamed herself. But in some ways it was harder. The knowledge that the chopping block could arrive at any moment made her job feel futile. She no longer deluded herself that Signor Tocci was a ticket to a better life. Then again,

Tomasso told her his friend at the cheese farm wanted to consult with her. Once she quit and lost her affiliation with the firm, would anyone want to consult with her?

Sometimes she mulled Francesca's words, "Aren't you worth more than that?"

She swung between yes and no with alarming regularity.

Antonella startled to find Signor Tocci's hand on her leg, his fingers skimming the edge of her skirt. He leaned so closely, Antonella could smell the garlic on his breath. He grinned. "You're thinking about it. Good."

"I . . . I'm sorry?"

His hand closed around her leg as the smile dropped from his face. "Antonella. You know how I hate it when you let your attention wander." Clouds filled his expression. Antonella knew what that meant. Once he got angry, she'd spend the rest of the day trying to soothe him, brushing up against him, trying to engage him with his work, while he pushed it away like a petulant child. Often, he couldn't get over his indignation until the next morning. She couldn't let that happen. Her time, it was so limited. She couldn't give him an excuse to fire her until she was ready. Until she had another job, another prospect, or something had changed to allow her the freedom to walk away.

He started to remove his hand when she placed her hand on his and tried to steady her breath. "I know, I'm sorry. It was just . . . your touch . . . I lost focus." She put his hand back on her leg. Closer to her knee than her skirt hem, but she hoped he wouldn't notice. She also hoped she would stop feeling like a whore.

At some time.

Any time now.

He looked doubtful. Antonella watched the warring expression on his face and realized. He didn't want *her*. Not really. He wanted control. Encouraging his advances wouldn't protect her position. In fact, that might get her fired.

Antonella's memory flashed to Signor Tocci's scantily clad photographs of Micia, frozen in time for his amusement. That's all he wanted from women, to be colorful insects pinned to velvet.

She shivered.

Now Signor Tocci smiled, his hand lingering on its slide, higher up her leg. "Finally, I have your attention," he murmured.

She sat woodenly, unable to move. Practically feeling her shoulders, like wings, adhered to a present, to a future that rang wrong. The room felt airless, and she gasped.

Signor Tocci misunderstood the sound. A wide, wolfish smile spread across his face. "That's my girl," he whispered, his hand stroking even higher on her leg, the leg he'd insisted be bare of pantyhose. She knew what would happen next. It had happened too often. He'd groan and bolt to standing. He'd watch her, perhaps run his hand over her hair, and make sure she noticed the bulge in his pants. Before he loped to the bathroom, only to return five minutes later, his face flushed.

His hand moved higher. Antonella remained frozen, lucid thoughts barely penetrating her awareness.

Higher.

Her heart beat wildly, wings desperate for freedom.

He pushed her legs apart and groaned, his hand inching further up her thigh.

This was different.

He groaned again.

Now is when he would stand.

Now is when he always stood.

But he didn't stand. Instead, he panted, "Get up."

She didn't move.

His voice rasping, his hand tight around her thigh, he said again, "I said, *get up*."

She couldn't move.

"Why won't you move?"

Antonella blinked slowly. "No."

"No? No what?"

She couldn't catch her breath. She couldn't free herself from the clinging sensation, pinning her into muffled stillness. In a soft voice, she said, "We're done here."

He sat back as if slapped. "Are you insane?" He watched as Antonella stood and gathered her things. "Where do you think you're going?"

She ignored his question.

His mouth worked. "Don't think you can go crying to anyone in this organization, and they'll take pity on you. Poor Antonella, with her tits bursting out of her tight shirts and her short skirts riding so high. Ask anyone! You made this happen."

"No. I didn't." She turned. "But I did take it for far too long."

"What job can you get if you walk out on me? You think I'll write you a letter of recommendation after this insubordination?"

She shrugged her purse over her shoulder and considered. "I literally couldn't care less. I would sweep streets from here to eternity to never be in arm's length of you again."

"What?" He yelped. "After all your innuendo and all your flirting. You wanted *me*. Maybe you still do," he wheedled, spying the red flush on her chest.

She buttoned her shirt one extra button while staring fixedly at him. Finally, she said, "Here's the thing you need to know. You are a tiny man." She strode toward the door. Her hand on the doorknob she stopped. And turned. "With a tiny dick."

It was Margherita's third tantrum of the day. Isotta wanted to let the child exert her will, but she couldn't be allowed to fling herself from the top of the slide. Especially given how wet the slide was from all the rain. Finally, Isotta bribed her with a trip to the *rosticceria*. As they exited, Jacopo reaching madly for the square of pizza while Isotta held it out of his grasp, she almost ran into Livia, who seemed to be loitering outside.

"Livia! *Ciao*. Enjoying our ten minutes without rain?"

Livia nodded but didn't answer. She joined Isotta, though, as they walked to a bench. Isotta dried it with a towel she'd brought along and settled Margherita with her mushroom pizza. Tantrum about the slide forgotten, Margherita munched happily. She swung her legs as she made up a merry tune to sing to the gathering pigeons.

Wordlessly, Livia gestured to the bench, and Isotta nodded. Livia sat down.

Isotta had never seen the woman so quiet. Pietro's double life must have shaken her. With a smack of her head, Isotta remembered what she should have remembered long before now. "Livia. I'm sure you've heard by now . . . I should have told you . . . "

"About Massimo?" Livia offered Isotta a bare smile of understanding. "It would be impossible to avoid. Aside from my troubles, it's the gossip *du jour*."

"I imagine so," Isotta said sheepishly. "But I should have told you myself, so you didn't have to hear it from others. I'm so sorry, Livia. You deserve better."

"I made my peace with his death months ago." Livia shrugged. "It's been easier than making sense of his life."

Isotta sat back, stunned. To have her thoughts laid out by someone else. "I've meant to thank you. For your help before the kidnapping, when Massimo was . . . "

Before Livia looked away, Isotta noticed her eyes shining with unshed tears. "To be honest, Isotta. I thought you blamed me."

"Blamed you! Why?"

"You didn't talk to me when he took the children. And when they came home, I wanted to help. I wanted to be with..." Livia raised her hand over Margherita's tangle of curls.

Isotta tucked Jacopo tighter against her lap as he lunged for a pigeon, his laugh cackling like a fall of rain. "And I denied you that. *Madonna mia*, Livia, I hope you can forgive me. I haven't been thinking straight."

Livia turned to Isotta, her eyes steady. "I understand."

Isotta shook her head. "I never blamed you...but I figured you wouldn't want anything to do with me with Massimo gone. He was our tie."

"Massimo was never our tie." Livia frowned. "Massimo was too broken to ever link anybody together. What connected us was..."

"Her," Isotta said.

Perhaps Margherita cottoned onto the conversation because she beamed at Isotta, her face smeared with tomato sauce, before appraising Livia on her other side with a smile only slightly less wide. Isotta held onto Jacopo with one hand while she searched for napkins with the other. Livia opened her purse and pulled out a packet of tissues, offering one to the child. Margherita looked at it suspiciously for a moment and then leaned her face down, shaking her mouth over it.

Isotta chuckled. "She hates getting her hands dirty."

"I remember that." Livia smiled. "Isotta, I'll be frank. I'd like to spend more time with her."

"Absolutely."

"Really?"

"I trust you." Isotta sighed dramatically. "Also, you should know, she's turned into a bit of a handful. I wouldn't mind the break."

Livia grinned. "Marvelous."

As if suddenly remembering, Isotta said, "Livia...you might be able to answer this question...Anna's money. Do you know what she did with it?"

"Did with it? Like what she spent it on?"

"Sort of. Massimo gave her a rather hefty allowance, but her bank account is all but empty. I haven't been able to get the list of transactions, I think that may happen now with the death being finalized. But I do know her account balance is low."

"She hardly spent any money. I can't think . . . " She paused. "Was it his mother Anna that the money went to? Maybe it was another Anna with the same last name?"

"Do you know one? Did Massimo? A family member, maybe?"

"I can't think of any. But Massimo had plenty of secrets. Anyway, the bank account numbers would have to match up."

"I'm sure Riccardo made sure it was the same Anna."

"It is worth checking. Massimo was capable of anything."

Isotta watched as Margherita shoved herself from the bench and threw herself belly first across the swing. "That is certainly true."

"Antonella . . . " Bea began. Antonella blinked and tried to focus on her grandmother. Bea continued, "Darling. You quit your job a week ago and you've been doing nothing but hiding in your room."

Antonella cast a blank look around her. "This doesn't look like my room."

Bea clucked. "I'm glad you came over. But what's going on?"

"Nothing."

"I've lived too long to believe that." Bea slid a chair out from the dining room table and dropped into it. "Tell me. Maybe I can help."

"You can't."

"Try me."

Antonella rolled her eyes. "If you insist. My boss harassed me at work. Sexually." She took perverse pleasure in her grandmother's shock.

Bea gaped, "Your boss...he made a *pass* at you?"

Antonella laughed bitterly at the antiquated word and then grew silent.

"Did you try to stop him?"

Antonella's mouth opened in horror at the question.

"You could have worn more modest clothes." Her cheeks reddening, Bea added, "I told you that skirt was too small!"

"Nonna! How could you? Do you think I wanted him to do those disgusting things! That I'm a...a..."

Bea put her hand over her granddaughter's gesticulating fingers. "Of course not."

"Whatever." Antonella nodded, uncaring. "It's no more than everyone else will say."

Bea frowned. "What do you mean?"

"How will I get work now? You know how people talk."

"Antonella, darling. People in Santa Lucia have known you forever. They won't—"

"You just did."

Running a hand over her face, Bea said, "Maybe for a moment. Out of surprise."

Antonella went on without hearing her grandmother. "Some people will be angry on my behalf. But others will titter about how they always knew these," she gestured to her chest, "would lead me to no good. They'll say I tried to use my body to get ahead. They'll say all that and more."

Bea shook her head. "They *won't.*"

They both regarded their intertwined hands, the young, tender hand held by Bea's wizened, strong one.

Bea asked softly, "Have you told your mother?"

Antonella shook her head, tears rising to her eyes. "Babbo's looking for work. Because of me."

Bea's voice was sharp, "He'll find it. Or your mother will. She always wanted to work, maybe now she will."

"She did? I didn't know that."

"She never told you? As a little girl, she always played 'work'. She'd dig around in trash bins hoping to find exhausted typewriter ribbons and white-out with the littlest bit of liquid remaining. She wanted to get dressed, go to an office. She once asked Giovanni for summer work."

"What happened?"

"She met your father," Bea shrugged. "He didn't like the idea. Then she got pregnant."

"Babbo didn't want her to work?"

"It made more sense back in the day. He said a real man supported his family. And he did. For years. Until his hands..."

"I know."

"But now... your mother will find something."

"Where though? The economy..."

Bea made a noise of dismissal. "People have worked in Santa Lucia for thousands of years. We'll weather the crisis. I wish Dante would do more..." She turned her gaze to Antonella. "Enough about other people. How about *you*?"

"What about me?"

"We need to get you working again so you can feel like yourself. Spring is around the corner."

Antonella smiled weakly. "What does spring have to do with anything?"

"New beginnings! Chickens will lay again, asparagus will appear!" Bea put her hands on her knees and stood. "Now, let's get going."

"Going? I'm not going anywhere," whined Antonella. "I haven't showered. I don't want to see anybody."

"The longer you go without seeing anyone, the harder it will be. No time like the present! Seize the moment!"

Antonella glowered but allowed Bea to hoist her off the couch. Bea cajoled her granddaughter into shoving her feet into shoes and pulling on her jacket against the rain.

As they walked up the street, Antonella grumbled. "So where are we going on this grand work tour of yours?"

Bea considered. "We could pop into every shop. But I think for today—"

"Today? You're making me do this *again*?"

Bea spoke loudly over her granddaughter. "For today, we'll start small. We'll go to Bar Birbo and see if Chiara knows of anyone hiring."

Staring at her scuffed shoes carrying her inexorably up the hill, Antonella didn't bother protesting. It seemed far easier to follow in her grandmother's wake.

Pushing Bar Birbo's door open, Bea called out a greeting to the room at large. She turned, helping Antonella off with her coat as if she were a child. Antonella jerked her arms out of the sleeves and faced the bar. She stopped.

Marcello didn't notice her walking in and did a double take. He straightened, planting his feet until he stood tall.

Bea bustled to the counter. "*Due cappuccini*, Chiara, *grazie*." Bea didn't seem to notice Antonella and Marcello studiously appraising opposite ends of the bar. "Chiara, Antonella is looking for work. Who is hiring?"

This got Marcello's attention. "You're not working in Girona?"

Bea said, "No she's not, and good riddance, you wouldn't believe—"

Antonella put her hand on her grandmother's and said firmly, "It didn't work out."

At Marcello's continued stare, Antonella lifted a hand to her lank hair, pushing it off her forehead. She attempted a look of bored unconcern, accepting her *cappuccino* with loud thanks. Then concentrated on gulping it so she could get home.

Edo and Francy shook like wet dogs as they strolled into Bar Birbo. Edo laughed, calling to the bar at large. "Sheets of water! It's ugly as hunger out there!"

Magda offered a thin smile and then returned to her conversation with Dante. "You have to defend yourself, Dante. You can't keep acting as if it's not happening."

Dante shook his head. "I won't give it validity by responding."

"Fine, but at least let people see you. *Talk* to people."

"No." He sipped his wine. "That would give them fodder for their little games."

Chiara leaned toward them. "Not everyone is in on this, Dante. Just a few."

"A loud few." His chin jutted. "I won't let them think they've gotten to me."

"But, Dante," Magda leaned closer, clasping his hand to get his attention. "Don't you see? It makes it look like you don't care."

"I *don't* care."

"No, it makes you look like you don't care about being mayor!"

Dante blinked at Magda. He turned to Chiara, who said, "She's right. The longer you keep your distance, the more people will doubt you."

Beside Dante, Fabrizio nodded seriously. "People need to know you are invested in them, Dante."

"I *am* invested in them, they should know that based on my years of service." Dante insisted. He swirled the wine in his glass. "If I keep my distance, nobody can say...things." He turned to Magda. "How can all the gossip be okay with you?"

She shrugged. "I guess I'm used to people saying awful things about me."

Dante cocked his head and gazed at her.

At the warmth in his eyes, Magda started to say more but stopped with a shake of her head. She turned to Edo and Francy, "How is the vineyard?"

Their heads ducked together, the men didn't hear her. Magda raised her voice, "Hey! *Ragazzi*! Any damage to the vineyard?"

Edo smoothed back his hair as he turned to Magda, the laugh still brightening his face. "Doesn't seem so."

Francy straightened Edo's collar and said, "Ale said that somehow, yesterday's hailstorm skirted right past the vineyard."

With Edo's attention on Francy's hands, he missed Chiara's stern expression as she turned away. Edo went on, "Luckily, Ale can't afford a tractor. With this insane rain, Bruno says tractors compact the soil."

Fabrizio's eyes followed Chiara as she bustled about, cleaning the shining La Pavoni.

A buzzing in Francy's pocket prompted him to pull out his phone. He whispered, "Marco. He's saying to call."

Edo took Francy's coat. "Go upstairs."

Francy shot a hesitant glance at Chiara whose attention appeared consumed by invisible flecks of milk foam. Edo gripped Francy's hand. "It's too loud in here, and if you are outside any longer, you'll get soaked through."

Francy grinned. "I'm already soaked through."

Edo said, "Help yourself to a change of clothes."

Francy nodded seriously. As he moved to the door, Fabrizio said, "Son, is everything quite all right?"

Francy glanced again at Chiara's back. "Marco."

Magda broke off her conversation with Dante. "Your friends who got a surrogate?"

Trying not to make eye contact with Dante, Francy said, "You have an excellent memory."

Magda nodded. "I hope they haven't hit any problems."

Chiara shook her head and viciously scrubbed the foaming wand.

Edo nudged Francy and said, "Go. I got this."

Francy turned and leaped the steep stairs three at a time.

Meanwhile, Edo turned back to Magda and said in a steady voice. "It could be good news."

No sound but that of grinding beans, sipping coffee, and the shove of a glass of wine. Dante said, "Another, if you will, Chiara." To her raised eyebrows, he added with a significant look out the window, where rain lashed like anger made manifest, "I don't want to go back out in that."

Francy threw open the door, wearing fresh jeans and a t-shirt, and an enormous grin. "He wanted me to know. They're having a boy."

Edo whooped, and Magda clapped. "How wonderful!"

Chiara stiffened and withdrew a clean towel from the drawer while Fabrizio chuckled to himself and said to Magda, "Wonderful people. You'll have to meet them."

She turned to Dante, who nodded over his wine. "Good for them."

The room grew quiet. Dante looked around. "What?"

Edo fumbled, "Before . . ."

"That was before." He grinned at Magda and touched his finger to her nose. "Before my Magda talked some sense into this stubborn, old man."

She chuckled. "You're not so old."

Dante regarded Francy with an open smile. "Seriously, Francy. Wonderful news. I hope you'll bring your friends to see us in Santa Lucia."

Francy laughed. "I will. Maybe once the rain stops." He glanced at Edo meaningfully. "Edo, did you want to come upstairs?"

Edo knocked back the last of his coffee. "Dry clothes never sounded so good."

Francy raised his eyebrows before he and Edo tumbled upstairs in a flurry of laughter.

Dante leaned down to listen to Magda as Fabrizio reached across the counter to snag Chiara's sleeve. "Isn't it marvelous?"

"What's that?"

Fabrizio's smile faltered. "Why, Marco and Reuben. Their baby boy.

Gender doesn't matter, of course, but it does help one visualize—"

"I don't know them," Chiara shrugged.

Fabrizio looked from Chiara to the closed door of the apartment. "Chiara? Is there a problem?"

She darted a look at Magda and Dante, now gathering their coats. "Why would there be a problem?"

He lowered his voice in return. "You seem angry."

"No more than usual," she bit off. She looked up with a merry wave as Dante dropped coins on the scuffed copper plate and the couple ducked out into the constant rain.

"I never said—"

"It's as if I can't have the right reaction anymore."

Fabrizio shook his head. "It's not about your reaction. I can't help but think some of your notions may be outdated."

"Outdated!"

"Can't you see? You bristle all the time anything comes up around—"

"I do not bristle," Chiara insisted.

His brows furrowed. "Then I don't know what you'd call it. You're surprising me, Chiara. And not in a good way."

She stepped backward, her hands on her hips. "Do we have a problem here?"

Fabrizio shook his head. "I do hope not."

Bea shook out her plastic hair covering as she stepped through the strings of beads to enter the *fruttivendolo*. Paola called out from her perch at the register, asking about Bea's family and the weather. They chatted as Bea hunted for potatoes with just the right amount of peeling skin. Bea paused at the boxes of leeks. She held one up. "Is it leek season already?"

Paola chuckled. "Every year, spring takes you by surprise."

Bea grunted her affirmation, resting the leek into her aged yellow basket.

At the sound of parting beads, Bea looked up to see Laura folding her umbrella.

Laura caught sight of Bea and paused. Not noticing the rising tension, Paola relayed a story she'd heard about Marcello giving a tourist a ticket for trying to drive through the arch, despite the posted signs forbidding vehicular traffic. Laura smiled tightly. Then she lifted her chin, grabbed a yellow plastic basket, and sidled along the other side of the shop, where mushrooms nestled in their boxes. Plucking up a handful and shoving them in a bag, she studiously ignored Bea.

Bea frowned. She strode toward the mushrooms as if she simply must have some. She reached into the same box as Laura and said, "*Buongiorno*, Laura. *Tutto bene?*"

"I'm as well as can be expected. This rain."

"Your heart?"

"Just fine."

Bea furrowed her brows in thought, heedless of the produce she'd planned to buy. Slowly she said, "And Marcello? How is your fine boy?"

Laura frowned as if Bea were teasing. "He *is* a fine boy. No need for sarcasm. Your granddaughter missed out."

Ah. That's what this was about. Bea nodded. "That's what I keep saying."

Laura startled and glanced at Bea as if checking for a trick. "Come again?"

"Not to Antonella, she's not in a state to hear it, but I told her mother that just last night."

Laura still looked doubtful. "You didn't tell Antonella he wasn't good enough?"

Bea flinched. "Who am I to have such opinions?"

"How many times did you say that Isotta and Massimo shouldn't get together or Fabrizio and Chiara shouldn't get together or—"

"All right, all right!" Bea smiled sheepishly. "I've had an opinion or two in my life. So have you, eh?"

Laura stared at the floor and refused to answer.

Bea went on. "But Marcello. You know I adore that boy."

Laura muttered. "I figured you didn't want your granddaughter with her fancy dreams to attach herself to a beat cop in her hometown."

Bea stared at Laura. "Laura. That would be my dream."

Laura stared back for a moment before she broke away.

"Where did you get this idea?" Bea asked.

Laura shrugged. "They were dating, he talked about her all the time. And then she shoved him over."

Bea said, thoughtfully, "She did." Though it was almost a question.

Laura sighed. "Well, girls can be teases. We know that, don't we?"

"She's not a tease!" Bea's voice rang with indignation. Paola looked up from sorting receipts. In a softer tone, Bea continued. "She's *not* a tease. She's had many obligations . . . "

Laura shrugged and picked up a head of lettuce, placing it into the basket beside the mushrooms she hadn't needed, but now had to find a use for. Maybe she'd throw them into that night's *sugo*. "Perhaps fickle then? I mean, what young woman ignores romance?"

"Don't spread rumors about her," Bea pleaded.

"Who said anything about rumors?"

"You know you can be a terrible gossip."

Laura glared hard at Bea.

Bea glared back for a moment before softening. "Okay, I can too. But please, *ascolta*, Laura . . . I shouldn't tell you this . . . "

Laura perked up.

Bea darted a glance at Paola, who pretended not to notice. "Antonella. She quit her job."

Laura went back to choosing the last of the season's radicchio with a knowing smile.

Bea shook her head and moved closer. "*Not* because she's fickle. Something happened." She breathed, "I can hardly speak of it . . . "

This got Laura's attention.

"Her boss . . . he . . . " Bea searched for the words, but she knew she didn't have the right ones to describe what she imagined must have happened to her granddaughter to make her so scared.

Laura watched the expressions shift on Bea's face. Comprehension dawned, and her mouth fell open. "Oh, *Madonna mia.*"

"Yes."

"This whole time? All these months?"

"Yes."

"How bad did it get?"

Bea began to crumple, her body nudging the stacked boxes in the middle of the store. Laura caught a bin of fava beans before it fell and then put her arm around Bea. She couldn't hold up the larger woman, but the touch seemed to fortify Bea, who still said nothing.

Laura said again, "*Madonna mia.* Poor Antonella."

Bea nodded sadly.

Laura thought for a moment. "So this is why she rejected Marcello."

"Laura, she's rejected everybody." Bea looked up at Laura with wide eyes. "She's been carrying this, this secret, all these months. It's eaten her alive. I don't know if she can recover. I'm trying, I am . . . "

Laura soothed. "It's hard to get children to listen to us, isn't it?"

"She's not a child. That's the problem," Bea sighed. "I'm out of my depth."

Ale watched Ava crest the stairs. His prepared grin and outstretched glass of wine suddenly felt foolish in the face of her pinched expression.

He put the glasses down and rushed toward her. "Ava? What is it? You're late and...what is it?"

She shook her head. "Is Elisa around?"

"No, she's at Isotta's. Livia brought Isotta's favorite cake from the *forno*—"

"Livia?"

He nodded.

"Right. Livia. Okay."

He ushered her to the table, set for a view of the groves through the open door. Since sitting outside had become an impossibility. Ale's mind worked, and he hazarded a guess. "Fabio?"

She gasped out a cry before wiping at her eyes with the back of her hand. "I shouldn't let him get to me. You don't have to tell me. But, the things he says..."

Ale watched her. "What happened?"

Pressing her eyes together, she whispered. "They had made such a point of saying he wouldn't be there. It surprised me." She stopped. "Actually, they seemed surprised themselves when he walked in with Morena."

Ale squeezed her hand.

She went on, "Anyway, he strode in all cocky with Morena behind him. He saw me and didn't skip a beat. Went on about gossip that I'd been after Massimo since I grew breasts." She turned to stare at Ale, aghast, "He said that. In front of my parents. I think that's what broke down my defenses. Who wants to talk about something like that, ever, let alone in front of her *parents*?"

A muscle in Ale's jaw worked.

She aimed for a lighter tone but sounded more leaden. "You can guess the rest. Somehow he wound up getting affronted on behalf of all men that I'd denied Massimo his daughter. And then to...how I had to sleep with somebody else's husband to feel..." her voice broke, "to feel good about myself."

"Oh my God."

She nodded without spirit.

"I can't believe your parents allowed this."

"They didn't. Mamma ordered him out of the house."

"*What?*"

"Not all bad comes to hurt, I suppose."

He paused. "I don't get it."

She looked up, wan. "It's an expression. Sometimes good comes from bad things."

He nodded. "Like silver linings."

She blinked. "What?"

"Never mind. So why now? After all this time?"

She shook her head. "I don't know. Maybe Massimo's death broke through something. Or maybe Fabio finally crossed a line."

"And he left?"

"Yes, dragging Morena behind him." She considered. "That was the other thing. My mother shouted to Morena that if she had any self-respect, she'd break up with my brother."

"Weirder and weirder."

"Maybe that's it. Watching Morena fade, maybe they are witnessing my life." Her voice cracked. "Ale. What if Elisa . . . what if underneath, she's like Morena? That emotionally stunted."

"She's not Morena."

"She's erratic. She's secretive. She gets so quiet."

"Ava, honey. She's a teenager."

Tears rolled down Ava's cheeks.

Ale wrapped his arm around her and pulled her close. "I should have been there today."

"You had to work. Did it go well? Did you work through your coding problem?"

"That's not important." He held her for a moment. "I hate that you were there alone."

She leaned into Ale for a moment, as if she wanted to melt into the safety of his broad chest. "It's okay. Anyway, I'm not sure my parents would have had their moment if you'd been there. With you supporting me, would they have felt the need?"

"Do you think it will last?"

"I wish I knew." She shrugged as she sat back up. "Maybe. His wounded pride might keep him away. Especially with the things Babbo said as Fabio walked out."

"What did he say?"

"It was bad. Babbo said they'd made excuses for Fabio all his life, but the truth was that he'd always been a twisted person and he had become a twisted man."

"Ouch." He shook his head, trying to keep up. "You think he'll hear it? Change?"

"Doubtful. It's more likely that he'll decide they're not worth his time."

"That makes sense." He stroked her knuckles with his thumb. "What happened after he left?"

"*Allora*, I haven't even gotten to that part." She ran her free hand over her forehead. "They didn't outright apologize or anything, but they acted as if we'd had some healing conversation and now we could move forward. And then we talked about the election."

"The *election*?"

"They think Fabio is behind Arturo's bid for mayor and the whisper campaign against Dante."

"I hear people at Bar Birbo say the same."

"Dante's not taking it seriously."

"No, he's not. He was there, and he kept laughing about it. He called it the 'carping of little children'."

"Somebody needs to get through to him. He's run unopposed for so many years, I think he's forgotten he could lose. And my parents...they said they've talked to lots of people who believe the rumors."

"Which rumors? I heard the one about him dating Magda, which last I saw seemed pretty true."

"But it's *not* true that she has ties to the Nazi party. If anybody does, it's Fabio. He took his beliefs straight from their playbook."

"The immigrants. I'd forgotten."

"It happened before you got here." Her eyes drifted to the scorch marks that she'd never been able to scrub from the castle wall. With a sigh, she said, "Oh, and there's this...he's also saying that Dante is secretly gay."

"*What?*" Ale sat back, shocked.

Ava said to herself, "Apparently there were flyers."

"How does that even fit with the Magda story?"

She lifted her arms. "I almost don't think it matters. People will believe anything if it makes them feel superior. Dante's been a good mayor for Santa Lucia in hard economic times, he's had a knack for bringing in tourism. But, he does act as if he's all-powerful. It's no wonder Fabio wants to take him down a peg."

"I can't believe Arturo would consent to this. I thought he and Dante were friends. And isn't Arturo's niece the musician-in-residence? Thanks to that program of Dante's, she lives here rent-free."

She shook her head. "Arturo loves drama. All that talk about his wife having an affair. You've met his wife, right? There's just no way."

He shook his head.

She sighed. "I can't believe you'd want to live here. To attach yourself to my crazy family."

"Hey. I love Santa Lucia. I love you. The crazy family is a bonus."

Spring blurred the rain with a frisson of warmth, layered between undulating bands of cold. Marcello admired the trees, blackened with moisture, but spangled with leaf buds. Soon the rain would end. And with it, he hoped, his loneliness. Ever since his brush with romance, he realized his mother was right all these years. Life was better with the promise of companionship. He'd dated before but had never been at risk of losing his heart to someone.

God, that sounded cheesy.

Even to himself.

But suddenly he *liked* cheesy things. He'd even found himself sniffling at movies he watched with his *parents*. And, truth be told, he'd been watching a *lot* of romantic movies—ones with weddings, ones with misunderstandings, ones with people realizing they loved their best friends. He seemed to have discovered a deep and abiding love for love. Just thinking about that Christmas movie, the one that ended at the airport with all the famous people falling in love, he felt tears rising again.

The moisture in his eyes impeded his vision, and he crashed into a villager leaving the *forno*. "Oh, *scusi!*" He said, blinking to clear his eyes.

Antonella.

Just his luck.

She avoided his gaze, leaning over to pick up the bread that had flung out of her arms. The damp bag securely in hand, she gave him a tight nod and made her way down Via Romana.

"Antonella! Wait!" He ran to her. He knew he should give her space. That's what his mother told him. "Give her time," she had said. "Antonella will come to her senses. But why should you take yourself off the market just because Antonella isn't ready? I hear Sonia, Pietro's daughter is single. She's pretty, don't you think?"

He shook his head to clear it of his mother's words. "Antonella . . . "

She regarded him warily.

"I wanted to tell you . . . " What? What did he want to tell her? That he loved her? No! He couldn't. That only worked on snowy New York streets.

That he felt bad for her? No! He knew from being a police officer that nobody liked to be pitied. He blurted, "Giovanni has Pan di Stelle cookies."

She frowned in confusion. "Cookies?"

He nodded, paralyzed by his foolishness. He muttered, "You said you liked them. You told me. But Giovanni hasn't carried them. I saw the bags last week and ... and ... "

"I know. Nonna bought a bag." She paused. "Anything else?"

"No. That's it." He hung his head.

She hitched the bag against her shoulder.

"That's not it," he said quietly.

Antonella stopped mid-step. She turned, watching Marcello levelly.

As if from a much vaster distance than the few meters that separated them, Marcello said, "I hate what happened to you. At your job."

Her lower lip trembled. "You know."

"Yes."

She thought for a moment. "My grandmother can't keep her mouth shut."

"No, she can't." He ventured a slight smile. "I know it's what you hate about Santa Lucia. But she wasn't gossiping. I don't think."

"What else could it be?"

He shrugged. And then said, carefully, "I'm glad you quit."

Tears sprung into her eyes.

He closed the distance between them, placing a hand on her arm.

She shook her head. "I should have left after the first ... " her voice trailed off.

"How could you know? I'm sure you thought each time was the last. That it couldn't get worse."

She regarded him, surprised. "Yes."

He nodded, his eyes trained on hers.

With a quavering voice, she said, "I tried wearing more masculine clothes. I tried making it a joke. I tried ... "

At the jagged tone in her voice, Marcello put his other arm on her. "I know you did."

"How . . . how do you know?"

He said softly, "Because I know you."

The tears spilled onto her cheeks.

He whispered. "I can't stand that he did that to you. That he made you doubt yourself."

She broke then, stumbling under the weight of her grief. He pulled her close and let her cry, glaring at Magda and Livia passing with quizzical looks. Glaring at the world that had broken her. His first love.

"Chiara, why haven't you renovated? You have all this unused space . . ." Fabrizio gestured to the kitchen doorway, which led to room after empty room.

She smiled tightly, "I guess I'm satisfied with my little life."

He nodded as if listening to a different conversation. "I need to talk to you."

Her arm, stirring the polenta, stopped moving. "Here we go."

He shook his head. "Here we go?"

"Ever since you stormed out that night, it's been . . . " She shook her head. "You've had more to say. It's obvious."

He sat back, arms crossed over his chest. "Is it? Then, pray tell me, what's the subject of our discussion?"

"That's an aggressive start," she muttered, turning back to the polenta. Catching his eye, she turned off the stove and sat down at the table. "Just say it."

Slowly, he said, "Since that night, I've been racking my brain trying to figure this out. And I can't determine if you have a problem with all gay people," he forced his voice to lighten, "or just my son."

Her mouth dropped open. "What are you accusing me of?"

"Neither would be pleasant," he said. "But I love you. I want to work through this."

"Maybe Francy has a problem with *me*."

"That's not true and you know it."

She shrugged and looked out the window. Or she tried to. But with the rain falling in sheets, she only looked to the window. Not out. Suddenly she felt suffocated, drowning in her desire to see, to breathe, fully.

He leaned forward. "As important as you are to me, Francy is my world. And I can't stand to see him slighted like this by the woman I love. You don't understand, perhaps, since you've never had children."

Chiara stood. "I think you should go."

"Go? Go where? We need to resolve this."

She couldn't catch her breath. "Not now, we don't. The things you are accusing me of . . . you need to think about what you are accusing me of."

He lifted his arms helplessly. "How could I help but think otherwise? I've watched you tense up, over and over. I've watched you dismiss him. Like you can't stand him. You can't stand him with your nephew. Or maybe you can't stand that Edo is gay."

"Please, just go. I'm done with this conversation. I can't . . . I can't bear more." Chiara's eyes filled with tears.

Fabrizio clasped her hand, but she shook it off and said, "Go."

He rose and looked back as he reached the threshold. But Chiara was staring at her fingers gripping the table and didn't notice.

Antonella stepped out of her house and almost walked right back into it. Each time she forced herself to walk about Santa Lucia, she felt the same fear of catching villagers smirking at her, as if they could see through her clothes.

But Marcello encouraged daily outings to get past the fear, even when she complained about the terrible weather. Each time, he insisted that hiding in her house would only convince her she should keep hiding.

She tried to ignore the shiver in her heart as she pushed open Bar Birbo's door, releasing the sound of the bell. Marcello spun around to greet her, his smile warm. She smiled tremulously at him before nodding at the villagers—Magda, Dante, Vito, Luciano, and Isotta—who nodded in return.

Maybe Marcello was right. Bea had also assured Antonella that nobody would judge her, but Antonella was too cross with her grandmother to give her any credit.

Antonella slipped beside Marcello and asked Chiara for a *cappuccino*. Chiara seemed distracted but nodded. Edo asked if she wanted anything to eat. Antonella shook her head, and he went back to stacking *espresso* cups from the dishwasher.

"See?" Marcello grinned. He swayed a bit as if he'd been about to nudge her hip with his own. Antonella swallowed her disappointment. She tried not to think about missed timing. And how Marcello no doubt would prefer a girl who was less . . . sullied.

She tensed when the bell chimed again, signaling new arrivals. Vito's son, Enrico, entered the bar, along with his girlfriend. Antonella couldn't remember her name, though she had talked to her once before.

Magda's and Dante's voices rose above the burble of the bar, each insistent and determined.

Magda practically yelled, "I'm telling you, she told me herself, so it's not up for debate!"

Dante shook his head, but Antonella couldn't miss his grin as he stroked Magda's hand. Were he and Magda really dating? Antonella had assumed that to be Fabio's rumor-mongering.

Magda scowled at the touch, but Antonella saw how she briefly put her hand over his before saying, "Somebody did it . . . who else could it be?"

Chiara smiled wanly. "Is there another mystery afoot in Santa Lucia? How could I have missed it?" A tremor of tension marred the bland curiosity of her voice. Antonella watched her. And watched how Edo watched her.

How much had she missed all these months?

Magda announced. "Carosello. And his sudden tidy appearance."

Antonella heard Enrico's girlfriend—Carla! That was her name!—ask from the other side of the bar. "*Carosello?*"

Enrico said, "The one-eyed dog. You've seen him."

Carla muttered with a laugh. "Oh, have I. What a disgusting animal."

The villagers darted looks between them.

Magda announced, "It was Livia. She's the one who cleaned him. She told me so herself, but Dante doesn't believe me."

Carla laughed. Antonella noticed how Isotta tensed at the sound before she reached into her purse to pull out coins. Her eyes on Isotta, Carla said, "I hope this Livia got a tetanus shot. That animal is revolting. Somebody should put it out of its misery."

Antonella's mouth fell open, and she looked at Marcello, who appeared equally stunned. He shook his head and returned to stirring his coffee.

Enrico, visibly tense now, said, "Carla . . . he's a *dog* . . . "

"Right. That's what I'm saying."

Isotta found Antonella's eyes, and the two of them exchanged appalled looks.

Dante said, "Why would Livia do it though? She's new to Santa Lucia, why take such an interest in a dog that none of us even notice unless he's rooting around our garbage."

Carla grunted a sound like, "See?"

Magda shrugged. "She said she felt bad for him. The matted fur. The burs and whatnot. Apparently, he looked *uncomfortable*."

Dante said, "Maybe she was lying."

"Livia? Doubtful. She sounded embarrassed about the whole thing."

Dante considered. "Maybe she's looking to appear righteous. After what happened with Pietro—"

Carla whispered loudly to Enrico, "Who is Pietro? What happened—"

He raised a finger to shush her, and she glared. Then she directed that glare at Isotta.

Magda shook her head. "She didn't say it like that. She said she missed having a bathtub and when I commented—do you know how much water bathtubs waste? It's ludicrous! Nobody should take baths! They should all be removed. You know how I feel about wasting water, right Dante?" Dante nodded, his mouth working to prevent his grin from distracting Magda from her diatribe. She stared at him for a moment before continuing, "Anyway, she agreed and said she wouldn't want a bathtub for herself, but a tub made it easier to keep Carosello clean."

Isotta murmured, "What a kind soul."

Carla remarked, "Of course you'd think that, Isotta. With your love of strays. So darling."

Eyes darted, meeting in confusion.

Isotta dropped her money in the scuffed copper plate. Luciano tried to stop her, reaching for his wallet, but she shook her head mutely before calling out a general goodbye.

Vito asked, "You'll be back for lunch?"

She nodded. "Yes. Elisa is at the house with them now..."

Vito grinned, "Please bring her!"

She smiled, relieved. "If it's okay with Ava. I'll check to make sure she doesn't have plans." She turned to Antonella, "It's nice to see you, Antonella, it's been a while."

Antonella impulsively strode forward to kiss Isotta's cheeks three times. "You as well."

Chiara hurried to the door and opened it for Isotta, snatching up an umbrella. "I'll walk with you and share your umbrella if that's okay. I need to pick up sausage for dinner and let Patrizia take mine."

Isotta nodded her agreement, and the women stepped into the rain huddled under Isotta's striped umbrella.

Enrico watched them dart up Via Romana before turning his gaze to Carla.

At his lingering stare, she asked innocently, "What?"

"Sometimes I wish..." He shook his head. "Never mind. I'm probably...never mind."

She trilled a run of laughter. "Oh, Enrico. You get so turned around in that enormous brain of yours."

He tried to smile and then caught Edo's eye. "Edo. Did you talk to Chiara about those documents? I meant to ask her today, but..." He gestured out the door.

Edo shook his head. "I haven't had a chance. But the other day I noticed a promising box in the storeroom. Let me grab it."

"I don't want to put you through any trouble."

Edo looked over at Marcello and Antonella deep in conversation with Luciano and Vito, and Magda and Dante with their heads ducked together. "It's fine. If anyone comes in, let them know I'll be right back."

To his receding back, Carla asked, "Documents?"

Enrico said, "For my research. Edo mentioned how Bar Birbo has been a bar for over a hundred years, I thought photographs or even order forms might give some context for my paper."

Carla nodded, but didn't seem to be paying attention, her notice caught on Ava and Ale coming down the stairs from the *castello*.

Meanwhile, Edo switched on the bare lightbulb of the storage room and located the box he'd found earlier. He flicked through the papers—receipts, a bill of sale for equipment. He paused. Should he ask Chiara before handing this over? He took out the papers and tapped their edge, before resting them back in the box. Maybe he'd let Enrico see them, and if he thought they would be useful, he'd ask Chiara before bringing them to Enrico before he left Santa Lucia that afternoon. He nodded to himself.

Maybe this would even give him and Chiara a neutral topic of conversation. It had been so long...

He hoisted the box into his arms and noticed below it a slim messenger box, closed with elastic loops. Could this be relevant, too? Listening out briefly for the bell over the door, he turned his attention back to the box, not much bigger than an envelope. He plucked the loops to free the front. He pulled out the papers, his eyes scanning the words. His breath caught. He started reading again, this time more slowly, flipping page after page.

He looked up, his eyes vague.

Edo shoved the paper back into the box and snapped the elastic loops over the corners. He put the box of documents on top and stood back to make sure it all looked relatively unmoved.

Dusting his hands on his jeans, he stepped back into the warming burble of the bar, an apologetic expression on his face. Readying his excuses that he couldn't find the documents after all.

Ava walked into her parents' house and felt instantly wary. Would Fabio be here? But no, the table was set for three. She smiled in relief and said, "Ale's sorry he can't join us. Elisa's art lesson switched at the last minute, and anyway he needs to pick up supplies for repairs in Girona, since he won't go to the hardware store here—"

Savia waved her hand. "That's fine! Just fine! He'll come next time." She lifted the lid of the pot and gave the ragù a stir. "How are the art lessons going? Her teacher thinks she's a genius, right? That child is a genius. My sister couldn't believe the postcards I sent her."

Ava said irritably. "She lives for those lessons." She tried to ignore her parents' too obvious exchange of glances.

Savia lifted the wooden spoon to her mouth and sipped. "Well, that's good."

Looking away, Ava let out a stream of muttering.

Her father led her by the hand into the living room. Savia returned the lid to the pot and followed, chatting about the upcoming election. "I spoke with Arturo's wife. Apparently, Arturo wants her to campaign for him. Can you imagine? After all the grief that man has given her over the years."

"It's his best campaign strategy to date," Ava sniped.

Frowning, Savia said, "What's gotten into you?"

Ava sighed. "Nothing. I'm sorry."

Savia narrowed her eyes at her daughter. "I heard about Ale's money troubles."

"Mamma!"

"What?" Savia lifted her arms innocently. "I can't help it if I overhear things."

Ava cocked her chin in thought for a moment. "Yes, actually, that's it. Ale's money troubles. I'm super tense about that."

Savia nodded. "It'll work out. You'll see. He owns a castle!" She laughed to herself before startling. "Oh! The pork roast!" She dashed back into the kitchen.

Bepe watched his wife leave. He turned to Ava and said softly, "No, you're not. Worried about money."

Ava stared at him.

He shrugged. "You're not. You never cared about money."

She sighed. "Since when can I not pull the wool over your eyes?"

He grinned, and then his face grew serious. "Elisa?"

She shook her head. "How did you—"

"Nothing makes a mamma more tense than trouble with her daughter."

Ava nibbled at the skin on the inside of her thumb. Seeing her father's eyes on her, she whipped her hand down and clasped them together on her lap. In a rush, she said, "I think Massimo messed her up and she'll never be the same."

He nodded.

She went on, "She makes these ghastly drawings. Like whatever's inside her is boiling. She can't keep a thought in her head. Most of the time it's as if she's not there even when she's in the room."

Bepe listened and reached for her hand. "Like mother, like daughter."

She looked into his eyes. "What in the world do you mean?"

Carefully, Bepe said, "Massimo hurt my girl, too."

"But I...I didn't do those things. I talked to you, or at least I wanted to." She looked at her father, accusation shining in her eyes.

He smiled sadly. "No, my dear. You didn't. Instead, you ran around town pulling up plants—flowers, weeds, it didn't even matter. Nothing green was safe. You left clods of dirt all over the house. And when we tried to talk to you, you yelled at us to mind our own business."

Ava's mouth dropped open. "That...that's not true." But flickers of memories shuddered across her mind. She'd written off her parents' response to her as uncaring, but now she remembered. Her parents huddled around her when she woke screaming in the night. Her pushing them away with dirt-streaked hands. Her bed filled with rocks that fell off the shoes she refused to take off, even in bed. "I got better. Eventually. Didn't I?"

Bepe smiled sadly. "In your own time. In your own way."

She shook her head. "What if something terrible happened to her and she won't ever tell me?"

"Ava," Bepe squeezed her hand. "She *is* telling you."

"Thanks for meeting me, Livia," Pietro murmured as he opened the door.

Livia nodded tightly before taking off her coat and putting it over her arm. "Where are your children? Word is, they've arrived." The living room had a few toys scattered around, but there was no way five children could be this quiet in a small house.

A muscle twitched in Pietro's cheek. "Nia took them to the restaurant. The playground is—" He gestured to the window, a view of pouring rain.

"Nia?"

Pietro shrugged, his eyes beseeching.

"Sonia. Right." She perched on the edge of a kitchen chair. "I suppose you called to talk about dividing our assets. Though you know," she glowered, "I can't divorce you."

He nodded in thought. "The church."

Frowning, she agreed, "The church."

"That's not . . ." Pietro shook his head. "You're the only person I can talk to about this. Any of this."

Livia looked up at him, her eyes vacant.

He sat at the table. "Now, without the secrets . . . things . . . they make more sense."

Livia shook her head, not understanding.

Pietro closed his eyes. "With Sonia, with having one foot out the door, we were doomed from the start."

"Am I supposed to feel sad? That your other marriage wasn't a fairy-tale because you made the mistake of marrying me rather than seeing if her fortunes changed and she somehow broke free?"

He put a hand over hers. She flinched and snapped it away.

"I'm sorry," he sighed. "What I'm trying to say is that with her death, I see what I never gave her. And what I never gave you."

Livia looked out the window.

Pietro said, "I heard about you taking care of Carosello."

She startled and turned back. "Somebody had to. That dog was beyond filthy. I worried for his health."

"It reminded me of how we met. Do you remember?"

"Of course, I remember." But she looked confused, as if attempting to put together puzzle pieces from different puzzles.

"You came into the restaurant. I was washing dishes, that's all they allowed me to do at the beginning..."

"And I asked for scraps. For the cats."

"I had never noticed the cats before. All of a sudden, I saw them. Before, they only annoyed me, their racket."

"I remember."

"It was your kindness, your goodness."

Livia stared at her hands and whispered, "Where is this going?"

He worked the corner of his lip for a moment and said, "You never told me you cleaned the dog."

She looked up, surprised. "Would that have mattered?"

"No."

"Then what?"

"Livia... I stopped seeing that goodness."

Livia huffed, and he put out a hand to stop her interruption. "What I'm saying is, like with Sonia, my double life changed you. Changed us. I see it now. I gave you half of what I had. And you had to starve yourself, me, *us*, to adjust to those scraps."

Livia's eyes filled with tears. She didn't want to nod, but the merest suggestion of a head tilt acknowledged the truth of his words. A truth she'd been unable to articulate for herself.

He gentled his voice further. "You tried to hang on harder. I resisted and pulled further back. You stopped wanting to show me your heart. I used this as a reason to stay away. It's clear as day."

Livia pressed her hands to her eyes. "I loved you so much, you know. I didn't want..." she flapped her hand, "any of this. I loved how you could make something from nothing. How you saw the pieces of me I didn't even notice, and loved them." Her voice turned ragged. "And you took it all away."

Pietro blinked back tears. "I did."

She wailed, "Every time I tried to get you to see how far off course we were, you blamed *me*!"

"But Livia, sometimes you made it difficult." She opened her mouth to protest but before she could, he said, "Which, of course, I understand. Without knowing what I was hiding, without being able to name the thing between us, you couldn't be the you I fell in love with. Kind and loving and always looking for the best in people."

She ran her hands through her hair and noticed his hands, resting on the table. Still.

He took a breath. "I'd like to try again."

Her mouth fell open. *"What?"*

"I'd like to try again. To give you what you should have had from the beginning. To give us both a real chance."

"You have got to be kidding me."

He wheedled, "The church won't allow a divorce, wouldn't God prefer it if we tried—"

"Oh my God, if you try to use my faith for your selfish purposes, so help me I'll—"

"You're right. I'm sorry."

She looked around, unable to look him in the eyes. Spying the abandoned block tower on the floor next to a scatter of trading cards, she said slowly. "You need someone to take care of your children."

"No!"

"It all makes sense. You're in over your head. And you think you can charm me with pretty words. Charm me into taking care of the children you had with another woman."

"I swear, that's not it at all. Yes, having them here has made me realize how much you did behind the scenes, how much work it is. Yes, it's difficult, but it's also been wonderful to connect with them. Now, I tuck them in every night—"

"How nice for you. Leo and Sonia, oh, I'm sorry, *other* Sonia, will be delighted to hear you've figured out how to be a father."

He shook his head, unable to find the words.

She stood. "I thank you for this. Most elucidating, I'm sure."

Vulnerability crept into his voice. "I've been a bad man. I want to be a good man."

She shook her head to break the spell.

"What do you want, Pietro? For once, be honest."

He looked into her eyes. "To start from scratch, to see if we can recreate the spark. Or find a new one."

Sadness tinged her words. "You are an insane person."

One more glare and she pushed past him. Without a backward glance, she stormed out into the afternoon light, slanting through the rain that seemed without end.

Even over the drumming of the rain, the sound of the floorboard cracking exploded like a shot. Isotta tensed. One more thing she didn't have the money to fix. She knelt and ran her fingers over the board with a sigh. She almost didn't care about the slivered wood as much as the noise, which would no doubt wake—

A lusty yell announced the end of Jacopo's ten-minute nap.

Her shoulder sagged, and she turned into Jacopo's room, resigned. She sat in the rocker and sang a shushing song. Margherita's head popped through the door "I done with my nap, too, Mamma!" Isotta had taken to putting Margherita down for a nap in her own room, hoping for the rare double nap that allowed her a few minutes to read a magazine.

She shook her head. "No, Margherita. Neither of you has napped at all. Go lie down."

"I's not sleepy."

Here again. How to get a child to nap who refused? She'd asked Livia, but the older woman had just laughed and said, "Enjoy them when they're small." Hardly helpful. Isotta didn't want to enjoy them. Isotta wanted a shower.

Margherita pulled a book out from behind her back. "You read me now?"

Isotta had to smile. She thought of her manuscript, sitting on top of the refrigerator. Tomorrow. Tomorrow Livia would take the children to her house for breakfast and then deliver them to Luciano's to give Isotta uninterrupted time to approve the illustrations the agent sent. The thought settled her aching heart. "Sure, honey. Bring it over."

Margherita handed her the book, and Isotta turned Jacopo so he could see the pages. Margherita leaned on Isotta's knee and listened intently as Isotta read the pirate story for what must have been the hundredth time. Jacopo nodded more and more slowly until his head hung. Asleep. As Isotta turned the last page, Margherita grinned at her and shouted. "Again!" Jacopo jumped but then closed his pudgy hands around his wide belly like some sort of Buddha and sank back into sleep.

Isotta whispered. "No, not again. I'm putting baby back in his bed. You climb into mine. I'll be there in a minute."

Margherita whispered loudly. "No. I's going to play more pirate! I found treasure!"

"Sure, sure..." Isotta said distractedly, as she settled Jacopo into his crib. She stayed for a moment, patting his back, before withdrawing without a sound. She leaned her back against the door with her eyes closed. Now, to Margherita.

Not in Isotta's bed. Isotta heard movement in the living room and sure enough, there was Margherita, sitting primly on the couch. "I's so awake!"

Isotta smiled despite herself. "Yes. You mentioned that." She sank onto the sofa. "I'm sleepy, though. Why don't you tuck Mamma in?" The ruse had worked before, Margherita curling up with Isotta to "help her sleep" until they both crashed together. It wasn't a shower, but it did make for a cozy respite.

"Okay, Mamma!" Margherita brought Isotta a pillow and handed it to her with her fists curled.

"What's in your hands?"

"Treasure!"

"Can I see?"

Margherita offered her hands, and Isotta unfurled the child's fingers from around a twenty euro bill. She looked over at her purse, knocked over on the end table. She laughed. "Well, sweetheart, I think that treasure will run out faster than we'd like." She lay down, her head on the pillow with dramatically closed eyes before opening them to say, "Will you help me nap?"

Margherita brought her face close to Isotta's and whispered, "I want to find more treasure."

Isotta opened her arms. "I didn't even know I had that much. Now, come snuggle Mamma, and then later we can plan a treasure hunt in the groves. Once this infernal rain stops."

As if in protest, the rain lashed harder against the windows.

Margherita considered. "I put treasure in the trees."

Isotta nodded, her face serious, "Of course you did."

Margherita climbed on the couch, snuggling against Isotta. She ducked her head under Isotta's chin for a moment before springing out. "When I find lots of treasure, I buy pink socks. Like Elisa."

Isotta caught on the words . . . another holdover from their time on the run with Massimo? Or was she referring to something more recent? Isotta's thoughts swung between that question, the always present memory of her few stolen moments with Enrico, and the endless worries of how she would balance making a living with taking care of the children. The thoughts whirled and spun, became whipped and airy. Before drifting away. Leaving Isotta and Margherita fast asleep, curled against each other, surrounded by the sound of falling rain.

Ava stepped into the kitchen, shaking herself like a wet dog. "Have you seen the marsh? It's completely flooded."

Ale looked up from his computer, the blue light reflecting off his face. "Marsh? Oh, the swamp below Santa Lucia? I know. When I picked up Elisa from her art lesson, it looked awfully close to the road."

Ava frowned, muttering, "I've never seen it like this. And those flowers trying to come up in the *piazza*? I'll have to replant all those seeds." She looked around. "Where's Elisa?"

"In the studio." He hesitated. "She's hinting that she needs more brushes."

Shaking her head, Ava said, "I told her. If she can't take care of the ones she has, I won't keep replacing them. How hard is it to clean her brushes?"

Ale pressed his lips together and began typing.

"You disagree?" Ava asked.

He shrugged. "It's not my place—"

"Ale," Ava sighed. "You're part of her life. My life. You get to have an opinion."

He closed his computer and smiled weakly. "All evidence to the contrary."

"Evidence?"

"Before . . . I didn't get to have an opinion," he smiled.

She dropped into the chair across from him and rolled her eyes dramatically. "That wasn't about you not getting an opinion. It was about you not letting me have mine."

His eyes dropped.

"Distinctions matter. So, you think I'm being too hard on her again?"

"Again?"

"Like with the art for the *castello*. See, you get an opinion there, right? You're all about not forcing her to produce something that doesn't feel natural for her."

"I only said that her work being different isn't a mark of some dysfunction on her part. Or yours."

"It amounts to the same thing."

He grinned. "Distinctions matter." He leaned forward, watching her intently. "So my opinion here is that you harping on her for her brushes is not much different from her parents harping on her for math."

"That's different! She *hates* math! She shouldn't have been made to feel terrible about not being good at it."

"Agreed. But she *wanted* to be good at it. And she wants to take care of her brushes. She's just . . . Elisa. She gets in a zone and she forgets."

Ava frowned. "So I should ignore it and keep buying her new brushes? Life doesn't work that way. People won't always step in and fix things when she messes up."

He said simply, "You've seen her with Margherita and Jacopo. When she takes care of them, she's not scatterbrained."

Ava considered his words. "That's true."

"I think helping her figure out a way to remember will be far more useful than punishing her for being forgetful."

"Not buying her new brushes when I bought her some last month is hardly a punishment."

He shrugged. "To her, it will be."

Ava considered. "You sure seem to get her."

"It's easier when she's not a reflection of me." Ale smiled. "Have you seen that oil painting she's working on?"

Ava nodded. "She and her teacher are discussing fruit in art history. Why?"

"He told me in a whisper as we left yesterday that Elisa is fearless with a canvas. She's not afraid of making mistakes, she's not afraid to push the boundaries. Anyway, this is all to say, because she's not mine, I guess I can see all that and not worry about her. She'll be okay."

Tears shone in Ava's eyes. "That means a lot to me, Ale. You don't even know."

He got up and kissed her cheek before carrying his cup to the sink. "Maybe the trick is to help her find a way to remember to clean her brushes. Like, we give her a warning when it's almost bedtime so she takes time to clean up."

Ava nodded. "Good idea."

"I'm full of them," Ale grinned. "Speaking of good ideas. At least, I hope..."

She sat straighter. "The app."

"Sì."

"It's done?"

"Mostly. I'm struggling with the interface, and how to connect that to branding and marketing. I wanted to hire Antonella to help as a consultant, but I can't afford her agency—"

"She quit."

"She did?"

Ava nodded. "Maybe she'll do a little consulting for you in exchange for something."

"That's a thought. We have all that olive oil and no tourists to give them to." He looked away for a moment, watching the rain pummel the window, streaking the warped surface into greater distortion.

Ava smiled. "So are you going to show me?"

Softly he said, "I don't know why I'm so nervous. It's as if I'm showing someone my baby."

She startled as if stung.

He rushed on, "I'm sorry! Bad choice of words..."

She shook her head. "It's fine."

"The doctor said to be patient. We've hardly started trying."

"I can't get the doctor's words out of my mind when I delivered Elisa."

He sat across from her and took her hand. "Which is why we started so early. But if it doesn't happen, Ava, it's okay. We'll deal with it."

"I'm fine, really. Most of the time I'm not even thinking about it." She smiled in an attempt to convince him. "It's just... never mind. Show me."

He took a breath and turned his computer. "Here's what I've got."

Her eyes scanned the screen, an expectant smile on her face. "What am I looking at?"

Nodding, he said, "See? The interface needs work. So what it is..." He ran his palms over his kneecaps before pointing at the screen. "It's an app for tourists to find local, traditional food experiences anywhere in Italy. The app pulls data from social media to see what foods people post about and uses that to make suggestions. This combines with the part of the app where users keep track of what they've eaten in different locations, rating them for their local appeal and also for quality. Tourists can use those ratings to locate a meal or a local specialty, anywhere they are in Italy."

Ava's eyes drank in the screen.

Ale went on, "It's different from TripAdvisor or other apps because it makes specific recommendations first based on this neat bit of predictive code I finally nailed, and then where to find iconic examples. So travelers learn about the local food customs, making that introduction to the culture the primary focus. Like, look here, if you are in Florence..." He typed for a moment and a new screen flashed up. "You'll get images of *lampredotto*—"

"I hate *lampredotto*."

"Intestine sandwiches not to your taste? I thought that was just me and my limited American palate." He grinned. "But look, there's also *ribollita*, *bistecca*, oh, I didn't know about this one... *Schiacciata con l'uva*. That might be a good bread to make when the grapes come in. Anyway, look, you can select any one of them, and find reviews and photos and location recommendations."

"Ale . . . that's . . ." She smiled at the tension forming in his cheekbones. "It's really, really great. But why just Italy?"

"I thought it best to start small. But if an investor comes through . . ."

"How likely is that?"

"Not likely, to be honest." He frowned. "But it's elegant. All my old classmates agree on that. One of my buddies is setting up a Skype meeting with an app development firm for Friday. I have a lot of work to do before then, though. I can't get this interface to work right."

"So I guess it's good the rain has kept you from working on the vines," she smiled.

He nodded. "Talking to Tomasso about the olives and Bruno about the vines is as close as I've been able to come to being in the thick of that."

Incredulity lacing her voice, she said, "You miss it."

"I seem to be working two ends of the spectrum. Creating a modern service while learning these old-world methods for wine cultivation and olive oil production. By the way, Tomasso said he'd bring me more barrels of last year's oil. We can do a bit of a demo in the castle. He said people love getting to pour their own into the tins. And the tins! With Elisa's painting . . ."

"Everything is coming together isn't it?"

"It seems like it. We just need a little luck on our side."

A trickle of water ran under the door. Unnoticed by either of them.

Livia refused to have Pietro pick her up at Magda's. "It would feel like a date."

"It *is* a date."

"No, it's not, Pietro. It's a conversation to divide up our lives since you wouldn't talk about it last time."

He grinned to himself; the phone clutched to his ear. "Call it what you will." He couldn't believe his luck that Livia had agreed to speak with him at all after last time. "Wouldn't it be easier if I picked you up?"

"I'll meet you at the car." She hung up.

He nodded to himself. Of course. Their separation had given her, not the notoriety she feared, but a certain level of celebrity. She didn't want anyone seeing them together.

Pietro arrived at the car ten minutes before their scheduled meeting. Just in case. He wouldn't put it past her to arrive early simply to complain about having had to wait. It was the kind of thing that had always annoyed him about her. He suddenly realized that had been her way of expressing anger at the thing she couldn't name.

She arrived right as the bells of San Nicola chimed the hour. Closing her umbrella with a shake, she slid into the passenger seat.

As she adjusted her skirt around her knees, he ran to close her door, hoping for a gallantry bonus. But she glared at him.

Chastened, he jogged to the driver's side. Turning the key in the ignition, he started the windshield wipers. They appeared ineffectual against the deluge. Vainly, he peered out the front car window, but the world dissolved into watery chaos. Livia held out her hand. "Stop."

He hadn't moved yet, but he obliged by turning off the car.

"We can talk here as well as Girona. I don't favor dying on the way."

He nodded while saying, "I wanted to take you to dinner though..."

"Pietro," Livia sighed. "I know you believe in the curative power of cuisine, but you can't erase years of betrayal by buying me a meal."

"I hoped for neutral ground. So we could—"

"Impossible."

"We could try..."

"No. We can't. In my eyes, you'll always be a—" she shook her head irritably. "I can't say it. The church wouldn't approve."

He offered, "I think the words you're looking for are 'a lying scumbag who destroyed everything that mattered to you'." His gaze fixed at some distant point, as if he were driving and not watching the window fog over, he missed Livia's eyes widening. "I'm not so dense."

Livia leaned back, listening to the rain pound on the roof of the car. "You want to forget what you did—"

"On the contrary."

She frowned at the interruption.

In a gentle voice, Pietro said, "I don't want to forget I'm capable of monstrosity, Livia. Only understanding my ability to lie to myself will eventually make me a happy man."

"I can't look at your face without feeling betrayed. Even if I could find that love for you again under all the hate and repulsion . . . the trust. It's gone."

He nodded, listening to the rain pound the roof of the car with such force, he expected pits to appear above his head like stars. "I don't deserve forgiveness, Livia. And I don't deserve a chance. But I hope you give me one. To see if someday you can look at me and see something better than what you see now. Something better in me now than you've ever seen before."

She looked at her hands, clasped on her lap.

He nodded. "As for the divvying our assets, Livia. I need to put food on my table and clothes on my children, but the rest belongs to you."

Edo checked the weather. Chiara, noting the motion, watched him. Slipping the phone back into his pocket with a frown, he caught her eye and shook his head.

She sighed. "The news said it would lighten."

Shrugging, Edo started to speak but then he turned back to the window. The streetlight illuminated water flowing between the cobble-stones like miniature canals, sluicing the rain toward some distant end. The rock walls looked as if they might well collapse under the weight of so much absorbed water. He looked back at Chiara, now bustling around the bar. He followed her with his eyes for a moment before joining her behind the counter.

At the bar, Bea nibbled her *cornetto* listlessly, casting accusing glares out the window. She brightened at the sound of the door. "*Ciao*, Ale! I heard you sold your vinegar to Pietro." She let off a peal of laughter.

Ale grinned uncomfortably. "Nice to get something for it. *Caffè*, Edo. When you get a chance. I can only stay for a minute, I have my meeting with the app development company in the morning and I'm afraid it will be a long night."

Edo nodded and the bar filled with the sound of grinding beans.

As he drummed his fingers on the bar, Ale looked around. "I'm surprised anyone is here so late in this weather."

Bea harrumphed. "By evening we decide that if we don't get out, we'll have been indoors all day."

As if in affirmation, Livia and Magda rushed in, their dark over-coats and clear plastic hair protectors at complete odds with their girlish laughter.

Bea asked, her voice stern. "Is the rain funny now? You know I saw several trees uprooted ... the ground beneath them just ..." she gestured to suggest the ground giving way, shrugging in resignation as it buckled under the groves.

Edo set the *espresso* in front of Ale and said, "It can do that?" His eyes drifted back outside as if he could see into the hills to monitor the strength of the earth holding up the gnarled ancient olive trees as well as the tender young saplings recently planted to replace the scorched ones.

Magda and Livia sobered, but when they exchanged glances they giggled again, muffled this time. Bea rolled her eyes and muttered. She made to get off the stool, but Dante entered the bar. If there was anything Bea liked more than fresh gossip, it was fresh romance. Though Magda and Dante didn't conform to her ideas about blooming love.   E v e n now, Dante regarded Magda with some haughtiness. "No umbrellas? Did you think the storm would pass?"

Magda smirked. "And your umbrella has done you so much good?"

Dante looked down at his miserable excuse for an umbrella. Several spokes had heaved themselves free. Leaving the fabric to flap uselessly.

Bea rapped the counter to get Dante's attention. "Dante! Did you talk to Giovanni? He said the delivery truck couldn't get up the hill this morning. The road is covered with rain and mud."

Edo said, "Sauro said the same. He had a truck coming to pick up bread for an event. Now he's swimming in bread. Well, swimming is probably an inopportune word."

All heads turned to the window.

Edo muttered, "And Francy comes tomorrow."

Chiara said, "I didn't know that."

Edo turned away.

Dante announced, "It's rain. What am I supposed to do about it?"

No one bothered answering, but Chiara, staring out the window, murmured to herself, "A biblical rain." She startled. "What is *that*?"

A line of pale figures marched down the street, like ducks—the tallest in the front, the second tallest in back, and in between a succession of poncho-clad waifs. Some children struggled against their umbrellas. Livia breathed, "Pietro."

Dante nodded. "And his children." He cast a sheepish glance at Livia. "I mean, his other . . ." His voice faded into the sound of rain.

The villagers watched the strange procession as the smallest of the children stumbled, falling onto the cobblestones. Boy or girl, it was impossible to tell; the child was so draped in protective gear. The child's mouth opened wide, releasing a howl of protest. Livia jerked forward instinctively before turning and placing her hands on the counter. "Not my problem," her firm lips seemed to imply. At odds with her eyes that couldn't stand the sight of the child tumbled in the street. A child that looked so similar to her own.

The tallest figure broke rank to prop the child back up. The little one refused to stand, instead flopping around like a boneless fish. Bea chuckled, "I remember that stage."

Pietro pulled the child into his arms and turned to continue walking down the hill, his face glancing into the bar shedding light into the street. He nodded at the bar patrons. Most nodded back, Livia with her hand to her mouth.

Pietro and his children disappeared into the darkness.

Livia leaned over the bar and asked Chiara for a glass of wine.

Bea spun back around on her stool and leaned to Magda. "I don't know how he's taking care of those children. Five!"

Magda tensed. As did Edo, shooting a glance at Livia, but she was thanking Chiara and hadn't heard. By the time Livia had turned back, Magda had engaged Bea in a conversation about how her chickens were faring in the rain.

Warmth rose in the bar. More villagers arrived, shaking beaten umbrellas. Chatter and laughter burbled. Bea kept her seat, asking now for a cup of hot milk and liberally sprinkling cocoa powder over the foam.

Right as Chiara apologized to yet another customer for her lack of hot chocolate, the lights flickered. The room grew quiet as everyone's eyes fixed on the ancient fixture hanging from the center of the ceiling. Nothing more happened and everyone laughed, their relief palpable. The words, "Can you imagine if we lost power" could be heard for only a fraction of a moment before a buzzing surged through the bar. With a crystalline pop, the lights snapped off.

A shriek from somewhere in the bar.

The shatter of broken glass.

A moment of waiting.

But the room remained dark.

Edo stumbled to the counter after locking the door. "How long do you think the power will be out?"

Chiara shrugged before remembering that Edo couldn't see her. "*Boh.*"

"I suppose we can wash the dishes by phone flashlight."

"You may not want to drain your battery."

A long pause greeted her statement. Edo said softly, "You think it will be a while."

"I don't know. But if a line is down, it could take time to fix. I think we should proceed as if we'll be living in darkness for a day or two, at least."

Edo felt his way to the sink and muttered, "If only there were moon-light."

Chiara's sigh alerted him that she was at his elbow, rummaging under the cabinets. "I think they're some old lamps in here from an old *festa*. Or . . . yes, here. And candles. We can prop them up in some glasses."

He nodded, and they spent the next few minutes arranging groups of candles to light the workspace enough to clean the bar. Soon the sound of running water took the place of conversation. Though Edo did mutter, "At least we have water, I suppose."

To which Chiara said nothing. The darkness expanded, obscuring the edges of the counter, the bottles, the La Pavoni. Softening it all.

Into the still bar, Chiara said, "There is something I want to ask you."

His tone was casual. "Sure. What's up?"

Running her finger over the ring of a mug, Chiara said, "Fabrizio and I. We had some words."

"About what?"

"That's not the point," she said sharply. "What's important is that in anger, he said something. I like to think it isn't true, but I don't know what to believe."

He paused. "If you're hoping that's enough to cue me, I hate to tell you—"

"He said that Francy saved the bar."

"Oh." She couldn't read his expression in the candlelight. "What a way to find out."

"Why did he do it? Why didn't anyone tell me? It feels like some cosmic joke. Like 'make the *barista* dance'. Was Riccardo in on it? Was *everyone*? Was the bar ever in danger?"

He held out his hands to stop the flood of questions. "Hang on. I know this is a lot to take in, but slow down. Ava knows. Riccardo knows. That's it. I only know because Ava accidentally spilled it. I suppose it's possible she told Ale, we haven't talked about that. Francy asked me not to tell you because he didn't want you assuming you owed him anything. In fact, I'm surprised Francy told his father."

Her voice emotionless, she said, "He didn't. They have the same accountant, who let it slip." She paused. "But why would he do it? To *woo* you?"

Edo stopped at her acrid tone. "No, Chiara, he tried to prevent my finding out—"

"Because to the casual observer, it appears that you are with him now because he saved your job."

"Not true."

She didn't seem to have heard him. "That he bought his way into your heart. Relationships built on that don't last, Edo."

"Chiara, how can you *say* this? Any of this?"

She put her hands on her hips. "I don't know, Edo. I'm mixed up. Walk me through it from the beginning."

So he did. About how Francy had discovered from him, Edo, about Chiara's ex-husband claiming the bar. And how he couldn't stand to think what this would do, not only to them, but also the village. So he stepped in, buying Chiara's ex-husband off to get him to never sully Santa Lucia again.

And she nodded. "How am I supposed to repay him?"

"You can't. That's okay. It's much easier to make your peace with it." He paused. "Speaking of secrets. I . . . I found something. And it raised questions for me, too. About you."

Chiara stiffened. "What is it?"

Edo smoothed his lower lip with his thumb for a moment. He took a candle into the backroom and returned with a slim box of papers. Gently, he set them in front of Chiara. "I know you hate talking about yourself. But I wondered if maybe . . . " His voice died out as Chiara turned one paper after another. Her face paled in the flickering light.

"Where did you find these?"

"In the back. I wasn't snooping, I promise. I was looking for old documents for Enrico, who is trying to piece together what Santa Lucia was like during World War Two."

Chiara put her hands on the counter and looked up at Edo, searching his eyes. Nodding to herself, she turned and walked to the end of the counter.

Edo shook his head. Just when he thought he and Chiara were repairing the impasse. He shouldn't have pushed her. But without talking about it, it seemed this would always hang between them. Chiara stopped at the end of the bar and pulled a bottle of wine from the shelf. She reached for a corkscrew and said, "Pull up a stool."

As the rain drifted up and down the darkened street, Chiara sat on the stool across from Edo and pushed the candles closer. Edo gulped a sip of wine.

Chiara spoke so softly, her words hardly disturbed the tender candle flames. "I always wanted children, a house full of them. This was like a million years ago, when we grew up assuming having children was a woman's duty, as well as her privilege. So when I got married, I got pregnant quickly. We were so happy." Chiara paused, her face stiff. "Before we'd told more than our parents, I lost the baby."

Edo reached for her hand.

She sipped her wine. "The second time it happened was worse. Then a third. And a fourth." The candlelight illuminated the tears in her eyes. "I stopped telling my parents, knowing each time would lead to disappointment. I guess you know all this. Seeing the records. But you can't know what it did to me. To feel at the same time so hopeful but so angry with myself for bothering to hope."

Edo pressed his lips together, leaning forward to better see his aunt in the half-light.

Chiara went on, "Sometimes the miscarriages happened early. Sometimes they happened much later when I'd given in to believing that this time, *this* time I'd deliver a baby. So many children I dreamed of holding against me." Chiara touched her chest lightly, eyes wide. She shook her head. "My husband. He blamed me. Told me I had to change how I ate, or my doctor, or my stress level. Finally, he declared I was bad breeding stock."

Edo's hand closed convulsively into a fist.

"I believed him. Why wouldn't I? My empty heart. My fault." She paused. "It wasn't until later, after he left, that I found out."

Edo hardly dared breathe. This he didn't know.

Chiara closed her eyes. "My husband, he had a younger sister. I never knew about her. Nobody did. She'd been born deformed and placed in a home. She died before she turned four. I can't even remember how I found out. Some family member must have let it slip, when they were trying to figure out how he'd gone so wrong. The sister, she'd had some rare disease.

After she was born, my mother-in-law was told not to have any more children. Because it was a miracle her son was normal."

She shook her head. "I told my doctor what I'd discovered. He said that all those miscarriages, that was my body's way of getting rid of a blighted fetus. He said I should consider myself lucky that none had been born. They would have been like ... her. But I never felt lucky. Not about that."

Running his hand over his face, Edo breathed, "Oh, Chiara ... "

"There was so much grief and anger by that point, so much to focus on. My husband was in jail. I didn't think about the miscarriages, the fact that I never had a baby. I enjoyed other people's. Filamena; I adored her like my own. All of you nieces and nephews. But now ... the deeper my relationship with Fabrizio, the more I realize what I'll never have. A family."

"Chiara. We *are* your family."

She wiped her eyes. "But I always wanted to create what I had growing up—children, loving parents."

He thought for a moment. "You kind of did, though."

She shook her head, not understanding.

He said, "This bar is your family. You take care of everyone who walks in, you make them feel full and loved and accepted, the way the best mothers do."

She shook her head. "That sounds nice. But it's not the same."

"I suppose not."

She smiled. "You though. Being part of your life brings me some of what I missed."

Blinking, Edo said, "Even though I'm gay?"

She shook her head. "Edo, as long as you're happy, I'm happy. I don't know how to convince you of that."

He spoke slowly, "So the surrogate thing ... it bothered you so much because ... "

She shrugged, "I don't know. I've tried not to think about it. Mostly I think it brings up babies. But also, I worry that you're jumping ahead. Moving too quickly. Which puts you at risk of losing it all."

"I love Francy."

"Sometimes love isn't enough." She straightened and took a breath. Defensiveness rang in her words as she said, "He thinks I'm homophobic. Fabrizio."

Edo put down the wine he'd been pouring.

She tried to laugh. "Well, aren't you going to tell me how crazy that is? After I told you all that? Did I tell you for nothing?"

Shaking his head, Edo started putting the saucers away. "It's not just the surrogacy. You get quiet every time Francy walks in here."

"Don't you see? I hated the thought that he rescued me. I'm not a damsel in distress. And neither are you."

"I don't buy it." He shook his head. "There are other things. All these little places where homosexuality comes up and you don't see..." He looked away.

"What? I don't see...what?"

He pressed his lips together. "Is it so impossible that maybe some bits of your upbringing have lingered? That you aren't as open-minded as you think you are?"

She winced.

"Well?"

"I'm thinking. After everything that's happened...It's a fair question. It deserves a fair answer." She let her gaze linger out to the street where the Madonna stood shrouded in rain and darkness.

He waited.

Chiara turned back to Edo. "I don't know, Edo. I like to think I am. I know I'm open-hearted, but maybe I do have habits of thinking."

Edo let his breath out in a rush. "I didn't think you'd admit it."

"I'm not perfect. I know that." She leaned forward, her eyes wide in the candlelight. "But when I tell you I wouldn't change you...wouldn't change Francy...I mean it. The rest...I guess I'll need you to help me. Point it out. Otherwise, how do I know?"

"You aren't exactly keen on feedback."

She chuckled. "I deserve that."

He added softly, "You aren't exactly keen on opening yourself at all."

"So Magda has been telling me." She paused. "I've kept a lot under wraps. I didn't want to broadcast my stuff. My life is already too public. But to tell you the truth," she chuckled, "Magda has been inspirational. If she can allow her private life to be public—her husband's evil twin, dating the mayor—well, maybe I can, too."

Isotta jumped at the knock. Jacopo, who had been dropping plastic shapes into a bucket and chortling to himself, screamed when Isotta picked him up to answer the door.

Livia's smile fell at the sight of the howling child. "Is he okay?"

Isotta stepped back to let Livia in. "He's crawling everywhere. Almost walking. I can't leave him alone for a minute, but when I pick him up he acts as if I'm ripping out his toenails."

Livia chuckled as she took off her coat and dropped it with her purse next to the door.

Isotta walked into the kitchen and then stopped. "I was about to offer you something, but I realize I don't have much."

"And I came empty-handed. Even if I had enough sugar to make anything, my cooking isn't winning me any prizes."

Isotta looked surprised and then said, "I can make tea. If I can find the matches to start the gas."

"I don't want you to go through any trouble."

"It's no trouble. I have to find the matches before it gets dark anyway. I couldn't find them yesterday and that was a scene." Isotta looked around.

Livia put her hand on Isotta's arm. "Please. I don't want to add extra work. I only wanted to see if you needed some help. I figure being cooped up with two children and no power for the last two days must be trying."

Tears rose into Isotta's eyes at the unexpected kindness.

Margherita strolled into the kitchen. "I'm hungry, Mamma."

Isotta said, "We have cheese. Would you like some cheese, darling?"

"No."

"*Cara*, we have to finish it before it goes bad."

"I'll take a Kinder cake."

Isotta shook her head. "Remember? We need to save those. Those last forever and the cheese—"

"I'LL TAKE A KINDER CAKE!"

"Margherita—"

The pitch of Margherita wailing at the top of her lungs drowned out Isotta's words. Isotta looked on in horror as the child threw herself across the floor. Not to be outdone, Jacopo flung himself backward and shrieked until his face resembled a beet.

Sure she could feel Livia's disapproval at her inability to keep her children behaving properly, Isotta reached into the cabinet and pulled out the box of Kinder cakes. Her voice pleaded, "Look! Margherita, here are the Kinder cakes. You can have one, okay?"

Margherita huffed a few more sobs before plucking the snack cake from Isotta's hands. "Okay. And I give some to Jacopo cause I good at sharing."

Isotta started to protest. Wasn't a one-year-old too young for processed foods? But at the sight of both children sitting quietly on the floor, Jacopo watching as his sister unwrapped the crinkling paper with fascinated eyes, she decided it was probably fine.

Isotta sagged into the chair. Not looking at Livia she said, "I know, I know. I should have given her the cake in the first place. Why fight about something like that when it's what she wants?"

Quietly, Livia said, "That's not what I was going to say."

Isotta regarded Livia with tired eyes.

"Look, I'm hardly the one to dole out lessons on familial relation-ships—"

"Livia. You're an excellent mother."

Livia shook her head. "My mothering days are behind me. But I do think you're making too much work for yourself."

"For myself?"

Nodding, Livia said, "You keep giving in to her and all she'll learn is how to push until she gets her way."

Isotta's cheeks flamed until they stung. She said nothing as she watched the children finish their snack. Margherita wiped the chocolate off Jacopo's face, smearing it into a garish grimace, before getting down on all fours to encourage him to crawl with her to the living room. Isotta heard Margherita "reading" to a suddenly quiet Jacopo, her sing-song voice filling the dim room. Biting her lip, Isotta said, "Maybe that's what parenting books say. But there aren't any books for children who have gone through what Margherita has gone through. She had everything ripped away, Livia. *Everything.* Shouldn't she have anything she wants now? So she can recover?"

Livia shrugged. "You could be right. I haven't read any books on being a mother. I learned from trial and a lot of error. A *lot* of error, Isotta. I'm not pretending I'm an expert, and I'm not saying you're doing it wrong."

Isotta muttered to herself.

"All I know is that children behave better when they learn that no means no. When the rules change and no becomes yes, well, they don't know what to expect anymore. It makes them willful. And you know," Isotta added with a smile, "Our Margherita has always been on the head-strong side, anyway."

Isotta considered Livia's words.

Livia went on in a quiet voice. "I'm not worried about Margherita, though, Isotta. I'm thinking of you. If you can't hold your line with her, I'm afraid she'll exhaust you. Jacopo, too."

Isotta nodded in thought.

Margherita peeked into the kitchen with a self-satisfied grin.

"It's awfully quiet." Isotta stood. "What are the two of you doing in there?"

"Playing explorer. We find new treasure!"

Livia frowned. "Treasure?"

"It's her favorite game. I keep telling her to stop getting money out of my purse, but when my back is turned, she's left another trail. She puts it in a dark room and then comes out with it. At least it's helped her fear of the dark, I suppose. And just in time, since dark is all we have. I'm only hoping she's not sticking any in the toilet." She cocked her head to the side. "But my wallet is empty." She strode into the living room. A careful trail of euro bills, larger than what Isotta ever carried, led from the kitchen through the living room to the front door where Livia's coat rested beside her purse.

Isotta blushed furiously. "I *told* her to stop."

Ava stepped into Elisa's room, her path lit by the taper candle she clutched in her hand. "Do you need any more candles?"

From the direction of Elisa's bed, Ava heard her daughter's voice, wan with tiredness. "Yes. This one is about to die, and I need to finish."

Ava brought the candle over and rested it on the nightstand next to Elisa. "Ale thinks he remembers a pile of oil lamps in the room attached to the *cantina*. Hopefully, we can move up a century. I can't believe you can draw by candlelight."

Elisa gave a noncommittal grunt.

Ava translated, "It's better than sitting in the dark?"

Elisa blinked. "Yes."

Nodding, Ava said, "I get that. I've been flipping through seed cata-logs. Chances are high that I've ordered a batch of zucchini seeds instead of zinnias. Or, that would be a possibility, if I could ever place an order."

At the annoyance in Ava's voice, Elisa looked up. "When will the rain end?"

"I wish I knew." Ava sighed in a way that suggested that her actual answer was a scream of "Never!"

"And the power?"

"Same," Ava said, flatly. "We'll have to use less water. All this rain, the system could back up. Or so say people on the street."

Elisa shivered. "Won't we run out of food?"

Ava set her jaw. She shook her head but didn't answer.

Elisa went on, "In books about floods. There are always problems, aren't they? Diseases, other things—"

"Stop worrying," Ava said firmly. She reached to tuck Elisa's hair behind her ear. Catching sight of the drawing taking shape beneath Elisa's hand, Ava stopped. Her hand clenched. Stiffly, she said, "What are you working on?"

"A drawing. I told you."

The words tumbled out before Ava could wish them back. "Oh, Elisa, when will you make happy things? You're so talented, and this is so . . . " Ava gasped as she noticed more details. "It's messed up, Elisa! Monsters in *movies* aren't this scary! Is that how you see the world?"

Elisa glowered at Ava. "Yes."

Ava snatched the drawing as Elisa yelped and lunged for it. Holding it to the light, Ava pleaded, "Elisa! Can't you see how grisly it is? Where do you *get* these ideas!"

Elisa lunged for the paper. "People are like that!"

Ava held the drawing out at arm's length and squinted in the bare light. "Their skin falling off? Empty eye socket?"

Elisa sobbed and snatched the sketchbook back. "Yes! That's how I see it! And you don't even care!"

"I do care, Elisa. I've tried to get you to talk about it since I got you back in my life!"

"I don't like talking."

"You have to! Or how can I help you?"

Elisa collapsed on the bed. "Why? Why would I? When everything I do is wrong?"

Ava sat beside Elisa and chanced a touch on her shoulder. "Everything you do isn't wrong, Elisa. It's not. But I don't understand why you have to fixate on the gloomy parts of life. Draw something pretty, for goodness sake. Maybe then you'll feel better."

"*Be* better you mean!" Elisa bolted upright, shouting, "Just leave me alone!" She threw her sketchbook on the floor and ran out of the room, sliding into the darkened hallway.

Dante rubbed his eyes, gritty from lack of sleep. Even when he found the time to tumble into bed, shoving his beleaguered pillow that was now more gaps than feathers, he could only close his eyes for a few moments before they flung back open at the thought of how this villager would find food when she was recovering from hip surgery or that villager would get his medicine. How much longer? How much longer until the rain stopped, the water receded, and workers began fixing the lines?

He didn't dare use his phone for anything but incoming phone calls, hoping to extend the charge as long as possible. After six long days, with almost everything disabled, his phone showed a battery of 4%.

Dante looked around. Where was he? Oh, yes. Bea's alley. He knocked, and she whipped the door open. "Dante. Thank you for coming. Especially so late."

"It sounded urgent."

"It is." She ushered him out of the rain, into the living room, where towels draped over the furniture in a vain attempt to outrace the mold. She sighed, her voice fragile. "It's my chickens."

"Your chickens."

She nodded.

He sighed inwardly. It was not the first urgent visit he'd made that did not seem remotely urgent. "What about your chickens?"

"I need them. The eggs, we all use them. Our family, and we supply others . . ."

"I know." He tried to keep the irritation out of his voice. *Chickens.* Of all things!

"Dante, they're starving. I'm out of feed! I've been frantic, wondering what to do! The sack, I shook out the last bit yesterday!"

"Could you turn the chickens into the groves, let them be wild for a while? Eat worms and whatnot?"

Bea's mouth opened, aghast. "Are you crazy?"

Dante stood still.

Bea shook her head muttering, "I'm sorry, Dante. This situation. It's getting to me. But my chickens . . . I can't turn them loose. Don't you see? They'd disappear. They'd never come home."

He rubbed his eyes. "I'll check with Sauro. See if he can help."

"I thought of that. All that bread that was never picked up. But Laura said he's been giving the bread to families. Nobody values my hens as I do . . ." Her voice trembled.

Dante said, "Sauro keeps those canisters of bread crumbs. I'll see how much surplus he has."

"Won't people need it?"

He stood. "I doubt anyone will make meatballs or fried veal right now. I'll bring you what I can get."

"Thank you, Dante. Thank you so much." Bea clasped her hands in front of her chest. "And...I want to tell you...I think you're a great mayor."

"Oh, well." Dante shifted his weight. "Thank you, Bea."

"Paola and I were just agreeing about it this morning. I went to her shop to see if she had vegetable scraps for my chickens. But she'd already given them to Graziano for his goats." She frowned. "She said something I meant to remember."

Dante checked his watch. "Perhaps you can leave me a note later, Bea. I have more visits to make and my phone won't last the night."

"Oh! That was it. Paola said she was going to call you. Her sink is backing up."

"Yes," Dante nodded. "I'm headed there next."

With her words still lingering behind her, Elisa appeared in the doorway. She sniffed.

Ava looked up, surprised. "You came back."

Elisa refused to look at her. "Where would I go?"

Ava nodded. Elisa perched stiffly on the edge of the bed. Her hair fell across her cheek, striped with a faint streak of blue paint.

"I didn't say any of that right," Ava said. "I'm sorry. I worry about you. Sometimes...it feels as if you're a million miles away, in some dark place, and I can't reach you."

Elisa wiped her eyes. "I always come back."

"I know. But each time. I'm afraid you won't."

Blinking, Elisa said, "You have to trust me."

"That's hard, Elisa. So much has happened to you. Your life hasn't been fair."

Elisa shrugged. "You can't make it fair by making me just like you."

"I'm not trying to make you just like me," Ava said, recoiling.

Elisa looked away.

"I'm *not*, Elisa. That's what my parents did, so I know what that's like." From somewhere in the back of her mind, she remembered her recent conversation with her father. And her discovery that, perhaps, her distance from her parents came not from their abandonment when she needed them. But from her pushing away their offers of church and meals and optimism. In their love and concern, they wouldn't leave her alone. When all she'd wanted was space to heal.

Space to heal.

Maybe that's what Elisa needed, too. Maybe Ale had been right all along, that Elisa had her own way of working through the hardships of her life. And that Ava trying to pivot that journey would only make the road harder for her daughter.

Ava wondered if all parents were doomed to repeat their parents' mistakes. Or if this all led back to Massimo.

"You're right, Elisa. I have to trust you. I'm sorry." At Elisa's quiet nod, Ava reached to stroke her hair. "This weather, the power ... it's making me edgy."

"Me, too," Elisa sniffed. "I shouldn't have snapped at you. Especially when you were so nice to clean my paintbrushes last night."

Ava shook her head. "I didn't clean your paintbrushes."

They looked at each other and said, "Ale."

Laughter filled the room. Elisa reached behind her to knot her hair out of her face as Ava leaned down to pick up the fallen sketchbook. "Here you go, sweetheart. It doesn't belong on the floor."

Elisa held the sketchbook in her tight hands.

"Your art is excellent, Elisa. It is. I'll work on believing you. Believing Ale. That you have access to the dark parts of us that we all have, but most of us are too scared to admit."

With shining eyes, Elisa said, "Ale said that?"

Ava nodded, the light reflecting in her daughter's eyes lifted a lump into her throat. "Yes. And he's right. For once." She added with a grin.

Elisa smiled. "I think I'll go to sleep. Maybe when I wake up, the rain will be gone."

Ava offered up a silent prayer as she kissed Elisa's forehead. "Want me to put your sketchbook on your dresser for the morning?"

"Sure." She yawned and handed it to Ava before crawling under the covers. Suddenly she stopped. "No, wait! Give it here! I'll put it beside me!"

Ava, staring at the dresser, didn't answer. The candle illuminated her stricken face.

"Mamma?" Elisa pleaded.

Ava turned, her hand filled with euro bills. "What is this?"

"I was going to tell you about that—"

"It's a hundred euros. At least."

"Yes, I know. I can explain."

"That's good. Because I'd like to know how a girl not quite fourteen can get her hands on a hundred euros."

"Margherita gave it to me."

"*Margherita* gave it to you?"

"Yes! She wanted to play explorer, you know how she's always going on and on about treasure. So we were digging, and she dug it up and brought it to me, saying now I could get us all Fonzies again, like I used to."

Ava ignored the window into her daughter's kidnapped life. "You're telling me you were digging in the grove with Margherita. In the rain."

"I guess it was before the rain." Her voice pleaded, her face tense in the flickering candlelight.

"And it didn't occur to you to wonder where Margherita got this much money? Did you think she actually dug it up?"

"No. I figured she got it from Isotta's purse. A few times she's given me other bills when we've been playing and I put them on Isotta's table. Margherita is in there all the time. Last week she found Isotta's lipstick and—"

"Don't change the subject."

Elisa dropped her eyes to stare at her hands clasped on her lap.

"I knew it." Ava laughed, addressing the ceiling. "I *knew* the darkness was real. It meant something. Everyone told me you'd get through it, that you needed to get through it, but they were wrong. I mean, you're a *thief*."

"No! Margherita handed it to me. I meant to give it to Isotta, but I *forgot*."

"For weeks. You forgot for weeks."

"Yes! You know I'm forgetful! I found it in my sweater pocket the other day and put it on the dresser to remind me, but with everything that's happened, I forgot again!"

The history lay between them—Elisa's long-ago story of how she paid Stefano with stolen money. Small denominations, she'd always insisted. Had she moved up to larger bills? Had she plucked this right from Isotta's wallet? She couldn't have taken it from Ava or Ale. They never had this much money. Come to think of it, Isotta didn't either. Maybe she'd just gotten some settlement. Or maybe her book had gotten picked up. Or maybe her parents had sent money to help. Isotta must be frantic, wondering where the money went.

"I'm taking this back to Isotta."

"*Now?*"

"No, not now. She has enough on her plate. I'll wait for the rain to stop."

"Don't tell her I stole it!"

"You did something wrong. You're going to accept the consequences."

"I forgot! I *forgot!*"

Ava shook her head. "Who forgets this much money?"

"I do! You know that!"

Ava left the room, as Elisa leaned her head on her bent knees, crying bitterly enough to match the rain.

Carosello hugged the side of Via Romana, his wet fur brushing against the stone walls. Spray flew from his body, blending with the falling rain.

He paused at doors cracked open for a bit of airflow, but none wide enough to welcome a wet and mangy dog. Snuffling around trash cans, he found no scraps. The villagers wasted nothing—every morsel, devoured. While bellies screamed for more.

The one-eyed dog trotted up the road. He passed Antonella's house, where she sat in her bedroom, trying to bat away the memories washing over her—her boss's fingers across her shoulders, his words across her breath.

The rain fell.

Bea stood outside her house, holding an umbrella over her chickens as she fed them from a battered tin bucket. Her mournful clucking twined with her birds', as she begged them to accept the sodden crumbs. Carosello's ears perked, and he paused, as if considering whether a detour past her chicken coop could prove fruitful. But he continued his jog up Via Romana.

He did a tour of the *piazza*, even though the cat food distribution had run out days ago. A stand-off with an orange tabby, prowling after a mouse, encouraged him to move back to the main thoroughfare and leave the last remaining dried and rehydrated bits of Simba cat food to Santa Lucia's starveling cat population.

Instead, he aimed toward L'Ora Dorata. He watched through the open door as Pietro and his children hung sausages to cure into salami. Where there was salami, sometimes there were leftover casings. Carosello sniffed around the edges of the restaurant, his ears tilting at a child's thin wail, "But I'm *hungry!*" And a shushing, an offer of hard bread softened with olive oil. Carosello waited. But no one invited him in.

The rain fell.

Outside Bar Birbo, the dog fared better. Chiara and Edo leaned over, side by side, to set out plastic trays with bits of old sandwiches, smeared with rancid mayonnaise. The two joked with each other about who was the most in need of a hot shower and who would most benefit from their sequestration diet—the relief in their old patterns palpable. Yet, there was an edge of anxiety in their voices. The constant whispered refrain, unspoken at Bar Birbo for the moment, but heard all over Santa Lucia, "Will it *ever* end?" Coupled with sparks of irritation. Before falling back into resignation.

Carosello, suddenly shy, waited for Chiara and Edo to turn back into the bar before wolfing down the beleaguered *tramezzini*. He startled, gazing up at the Madonna. As if she had called his name. He sat briefly, allowing his tail to thump, once. Twice.

And the rain fell.

His head cocked as he gazed at the steps leading to the *castello*. Where Ale flipped through sketch after sketch of an interface that wouldn't come together while shooting dark looks at his computer gathering dust. As Ava and Elisa ignored each other.

The dog stood and, as if suddenly remembering an appointment, he jogged to the *macelleria*. A gold mine. Giuseppe had left him scrap after scrap of soured meat. Probably whatever was leftover after sharing what he could with Pietro, both men mixing and drying the meat into a variety of salumi. Salumi that would prevent the meat from going to waste, but wouldn't be ready for months. And please, *Madonna Mia*, let the rains end before that. Let the power return. Let life resume.

Rather than this shell of an existence.

Carosello jumped aside at the approach of a man. Out in this weather?

Dante's even tones rang through the street. "It's quite all right, old fellow. You getting enough to eat?" A beat. "Ah, I see Giuseppe looks out for you. Good man. If only our digestive systems were as tough as yours."

The faintest of brushes over Carosello's ears before Dante strode forward, to Luciano's. Isotta hadn't seen her friend in days and worried about him remembering to take his heart medicine. Dante had promised to check. As Carosello watched, Dante's eyes lingered on the alley that led to Magda's. Where she sat at the table, turning a can of beans over and over in her hands. Sighing, Dante continued his walk to Luciano's.

Carosello took one last pass over Giuseppe's offerings. He trotted, more slowly now, up the hill to the arch that led out of Santa Lucia.

While the rain fell.

Isotta looked up at the sound of the door. She instinctively checked her phone to see if anyone texted that they'd be by, but her phone remained blank and impassive. Isotta rolled her eyes. Her phone had been dead for days. She stood up, commanding herself to not even bother reaching for the light switch. There was no power, there was no power, she repeated to herself.

Yet, once she reached the door and tried to peep through the peephole, she noticed her hand reaching for the switch.

She threw open the door and announced to Ava. "I am ill-equipped for primitive conditions. I'm desperate for real food and a hot shower. Please tell me you come bearing news of power."

Ava eked out a smile as she held aloft a tin of olive oil. "Unfortunately, no. But we have all this oil. We're using it to soften stale bread. Makes it more bearable. I thought—"

"Thank you!" gushed Isotta. She held the tin with two hands and gazed at it lovingly. "The fat, too. We've had so little since we ate the last of the salumi and cheese. And Giovanni's shelves are bare." Looking up, she caught sight of Ava's serious expression. "What is it? Is everything okay?"

Ava shook her head. "Where are the children?"

"Napping. Or Jacopo is napping. Margherita is singing to her dolls on my bed. She seems to have outgrown naps, but Livia said it's better for children to at least have some quiet time and that even when she complains she's bored, I should—"

"I need to talk to you. I've needed to for the last week and a half. I planned to wait until the rain stopped, but," Ava gestured outside with a harsh laugh. "That may be never."

Isotta regarded her friend for a moment. She nodded and walked to the kitchen.

Ava followed her. They sat at the kitchen table in silence for a moment. Ava drew a handful of bills from her pocket and laid it on the table. Isotta looked at it curiously. "What's this for?"

"Elisa stole it from you." Ava started to cry. "I don't know where I went wrong. I've tried, I have. And then she does this . . . what's *wrong* with her?" Ava dropped her head in her hands. "My father told me I struggled, too, after . . . but I got through it. Why can't I fix this?" She shivered, once again feeling her skin chafed by grit and rocks in her bed.

Isotta put her hand on Ava's shoulder. "Elisa didn't steal that from me. I can't remember the last time I had that much money."

Ava sat up. "It was a while ago."

"Even so. Why would you assume she took it from me?"

"She said," Ava wiped her eyes, "oh, she said that Margherita gave it to her for Fonzies. But see, that's ridiculous. Where would Margherita get it if not from you?" Ava's face paled. She whispered, "This is worse. She's lying about whose money it is."

"Is it possible someone gave it to her, and she doesn't want you to know?"

"Who would give her that kind of money? If someone is paying her that much for something she can't admit to, that's even scarier."

Isotta closed her eyes in thought. "Okay, let's take this one step at a time. Tell me everything Elisa said. We will figure this out."

Ava wiped her eyes and then rubbed her hands across her jeans. "She said that she and Margherita were in the groves playing explorer."

"So far so good. Margherita wants to play explorer all the time."

Nodding, Ava said, "Elisa said that Margherita pretended she had found buried treasure, and then gave the money to Elisa. Elisa claims she figured the money came from your purse, and she *meant* to give it back, but then 'forgot'."

"Treasure . . ." Isotta said, thoughtfully. "Like pirate treasure."

"Right, Elisa mentioned that. Oh, Isotta. How do I even figure out where she got it?"

Isotta spied Margherita's face peering out from behind the door. "I think I may know."

"Come here, Margherita." Isotta wheedled, her voice lilting like a song.

Margherita shook her head. "I's not sleepy."

Isotta smiled. "You can be done with your nap."

Margherita hesitated.

"Come sit on my lap and say *ciao* to Ava."

"*Ciao*, Ava," Margherita grinned before bounding onto Isotta lap. She snatched up the money on the table.

Isotta asked gently. "Look at this treasure! Do you like treasure, Margherita?"

"Yes."

"Shall we play pirates? Or explorers?"

"Yes! Pirates!" Margherita sat up straight as if she'd already won the game.

Ava whispered, "What are you doing, Isotta?"

"Bear with me." She put Margherita down with a noisy kiss on her forehead. "Okay, love, why don't you be a . . . a . . ." she searched for words,

"A pirate princess. And Ava and I, we're your helpers. We need to find your most special treasure."

Instantly, Margherita looked suspicious. "Why you need my treasure, Mamma? Let's get yours." She reached for Isotta's purse.

Ava closed her eyes in resignation.

"Mine isn't special enough," Isotta shook her head. "You see, there's a dragon—"

Margherita yelped and clasped her hands in front of her chest.

Smiling, Isotta went on. "If we can find the dragon's treasure, we can get some sweets."

"Lion bars?" Margherita asked, considering.

"Lion bars *and* lollipops." Isotta amended under her breath, "Once the blasted rain stops."

Margherita cocked her head to the side and tapped her toe. If Ava hadn't been so tense, she could have laughed at the outsized drama in this little person. Frowning, Margherita said, "It's hard to see treasure in a dragon's cave. It's so dark, Mamma."

"Aren't we lucky that you are so brave in the dark now? Isotta smiled. "I'll bring a candle. Ava will, too. Right, Ava?"

"Absolutely."

Another moment of thought and then Margherita said, "It's very, *very* spooky. So we have to be very, *very* quiet."

Isotta nodded seriously. Ava followed suit and added, "I won't make even a little sound."

Margherita grinned, pleased, before she pursed her lips. "Follow me." She spun theatrically and then whispered loudly over her shoulder. "Bring candles!"

"We've got them!" Isotta assured her. She handed one to Ava. The two women tiptoed cartoonishly after Margherita. Margherita got partway down the hallway and peeked over her shoulder. She grinned and danced a little caper before continuing to the bathroom. She stopped and swung the door open. Creeping inside, she knelt in front of the sink. Putting a finger over her mouth, she stared meaningfully at Isotta. Isotta mimicked the gesture.

Ava lifted her finger to her mouth as well and then turned back to the kitchen. Isotta stayed her hand, "We need the light."

Ava said, "This is fruitless, Isotta. There's no dirt in here to bury treasure."

"You haven't read enough treasure books," Isotta grinned. "Wait."

"Fine." Ava held her candle higher, creating a halo of light around Margherita as she crawled into the cabinet. From within, they heard a rustle. Margherita's hand waved behind her now, clutching a euro bill. Isotta took it and held it to the light. "A twenty."

Ava nodded. "She must squirrel money back there. Anything she finds."

Isotta crouched down beside the child. "Can I see, *cara*?"

Margherita backed up and put her head close to Isotta's. "Quick before the dragon comes."

Isotta held her candle in front of her face and ducked into the cabinet. The back wall seemed . . . furry, like an animal. Mildew? Isotta hesitated before brushing her hand against it. The whispery feeling, not at all what a wall should feel like, made her exhale and recoil. The candle extinguished, leaving the faint scent of smoke seeping into the darkness. "Ava! Your candle!"

"But then I can't—"

"Now!"

Ava hunched down next to Isotta and handed her the candle.

Isotta said, "Careful. We need to keep it lit." She held the candle to the back wall. Only, it wasn't a wall. Not in a proper sense. Where a wall should be were stacks of bills. Stacks and stacks and stacks of bills.

Ava breathed, "*Madonna mia.*"

Isotta started removing stacks. More piles lay behind. The wall seemed to have been hollowed out and then filled in with cash. Quietly

Isotta said, "I think we figured out where Anna hid her money."

Beside her, she heard Ava whisper, "Crazy bitch. What's wrong with the bank?"

"I guess she didn't trust anyone." To Margherita, Isotta said, "Thank you, little one. For showing me the treasure."

"One." Margherita lofted a finger into the air proudly.

"One what?'

"One treasures." Isotta's legs gave out, and she slid onto her bottom. "Counting can be hard, Margherita. Are you sure there are more?"

Margherita threw her head back and laughed.

At the noise, Edo sat up in bed, his hand reaching for Francy. Before remembering he hadn't seen Francy in over a week. Thank goodness he'd alerted Francy to Santa Lucia's power outage before his phone died. Their connection seemed sound, but who knew what assumptions Francy could make if his texts and calls were met with silence. Instead, Francy promised to come. Even though Edo had insisted, "I told you, the road, it's washed out. There's no way up."

Francy's response? A shrug emoji, a heart emoji, and a crossed fingers emoji. Followed by a message. "Love finds a way through paths where wolves fear to prey."

To Edo's question marks, Francy had typed, "Byron. Save your battery. Take care of each other. I'll see you soon."

But of course, he hadn't come. How could he? Santa Lucia had become an island.

Edo lay back down before his eyes flew open. The sound . . . clearer now. Like crystals wincing against blackened cobblestones. A split second and then the sound of hooting, laughter—rough against the continual patter of rain—falling, falling, falling.

A moment of stillness rang through the darkened streets.

And then...another whoop, winnowing into the night air. Followed by the sound of splintering glass. Footsteps rustling, forcing open swollen doors, while objects hit the floor.

Then...no more moments of stillness. Just a constant rush of footsteps, interspersed with glass fragmenting into shards, scattering, tumbling into the shadows.

This time, close enough that it seemed he could make out the sound of individual splinters of glass hitting the street. His heart stopped. Who would break windows in the middle of the night, with everyone vulnerable, weak, and scared? He couldn't breathe.

Chiara appeared at his doorway. "Did you hear that?" She flinched and clapped a hand over her mouth to keep from shouting as another window smashed. She whispered. "Is that the bar? Did someone break our window?"

Edo jumped as another window shattered. Catcalls and hoots followed. He shook his head. "I think it's the *macelleria*."

Her face shone pale in the dark. "Oh my God, we need to call Giuseppe and Patrizia."

His hands tightened. "No phones, remember? So unless you want to go out there—"

She blanched. "What if they break in here?"

Edo stood and crept to the window. He lifted back the curtain to peer into the street. Figures rose darkly before collapsing back into the shadows. "I'm going down."

"No!" Her voice tensed.

"Chiara," he said, moving toward her in the darkness. "The La Pavoni."

She staggered backward. And then nodded, mute.

He nodded and grabbed a broom—

"A broom?" Chiara whispered, incredulous.

"It's not like movies, where there's a baseball bat lying around. Or andirons." His voice shook with forced bravado.

"Don't go yet!" She flew to the kitchen and grabbed a pasta rolling pin. How long since she'd rolled pasta with the three-foot long pin? And was this the time to ponder such inane questions?

She shook her head and readied the pin over her shoulder. Tiptoeing to catch up with Edo, she met him at the landing. They crept down the steps and then stopped at the burst of splintering glass immediately below them.

"*Madonna mia*," breathed Chiara.

"Holy hell," muttered Edo.

He ran down the remaining steps, broomstick ready over his shoulder. At the sound of the door banging open, the darkened figures in the bar stopped mid-motion. Edo could barely make out a man at the register, another at the shelf with the liquor bottles, and another standing with one hand on the La Pavoni.

Waving the end of the broom as if ready to strike, Edo shouted. "Get out! Get out of here!"

A snickering laugh cut the darkness.

Then a crash, as one looter used a half-filled bottle of Aperol to shove the wineglasses off the shelf.

Edo stepped forward, brandishing the broom menacingly. He wished he wore something other than pajama pants and a ratty t-shirt. And bare feet. He could see the shards of glass winking in the moonlight. At the sound of the La Pavoni scraping its way to the edge of the counter, Edo forgot about his feet and rushed into the bar, Chiara behind him, waving her rolling pin wildly. Hoping the looters would misconstrue the inherent danger of her improvised weapon.

Ignoring the shards of glass slicing his feet, Edo whooped and charged toward the looters. He swung his broom handle, knocking more glass onto the floor. Chiara joined in the shouting. Together they waved their weapons and their arms, appearing as a single mass of noise and chaos.

The looters jumped over the counter and for a moment stood silhouetted against the broken windows.

Without a word, they melted back into the rain.

Morning dawned . . . rainy. Again. Villagers glared at the sky.

"I think it's lighter today."

"You said that yesterday."

"I mean it today."

"Wishful thinking. Look at all that water running down the street."

Indeed, it was impossible to miss. The water flowed like a river spangled with broken glass.

"How are we supposed to clean all this up?"

"Never mind that. Who would *do* this?"

Grumbles up and down Via Romana as villagers studied the damage. Mostly to Santa Lucia's shops, but more than a few villagers had spent the night huddled in their beds as their living room windows' shattered.

Magda joined villagers standing beside the Madonna's niche, where the castle steps met Via Romana. "I can't believe we have to walk around town now, wondering who attacked us."

Ale, walking down the stairs, said, "The *castello* was spared. Surprisingly enough."

Giuseppe, wan from the long night, added, "The *castello* is out of the way, and harder for looters to escape from if caught. The *macelleria*, however . . . "

Edo picked his way through the damage to Bar Birbo, wincing as he walked. "How much damage, Giuseppe?"

"Enough."

A figure appeared from the *piazza*. Not until he was closer did the villagers recognize Giovanni. He cast a hopeful look into Bar Birbo. No coffee, of course, and the shattered glass covering the floor precluded even a simple gathering indoors. He sighed. "They ransacked my shelves. Not that I had much on them, but..."

Everyone nodded gloomily.

Chiara popped open an umbrella and joined the assembled villagers. "What a night." To Edo, she said, "How are your feet?"

Ale said, "What's wrong with your feet?"

Edo shrugged.

An edge of pride in her voice, Chiara said, "Edo scared the looters off last night—"

"You did, too," Edo interrupted.

More loudly, Chiara went on, "It all happened so fast. He ran in there with bare feet. We spent the next few hours hunched next to a candle with a pair of tweezers."

Giuseppe looked serious. "You don't want to risk infection. Get someone to look at those cuts."

"Who?" Edo asked, simply.

Everyone stood silent as the rain tapped a steady clacking drumbeat on the road and a muffled cadence on the umbrellas.

Giuseppe said, "Pietro told me that Livia used to volunteer at a clinic..."

Edo said grimly, "We all have enough to deal with. It's fine."

Chiara said, "But Edo—"

He turned to Giovanni. "What's the damage on the other side of town?"

Giovanni pressed his mouth into a straight line. "What you'd expect. L'Ora Dorata has no damage, thanks to those wood shutters Pietro installed. But the flower shop, the *rosticceria*. A few houses in between. The church is fine."

Edo frowned. "With no money coming in, how in the world will we ever fix it all?"

Chiara wondered, "Any rhyme or reason to the houses? Why some are hit and others not?"

Giovanni hesitated, shooting a glance at Magda. "You haven't heard?"

Chiara ran her weary hand over her forehead. "Heard what? What more can happen?"

Nodding, Giovanni said, "Rumors have already started. While no one is *saying* Dante did it, there's grumbling that his house, Magda's house, his buddy Ale's house, and the *comune* . . . none of them sustained any damage."

Magda huffed, "How does anyone know my house didn't get looted? Nobody has been by to check on me!"

Giovanni turned to Magda. "Did your house get looted?"

"No," Magda grumbled. "But it could have. You don't know."

"*Nobody* knows. That's the problem."

Chiara said, "This makes no sense. Dante is at Bar Birbo more than he's at the *castello*." She gestured to her bar, gathering rain through the smashed windows.

Giovanni shook his head. "Ridiculous sells around here, nowadays." He sighed. "Anyway, there's more."

"More?" yelped Chiara and Magda.

"More," affirmed Giovanni. "Even those who aren't buying the rumors that Dante planned this, that gossip greased the gears for spreading a milder version. That, if Dante had been a strong leader, none of this would have happened."

Chiara frowned. "How can so much nonsense be circulating when the sun has just risen. Theoretically, anyway." She glared at the subtle circle that flickered through the cloud cover.

Magda choked on her words until she spat out, "Dante has worked tirelessly. The man has gotten *no* sleep, *no* food in close to two weeks. And now a pack of ruffians adds even more discord to Santa Lucia? Doesn't anyone remember how Jacopo was born right there," she gestured to Bar

Birbo. "There, on the floor! And doesn't anyone remember how we all came together when that blasted fake husband of mine was mucking around? This is a *good* town with *good* people, and I'm furious that a rowdy bunch of thugs would make everyone forget that! And forget how much Dante has done for *all* of us?"

Giuseppe shook his head. "Maybe that's why Fabio's band is blaming Dante. Trying to diminish the goodwill people have for Dante now."

Edo rubbed his eyes. "You think Fabio is behind this?"

Giuseppe shrugged. "Not the damage. Too low even for him. Has to be stir-crazy teenagers. But Fabio must have started the rumors. He'll take any opportunity to twist things to suit his story. To get Arturo elected."

Chiara shook her head. "I still don't get it. Why does Fabio care about Arturo?"

Giuseppe shook his head. "Who knows, Chiara? Maybe because he thinks it'll be easy to pull Arturo's strings. Maybe he wants to stick it to the police, who laughed at him. All Fabio wants is power."

Chiara muttered, "What he wants is prestige. Power is a substitute."

Giuseppe said, "And if he wins. Disaster. Did you hear he wants to take money out of the schools?"

Chiara recoiled. "He does? And do what with it?"

Giuseppe shrugged. "Start a police task force to root out illegal immigrants selling drugs."

"Huh," Chiara said. "Do we have any of those?"

Giuseppe grimaced. "Who knows? But we'll have a hard time convincing Filamena to move back if he takes even a little from the school system."

Chiara stared into the foggy piazza, thinking of Marco and his extra aide. "Dante has to win."

Nobody answered as they sat with their thoughts, the rain swelling around them.

Elisa rubbed her eyes as she stumbled down the hall. It had been a long night. The sound of crashing glass up and down the town had kept her up half the night. Ale had warned her early into the power outage that restless teenagers might turn to looting as a way to blow off steam. So she knew to stay quiet, safe in her room behind windows laced with exterior stonework.

She would have been awake even without the sporadic shouting and crashing. Though she'd feigned sleep to avoid the confrontation, she'd heard Ava creep in after her visit to Isotta. What if Isotta believed Ava, that Elisa had taken her money? Would she not allow Elisa to be with Jacopo and Margherita anymore? Elisa's gut twisted.

And how could she look Ava in the eye, knowing that her mother believed her to be a liar?

Tears rose again in Elisa's eyes.

Stupid.

She was so stupid! If only she'd remembered right away to give Isotta the money.

Elisa rooted in the kitchen cabinets, hoping to find a package of anything. She was so tired of bread. Bread salad, grilled bread, toasted bread topped with garden greens.

Her eye caught on a piece of paper on the kitchen table. Tidy Ava never left *anything* on the kitchen table. She must have gotten home from Isotta's too distracted to clean up. That couldn't bode well. Elisa startled, realizing that the paper had her name written across the top. She drew closer and read—

"*Elisa. I'm sorry. You're right. I treated you like you were me, completely forgetting how wise you are. I know you won't want to talk about it. So instead, I thought I'd use the power of your language. I 'drew' you this picture. Please ignore what an artist I'm not and instead remember how very much I love you.*"

Elisa's eyes scanned the drawing, and then she slowed down to take it in. She had to smile at the roughness of the crayon work—the wavering lines, the crudeness of the image. Her art came so naturally, sometimes she forgot that not everyone felt more comfortable with a pencil than with a fork or spoon. She supposed that the figure with her hair in the ball was Ava, the one with hair drawn as straight lines must be her, Elisa. The figures stood side by side, though given the road they seemed to be on, Elisa supposed they were meant to be walking. Hearts surrounded the figures, drawn with every color of her crayon box, even black and grey. How it must have pricked Ava to draw hearts with such gloomy colors.

No more to it. But Elisa clasped the image to her chest. She stood before she could talk herself out of it and strode to Ava and Ale's room. She knocked and opened the door tentatively at Ava's, "Come in." Ava sat at the desk she had scooted to the window, scattered with gardening catalogs.

Elisa asked, "Ale?"

"He went to check the damage."

Elisa nodded. Shyly, she held out the picture. "Thanks for this."

Ava blushed. "I know it's awful."

Elisa gazed down at it. "It's perfect." She looked at Ava. Who studied her hands clasped in her lap.

"I never should have doubted you. You've always been honest with me, even when I didn't make it easy."

Elisa worried her lower lip between her teeth. "And my art?"

"I'll come to terms with the fact that my daughter can somehow with-stand the darkness better than I can." Ava offered a tremulous smile.

Elisa asked quietly, "You feel it, too?"

The words stalled Ava. She pressed her hands against her eyes before she lifted her gaze to Elisa. "Less and less. But it's there. I feel it when I'm alone, sometimes."

Hesitating, Elisa said, "I feel it when I'm alone, too."

Ava nodded. "I guess it makes sense." She shook her head, hoping to clear the tears from her eyes. "I cover up my dark feelings with flowers. I'm done trying to get you to cover yours." To Elisa's blank expression, she smiled. "I'm talking too much."

Elisa nodded. "Can we be done now?"

Laughing, Ava said, "Please. How about last night . . . did you hear any of that?"

"What's it like out there?"

Ava shook her head. "Ale should be back soon with a report. But I can say one thing for certain. It's still raining."

Elisa huffed. "Will it ever stop?"

"Doesn't seem like it, no." Retying the bun at the back of her neck, she added, "I'd suggest asparagus picking to add to our food stores, but Marcello went out a few days ago and fell down the hill. It's treacherous."

"Our food . . ."

"We'll need to limit it a little more."

Elisa nodded and then said as if realizing, "Oh!" She blushed. "The money . . . you gave it back to Isotta? How did you figure out I didn't . . . "

Ava drew her knees up to her chin and grinned. "You're not going to believe this."

Marcello strode up and down Via Romana. It seemed he'd never, ever stop pacing this blasted street. He paused and looked around. It really did seem like a blasted street. What with the shattered glass and debris strewn every which way, and the rain that covered everything with grey.

His stomach growled.

Stepping into Bar Birbo, he nodded grimly to Edo and Chiara, who paused in their sweeping. Marcello blinked at the misty, almost green, half-light. Nowadays, every moment seemed to unfold underwater.

Rubbing the back of his neck, Marcello said, "Dante asked me to come by. He's creating a new list of what people's needs are and who has supplies or labor to offer. After the looting yesterday, the old list is—"

"Defunct," Chiara supplied. With a sigh, she added, "I expect so."

"What can he or you or anyone else do?" Edo asked irritably. He caught Marcello and Chiara's exchange of glances and sighed. "Sorry," he muttered, picking up a piece of trash and tossing it across the bar. "I'm just sick of this. All of this." His eyes raked the floor for something else to throw. "And I'd kill for some protein."

Marcello flipped open his pad of paper. "Ale still has oil. Loads of it. Thank the Madonna, Tomasso delivered it before the road washed out. That adds calories. Vinegar, too, but I don't see that being useful for anyone. I tried hunting for wild greens, but—"

Chiara nodded. "We heard." She gestured to his mud-stained pants.

Marcello said, "We can't wash anything."

Beginning to sweep again, Edo said, "We still have plenty of bottled water if anybody needs that."

Marcello said, "Water is what we don't require." He glared out the shattered window.

Stepping over the pile of glass splinters, Chiara said, "I heard Sauro still has flour."

"He does." Marcello nodded. "So does Pietro. Pietro also has eggs. Some vegetables. Anyway, he's cooking it all up, having as many people as possible for dinner tomorrow. Giuseppe is bringing the last of his cured meats."

Edo groaned and held his stomach. "I miss proper food."

Chiara grinned, "I won't take offense."

"Your pasta with oil and pepper flakes has been divine, Chiara, but after the millionth time?"

"I'm joking," Chiara said, gently. "I miss it, too. Plus light. And hot showers." She lifted a hand to her lank hair.

Edo sagged. "And phone. And internet. And television." Shaking his head, he turned to Marcello. "Any word on who did this? Nobody still accuses Dante, do they?"

Marcello shrugged. "A few. But many say he didn't do enough to prevent it. I'm afraid it will hurt his chances."

Edo huffed, "This town is nuts."

Marcello shrugged again. "Dante himself is ignoring it. He's been all over town, working, listening, chipping in with clean up."

"How can that not convince people?"

Sweeping toward the window, Chiara said, "It probably has. The question is, will people choose to believe the good they see or the bad they gossip about?" She stopped and stared at the pile of glass accumulating under her broom. "Edo, are you smoking again?"

"What? No, I quit last year when—"

"Nobody else has been here. And I wouldn't blame you, it's been so trying—"

Edo shook his head, "What are you talking about?"

Marcello hunched over the glittering shards of glass. Carefully, he picked up a cigarette butt. "The looters must have left it."

Edo frowned. "They stopped to smoke a cigarette? Wouldn't a horde of teenagers have been racing around, adding insult to injury? Damn jerks."

Marcello picked up the butt and held it to the light. "Maybe they weren't just a horde of teenagers." He looked up with a grin.

Chiara and Edo looked at each other, confused.

Laughing now, Marcello said, "It's a MS cigarette butt. Fabio's calling card."

Pietro held the door open. Edo, his arm slung over Chiara's shoulder, sauntered into the *trattoria*. He lodged his umbrella in the corner and greeted Pietro, "Thanks for inviting us. We ran out of pasta yesterday and have moved onto *risotto*. But we're just boiling the rice in water."

"Thank goodness for gas stoves, anyway." Pietro nodded. "I'm glad you're here. I can think of no better way of using up ingredients before they expire."

Chiara asked, "Is there anything I can do to help?"

Pietro gestured to Ale at the counter. "Perhaps see if Ale needs help lighting his oil lamps?"

Edo frowned. "He has oil lamps? Or even oil?"

"He found the oil lamps in one of the rooms of the *castello*."

"And the oil?"

"Last year's olive oil."

Chiara laughed. "That works? I thought you'd need a particular oil for lamps."

"It smoked a lot," Pietro conceded. "But Dante asked the old-timers on his rounds and discovered we just needed to adjust the wick."

Chiara asked, "Is Dante coming?"

Pietro smiled. "He's already here. In the kitchen."

"In the *kitchen*?"

"For a man afraid to get his hands dirty, he works hard." He seemed to lose his train of thought as he noticed Magda pulling a reluctant Livia down Via Romana. Livia looked everywhere but at Pietro. As they approached, Magda offered a polite and stiff, "*Buona sera*" as Pietro said softly. "You came."

"It's a free meal," Magda muttered. "Of course we came."

A blush suffused Livia's fine features as she gave Pietro an embarrassed nod. Magda, spotting Luciano's mane of candy floss hair, hurried across the restaurant, calling inquiries about his health. Livia tried to follow, but in her haste to escape Pietro's beseeching expression, she ran headlong into Nia.

Livia stopped and pretended interest in the oil lamps, hoping Nia would slink away. But when Livia chanced a glance, she found the young woman staring at Livia. Did she have to make small talk with her husband's daughter? She resorted to a mere nod before sidling past. But then she caught sight of Nia's downcast eyes, the red of her cheeks. Livia paused. She hesitated for a beat before saying, "Such a hard time to settle into a new town."

Nia met Livia's eyes with surprise. She nodded, mute.

Livia tried not to notice how much Nia's eyes resembled her Sonia's. How her shoulders jutted like angles within her shirt. Livia frowned. "That shirt. It's far too small. How can Pietro—" Her eyes darted around the restaurant, but she couldn't see anything in this dim light, and anyway, what could she say?

In a small voice, Nia said, "I told him already. Mamma was so sick and then . . . "

"He forgot."

"He always forgets. Or doesn't tell me." Livia watched the youthful indignation spread over Nia's face. "I didn't know. I swear. When I asked you how to find him . . . I didn't know. Nobody told me." Her face collapsed. "I'm sorry. I'm so embarrassed." She covered her face with her hands and turned away.

Livia put a hand on her shoulder. "Wait."

Nia stopped, but kept her face covered. Livia's words stalled at the sight of those hands, as exquisitely wrought as the Madonna's. Fine and sensitive, waiting to offer a gesture of solace, ready to accept a gesture of grace.

Nia looked up at the silence, her eyes flashing. "You must hate him. Hate me. Hate all of us."

Livia shook her head. "I don't hate you, child."

"I hate him." Nia set her jaw. "For what he did to us."

"He made a mistake. I hope he makes it right. For all of you." Where were these words coming from? She had no idea, but as the words fell from her mouth, she sensed the path before her, once cluttered with brush, clearing. Making way for drifting sunlight.

Livia noticed Magda approaching, her face aghast at seeing Livia and Nia together. Before Magda could reach them, Livia leaned toward Nia. "There are clothes. In my closet. My old ones, Sonia's too. Outgrown. Take them."

Nia's mouth worked. "Take them?"

Livia smiled and tucked Nia's loose tendril of hair behind her ear. "Take them. They're yours."

"You're helping her?" Magda hissed in Livia's ear.

Her eyes not leaving Nia's, Livia said, "The girl doesn't have a mother."

Livia patted Nia on the shoulder before Magda offered the young woman a bland smile and tugged her friend away. Magda shook her head, "I think you're carrying this charity thing a little too far."

Livia shrugged. "It's just clothes. That's all."

Magda rolled her eyes. "If I know you, it won't be just clothes." She returned to her seat at Luciano's table, forcing Livia to sit beside her. Isotta and Ava had joined Luciano, engrossing him with their tale. Margherita mimed digging, but Luciano hardly noticed. Elisa had heard this story several times, but she listened with as much fascination as Luciano.

A bustle from the kitchen signaled the arrival of dinner. A hodge-podge dinner, to be sure, made from cured meats and limp vegetables. But eggs last a long time, and flour lasts even longer. So there was pasta upon pasta from wide *pappardelle* to thin *tagliatelle* to kinky *stringozzi*.

Unlike the elegant dinner that brought them all together for the soft opening in the autumn, this was familial. With trays set over Sterno lamps and everyone helping themselves. Villagers heaped food onto their plates and then joined their neighbors at tables illuminated by ancient oil lamps, filled with oil from the surrounding groves. Marcello, last in line, found there were no more plates.

Antonella, who had taken the last one, realized with a laugh. "I guess I got you back for the cookies."

He shrugged, pleased that she remembered. "I'm hungry enough, I'll just eat from the serving spoons. That wouldn't be ill-mannered, would it?"

Antonella held out the plate with two hands. "I'm only joking. You take it, you've been working so hard."

Taking a step closer, he put his hands on the plate. Antonella thought for a moment he might run his thumb over hers. She shivered in anticipation, but he only said, "You okay?"

She pushed her lank hair off her face, wishing she'd been able to wash properly. "Please have it!" she said brightly. "I'll use Nonna's plate when she's done."

Marcello looked around for Pietro. "He must have miscounted."

Antonella stepped out of the line. "His hands are full, let's not bother him."

Reeling her back by the arm, Marcello said with a smile, "You didn't think I would let you give me this plate did you?"

She bit her lip.

His grin broadened. "And let you lord it over me, later? We'll share."

"Sh-share?" She stuttered.

"Sure, why not?"

Antonella tried to convince herself Marcello was being friendly. That spark in his eye? Only his good humor. She tried to laugh with him. "It's a deal."

They sat together, Antonella careful not to touch him. But somehow, they wound up hip to hip. A zing raced through her body. She ignored it and focused on him trying to get her to eat the last of the *tagliatelle*. "It's your favorite!"

Bea called from the next table, "It's not her favorite. She likes mine better. With white sauce."

Marcello and Antonella ducked their heads together and giggled. Antonella pushed the *tagliatelle* toward him and said, "I promise. I mean it. You take this. You need the calories more than I do."

He touched his tongue to his upper lip. "Antonella. I don't know how to do this."

"Do what?"

"Flirt. With you. I keep fumbling and now I'm scared to blow it."

She blinked. Touching his hand, she said with a smile, "I wouldn't worry about that."

His eyes widened. Tentatively, he leaned forward, and she pulled back in alarm. "But not now! I ran out of deodorant last week, and Dante said it was *not* on the list of essentials. Wait until I've had a chance to clean myself up?"

A grin spread across his face as they gazed at each other. "Oh, I think—"

Ale pulled a chair up beside Antonella, completely missing their unfocused eyes. "I hope I'm not interrupting. But I've been wanting to talk to you."

Antonella turned slowly. "Me?"

Nodding, Ale said, "Have you gotten another job yet?"

"No." At the iciness in her expression, Marcello reached for her hand.

Ale smiled, his enthusiasm blinding him to the exchange. "Good!"

In unison, Marcello and Antonella said, "Good?"

"Would you consider working for me?"

Antonella narrowed her eyes. "For you? Like, in the *castello*?"

Reading her expression, Ale rushed to clarify. "Not washing sheets or anything like that. You see, I have all these projects, and the *castello* is the lynchpin of them all. You know about my work with the *frantoio*?"

"Yes . . ."

"Right, you were instrumental to that. Then there's the wine."

Antonella nodded, trying to see where this was all going.

"And after you and I had that conversation in the street. I got this idea.

For an app that helps travelers find local specialties wherever they are in Italy."

Marcello watched as Antonella sat back, her face still as she processed his words. "That's . . . that's a great idea."

"Of course you think that, I stole the idea from you." Ale grinned. "I figured the least I could do was offer you a job. I'm struggling with interface and branding, so I'm not getting enough notice from investors. I finally set up a meeting with an app development company but then the power went out. I barely had a chance to text them to cancel, and I'm sure they think I'm weaseling out of it."

To blank looks, Ale added, "Americans will have a hard time wrapping their mind around a town essentially surrounded by a moat of water. With no power, vanishing food, and, the *horrors*, no *internet*." Marcello chuckled and Ale went on, "Anyway, I want to tie all these projects together. Which is tricky, it's an odd combination of old and new methods of income generation." He stopped and looked up at the ceiling. "Is it possible to be *too* diversified? But I don't see a way around it. One bad season and there goes my olive crop or my wine crop. Or both. But one bad turn of the market and there goes any tech development I've created."

Feeling all surrounding eyes on him—Dante watching from the next table, Edo leaning back to hear—Ale chose his words carefully. "For me, the solution lies in bridging the two. The old and the new. I want you to help me build that bridge."

Pietro stood. His fingers started to flick like marching soldiers, but he shook his hands and walked to the kitchen.

Antonella considered Ale's words. "This is a great opportunity for me, Ale. Seriously."

"Now, don't get too excited. I haven't told you about the salary. Which right now is nothing." He ignored Marcello's black expression. "But I hope we can agree on a percentage. Once I start making money, you do, too. And you'd be welcome to look for proper work at the same time."

"Thank you, Ale. I'm flattered. I'd love to see what you have."

He snorted. "We'll need to wait for electricity."

In an undertone, Antonella said, "I have to know. Is this a pity hire?"

"A pity hire? What do you mean?"

Antonella stared at her plate. "I figure you heard. I mean, I figured everyone's heard why I left my last job. The harassment."

Ava dropped her fork. "Sorry," she muttered, leaning over and taking more time than required to pick it back up. Elisa knelt on the ground and held it aloft saying, "It's right here. I'll clean it." She handed Ava the wiped fork before plucking Jacopo from Isotta's lap.

Softly, Ale said to Antonella, "I hadn't heard. I know this is terribly insufficient, but I'm sorry that happened to you."

She shrugged. "I'm sorry the situation has made it complicated to pick up my last paycheck. We could use it. Especially now, with nobody working."

Ale nodded thoughtfully. "Maybe we can get our work started even before the power returns. I might have one last legal pad I can use for sketching ideas. Can we meet tomorrow?"

She nodded, a smile lighting her face.

Ava blurted, "You deserve that paycheck, Antonella."

Antonella's smile evaporated. "Every time I think about walking in that building, I get sick. Imagining them all speculating about why I left."

Ava's eyebrow creased in confusion. "You didn't tell anybody what happened?"

"How could I?"

Ava looked at her plate and said nothing.

Lamplight flickered across Antonella's face as she whispered, "You think I should have said something."

"Nothing of the sort." Ava shook her head. "I can imagine how scary it is to talk about it here, let alone . . . there. Only, I can't help thinking . . ." Her words drifted away.

Antonella sat back, her eyes wide as she whispered, "The next girl."

The door blew open, and a figure appeared in the threshold, unrecognizable in the dim half-light. A voice boomed. "Is there room for a party crasher?"

Edo trembled at the sound.

The figure moved further into the *trattoria* where the concentration of lamps threw his face into stark relief.

"Francy," Edo yelped, "It's you!"

Francy laughed, throwing his arms around Edo.

"But ... how did you get here?"

"I walked."

"You *walked*?" Edo asked, incredulous.

"Yes. Did you know the road is washed out?"

Everyone laughed.

Francy went on, "I pulled over and used my iPhone flashlight to climb through the groves."

"Walking in the dark, in the mud, with all the loose stones ... it's a miracle you didn't fall and break a leg!" Edo said.

"I admit I felt nervous setting off. There's so much water flowing around the base of the mountain, and the ground seemed ... like soft cheese."

"I knew there'd been a landslide!" someone called from the back of the room.

Francy grinned. "But once I set off, the danger seemed to evaporate." No one spoke, every eye trained on Francy. He went on, his voice reverent, "The path cleared before me, every one of my steps landed as if preordained. I don't know how to explain it, but getting here seemed ... easy. I moved as if in a dream."

Silence met his words.

"I brought extra portable chargers, by the way," Francy announced, looking around. "For anyone that needs them."

Edo shook his head, dumbfounded. "But Marcello tried getting down the mountain before the looting—"

"Looting?"

"There's so much to explain. He didn't get more than a few hundred meters before he fell—"

"Handsomely, it should be said," interjected Marcello. "Really, quite fashionable, that fall." He put a careful arm around Antonella. Who beamed at him.

"But," Edo's eyes searched Francy's, "how did you make it through the rain?"

"What rain?"

All heads turned to the window, black now. Obscuring what lay beyond.

Dante stood. "Are you quite certain?"

Francy shrugged, "See for yourself."

Dante stepped to the open door and tentatively lifted his hand, palm to the sky, to feel the precipitation. He turned to Magda and grinned before calling to the room, "*Tutti!* The rain!"

Everyone rushed the door.

"It's lighter!"

"Gone, I'd say!"

"Hey, Luciano! I bet your brother can make the move to Santa Lucia now! If he still wants to come to our blighted town..."

"Is that...*starlight?*"

"Temporary. The rain will kick up again when we're all walking home, mark my words."

"*Uffa*, always with your depressing fortune telling!"

"Is there any way to know? Since we can't check our phones?"

"Watch the sky."

Groan. "So old school."

"I bet there will be power soon, though. If the rain is stopping."

"Do we know why we lost it in the first place?"

"Dante thinks the flooding swamp fried the transformer at the bottom of the road."

"Why would they place a transformer by a body of water?"

"How could anybody have predicted a storm like this? Not even the old-timers have ever seen the water rise this high. But maybe lightning hit the transformer. Or I heard Luciano say that the landslides might have exposed a power line. Could that be it, Dante?"

"Dante?"

"Where's Dante?"

The villagers watched as what must be Dante's silhouetted figure made its lonely way up Via Romana. Before falling at the Madonna's feet. Head ducked in prayer or praise or supplication. Or maybe all three. Suddenly, they saw Dante's form unfold and rise, tall. His fingers whispered against the hem of the Madonna's skirt, lit by moonlight. Trailing off the pedestal, Dante's hand drifted to his side as he hurried up the steps to the *castello*.

In the quiet, they heard the breeze winding its way through Santa Lucia, light and airy.

The rain had truly ended.

Edo squeezed Francy's hand as the two of them walked down the road. "I can't believe you're here."

Francy grinned. "If Mohammed won't come to the mountain..."

"Hey, first of all, Mohammed wanted to come to the mountain. Second of all, mountain? You don't think you're flattering yourself?"

Francy laughed before saying, "How are your feet?"

"Fantastic."

"I can't believe how much you tore them up."

"If you'd seen all the glass, you'd believe it." Edo tipped his head back. "Sun, how I've missed you."

Francy pulled Edo into his chest, wrapping his arms around him before pulling back to run a finger down his cheek. Edo bobbed up on his tiptoes to press a kiss onto Francy's lips. He pulled back, his eyes teasing. Grabbing Francy's hand, he tugged him down the road. "Come on, I want to see if the swamp water is receding. I hope your car didn't flood."

"How could it? I parked far from the water."

"Listen, nothing surprises me anymore." He paused. "You should know, Chiara found out about you saving the bar." At Francy's patient smile, Edo added, "I didn't tell her! Fabrizio did!"

"He did? How did he know?" Francy turned his gaze out to the distant hills. "Our accountant. I should have anticipated that. Is she angry?"

Lightly, Edo said, "She had a lot of questions. And she can't help feeling she owes you something—"

"She doesn't."

"That's what I told her."

Francy stopped walking and pointed across the clear and shining air. "Look at that."

The flooded wetland gleamed in the early morning sun, reflecting the mountains and the pink sky streaked with clouds, fresh in their innocence.

Edo breathed a sigh of relief. "Those clouds can't hold any rain." Suddenly he yelped. "Look at that!" He pointed at a group of men in waders trudging through the water that flowed over the road. They gathered around the grey metal box that stood on the Santa Lucia side of the road.

Edo hurried down to meet them. "*Ciao! Ciao! Salve!*"

The men nodded.

Edo asked, "So it was the transformer box? Flooded?"

One of the men looked up from laying out his tools. In a sharp voice, he said, "That's what your mayor thinks. And seemed intent on our knowing at five o'clock this morning when he began banging on all of our doors."

"Dante? Was in Girona? How did he get there?"

One of the other men yawned and said, "Judging from the amount of mud he was sporting, I'd say he walked."

"He walked? All the way to Girona?" Edo couldn't keep up. "Why didn't he call?"

The men looked at each other and burst out laughing.

Edo looked confused. "What?" He turned to Francy, "You gave him a portable charger, right? He could have called . . . "

The first man shook his head, still chuckling. "He called all right. I don't know how he got all of our numbers, he must have an in with the power company. He blew up each of our phones. We told him we'd come later in the week. We have a *lot* of outages to attend to. So he showed up. On each of our doorsteps."

Edo looked at Francy with wide eyes. "Wow." To the men, he said, "Can you fix it?"

They grumbled. "We're trying. Probably could work faster without interruption."

Edo grinned. "Okay, okay, we can take a hint."

He pulled Francy's hand. One of the men stared at the gesture with curiosity, but most of the men shrugged and got to work.

Edo took off his sweater while they walked, as the sun burned off the early morning coolness. He enumerated all the things he would do once they had power. Make a proper cup of *espresso*, rather than coffee from the moka. Watch television. Take a hot shower. Read by an actual light.

It was hard to tell in the throbbing morning light, but in that moment, the electricity surged, powering the homes of Santa Lucia.

The bell over the bar tinkled and Chiara called from her hunched position behind the counter. "Not open yet! Still no milk...Or much of anything," she said to herself, standing while straightening the kerchief she'd tied over her hair.

"Actually, I brought *you* coffee," Fabrizio said, holding out a cup.

Suddenly, the entrenched gloom of the last two weeks lifted like a curtain and Chiara's face reflected the full glory of the nascent sun. She had to stop herself from running to him. "Fabrizio."

"Francy told me the road opened. I'd been in Girona, waiting."

Chiara rubbed the back of her hand across her forehead, leaving a grey streak.

He went on, "I've missed you."

She looked down, unable to form the words.

He paced the bar, taking in the state of things. "The looting...was it Fabio?"

"We can't prove it, but..."

"Does this mean he's backed off of Dante?"

She blinked, still getting used to sunshine drifting into the bar. "This can't be what you want to talk about."

"So, we're diving in," he said. "I know I'm overprotective of Francy. And there were these places where it felt as if you refused to see—" The squeal of the door opening from the apartment cut off his words.

"We need to oil this door," Edo announced before noticing Fabrizio standing in the middle of the bar. "Fabrizio! You're here! Just in time to help with the cleanup. Francy went to Girona to get some cloth that's better for picking up glass shards."

Fabrizio stared at the ground, looking up as Edo cross the bar and kissed his aunt's cheek. "*Buongiorno*, Zia. I'm going to meet him at the lot to help him carry."

Chiara nodded.

Edo smiled easily before strolling out of Birbo, whistling.

Fabrizio watched him go, "He's happy."

Despite herself, Chiara grinned. "The rain stopped. The power is on. And best of all, Francy's here."

Fabrizio searched her face.

Chiara went on. "You made a lot of assumptions about me. It's what people have done, my entire life. Assume they know all parts of me, because I stand here in the public eye every day."

"I know. I'm sorry . . . but when you closed up and got defensive—"

"I did, and I'm sorry. There's a lot there. None of it what you think. Or maybe *some* of what you think. After all, I'm a work in progress. I can admit that. Edo has been telling me how to wake up. Or get woke?" She grinned, weakly. "But one thing I need you to know. It was never about Francy. I think the world of him. I just didn't want him to hurt Edo. Or Edo to hurt him."

He breathed deeply and then looked up with an enormous grin. "Chiara. These two weeks without you. My life has no color."

She smiled. "Well then, grab a broom."

Ale leaned back, his face haggard from working through the night. "I can't believe it. The answer was in front of me this whole time."

Antonella shrugged with a small smile, collecting their papers into a stack.

"You asked three questions and boom! The whole thing came together. The interface, the predictive code . . . I think we have something here."

"You needed to talk it through, that's all."

He shook his head. "At the time, it killed me that I'd worked so hard for this meeting and then had to cancel. But now . . . "

"No, you weren't ready," Antonella chuckled.

"I would have blown that one chance, and that is no lie."

"Did you have trouble rescheduling for today?"

"It took some pleading," Ale said. "And throwing in references to newspaper articles about the outage. Plus, I think my buddies pulled some strings."

Ava stepped into the office. "Ale, you asked me to tell you—"

"Oh, my God! Is it time already?" He looked at his watch.

Ava and Antonella exchanged amused glances before Antonella picked up her purse. She ordered Ale, "Stay calm. Keep to the script. Hit those points I underlined." She smiled. "You got this."

He shouted over his shoulder as he ran to the bedroom. "Thank you, Antonella! I'll call you!"

Antonella chuckled to herself.

Ava smiled after him. "Think he can do it?"

"The app is great, he has to trust it to impress, so he doesn't oversell." Antonella looked around with a grin. "Okay, you might want to make sure he puts on a tie. I imagine it's been a while."

Ava laughed. "Thanks, Antonella."

"No problem. I'm glad I could help." Her smile dazzled, even in the sunlit office. "Speaking of help, I want to tell you—"

A crash sounded from the bedroom.

Antonella shook her head. "I'll tell you later. Go!"

Ava rushed into the bedroom where Ale was throwing clothes all over the bed. "Ava! Where is that shirt I ironed?"

"Ironed? You didn't iron any shirt."

"I did! I—" He stopped. "Oh, *Madonna mia*. I reminded myself to iron so many times my brain must have convinced myself I did it."

She picked up a shirt from the bed. "They won't be able to see wrinkles over the screen, right. This one should—"

"No! Ava! Don't you know how important this is? They aren't going to invest in my app if I look like some sort of street urchin!"

Ava looked at the shirt in her hands. "It's Dolce & Gabbana." She held it out. "Even if it's a little wrinkled—"

He shook out one shirt after another, flapping them like a bullfighter calling danger as he muttered, "You don't understand."

She put a hand on his arm. "Hey. I do understand. This is important to you. You've worked hard. But if it doesn't work, Ale, you'll be okay. I hope you've learned these last months that you are smart and capable enough to come up with idea after idea until something sticks. I trust that. You need to do the same."

The fight went out of Ale.

"Thank you. I needed that." He grinned and took the shirt from her. "I'll not only wear this one, I'll *own* it."

"Yeah, you will."

He pulled his t-shirt off over his head.

She gave a low whistle and sat back on the bed. "My *man*."

"Hey now. No time for that." He shrugged the shirt on. "Raincheck?"

She grinned. "Promise?"

As he buttoned the charcoal-grey buttons, he leaned down to kiss her.

Her lips parted as she pressed herself against him, her hands reaching into his hair.

He straightened with a glint in his eyes. "Hey, watch the hair. I've cultivated a style."

"You mean by not getting a haircut in ages and then not showering for two days while you've been working around the clock?"

"That's the one."

"It's working for you." She nodded and then stood to straighten his tie. "Now, tell me. After today, when will you know?"

"If they like it, they may want to invest within the next few weeks."

"Just think of it. A salary!"

"Sounds like a dream," he laughed. "Okay, how do I look?"

She stepped back as he lifted his arms and twirled. "Like the person I want to buy an app from."

He grinned and opened the door to run down the hallway to his office. "Go get 'em, Tiger!" She called after him. In English.

He spun and ran backward. "Where did you get that?" he said with a laugh.

"From you."

As he disappeared into his office, she whispered, "*In bocca al lupo.* Good luck, my love."

Isotta watched as Livia followed a sprinting Margherita down Via Romana and held fast to Jacopo, lunging to get his little feet on the ground. Tapping the (charged!) phone in her hand, Isotta planned out her next hour—the phone call with Riccardo, moving the cash to the bank, the accounts to set up for each of the three children. There would be enough leftover so she could delay returning to work until Jacopo started school.

Her book . . .

She couldn't count on that for income. But having it to focus on had gotten her through these last few months. She loved having a way to access a part of her she hadn't known existed. No matter how strained things became with Enrico, she felt grateful that he'd given her this gift. She just wished she could see her work in print. Her agent had shipped proof copies during the flood, but with the road washed out, the postal service returned them to the publisher. Hopefully, they'd be sent back soon. She couldn't wait.

She watched the sun sparkle against the walls, a play of light against dark stones. Carosello jogged past, looking remarkably clean. Livia must have gotten to him again. Grinning, Isotta turned to walk up Via Romana, only to come toe to toe with Enrico.

He grabbed her arm to keep her from stumbling backward.

Catching her breath, Isotta said, "I didn't know you were in town."

"Babbo and I arrived this morning."

She nodded. "The two-week flooding fiasco didn't change his mind?"

"He's committed to moving in. Luciano, though, might have some regrets when he sees both of our cars packed to the brim. They got distracted before we could bring in more than a few boxes and now they're wandering around town looking for damage and discussing floods of yore."

"That sounds about right." Casually she asked, "Carla isn't with you?"

"We needed every inch of space in both cars."

She nodded.

He ventured, "I understand congratulations are in order."

"Congratulations?"

"You found the missing money."

"Some of it. I suspect more will turn up once we begin renovations."

"You'll get to make the house yours."

"Yes."

"Now you have everything you ever wanted." His smile didn't meet his eyes. "Right?"

She looked at the ground and said nothing.

"Right?" He prodded.

She avoided his gaze. "How am I supposed to answer that?"

"How about the truth?" He added bitterly under his breath. "For once."

Isotta lifted her eyes, her expression challenging. "What do you mean?"

"Never mind." He turned into Bar Birbo but then whipped back around. "Do you even like me at all?"

Isotta stared at him blankly.

"You act sweet and interested when I'm with you, then you laugh at me behind my back about how boring I am, then you throw yourself at me. I can't keep up."

"Laugh at you . . . what do you mean?"

"I don't know the games you're playing at, but it's unfair of you to treat me like this when you know how I feel about you."

"Feel? As in, present tense?" Her eyes widened.

"I misspoke. Felt." He frowned. "But our lives intersect. We have to get along. Have some respect."

Isotta frowned. "Listen, it wasn't just me that night. You were there, too."

He lifted his hands. "I'm only a man, Isotta. I show up for you because I care. Even though I know how boring you find me. And then you—"

She shook her head angrily. "That was you as much as me. And where do you get that stuff about me finding you boring?"

A muscle worked in his jaw.

"Oh," She drawled out the word and then laughed mirthlessly. "Carla."

"What about Carla?" He spat out.

She studied him for a moment. "I haven't wanted to say anything that would risk hurting our friendship. But without my being honest with you, we don't have a friendship to protect."

"Well?" He practically stomped his foot in impatience.

"Your girlfriend is a snake."

His mouth dropped open.

"I'm sure she has some perfectly lovely qualities, but honesty and generosity of spirit are not among them. At least not as a rule. I don't blame her for being territorial. But there are adult ways to deal with that, and then there is Carla."

"She said when you met me—"

"Believe me or don't believe me. You know what was happening in my life when we met. My first romance was with *Massimo*. Can you imagine what that does to a woman? Yes, I considered you a friend for months, but, Enrico, I don't think that's a bad thing. It means I fell in love with you because of *you*. God, Enrico, isn't that obvious from that night? What did you think that was about? I couldn't fake that kind of…" Her voice trailed off as she blushed.

He stared at the ground.

Shaking her head, she said, "I know I shouldn't tell you any of those things. It'll make it awkward. But honestly, I think it's been more awkward to have it hidden away as if my feelings don't matter. When you're the one who showed me they do."

Finally, he whispered, "Tomasso?"

"Oh, Enrico," she sighed. "You see what I mean?"

With that she stepped past Enrico and walked up the street, her arms around her body, trying to keep it together until she rounded the corner and disappeared into the alley.

Only a few puddles remained beside the marshland. The air shone as if all the moisture had filled the atmosphere, swelling each unseen particle. Trucks made their winding way up the hill. Bringing produce to restock the depleted *fruttivendolo*, packets of pasta and yogurt for Giovanni's *alimentari*, and flour for Sauro's *forno*.

Waiting for the trucks to pass, Antonella drove quickly past the wetlands. She knew the water couldn't rise and take her car into the swamp. But she couldn't shake the tremble of nerves.

Her phone buzzed. She ignored it, eyes on the road. That phone had been buzzing all morning. All weekend, in fact. Ever since she'd walked out of her meeting with Ale the day of his pitch and called Francesca. She didn't have time now for cold feet. She had no energy to carry anybody over the finish line. As she approached Girona, she popped a mint in her mouth, hoping it would settle her stomach.

Before she knew it, she arrived outside the office building. She parked across the street, gathering her purse, her keys, and her courage. As her heart beat emphatically, Antonella wrapped her saffron scarf around her neck. A gift from Marcello, who had said that some religions considered the color holy. She didn't know where he got his information, but she wore the sunshine like armor.

As she stepped out of her car, she noted the gutter, running with water at least a meter wide. Her eyes scanned until she found a wooden plank set up on the corner to allow pedestrians to access the sidewalk. She heard Francesca's voice behind her, and turned, ready to greet her. Until her mouth fell open. Francesca held point position, leading what seemed a battalion of beautiful women. Eight? Twelve? Antonella couldn't count them all.

They approached her, faces resolved. All of them wore their hair sleekly styled with suits that announced power and elegance while not hiding the very obvious fact that they were women. Their shoes underscored the fact, calves shapely with the lift the heels gave them.

Francesca asked, eyes flashing. "Are you ready?"

Antonella answered, her voice grimly determined. "As I'll ever be."

Francesca called over her shoulder. "All right, ladies. Here we go." She stepped beside Antonella and clasped her hand. The women marched forward, united, and threw open the glass double doors with their free hands. The women poured into the office and hesitated for only a second at the sudden stilling of office chatter. Antonella inclined her head toward the glass corner office, the seat of power.

Francesca nodded in agreement and they stormed forward. At the desk outside Signor Marconi's office, Francesca offered a tight grin to the secretary, who blinked in understanding before standing to announce their presence. Her voice could be heard from outside. "You have some people waiting to see you, sir."

"Who?"

"Former assistants of Signor Tocci."

"What do they want? Actually," he cut himself off, "tell them to make an appointment."

"They have one."

"They do?" His voice rose. "How do they have an appointment? I didn't authorize that."

The secretary's voice, innocent, "I can't imagine, sir. But there they are. On the schedule."

"Send them away. I don't have time—"

Antonella and Francesca nodded to each other, Francesca signaling the women behind them with her eyes. They strode through the door.

The secretary shot them a knowing grin before backing out of the room, saying, "I'll just leave you to it, shall I?" She closed the door.

Signor Marconi sat at his desk, staring as his office filled with women, standing above him like amazons. Weakly he said, "Have a seat."

They looked around at the three chairs. Francesca said, "We'll stand, thank you."

Antonella said, "We're here about Signor Tocci."

His forced chuckle fell flat, hard stones onto his polished desk. "Signor Tocci. Always a treat for the ladies. If you let him take that too far, well, that's hardly my concern."

From behind Antonella, one woman said, "So you know. About him. And what he does."

He shrugged. "He is a terrible flirt. Everybody knows that."

Francesca scowled. "Flirt. Is that what you call it? When he puts his hands all over you?"

"Ladies, ladies. "Signor Marconi winced. "Let's not get overly emotional. It's hardly my job to police what happens behind closed doors."

Signor Tocci burst in, his tie askew, shoving his shirt into his pants. He had clearly been alerted to the women's arrival while servicing himself in the bathroom. "Whatever they're telling you, it's not true!"

A woman's voice boomed, "He made me sit on his lap."

Signor Tocci protested, "That was your idea!"

Another woman said, "All of our ideas? Each of us decided, unbeknownst to each other that we would like nothing more than sitting on your lap while you fondled—"

"I did not!"

Antonella said, "You made me try on underwear."

Francesca whispered. "He made me do that, too." Her voice rising now, she added, "The touches, the innuendos, they started small. Then he began . . ."

From the crowd of women, one shouted, "Then he began getting off. First right after touching us, on his own. Then right in front of us. While he made us watch."

Antonella shivered.

Her voice rising, Francesca said, "He forced several women in this room to have sex with him."

Signor Marconi gasped as Signor Tocci bellowed. "Lies! All lies! I'm married to a beautiful woman. Why would I want to have sex with my *secretary*?" His voice resembled gunfire. "What am I? A cliché?"

The women, as one, turned to stare at him. He sank into a chair and turned to his boss. "They're lying."

His boss regarded him levelly and quietly asked, "All of them?"

Signor Tocci flinched. "Yes! A bunch of talentless, poorly educated women trying to climb the corporate ladder! They . . . they came onto me! And when I declined, they decided to . . . to do *this*. This is retribution for their feminine egos!"

Signor Marconi shook his head. "Stories have been circulating for years, Claudio. I didn't know it had gone this far. A little harmless flirtation, a little charged banter, sure, but—"

Sounds of derision exploded from the women.

Francesca said, "Sexual harassment is acceptable as long as it doesn't include sex?"

He shrugged. "You women take everything too seriously. Sexuality is

352

part of life, it happens on the street, on the beach, in the office..."

Antonella shook her head. "So what you're saying is that a man can touch a woman to satisfy his sexual urges, irrespective of her own?"

He glared. "I'm saying you women need to lighten up." He gestured at Signor Tocci. "You're so overwrought you're missing the fact that I'm giving Signor Tocci a reprimand."

"A reprimand!" They shouted.

"Yes. A reprimand." He turned to Signor Tocci. "Claudio. It's gone too far. Surely you can see that. Apologize and we can—"

Antonella leaned over the desk and looked directly into Signor Marconi's eyes. Her heart jackhammering in her chest she said softly, so softly he could hardly hear her over the rustling in the room. "Don't you have a wife, a daughter, a sister... you must at least have a mother. Imagine a man pawing at a woman you love as if she gets no say. Telling her over and over that she's only worth the number of buttons she unfastens. Can you imagine how trapped she must feel? How terrified? Can you see how, caught between sacrificing her job or sacrificing herself to each increasingly intimate touch, she might lose all sense of who she is? A word or a touch might seem small stakes to you, Signor Marconi. But even small jabs can kill a person." She stepped back and gestured behind her, even as she noticed Signor Marconi's gaze flicking to a framed photograph on his desk. "This is the fallout. It's been coming for a long time."

Signor Marconi watched his thumb rub across his knuckles as crosstalk filled the room. He scanned the women in front of him. Wall to wall women, arms crossed, shoulders taut.

He hesitated before turning to Signor Tocci. "Claudio. I know you had that one great account years ago—"

A sound of exasperation followed by a woman's voice. "Visia? That was me."

Signor Marconi grimaced. He sat back. "I see."

Signor Tocci shouted, "She's lying! You know she is."

Clasping his hands on the desk in front of him, Signor Marconi shook his head. "I don't know that. I do know that when she left, chased out as it now appears," the woman drew herself to full height, a smile playing around her lips, "Your creativity seemed to go with her."

Signor Tocci sputtered. Meanwhile, Signor Marconi turned to the women. He stood slowly, letting his eyes move from one to the other. "I looked the other way. I knew...at some level I must have known. As much as I told myself it was nothing. I let it happen, ladies," his eyes darted to Antonella, "and for that, I apologize."

The room erupted, and Signor Marconi put up his hands. "I know that's not sufficient."

"What are you saying?" Signor Tocci whispered.

Signor Marconi turned to Signor Tocci. "I should have thought that would be obvious. You're finished. Pack your things, I want you gone. Now. Five minutes ago." He watched, they all watched, as Signor Tocci opened his mouth to protest but stopped at the fury on Signor Marconi's face. He spun on his heel and darted out the door.

Turning back to the women, Signor Marconi said, "Sit down, please, ladies. We need to talk about how to make this right." They looked around, faces awash with relief but confusion about where to sit.

Signor Marconi nodded. "Let's adjourn to the conference room if that's quite all right?" As they followed him out the door, Antonella heard him mutter to himself, "The least these women deserve is a place at the table."

Ale spun around in his kitchen chair. His haste eradicating his knowledge that the chair was a regular chair, a kitchen chair, not a spinning chair.

"Ava...*Ava!*"

She came running into the room. "What is it? Is everything okay?"

"The app. I got it. An *offer*."

"Oh, that's marvelous! Now you'll get a salary and—"

"No, you don't understand," he laughed. "This isn't just an investment offer. With an investment, I'd be funded to continue working on the app, until it eventually made money or I sold it. Or ideally, both. But this . . . it's total buyout. They give me money. I give them the rights."

"How . . . how much money?"

Elisa peeked into the room. "I heard shouting. Is everything okay?"

Ale grinned and waved her in. "Very okay. You should be here for this, too. It impacts all of us."

She stepped in and put her hand into Ava's.

He took a breath and said, "The company wants to buy the app. Partly for the app itself, but it turns out that predictive code I labored over is worth more than I knew."

Elisa darted a look at Ava who said, "Ale, you're losing us."

"What matters is this, my non-tech savvy ladies. It's time to celebrate."

Elisa shook her head, "What are we celebrating?"

Right as Ava said, "Are you sure you want to sell it, Ale? You worked so hard. You don't want to see it through?"

He shook his head. "Oil and wine, I'll see to fruition. For tech, the idea generation was fun, but I'm more than happy to hand over the reins. Especially for two million euros."

"*What?*" Ava and Elisa shouted at the same time. They looked at each other. Ava whispered to Ale, "It's not funny, Ale. You shouldn't mess with us like this."

"I'm not! I have the offer right here. I sign over all rights and send them the tech, and they'll transfer two million euros into a bank account of my choice."

Ava shrieked and leap into Ale's arms while Elisa threw her hands over her head and ran in a circle, landing in a hug with Ale and Ava. The three of them jumped up and down, yelling and shouting.

They pulled apart and stared at each other. Ale said softly, "Think of it. We can get married."

"I would have married you without money, I *told* you," Ava murmured.

He shook his head. "Not until I could take care of you. I told *you*."

She muttered with a smile, "So old-fashioned."

"Tell me about it. Bruno says I have the makings of an excellent crotchety old farmer," he mugged. "We'll finish the *castello*. All of it. Ava, we won't need to rent out rooms. Instead, we can build that arts and retreat center we dreamed about doing someday. With flowers every-where." He turned to Elisa, "Elisa, your art teacher, we can pay him now, instead of bartering. So you can have lessons a couple times a week, rather than a couple times a month. And, think of it, *art school*."

"A whole school? For art?" Elisa looked dumbfounded.

Ava said, her voice suddenly worried, "Already?"

Shaking his head, Ale said, "High school. She's got two years. There are fantastic ones in Florence and Bologna. And Rome, of course."

They looked at him curiously. He shrugged, "I did some research. This town can't contain a talent of Elisa's magnitude."

Ava and Elisa looked at each other, their eyes full of tears. With their hair back from their heart-shaped faces in almost identical knots, they suddenly realized how they mirrored each other. Though Elisa's hair, sev-eral shades lighter, looked even lighter with the streaks of yellow paint. That enormous canvas of sunflowers . . .

Throwing her arm around Elisa's shoulders, Ava grinned. "This is amazing. So other than completing the *castello* and art lessons, do you have any other plans for the money?"

"Funny you should ask." He looked from Ava to Elisa and back to Ava, unable to suppress his grin. "Lately I've been thinking of how much fun it would be to own a hardware store."

One by one, villagers filed into the middle school. As they entered, they accepted their special pencil with no eraser and the enormous paper ballot with two names on it. Two names. One had been mayor since what seemed time immemorial, and the other seemed a little confused, frankly, as to what he was doing there. He stood in the *piazza* waving at people as they entered. Darting glances at the police officers standing at attention to keep the peace.

Almost all the villagers had decided on their candidate before walking into the school. Indeed, many had decided from the moment Arturo had announced his candidacy. But many had been swayed, back and forth, over the intervening months. They had argued with their neighbors until the two men's names floated in the very atmosphere of Santa Lucia.

"Arturo has no experience!"

"Who needs experience? Italy is in crisis, we need someone bold."

"How, exactly, is Arturo bold?"

"Well, he . . . I mean . . . He really laid into Dante in those flyers."

"That was Fabio! And anyway, how is attacking someone on paper the same as having bold ideas?"

"You two talking about the election? I agree! Dante has kept the crisis from hitting our doorstep. My cousin in Le Marche told me how much they're suffering. We get by in Santa Lucia."

"He didn't protect us from the looting."

"The looting? Didn't you hear? Fabio planned that whole thing."

"Fabio!"

"Trying to pin it on Dante. Make him look bad."

"Are you sure?"

"That's what Marcello says. They found an MS cigarette in Bar Birbo."

"That could be anyone's!"

"Who else smokes MS cigarettes?"

"I'm sure lots of people!"

"In Santa Lucia?"

"Oh. Well, I suppose if Marcello says so, that's good enough for me."

"You all talking about Dante? Listen, I wasn't sure what to believe, especially since he wouldn't even say anything about the rumors. But during the flood... he was our *mayor*. Nobody else would have done what he did."

"Right! He showed *up*. Every day. And that walk..."

Silence.

"Plus. What Arturo did? Framing him that way?"

"That wasn't Arturo though, was it?"

"*Boh*. May as well have been. Arturo said nothing about it. Just stood there grinning like an idiot."

One by one, the villagers collected their pencils and their ballots and evaluated the worth of a man based on what they heard at the counter of Bar Birbo.

Dante nodded at the villagers as they sauntered past the police officers and into the middle school. And he nodded again as they left. He stopped trying to greet the villagers. His voice always croaked. Magda soothed. "It's okay, Dante. You'll win. You always win." She noticed one villager shooting an overly curious look at her. "But to be on the safe side, I think I'll go. You don't want to remind people you're dating the German outcast." Though she intended her last words to be light, Magda herself was not light, and instead she sounded annoyed.

"I told you. I need you here with me. You're the one person who knows how hard this has been. Not just the election... everything."

"Your epic walk to Girona." She reached for his hand.

He squeezed her hand. "Any mayor would do the same."

"Think what you want. But I heard Graziano is writing a song."

He watched people walk past him, some waving a cheerful greeting, some looking away and shuffling quickly into the middle school. He said softly, "I can't stand the waiting."

She said nothing.

He said, as if to himself, "I'm glad you're here, Magda. If I win—"

"You *will*."

"I need people to know that one rumor, at any rate, is true. I won't hide the fact that we're dating."

"It's a funny thing, isn't it, *caro*— all those rumors are about what you're hiding, but you are the most forthright person I know."

He grinned. "*Caro*? We're doing words of endearment now?"

She shrugged and beamed up at him. "I figured it was time."

A rowdy group of new voters strolled into the *piazza*, arms slung over each other's shoulders. Carosello threaded between their legs as he jogged up Via Romana. They ignored the dog as they joked with each other.

Dante watched them. "The youth vote. I didn't campaign enough, Magda. I'm afraid I didn't realize the seriousness of the threat until it was too late."

Some flashed smiles at Dante with a thumbs up; some ran to Arturo, flinging an arm around him and straightening his tie. Dante couldn't count the proportion. He muttered, "If I get this, I have to do a better job. Listen to people, not just write them off when I think they're being a nuisance. I'll endeavor to deserve this."

His words hung in the air. They stayed with him throughout the day, into the evening as the polls closed. They stayed with him all the times he ducked into Bar Birbo throughout the day. Each time Chiara smiled and served him his coffee with a compassionate smile. She leaned across the counter and murmured, "Dante, you're our mayor." As Fabrizio clapped his shoulder, his smile broad and reassuring.

The sun faded from the sky. The lock on the middle school twisted closed. The election manager took it in turns to clasp both Arturo and Dante's hands and say, "Tomorrow morning. No later than noon, I should think."

Arturo offered Dante a wavering smile before walking up Via Romana.

The sun broke early the next morning. Or at least it seemed to, for those awake enough to notice.

Dante pushed open the door to a hail of cheers.

"Signore Sindaco! Mr. Mayor!"

"*Auguri*, Dante!"

"*Auguroni!*"

He beamed and bowed slightly, tipping his hat before hanging it on the post. Still grinning, he leaned over the counter and asked Chiara, "Has Magda been in yet?"

"Not yet."

He nodded and turned to face Rosetta, the school principal. She kissed his cheeks and smiled into his eyes. "Dante. The right man. I'm so relieved."

"Did you have any doubt?" He asked, his eyebrows lifting playfully.

"None at all," she responded, her innocent words belying the relief she felt at preserving her school's budget.

Luciano strolled into the bar, arm-in-arm with Vito, and announced, "The sky is clear!"

Rosetta turned to them. "I can't believe how quickly the marsh receded."

Arturo slipped into Bar Birbo before the door closed, declaring, "Nature takes back her own."

The room grew quiet, eyes gazing around uncomfortably.

Arturo hung his hat beside Dante's and turned to the mayor. With a smile he said, "The better man won. Congratulations."

Dante shifted his weight. "You put up a good fight, Arturo."

"I put up a fight, or at least I let others battle for me," Arturo said. "But it wasn't a good fight and it wasn't a fair fight. I convinced myself they believed in me. I'm afraid it went too far."

Vito whispered a question to Luciano who whispered back, "Giovanni heard Fabio laying into Arturo this morning. Blaming him for being such a weak candidate. Mocked Arturo for his wife cheating on him."

Vito whispered back. "But you don't think she is, right? Cheating on him?"

Luciano shook his head. "Nobody does. Perhaps now Arturo will retire that particular card."

Dante inclined his head no more than a few centimeters to catch this conversation. He straightened and stepped toward Arturo, placing a hand on his shoulder good naturedly. "Many people believed in you. And I will be a better mayor because you gave me a run for my money."

Arturo's expression registered disbelief—could he trust Dante's words? But Dante's steady gaze and warm smile convinced him. He impulsively leaned forward and pressed his face against Dante's, kissing his cheeks. "*Auguri.*"

Dante smiled. And the ripples from his grin filled the bar.

The bell over the door announced Ava and Ale's entrance. "Did everyone see the poppies?" Ava asked the room at large. "I thought they would be too waterlogged to ever bloom, but we just took a walk to the vineyard and the hills are a carpet of ruby red!"

Luciano asked, "The vineyard. How did it fare?"

Ava looked up at Ale, who wrapped his arm around her waist and pulled her close, their happiness palpable. "Just fine. Bruno said it must lie in a protected position, shielded by the hill from getting too much rain. On the slope to keep water from accumulating around the roots. Just fine."

Chiara said, "Thank the Madonna."

Ale said, "And we're having a celebration! Everyone is invited. Monday, when the bar is closed."

Edo asked, "What are we celebrating? The vineyard's weathering the storm?"

Ava and Ale shared a private grin. His eyes didn't leave hers when he said, "Among other things."

Fabio hauled an overflowing box across the street toward the waiting Ape. Carosello appeared from the alley and brushed Fabio's leg. Shouting, Fabio executed a poorly balanced kick at the animal, sending Carosello cowering across the street, and flinging Fabio himself into a circle that landed him on his knee. He cursed, yanking up the socks that had fallen out of the box.

His parents appeared with Morena. Savia said, "Morena said you're moving today. Fabio, why didn't you tell us?"

He shoved the box on the bed of the Ape and said, "You made it pretty clear that you can be loyal to only one of your children."

Already exasperated, Savia said, "The world is not black and white, Fabio. We can love you and not want you to be cruel to Ava."

"Oh, I see, but Ava being cruel to me, that's just fine."

"She's not—" Savia cut herself off at the touch of her husband's hand on her arm. "It doesn't matter. It's useless. We only want to say you don't have to leave. Just because Dante won the election."

Noticing a sock on the ground, Fabio picked it up and held it in his fist as he gestured. "I don't care about that. This town is a bunch of losers." He shook his head. "I happen to have gotten a really excellent job opportunity in Naples. My buddy Giorgio has a shop, everyone says it's the best in Naples. But it's not making money, and unlike some people who are too stupid to see my worth, Giorgio knows that I'm the only person who can turn it around."

Morena said in a befuddled voice, "I thought you were fired."

"Morena! Who asked you for your opinion!"

Morena ducked her head, drawing her hair across her face as she said in a small voice, "That's what you said when the owner of the hardware shop called you . . . that's what you told me."

Fabio began to shout a response when his vision caught on Ale and Ava walking down the street hand in hand. Crossing his arms in front of his chest, Fabio snarled, "Well, isn't this a cozy family reunion? Come to see me off, dear sister? Come to finally admit what everyone knows, that you've been unfair to me and turned everyone against me?"

Ava cocked her head and stared levelly at Fabio. "Is *that* what everyone knows?"

Ale chuckled. "Actually, we're checking out our new property."

Savia said in a rush, "You're not selling the *castello* are you? I know money has been tight—"

Fabio snorted and mumbled, "Stupid American doesn't even know how to make money from an honest-to-God *castello*."

Ale shook his head. "Oh, don't worry, Savia. It's the hardware store we're headed to now."

Fabio spun around. "Why? It's closed."

"It's closed when I say it's closed."

Fabio scratched his head and said, "The owner hired you?" He chuckled. "Guess the *castello* isn't doing that well if you have to get a job like us regular people, right?"

"Oh, Fabio. Always a little slow on the uptake." Ale shook his head and clucked. "I *am* the owner."

Savia yelped, "You *bought* the hardware store?"

"I did. It's a little rain-is-over present to myself. And to my Ava." He put an arm around Ava and squeezed. She grinned up at him happily. Pretending to frown, as if suddenly realizing, Ale said, "Say, Fabio. I guess that puts you out of work, doesn't it? That's unfortunate. I'm sure you can get another job in Santa Lucia . . . unless you've burned every bridge."

"He's moving," Morena said.

Fabio glared at her.

"What?" Morena asked, innocently. "It's true. And he can see the boxes, same as everyone."

Fabio shook his head. "Bitch."

Through gritted teeth, Ale said, "What was that?"

For a moment it seemed as if Fabio would turn and walk away, but he whipped around and shouted, "I don't know why it's my curse to be surrounded by conniving women. Ruining my life!"

Ava looked up at Ale and jerked her finger toward Morena, who had turned away with her arms crossed protectively over her thin chest. "What did *she* do?"

Spittle flew from Fabio's mouth as he shouted, "All of you! No loyalty!"

Ava lifted her hand to her mouth to stop herself but couldn't, and the laugh flew out. "I'm sorry, but... come on. You can't possibly expect anyone to take this rant seriously."

He narrowed his eyes. "All I can say, sister, is that you must be a wildcat between the sheets to get this guy to fall for your cheap antics."

He turned away, until Ale yanked him by the shoulder, forcing him to spin around. Seeing it before it happened, Ava shouted as Ale threw a punch that landed squarely on Fabio's eye. Grunting, Fabio hunched over, pressing his hand over his face. Morena turned at the crushing sound, in time to see Fabio glowering and cursing and curling his fists.

Ava held Ale's hands down. "Don't solve my problems—"

"I'm not. I'm solving mine. This guy breeds poison wherever he goes. It's about time he got some."

Savia moved to help Fabio, but he held up an irritated hand. Morena's gaze flitted between Ale and Fabio, trying to make sense of the scene.

Perhaps Fabio considered fighting back. Perhaps Ale's taller, stronger form convinced him not to. Didn't all those Americans do wrestling or kick-boxing? Instead, he sneered, "Big shot, huh? You're lucky I'm in a hurry. I'd wipe the floor with your ass." He muttered, "Morena, let's go. Where are your suitcases?"

She shook her head. "I didn't bring suitcases."

He rolled his one good eye, his other still covered by his hand. "What kind of idiot are you?" his gaze quickly cut to Ale who pitched one shoulder to Fabio aggressively. Fabio flinched.

Morena said, "You didn't ask me to come."

"You need an invitation? "

She licked her lip, "How would I know you wanted me?"

Grumbling, Fabio said, "Go get it, then."

She shook her head. "I can't." She peeked up at Ava through her lashes. "I like it here."

Edo strode into the bar. "Chiara! Ale's new vines, the ones he planted from cuttings, they're leafing! As soon as the ground is dry, we'll go out there for a picnic." He stopped at the sight of Riccardo, tapping a stack of papers on the counter before slipping them into his satchel.

Nodding at Chiara, Riccardo said, "And you'll let me know."

Chiara nodded, her face serious.

Riccardo patted Edo on the arm as he strolled out, calling over his shoulder, "It's a gorgeous spring day! Probably my imagination, but I can practically smell the almond flowers blooming." He turned back. "Is Giuseppe up and running? I'd love to bring home chicken sausages."

Putting the pens away, Chiara nodded. "He may be out of them, though. This town seems to have developed an insatiable desire for chicken sausage."

Chuckling, Riccardo said, "I'll bet." He stepped into the sunshine, up Via Romana, toward the *macelleria*.

Edo watched him go and turned to Chiara. "Is everything okay? Your ex isn't back, is he?"

"No." Chiara smiled weakly. "I asked Riccardo about that. If the

bastard lays any claim to the bar again, or even contacts me, he's in viola-
tion of his agreement with Francy. Your boyfriend closed every loophole."

Edo removed an apron from the drawer and began tying it around his
waist. "That must be a comfort."

"It is," Chiara said. "That's not why I invited Riccardo."

Edo glanced up, waiting.

Chiara took a breath. "I want to leave the bar to you."

"Is something wrong?" Edo paled.

"I'm fine. But the flood... I can't pretend I'll always be fine. When I'm
no longer able to take care of Bar Birbo, I'd feel better knowing it's in your
hands."

Edo leaned against the counter, watching her intently. "Wow, Chiara.
This is... I mean, have you thought this through? You know that any children I have—"

"I don't care about that."

"Are you sure? Because Francy and I have started talking about it a
little... and I'm not a betting man, but I'm betting on us."

She grinned. "I know it's deluded, but I keep thinking you two would
have the most beautiful babies."

Edo guffawed.

"I mean it, Edo. Adopt, use a surrogate... I'll love any child of yours
like a proud nonna." Her voice trembled.

"You will be. As much a grandmother as our mothers." Edo clasped her
hand in his. "You're not angry anymore? About Francy buying the bar?"

"I'm not sure I ever was. I just didn't like being the only person who
didn't know."

"For a woman in on everything..."

She grinned. "Exactly. He's good for you, Edo. And I worried, for a
bit, about growing attached to the idea of you being with him. With the
history—"

"Say no more," Edo held up a hand with a grin. "I'm fully aware that I haven't always acted the mature part, here."

"But it's different now. I see that. He's good for you. You're good for him. You're good together."

Edo blushed. "We are, aren't we?"

Chiara put her hands on Edo's shoulders and searched his eyes. "But you need to think about this. You may not want to tie yourself to the bar. Francy might not want that either."

"Oh," Edo said lightly, "We've talked about where we'll settle. The musician life is so scattershot, he agrees he wants his off days to be quiet. Slow. We want to be here."

She grinned. "*Sono contenta*. That makes me happy."

"I thought you wanted me to get out of here."

She shook her head. "I only wanted your happiness and wondered if you were cutting yourself off from it. There's a wide world to explore."

He studied her for a moment. "Do you still think about leaving?"

Chiara put down her dishcloth and gazed out the window. "I need to do it when it's for me, not because I fear losing Fabrizio. I'm feeling more ready, though." She smiled. "For some reason, knowing that this bar, its future is ours, yours and mine . . . it makes it easier to consider taking some time away."

He laughed. "We'd have to hire someone. Again."

She nodded. "Once the baby is a little older, I think Patrizia's daughter would love the work."

"Filamena?"

Chiara nodded.

"I like her, she's steady but not too serious." Edo said, "Francy and I, we're talking about taking a trip when his tour wraps up."

"Where?"

"He suggested an ashram in India. 'A week of breathing'." Edo rolled his eyes with a grin as he added the air quotes.

"You don't sound convinced."

"*Allora*, the sunshine sounds good after the last few months." He stared at the floor as he added, "But I worry about the food. I mean…" Edo looked at Chiara and they both broke into peals of laughter before saying, "they don't even *have* pasta."

As Ava piled bottles of wine into metal tubs, she asked Elisa, "Any word from Fatima?"

Elisa shook her head. "I texted her, telling her about the party today, but I didn't hear back."

"It's like she's still a villager. None of us have gotten back in the habit of using our phones." Ava laughed and rearranged the bottles as she said, "By the way, I left you new brushes in your studio."

"I saw them," Elisa grinned. "Did Ale show you the new plates?"

"He did. The blue one is my favorite. With the *castello*, but the *castello* is wavering as if you're seeing it through old glass."

"I thought you would hate that one."

"Maybe I would have at one point. It's not how I see the *castello*. But now…" Ava shrugged.

"It might not sell well."

Ava shrugged. "The shirts will, thanks to Fatima."

Edo stepped into the kitchen. "I wanted to see if you need help."

Ava grinned. "We ordered food from Pietro, so there isn't much left to do. But keep me company? Elisa, look, here comes Isotta."

Elisa's face blossomed, and she ran toward her siblings.

Edo mused. "I keep thinking she's turned into such a little adult, but then she sees those kids and becomes one herself."

"Have you seen her help Jacopo walk?"

He shook his head.

"It's hysterical."

Edo watched Jacopo as his arms stretched toward Elisa while Margherita tugged her older sister's leg. "They sure love her."

Ava nodded, her eyes suddenly seared with the rising sunshine. Blinking, she and Edo carried the bins of wine to the tables scattered over the *castello* lawn. Small vases of wildflowers held down the rough white cloths, billowing now and again in the afternoon breeze. The air smelled like blue sky waving toward a yielding earth.

"A beautiful day," Isotta said, pulling Ava toward her to kiss her cheeks. "Do we get to know yet what we're celebrating?"

Ava grinned. "Who says we're celebrating something? Can't it be about the end of the storm?"

Isotta laughed. "Sure."

Edo lowered his voice. "Is it true? Ale bought the hardware store?"

Ava pressed her lips together to keep from laughing.

Edo whistled. "Ale is something else."

Softly, Ava said, "Remember when he first came to town?"

Isotta said, "With his academic accent."

Ava laughed, "I'd forgotten about that." She slipped her hand into Isotta's and the women grinned at each other.

The moment broke as Edo said, "Is that Enrico? I didn't know he was coming."

Ava shook her head. "I didn't either." She whispered to Isotta, "I would have told you."

Isotta shrugged. "That's okay. At least I don't have to pretend anymore. I told him what I needed to tell him."

Ava frowned. "I want everyone to be happy."

Isotta squeezed Ava's hand. "I heard a rumor that Pietro is making *tagliatelle* with wild asparagus."

"He is. I saw him walking with his children to pick asparagus yesterday. Livia, too. They came back with baskets full."

Isotta didn't register Ava's words as she watched Enrico scan the yard.

He caught sight of her staring at him and startled. Sheepishly, he grinned and made his way across the lawn as Ava and Edo slipped away.

Within a moment, Enrico arrived in front of her, his hands clasped around a paper bag. "I tried texting... I didn't want to surprise you."

Isotta patted her pocket. "I guess I forgot my phone."

Enrico nodded but seemed distracted, his gaze fixed over Isotta's shoulder. She turned to see what had caught his eye. "What is it?"

His mouth opened for a moment before he said, "The swallows. They've come home."

Enrico and Isotta stood together for a moment, watching the birds wheeling and weaving, inscribing eternal arcs across the azure sky. In a hushed voice, Isotta said, "They're back. I hadn't noticed."

She looked back at Enrico, who grinned and said, "Am I the first?"

She shook her head, not understanding.

Enrico dipped his hand into the bag and withdrew a slim volume, the cover illustrated with a rabbit painted in bold watercolors. Softly he said, "I'd love to have you sign it."

She reached out, her breath stalled in her lungs. Lightly, her fingers skimmed the cover, tracing the rabbit, the words... her name. Her voice full of wonder, she said, "How... how did you get this?"

Grinning, he said, "Babbo told me your box of books hadn't arrived, but I figured there must be copies available somewhere. I called the publishing house, and they directed me to a shop in Rome."

"Rome? You went to Rome? My book is in *Rome*?"

"It is. I took photos of the shelf, I thought you might get a kick out of it."

She looked up at him, tears shining in her eyes. "I can't believe you did this."

He stepped closer. "Isotta, I need to tell you..."

Her heart clenched.

"I ended things. With Carla."

She started. "You did? Because of what I said?" Her stomach lurched.

He shrugged. "It made me realize how much I had forced myself to ignore. I kept giving her a pass because . . . well, I figured she picked up on my feelings for you. I could hardly fault her for reacting. When you and I spoke, I realized it wasn't fair to Carla to pretend to be wholly hers, when I'm . . . " He blushed. "I'm wholly yours."

Isotta's breath caught.

Enrico moved closer. "But if you are dating Tomasso, I understand. I shouldn't be with Carla, anyway. I shouldn't be with anyone until I feel about them the way I feel about you."

She whispered, "I've spoken with Tomasso like twice in my life, always at Bar Birbo and never about anything of substance, just the weather and the groves."

He murmured, "So you're saying . . . "

She shook her head. "I'm tired of saying." She put the book back in his hands and lifted her arms to pull his head down to hers, her fingers wound into his hair. She kissed him intensely, ferociously. Drinking him in. At the sound of catcalls, they pulled apart, gasping. Marcello called out, "It's going to be that kind of party?" He looked down at Antonella and said, "I'm good for that."

Isotta blushed and grabbed Enrico's hand, taking him to where Elisa, Margherita, and Jacopo picked flowers to turn into chains. As they walked, Enrico said, his voice strangled. "Can we be alone?"

"Soon." Isotta grinned, lifting her eyes to his. "Oh, very soon. We have all the time in the world."

Marcello and Antonella watched them leave. He leaned down slowly, before brushing his lips against hers. She shivered, succumbing for a moment before she said, "My grandmother will be here any moment."

He grinned. "She approves of me."

"I don't think she'd approve of me locked in an embrace in the middle of a celebration."

"Fair enough." He looked around. "What are we celebrating?"

"I figured the app selling." She shrugged. "But Ale has all kinds of global schemes I can't talk about."

Wrapping his arm around Antonella, Marcello said, "He won't lure you away from here, will he? With promises of fame and salary?"

She laughed. "No. With the app sold, his focus is here. The groves, the vineyard, and his plans for the *castello* as a community space. Plus, making all those work under one brand." She adopted a stern expression. "I've already said too much! Details given on a need-to-know basis."

He swooped her up, nuzzling her neck with kisses until she squealed. "I'll tell you what I need to know," he murmured, happy for the excuse to hold her close.

"*Ragazzi!* What are you doing?" Bea's voice boomed across the lawn.

Marcello and Antonella pulled apart, blushing, as Antonella straightened her dress, which had twisted in Marcello's playful embrace.

"Nothing," they said in unison. Before collapsing in a fit of giggles.

"Those two," Bea complained cheerfully to Patrizia arriving at her elbow.

Patrizia nodded, her attention focused on the bundle in her arms. Bea hooted as she caught sight of the pink blanket. "Your grandbaby! Filamena's here?" Bea scanned the guests cresting the top of the stairs.

Patrizia's smile widened. "They're moving the last of their boxes in now. Giuseppe is behind me with our grandson." Her chest swelled with pride.

Bea chuckled, "The flood didn't scare them away?"

Shaking her head, Patrizia said, "On the contrary. Being out of contact for so long made them realize what's important."

Magda overheard and said, "A flood like that happens once in a century. Or less! I'd say Santa Lucia is preserved from any flooding for a good long while."

Dante nodded and shifted the boxes in his arms. "And fires. And kidnapping. And childbirths in bars."

They all laughed, and Dante called out to Ava, over the burble of the arriving guests. "Ava! Where do you want the apricot tarts?"

Ava untangled herself from the conversation and practically skipped toward Magda and Dante. The older woman frowned. "You're happy today. Will you finally tell us what we're celebrating?"

Ava leaned forward confidentially. Magda leaned to meet her with a grin of her own. Only to hear Ava whisper, "Not a chance."

Magda remained still for a moment before guffawing. "Suspense, huh?" She turned to Dante and said, "Well, some things are worth waiting for."

He grinned and dropped a kiss on her nose.

She pulled back and looked around. "What if your children put in a surprise appearance?"

He held her close to himself and leaned down to whisper in her ear. "Then they'll have another opportunity to get used to it. I'm not worried." Taking her hand, he said, "Look, Pietro put out a table of *antipasti* . . . let's see if there's that *bruschette* you love. With the truffle oil."

Her laughter pealed through the assembling crowd.

More guests filed in.

Luciano and Vito, arm in arm. Stopping every few steps to finish a joke.

Chiara and Fabrizio, hand in hand. He pulled her close. "I've missed this."

She grinned up at him, "And I've missed you. Stupid flood."

With a saucy smile, he said, "So I'm thinking . . . my next book. I think I'll write about Santa Lucia."

Her mouth fell open and she laughed. "You wouldn't dare."

He shrugged. "You got to admit, there's plenty of material."

"As long as I'm not in it."

"We'll talk about it." He leaned down and kissed her. "We'll talk about it."

Francy stopped beside them with his box of bottled water. "Okay, lovebirds, do you know where Ava wants this?"

Chiara blushed and then pointed to the tables. "Probably over there? I can ask."

Francy's face lit up. "There's Edo."

More villagers arrived—Paola, the fruit and vegetable seller; Rosetta, the principal; Bepe and Savia, Ava's parents.

Ale and Ava nodded at each other. He used a chair to stand above the crowd and shouted for attention. "Welcome, dear friends and family. We're so glad you could be here today on such short notice."

From the crowd, someone shouted, "Where else do we have to go?"

Laughter.

Ale gazed down at Ava, his eyes full of love, as he tucked the tendril of hair back behind her ear. He pulled his vision back to the guests and grinned. "We wanted to share with you the first taste of our *passito*."

Ava poured a thimbleful of wine into plastic cups.

Someone in the crowd grumbled, "This is all we get?"

Ale grinned. "We need to hold some back to win over distributers. And it's not technically ready yet." As the last of the cups got handed around, Ale said, "In this wine, I hope you sense your collective history. *Our* collective history. It's sweet, but according to Gaetano, our expert in Perugia, it's got some backbone. Unusual for a *passito*. It's layered and nuanced, but it comes together in a powerful way."

Murmurs in the crowd as everyone sniffed their *passito*.

Ale raised his cup. "And so we're here to celebrate the wine. To feeling our roots in the past but blooming today. And we also want to announce that, as of this morning... Ava and I are husband and wife."

The crowd erupted.

"Married!"

"I thought they were already married!"

"No, you numbskull, they've been living in sin. Her mother was outraged, only allowed it because of the kidnapping and the Fabio situation."

"Good for them! They make a beautiful couple!"

"What are they saying? Have you tried this *bruschette*? Where did Pietro get ripe tomatoes this early in the season?"

Ale leaped down from the chair to plant a lingering kiss on Ava's mouth. Everyone whooped and cheered. Elisa pretended to roll her eyes in disgust, but a knowing smile gave her away. She watched her mother and Ale, lost in each other's eyes before she felt arms surround her and kisses on her cheeks . . . Luciano, Isotta, Enrico, too many congratulations to count. Looking up, she startled at the sight of a figure loitering at the top of the stairs. Yelping, she raced forward. "Fatima!"

The girls, or really, young women now, ran into each other's arms as if they were once again middle schoolers celebrating the end of the school day with a hug and promise of *gelato*. Fatima hung onto Elisa, a tear coursing down her cheek. "I felt nervous the whole way here. Maybe I shouldn't have surprised you."

Elisa held Fatima's hand and looked into her eyes searchingly.

Fatima grinned. "I heard the news. On my walk up."

Elisa grinned. "Isn't it great? I've had to keep it a secret."

Fatima nodded.

Elisa leaned toward her to whisper in her ear. "Speaking of secrets, Mamma is pregnant."

"She is?" Seeing the grin on Elisa's face, Fatima laughed aloud. "Soon you'll have enough siblings to fill a soccer team."

Elisa laughed.

Fatima gestured with her head. "Fancy a walk?"

Elisa nodded. "Yes. I want to hear all about Japan."

"That can wait. I want to hear all about Santa Lucia."

Meanwhile, the one-eyed dog appeared at the base of the *castello*

stairs as if created from the warping blue light. He lifted his paws against the wall, stretching high, his one eye fixed seriously on the Madonna's serene face. Her hand seemed to bend in greeting. A trick of light, surely. The dog patted the wall with one paw before returning to all fours and trotting up the stairs to the *castello*.

He threaded through the villagers who gathered to pile fresh pasta onto their plates. Only a few noticed him. The rest moved around him like creek water around a stone.

He nosed around for scraps and then seemed to decide the pickings would be easier, and more fruitful, later. Turning, the dog leaped over the low wall of rosemary to find his path into the groves. The light warbled as he entered the groves, dimming and shushing as it closed behind him.

The dog ignored the tender leaning of the olive boughs, the magic of the papery light. None of this surprised the beast as he jogged down the slope and around the bend, to the path that led to the hill overlooking the castle lawn. As he rounded the corner and crested the hill, the noise of the party faded away. In the hush, only the dog's footfalls could be heard, a staccato beat underpinning the free song of swallows, carving their way across the sky. Their wings blurred with dark and light.

Threading between each of Carosello's steps rose the scent of wild mint and thyme, a hint of yellow jasmine. But . . . *aspetta*. Wait. Beneath the padding cadence of the present thrummed sounds that ran before, sounds that run ahead. The call of farmers picking grapes generations ago, the sound of wedding bells to come lingering over the castle turrets. The strands of time wove together with the gentle, patient padding of the one-eyed dog.

Carosello picked his way to an olive tree with roots so gnarled, they formed a bed, rising above the earth, still thick with recent rains. He turned—once, twice, and then, for the first time since our tale began, he rested. Crossing his paws stretched in front of him like the image of a beast so regal, artists painted him in oils over and over and over again.

His head drifted down to his crossed legs, his one eye fixed on the scene spread before him.

He watched as two young women disappeared into the groves, their heads silhouetted with crowns of fiery sunlight. Fatima and Elisa. One with a wave of hair tumbling down her back, the other with a low, untidy twirl at the nape of her neck.

Carosello's body leaned slightly to accommodate the tilt of the spinning earth. The dog watched the banter of old people surround the villagers like vines. His eyebrows cocked, one after the other as he blinked, following the steps of a young boy stumbling to stand and an older girl laughing, her curling hair haloing her head as she held her brother's hand. He watched Livia, the one who washed and brushed him, bring forward two young children to play with Jacopo and Margherita. Two children of the five, the rest waiting with their father against the castle walls. The four children played, their laughter rising like streamers into the air. They called their invitation to the older children who abandoned shyness to join them in a game without rules or form.

Their voices tangled with the voices of children not yet born.

Ava and Ale's two little girls, one growing even now in her mother's womb, heedless of the love that awaited her birth. Edo and Francy's twin boys, born to a surrogate in the United States. A surrogate of Italian descent. Isotta and Enrico's three children. A boy, a girl, and another boy. Antonella and Marcello's one boy, born and raised in Rome until his parents decided novelty and stimulation had their place, but they wanted their son to lean into the arms of the people who loved him most in the world.

The dog watched the scene of today's villagers blend with yesterday's filmy ghosts and tomorrow's images, wrought from sunlight.

Rays of waving blue fell around him. Surrounded him. The dog's breath slowed, hewing to the vibration of the earth.

In front of Carosello, the stage blurred. The edges ran together into a rhythm, a spectacle of light and shadow. Echoed in the whirling shapes of the swallows calling overhead. The light, the sound, twirled into a lullaby. A lullaby for a dog, who sank into the roots of Santa Lucia's oldest olive tree.

His single eye fell closed, and his breath, his slowing heartbeat, twined with the breeze that brushed past his fur, before that breeze rose to lift the branches of the olive tree. Scattering flecks of gold and green, grey and silver.

His single eye fell closed.

As if it were the end of the story.

DEAR BEAUTIFUL READER,

Thank you for following the tales of *Santa Lucia* to their conclusion. But...are they really over? I'm already a little lonesome for my friends in Santa Lucia, so I'm mulling a spin-off series. Make sure you sign up for my newsletter at *michelledamiani.com/grapevine* so you catch it when it reaches fruition.

I hope you consider leaving a review of *Into the Groves* (and the other books in the series). Reviews are an excellent way to help independently published authors, as they help encourage new readers to discover our work. Priceless!

It's with some sadness that I wind up the last of these farewells. So instead of goodbye, I'll say "until next time."

Alla prossima,

— Michelle

ITALIAN WORDS IN THIS TEXT

CONVERSATIONS

a dopo/ a presto/alla prossima volta	see you later	*buongiorno*	good morning
		cara	dear
allora	well now	*castello*	castle
amore mio	my love	*che c'e?*	what's up?
anch'io	me too	*che succede?*	what happened?
andiamo	let's go	*ciao*	hello and goodbye
arrivo	I'm coming	*come no?*	why not?
ascolta	listen	*comunque*	anyway
aspetta	wait	*davvero?*	isn't that right?
(un) attimo	just a moment	*eccoci qua*	here we are
auguri	congratulations	*fa un freddo cane*	literally "it makes a dog cold", used to express that it's freezing outside
Babbo/Papà	Dad		
basta	that's enough		
bella	beautiful	*fidanzato/a*	fiance/e
bentornato	welcome back	*gita*	field trip
boh?	no real translation, similar to "who can say?" and often given wth a shrug	*grazie*	thank you
		lo so	I know
		ma dai!	Come on!
bronzato	tanned	*maestro*	teacher, often used as an honorific
buono/a	good		
buonasera	good afternoon	*moda*	fashion

nascondino	hide and seek	*salve*	greetings
nonno/a	grandfather/mother	*senza peli sulla lingua*	without hair on the tongue (plain speaking)
paesano	country boy		
per favore	please	*sono d'accordo*	l agree
piacere	nice to meet you	*stronzo*	bastard, piece of crap
poverino/a	poor	*tesoro mio*	my treasure
prego	you're welcome	*tutto bene/ tutto a posto*	everything's okay
pronto	literally "ready" but used as "hello" when answering the phone	*va bene*	it's okay
		vuoto	empty
ragazzi	guys	*zio/zia*	uncle/aunt

❧

ABOUT TOWN

alimentari	shop that sells cheese and cured meats, as well as some other basic foodstuff and household supplies	*palazzo*	palace
		palazzo comunale	seat of civic authority, like a town hall
Ape	a three-wheeled truck with a small motor	*Perugino*	Umbrian Rennaisance painter; his paintings (or those of his students) adorn many Umbrian buildings
comune	where administrative aspects of the town happen		
		piazza	town square
farmacia	pharmacy	*polizia municipale*	police department
festa	celebration/party		
forno	bakery	*rosticceria*	shop to buy pizza by the slice, and sometimes cooked items for takeaway like fried rice balls (arancini)
fruttivendolo	produce shop		
macelleria	butcher shop, often with other fresh items		
		trattoria	informal restaurant

FOOD & DRINK

albicocca	apricot	*frutti di bosco*	literally fruits of the forest, mixed berry
aperitivo	cocktail		
Barolo	a red wine from the north of Italy	*lampredotto*	tripe sandwiches
		latte caldo	hot milk
biscotto/i	cookie/s	*mandarino*	mandarin orange
buono/a	good	*panino*	sandwich
cacio e pepe	pasta with grated cheese and pepper	*pecorino*	sheep's milk cheese, sold at different levels of ripeness; Pecorino is also a kind of white wine from Le Marche
caffè	espresso specifically, or coffee more generally		
caffè lungo	espresso pulled slowly so that there is more water and a fuller cup	*lumaca*	snail
		normale	my usual
cappuccino	espresso with milk	*prosecco*	bubbly wine, Italy's version of champagne
cenone	a big, festive dinner (typically on New Year's Eve)	*salumi*	cured meats, like salami and prosciutto
ciambella/e	donut/s	*tagliata*	sliced, grilled beef, often scattered with rosemary and olive oil
cornetto/i	Italian croissant/s		
cornetto con marmellata	Italian croissant filled with jam	*tagliatelle*	fresh pasta, cut similar to linguini
cornetto con crema	Italian croissant filled with cream	*tartufata*	black olive and truffle
		torta	cake
farro	an ancient grain, similar to barley	*vino*	wine
frizzante	bubbly water		

A WORD ON ITALIAN MEALS

Italian meals are divided into appetizers (*antipasti*), first course of pasta or soup (*primi*), second course of meat or fish (*secondi*), side dish of vegetables (*contorni*) and dessert (*dolci*).

ALSO BY MICHELLE DAMIANI

Il Bel Centro: A Year in the Beautiful Center

Santa Lucia

The Silent Madonna

The Stillness of Swallows

*The Road Taken: How to Dream, Plan, and
Live Your Family Adventure Abroad*

More on these books and works in progress can be found at
michelledamiani.com

ACKNOWLEDGMENTS

This book, more than any of my others, called for the collective talents of my circle. Paul Ardoin once again offered the wisdom of his discerning eye to improve my pacing and character development. Kristine Bean has edited every one of my books and somehow always acts thrilled when I ask. My advance reader team identified niggly little errors that get lost as eyes turn bleary from too many read-throughs; I can't thank them enough (particularly Nancy, Sue, Julia, Janet, Midge, and Natalie).

This book required my writing about topics of which I knew embarrassingly little. I leaned hard on Dwight Stanford's knowledge about wine and winemaking to create Ale's journey. I met Dwight years ago, when he came to a Thanksgiving we hosted in Spello for Americans living in Italy. Later, we visited his winery in Le Marche; I'll never forget, at the end of a dinner that the ten of us worked together to make, when he ran downstairs and brought up a bottle of passito. Our laughter twined with the candlelight as he reenacted the backbreaking work of squeezing juice out of what were essentially raisins. With indefatigable patience, Dwight answered every one of my naïve questions and shepherded me through the trials and joys of winemaking. I now sip wine with a sense of reverence.

I'd like to take a beat to also thank Robin Albertson-Wren. In this time of global pandemic, she provided twice-weekly Zoom mindfulness classes, an oasis in a prickly and panicked world. Robin, you are a light in the universe and I'm so grateful for you.

And I want to thank Nell for her belief in me. Without her pushing me to get my work into the hands of readers, I'm fairly certain each of my books would be half-done affairs, languishing in a drawer somewhere. I'm so lucky to have her in my corner.

My husband Keith not only makes my gorgeous covers and designs my books and mulls with me when I hit a difficult plot point, but for this book, he also offered the wisdom of his experience in app development. I'll never forget walking cloudless Manhattan streets together, bantering about my imagined food and travel app. Little did we know we were inadvertently picking up the coronavirus that would derail our plans for a worldwide adventure. But that's another story.

Printed in Great Britain
by Amazon